Drown Deep

The Blood Scouts

Book 2

PHIL WILLIAMS

MMXXIV

ISBN-13: 978-1-913468-26-2

Cover art by Stefan Koidl
Cover design by P. Williams

Published by Rumian Publishing

Visit **www.phil-williams.co.uk** online for more information and regular news regarding the writing of Phil Williams.
Join the newsletter to be the first to hear about new projects.

Map of Boldarow, c. 720

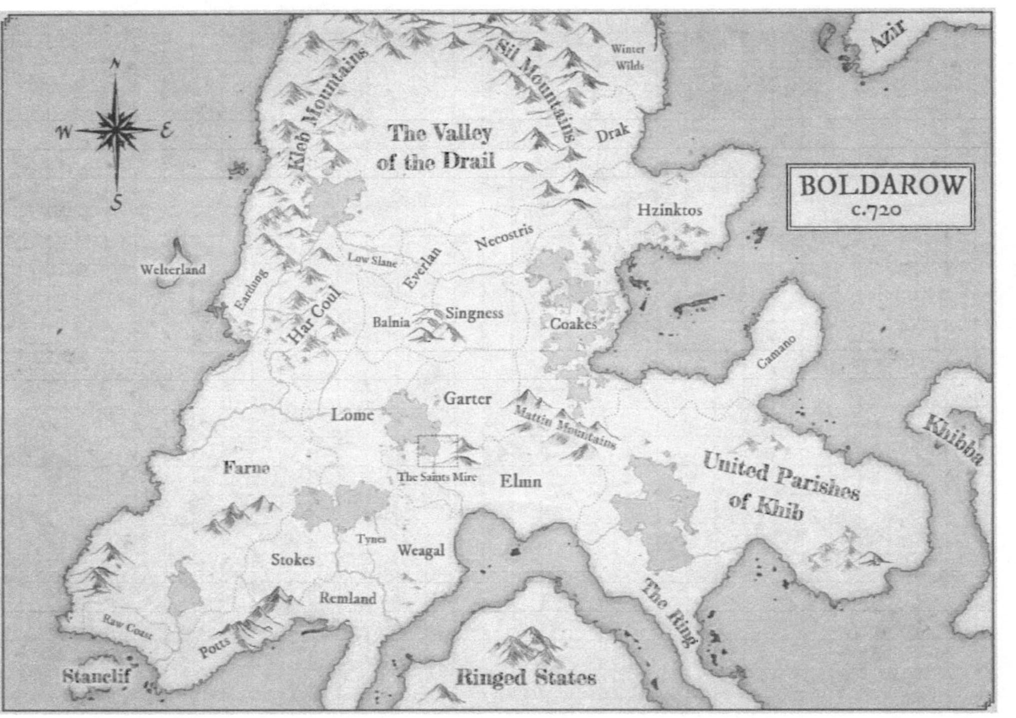

Map of The Saints Mire, c. 720

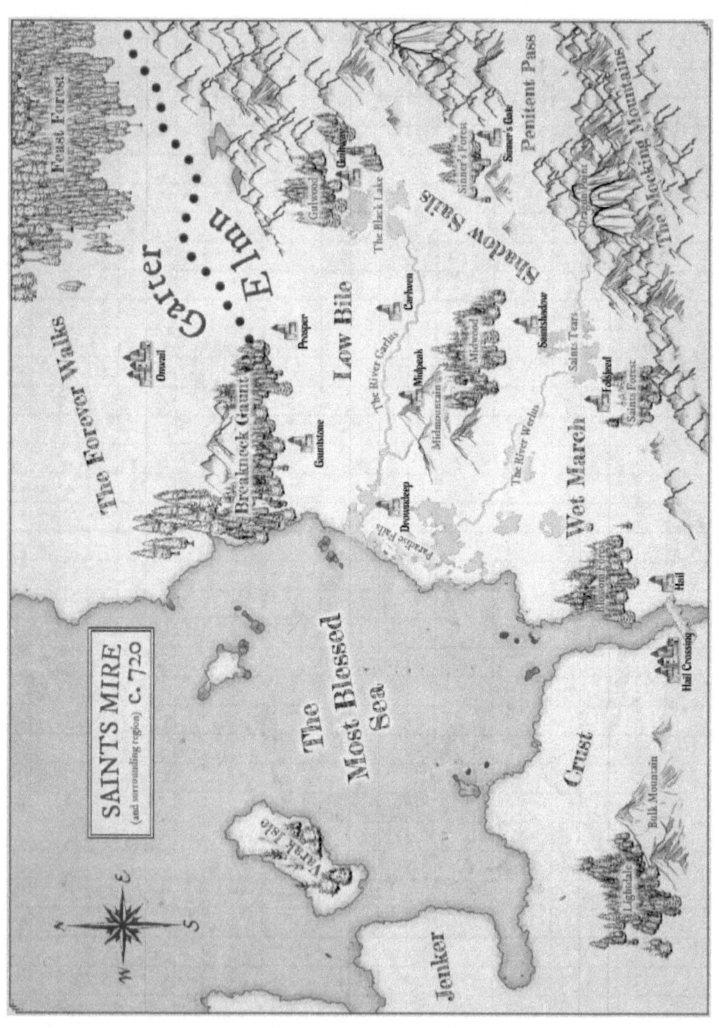

Languid's Recap

Abridged from "Languid's Recap", *Languid's Everyman Guide to Fierce Women of The One War (Issue 6: Havikare Eens)***, p. ix-xi**

Alright, so you want to know about Havikare Eens, the Chaos Librarian, Little Miss Malicious, the Goblin Princess and all them other monikers. Before we get into that, it's worth your knowing the force she encountered in the Blood Scouts, and the state they were in after the Battle of Wick. If you don't recall my full treatise on that crazed platoon, I'ma take care of you right now.

So – we all know how Captain Brade, famed adventurer, spy and gentleman, single-handedly thwarted Dr Vorhale, a lunatic Slanik scientist who sent the Dread Corps to the front with one hell of a bomb? Brade sabotaged that bomb in their back pocket and it blew all hell out of them. Right?

Wrong.

Those of us in the know give the real credit to the Blood Scouts, a platoon of two score fierce women who escorted Brade into Low Slane. In particular, you'll want to remember the sniper Wild Wish, who took over Boot Squad when her beloved Sarge got crushed by a hawk giant. It was her and her girls who really went up against Vorhale.

Wild Wish had quite a time on that campaign: let's take you back to the Battle of Green Rise, where she swayed the tide by clipping a few hundred men with a machine gun, and lost her friend Loose. She and her mates were then sent behind enemy lines, on one nasty long journey – up through rocky Har Coul, across the Little Step River into Eardung (that's barkmen territory), over Heaven's Eye Lake, via the windy Horns of Heaven tunnels, and finally down the Devil's River to Reeve Abbey.

We lost a lot of scouts on the way, the total never fully established, but there was Sarge and Small, killed by the hawk *giant; a few who got unlucky when the barkmen's boat got fired on; most of Rock Squad who got torn up by giant insects; Pound and Fixit from Boot who died around Reeve Alley; and a bunch who got intercepted by the Drail's Constans Maringdale, a Purification agent gone rogue.*

Oh yeah – about her: Maringdale's activities aren't all that well recorded but a few inferences here and there say she was a world-class intention mage reduced to a second-rate role. She had a burning desire to stop whoever was coming after this Dread Corps project, and she cut some of them off alright. We're pretty sure she punched her ticket on the Iron Barge, where the scouts set off the bomb on its way into Wick. Maybe she ran into Wild Wish herself and the pair came to heads. If so, Wish came out on top.

See, Brade wasn't alone in Low Slane and he sure wasn't alone on that murder train: after Boot Squad raided Vorhale's lab at Reeve Abbey, Wild Wish, the dirt-minder Emi and a small Gonish guy called Colm Hightower flew after the bomb on a wyrling. Wish actually stopped the bomb from properly activating – against Brade's will – or it could've done a lot more damage. As it was, it just decimated everyone on that train and about half the city of Wick, leaving it vulnerable for the Stanclif forces to charge in.

At this point, Wish had lost pretty much everyone she knew: her thuggish best mate Rue was all burnt up at Reeve; her new paramour, the ringer Newk, got a nasty head wound; her cynical pal Dakoda had her stomach cut open; and her rival sniper/best pal Oksy was left behind to look out for them. The entirety of Sun and Sabre Squads, including the witlacer Dollemore and sniper Four Skills, never even reached the abbey.

So Wild Wish ended up back in Wick, just her and Emi left from the whole platoon, as far as anyone was aware, and General Easter himself, head of the Stanclif efforts out west, said she was to put the Blood Scouts behind her. He had a new assignment, considering the competence she'd shown: off to Lome to train more hopefuls in the sneaky arts. That's where we can rejoin the scouts, see, because it's from there, with Wild Wish carrying the baggage of a hellish campaign, that this sniper set out on a collision course for our real lady of concern here, Havikare Eens.

And it's no exaggeration to say that from innocuous beginnings, between them, this pair were gonna change the course of the One War for everyone.

Languid's Glossary

Abridged from "Languid's Glossary", *Languid's Everyman Guide to Fierce Women of The One War (Issue 6: Havikare Eens)*, **p. vi-viii**

Hey. Want a bit of briefing on this world, and the people in it, before you dive in? The what and the where and the why and the who of this particular stage of The One War? Then, mate, I've got your back.

As well as focusing on the Chaos Librarian herself, our scope's gonna include the fabulous Blood Scouts post-Wick, getting on to the fall of 720, and a chunk of time spent in the Saints Mire, so here's everything you need to get started. It's not essential reading, just a primer for if and when, see? But I'm gonna assume you know nothing because let's be fair, some of you don't. Not judging; I'm here for the everyman, as always. Right – here's what you're dealing with:

Lay of the World

__The Rocc:__ the stone we stand on; everything, this whole world. You know this.
__Boldarrow:__ the biggest and baddest central continent of the Rocc.
__The One War:__ global conflict where empires clashed, 719-728.
__The Drail Empire (people: Drail / the Drail (collective), adj: Drail):__ an empire comprising (dominating) seven nations in the Valley of the Drail, headed by Drail itself and bolstered by Low Slane, Har Coul and that lot; these fiends promoted "Purification", meaning, the more you stuck to their ideals the safer you were.
__The Comity:__ countries unified in taking down the Drail, led by Stanclif and Khibba.

Imperial Stanclif (people: Cliffer(s) / Stain(s) (derogatory), adj: Stanish): an empire with a seat of power in the small southwestern isle of Stanclif. These lads promoted the secular "Civilisation" movement, essentially putting material wealth and snooty values above all.

Khibba (people: Khib(s), adj: Khib): a monstrously big empire way off in the Eastern Continent, with old-fashioned religious values and a big melting pot of inhuman races.

Garter (people: Garter(s), adj. Garter): large central nation overrun by imperial fighting, previously the seat of the hugely powerful Holy Garter Empire (of the Ven church).

Elmn (people: Elmish, adj. Elmish): expansive rejoin adjoining Garter, with borders heavily contested before, during and after the war.

The Raw Coast (people: Rawboys/Rawgirls, adj. Raw / Rae): long-contested coastal region near Stanclif; part of the Empire at the start of the One War.

Lome (people: Lomen, adj. Lomian): large central nation subject to heavy fighting during the One War, previously a seat of high culture.

Har Coul, Balnia, Low Slane and Coak: countries within and around the Drail Valley.

The Saints Mire

A holy borderland between Garter and Elmn, technically under Elmish sovereignty at this point, but ruled by the Church of the Venerate Flesh.

The Ten Priories of the Mire (old names in brackets): Midpeak (Venstar); Prosper (Soway); Saintshadow (Ghutace); Guiltway (Tikace); Hail (Nael); Gauntstone (Militace); Carlwen (Castorly); Sinner's Gate (Azristar); Folsfeed (Tuskace); Drowndeep (Bonstar).

Tribes of the Mire: Shore Stalkers, Gaunt Lanterns,

Shadow Farmers, Woodwings, Mock Mirians, Little Tears, Big Tears, Wet Walkers
(See map for more locations within the Mire.)

Other Places of Interest

Vasseer: *capital of Stanclif.*
Hail Crossing: *gateway city to the southern Saints Mire.*
Onwail: *gateway city to the northern Saints Mire.*
Tynes: *city state known for its finance and neutrality, southern Boldarow.*
Wick: *walled city on the border of Farne and Har Coul.*
Rock Stable: *Stanclif training ground in Lome.*
Swelig: *a small village in Stanclif.*

Institutions

The Church of the Venerate Flesh: *once dominant religion that followed prophet Bly Castor's Book of the Body; accolades commonly called "Vens", priests "Venerators".*
Revery of the Cane Saints: *ancient religion that personified a host of saints through the teachings of the Ten Prophets, later partially absorbed into the Ven church.*
The Movement of Knowledge: *secular revolution placing science and materialism above religion and magic (underpinning "Civilisation" and "Purity" to supplant the church).*
Mortal Magic (or witlacing, flesh weaving, blood corrupting): *magical practice relating to living flesh and consciousness. Broadly grouped into four schools: intention, will, flesh and parsing.*
Earth-touching (or dirt-minding, mindlessness): *magical practice concerned with manipulating the physical world, of and relating to the environment.*
The Arbitration: *international regulators of safe and proper magic use.*

Leaders of Interest

Statesmen Dowel: *the nominal head of Imperial Stanclif (supported by lords).*
Patrain Vinkent Narroway: *head of the Drail (supported by Prognanes (lords)).*
General Easter: *commander of Stanclif's 6th ("Sick") Brigade.*
General Macwest: *commander of Stanclif's 3rd Brigade.*
General Foul: *commander of the Drail's 3rd Division.*
Colonel Dedicus Atmoor: *commander at Onwail.*
Lieutenant Colonel Nasim: *commander at Hail Crossing.*
Captain Brade: *famed Stanclif adventurer.*

Notable Members of Atmoor's Legion (Drail 17th Division)

Section leaders: *Major Weles (Section 1), Captain Hollery (Section 2), Wideskull Bleacher (Section 3), Sgt. Major Salfesk (Section 4), Lt. Ilscot (Section 5)*
NCOs: *Sgt. Mac Carrow (Section 1), Spt. Hissle (Section 3)*

Notable Members of Kin Kasidee's Irregulars (Comity Partisans)

Leaders: *Kin Kasidee, Havikare Eens, Raltman, Larrist*
Marksman: *Lost One*
Foot-soldiers: *Bodi, Colen, Brocken*

Notable Members of the Blood Scouts Platoon

Leaders: *Captain "Tenacious" Tate, Lt. "Wild Wish" Evans*
Magic support: *Emi (dirt-minder), Dollemore (witlacer)*
Snipers: *Four Skills, Oksy, Dalliance, Fawcet*
Urlian squad: *Caracker, Runt, Ohno, Toothless*
Rawboys: *Macmiddan, Graveguard, Latebite, Ptrangus, Basing*

Notable Races/Species

Coakels (worm-eyes): *part invertebrate part fish, from the Coak wetlands.*

Degrebus: *leathery, devious winged creatures found in mountainous regions.*

Giants: *enormous bipeds of various types, including skalk, hawk and swamp.*

Goblins: *green-skinned bipeds, about half human size and low in intelligence; including harker, lowbite, pack and weed. Notable vocabulary: 'wideskull' (general), 'sharptooth' (lieutenant), 'thins' (regular soldiers), 'talls' (humans)*

Grekkels: *part lupine (wolfy), part lacertillian (lizardy) bipeds.*

Grescinds: *huge crustacean (crablike) creatures native to Paradise Fails.*

Humans: *the prominent, powerful and most common bunch of bipeds.*

Urlians (ogres): *bigger bipeds, known for their great strength and less great wits.*

Trudge horses: *massive long-haired horses bred for swampland.*

Wyrlings: *big flying worm things.*

1

Though the stages of escalation in the One War were many and interwoven, plenty of crucible moments can be agreed upon. These were often minor events that chance might otherwise have overlooked. For example, a set of incursions into the Saints Mire was almost entirely ignored at the time, yet the war that followed would have been very different if the region had remained untouched.
Unfortunately, nowhere was untouched by this war.

Dueley's Comprehensive: The One War in
10 Volumes (Vol. 5), p. 25

Brother Poliset, Monk Adept in Guiltway, the Third Priory of the Saints Mire, and Assistant to High Venerator Venlain, considered the soldiers at the tree line and whispered, "Bollocks to this."

Despite what his mother always told people, Poliset had not taken up the calling of the Cane Saints and a life of solitude because he was brave. Quite the opposite: he'd seen war coming and believed this miserable land was so hallowed, and so undesirable, that there'd be no fighting here. The priory of Guiltway, in particular, nestling between brittle trees, jagged mountains and a sinister dark lake, was attended by only the most dedicated penitents. A location with zero military value.

So why, after ten months of hardship in this saints-forsaken keep, were there soldiers coming?

High Venerator Venlain gave Poliset a disapproving look for his curse, but for once Poliset didn't shrivel under his gaze. The venerator was wider than most, and louder, and presented himself as royalty, with his thick gold chains and scarlet robes. His eyes bulged indignantly as he quoted, *"Waste not the power of words, for they are the gift that separates us from the beasts."*

Scripture from the Prophet Azri. Poliset resisted saying bollocks to that and all. He suspected that the venerator, pompous as ever, was leaning on his everyday scoldings to avoid acknowledging the grim reality before them.

From the battlements of a stone wall over a thousand years old, they had an excellent view of the Wither Plain, a patchy grassland that separated Guiltway from Gulwood, where the creepy woodland created a barrier from the rest of the world, running all the way to the abyss of the Black Lake to the south. The plain, usually drearily empty, was gradually filling with people emerging from the trees.

There were hundreds of them, led by a group of soldiers on horseback in unmistakable military coats, sheaths of weapons hanging off their flanks or strapped across their backs. One of them held up a tall wooden cross with a scrap of material flapping from it, partly torn. Once a proud company standard, presumably, but in the dark, at this distance, and with its rips, it was indiscernible. The bulk of the soldiers passed the horses on foot, carrying rifles. Poliset had never seen such weapons before; the war had only briefly touched the Saints Mire, right at the start of everything, with an abortive campaign that barely even crossed the borders. Both sides had then quickly agreed to leave the Mire to its bogs and prayers. Not worth it.

Yet here they were.

Poliset swallowed as the line of horsemen raised torches, which ignited one by one in a display that would've been impressive if it wasn't so dreadful. They held the flames high, putting themselves on fearsome show as it cast bright-lined silhouettes and deep shadows.

"What madness is this," Venlain grumbled, at last acknowledging the threat. When the bell had rung, he had bumbled his way up here, bunching up his robes and plodding unevenly over the stairs, unused to the climb. Poliset and three other adepts had followed, joining another half dozen monks who had already reached the wall's highest point. They'd all been waiting for the venerator's assessment. For him to make this go away. But minutes had passed as he watched with disdain, and now he said, "These lands are protected by the Saints and the Flesh. Have they no idea what they are doing?"

The army looked very much like they knew what they were doing, Poliset thought, considering how neatly the soldiers were lined up. There was movement in the centre, as some made way for others to bring forward a large object.

"Can you see their colours?" a young adept asked. "I can't see their colours."

"Whoever they are," Venlain huffed, "their presence is a blasphemy."

"And against international law," Rimpert, an older adept said, importantly, but with clear nerves.

"Should we call on them to withdraw?" the young adept asked. Because a huge army who'd put themselves on show just needed to be told to move along, please, you're not welcome. Poliset rolled his eyes.

"Let them make their case," Venlain sneered. "Stand brave, my brothers, my sons. This is Guiltway, as unassailable as any priory in the Mire. No enemy force has ever successfully laid siege to this fort. This is a castle thrice blessed by the Saints and their Prophets. Woe upon any who challenges us here."

His proud words warmed the adepts, whose scared expressions turned hopeful in the flickering light from the nearby brazier. Then one of them gasped, drawing attention to fresh movement in the plain. Poliset squinted at a group of soldiers tramping forward with raised rifles. Where they had parted the line, the large object was now properly revealed, boasting a long barrel: some kind of cannon. A mounted soldier raised a hand.

Poliset considered that it might be true that Guiltway had never been successfully taken, but there were two good explanations for that. Firstly, no one *wanted* it. Secondly, he was quite sure no one had brought a cannon here before.

He checked over his shoulder, taking in their modest home. Though the keep was substantial and the walls were indeed thick, it was essentially a ring of stone with scant living quarters and storerooms between empty chapels. They had pikes and spears with more historical value than practical purpose – no one was trained to use them. They might repel invaders for a few moments, at best.

Poliset's eyes ran up to the keep's eagle's nest tip, joined to the battlements by a rickety wooden stair-bridge the monks rarely ventured up. Their greatest brazier sat up there, the last place invaders were likely to reach. If they did break in, he supposed, the killing might stop by the time they fully secured the priory. He had retreated this far from the war, what was a little further? And besides, their best – only – hope was to alert the next nearest priory for help.

"Should we light the beacon?" Poliset asked loudly, interrupting the others' frightened muttering. He was already edging towards the stairs. High Venerator Venlain threw another disapproving look his way, rightly suspecting he wanted to flee. Venlain had always considered him an unworthy coward, from the amount of work he gave him.

"Why would we do that? Do you doubt the Saints' protection?"

Poliset hesitated, because yes, he very much doubted any holy force was going to stop those soldiers, but the venerator's glare warned him not to answer.

"No," Venlain said. "We will not appeal to them, nor will we hide, nor will we cry for help. We will let the Saints answer this sin. They will sink in the mud. Their weapons will bounce off our armour. This is Guiltway, a blessed sanctuary, and they will know it!" His voice rose as he spoke, the defiance swelling his chest, and his adepts' faces brightened again.

Poliset stared. However passionately he said it, the man *had* to know it was ratshit. The Rocc had broadly rejected most faith centuries ago, leaving these priories and orders alone out of politeness or pity more than reverence. As a monk, he appreciated the calming nature of prayer and the hope of beings more powerful than himself, but Poliset always believed that the Saints only helped those who helped themselves.

As High Venerator Venlain faced the horde with a glare fit to drive the entire war back into whatever hole it had crawled out of, Poliset gave the wooden stairs another look.

"They think the Saints no longer matter," Venlain went on. "Their weapons get stronger and more horrific, but they will never develop a machine that can match the power of the one, true –"

The battlements erupted in an explosion that threw Poliset down, a thunderous boom following a moment later. He landed hard, ears ringing, and blinked as he tried to understand the changed scene before him. Where High Venerator Venlain had stood, on the thick, impenetrable wall, there was now a crescent curve, a gap with smoke and dust clearing and rubble crumbling. A dark splatter coated the stonework before Poliset and another monk lay crumpled over the edge, not moving.

The venerator was gone. Completely gone.

Poliset looked around as if he might find him somewhere further back, in the air, but there was nothing but a thin trail of smoke and little specs of stonework raining down. As his hearing returned, he heard screams. Someone shouting. Rimpert was jumping up and down on the other side of the gap. His words slowly became clearer: "Light the beacon! For Tikan's sake, light the beacon!"

Poliset nodded and confusedly crawled along the rampart, stumbling as he tried to stand. He fell against the wall and looked out over the plain, blinking the stinging smoke from his eyes. The amassed army was swarming over the grass, lit in patches by the torch-wielding horse riders, and a collective shout came ahead of them. A battle cry borne by a mob of feral people. They had fired on Guiltway with a tremendous weapon that had torn through the wall and eviscerated High Venerator Venlain. They had attacked without warning and without quarter, not even giving the priory a chance to surrender. Why?

The plain sparked with small flashes, and the wall was peppered by loud impacts. A bullet rushed past Poliset.

"The beaco –" Rimpert shrieked and Poliset turned to see the monk's head erupt as a shot caught him in the temple. He flopped limply over the battlements, dead face fixed in surprise.

Shaking out the confusion and terror, Poliset ran. He ducked and held his hands over his head. The sound of soldiers' yells and gunfire was quickly approaching, building in volume, as he scrambled for the stairs. He used both banisters to propel himself, and was halfway up when the structure quaked violently. Another clap of thunder followed, out near the trees, the cannon so powerful that it struck before its sound reached them. He heard screams below, the crunching of broken brickwork, where the weapon had breached the walls near the ground.

Gritting his teeth, Poliset kept climbing and staggered into the keep's nest, grabbing the beacon's cage to stay upright. He fumbled through the kindling for the spark box and flinched as more shots whipped by, nearer and nearer. Screams came from his kin being slaughtered, and from the killers charging inside. They were demons, mixing laughter in the shrieks.

Poliset cranked the spark box. It flashed but didn't catch. He cranked it again, desperately. No one could save them, he already understood. But someone had to *know* of this horror. The shouts were rising, soldiers climbing stairs, monks screaming as they fell.

The box flashed once more and the beacon lit. Poliset stepped back with a rush of relief, the fire spreading through the caged wood and coal to form a pillar as tall as him. The ferocious blaze immediately made him sweat, its roar matching the battle noise, promising salvation.

Poliset laughed giddily, flicking a look from the fire to the violence below. Monks were being murdered everywhere as soldiers piled in, smashing whatever got in their way. He saw an adept stabbed through the eye. But the beacon was lit. This brutality would be answered. He might even be saved.

The ground quaked again and Poliset almost fell over, bracing himself against the beacon cage. He stepped back with a shriek of pain as his hand burnt, and the rolling thunder of the cannon's boom blended into the sound of stonework splitting. He knew what was coming – the tower itself was hit – but he didn't want to look, to make it real. The floor shifted again, scattering fire from the beacon.

Poliset saw a broken gap in the wooden stairs, a few metres down. Too big for him to jump, leaving no way down. The tower moaned again and he peered over the edge at last. The blast that had torn through the stairs had torn through the tower, too, leaving a great chunk missing, and cracks spreading. On the battlements, soldiers looked his way, rifles in hand, macabre fire-lit grins on their faces. Poliset shakily looked away from them, to the beacon. Chunks of it had already spilt out, the cage broken, light dimming.

He had left the war as far behind as possible. He had done everything he could, hadn't he, to stop it from reaching him – why hadn't it been enough? He closed his eyes and offered one last prayer to the Saints, wishing harder than ever that the faith was real.

The tower broke apart. He tumbled into a cascade of stone and fire.

2

In 720, while Khibba outriders still trained with bows and spears, weapons were being devised that could destroy entire neighbourhoods in one blast. Consider, too, the sniper schools of central Boldarow's repurposed country estates: young hopefuls were taught how to fire rifles as far as the eye could see, mere paces from peers training in traditional husbandry.

A Fine & Baffling War, Flegherty, p. 4

Wild Wish watched her newest recruits getting into formation, idly shuffling, breath misting the air. They weren't all nervous, exactly – some looked decidedly cocky – but they didn't know how to manage their knobbly knees and elbows or steady their feet. If they weren't unsure, they were impatient. It was her third class of trainees and she was used to the signs now: they wouldn't be sent to her if they were already fully competent soldiers. Her task should've been to take accomplished riflemen and make them expert snipers, but she suspected the ones with most promise were being sent to more seasoned trainers, like those at Killen's Estate, while she got the iffy hopefuls. Immediately, she ranked these newbies: Blond Curls, likely to crack under pressure; Ponytail, probably squeamish about mud; Moustached Ringer, not serious.

They were all men, of course – another disappointment, as expected.

Yet despite this rabble, Wish couldn't complain. The barracks at Rock Stable were sturdy, warm and well stocked with food and drink, more traditionally used for training winged degrebus. They were a long way from the fighting, on a mountain plateau that overlooked a great swathe of flat Lome farmland. Wish only had to train people for half the day before their attention waned, then she was free to wander the woodland, loiter around the officers' quarters or read quietly in her room. Her room, in fact, was the most comfort she'd had since enlisting. The bed alone was a luxury, never mind the chair, ceiling, walls and view. She also commanded a modicum of respect here, with officers and recruits alike gradually accepting she knew a few things worth teaching. Everyone still gave her uncertain looks (why was there a woman in uniform here? Or at all?) but no one gave her trouble. Sergeant Bix helped with that.

On the other hand, this comfort meant she had a lot of time to think, and the thoughts were seldom pleasant. Taking in the fresh faces, she wondered which of them would survive longest. Would any of them survive at all? The war had lasted well over a year already and it wasn't slowing down. The average life expectancy of a sniper was three weeks, she had been told. She'd survived more than half a year herself, so she wondered if she'd used up approximately . . . eight other snipers' complete time? Were these guys going to step out of training right into a bullet to balance out her luck?

Sergeant Bix cleared his throat.

It was a sound she'd got used to: a short cough that warned her to focus. Wish flashed a brief smile. Bix offered no judgement, his scarred face always steely in default moodiness. He was an older soldier with an average height and build, and a head of badger-striped hair, but his presence commanded order. He rarely needed to speak to get his way.

"Okay, right, yes," Wish said, and the hubbub quietened. She smiled again then forced herself not to. Not here to make friends, people kept reminding her. She needed authority to teach effectively. She straightened her back and shored up her voice. "So you all think you've got what it takes to be a sniper?"

The two rows of eight skinny men (and they were all skinny) stared with suspicion. They knew who she was, but that was never enough to demand respect outright. She continued with a short speech she had prepared for her first class and since perfected. She walked along the line, hands behind her back, eyeing each recruit in turn, as she told them this was going to be a tough few weeks. They were going to be held to a higher standard than anyone in the Stanclif military. They were going to come out as the best or not at all. (That got some shocked muttering and she wondered if it needed rewording.) She went into a spiel about the guns they'd be learning to master: the Long 0.48, her preferred weapon, and the Hallwood 0.42, Oksy's weapon of choice. She explained these weapons were unlike anything they'd used before, and her mind wandered.

Where *was* Oksy?

Where were any of them? Wild Wish was so alone. Bix and his silent scowls and a couple of polite nods from other officers was a poor substitute for the distinct lack of friends. It was all men marching about with rifles or managing unruly degrebus in the stables. There was one nurse, best described as matronly, and one male doctor. A half dozen male orderlies. The female cooks were unpleasant; they didn't speak Stanish and made their disdain for Wish known with disapproving looks. It was her village of Swelig all over again, except back home she could at least exchange hellos with mums and old women. She felt a return of some of the deep regret and panic that had gripped her when she first joined the war. This was a boys' club isolated on top of a rock, and it made the absence of the rest of the Blood Scouts a constant, painful reminder.

Wish asked everyone who came through if they'd heard word of the girls she'd left in Low Slane. Most people had no idea what she was talking about, the existence of the Blood Scouts not being especially well known to begin with. General Easter himself had mentioned some female scouts were reported to have been travelling south, before she came here, but he hadn't elaborated. Wish had dozens of friends unaccounted for: the entirety of Sun and Sabre Squads, and her own injured companions, Rue, Dakoda, and dear, dear Newk, with only Oksy and a couple of others to look out for them. It had been almost two months. Had they made it back? Would they ever contact her?

The questions and accompanying memories filled Wish's mind in her idle hours. And most hours in Rock Stable were idle.

Bix cleared his throat again and she focused on the crowd of waiting men. Had she finished talking? From the look on their faces, yes. Wish brightly asked, "Any questions?"

The dark-skinned moustached trainee's hand went up. He had a glint in his eye, an arrogant half-smile under that untrustworthy thin moustache. But he was a ringer, like Newk, so maybe he was alright. Wish gestured for him to go ahead and he said, "How old are you?"

A few braver recruits laughed, quietly, and he looked self-satisfied for two seconds before Sergeant Bix drove a fist into his gut. That left Moustache wheezing on his hands and knees, eyes shimmering with tears. Bix stood pillar-stiff, daring anyone else to speak. His lips peeled back to say something but Wish intervened.

"Alright, Sergeant." She needed to handle this herself. It wasn't an unreasonable question, really. She was probably younger than most of these men, and softer-looking, without any of Bix's mean aura. But they needed to know that she was also formidable. She had practised this, too. "My age isn't important. Count the number of people I've killed instead, it's probably more than anyone you know. You want to benefit from that experience, you're gonna have to earn it."

It sounded good. Wise. Something she could say with a knowing smile even if the weight of it made her heart ache. She stood over Moustache as he looked up, a little afraid? She wasn't trying to look tough. She'd tried that with her second class and saw them hiding smiles. She wouldn't kick or shove them, as Bix once suggested she do. She just stared into their eyes to let them know she meant business. Besides which, cheeky as Moustache was, it didn't seem right to pick on the only ringer in the group. The only one she'd seen, in fact, since abandoning Newk.

He nodded obediently, as if she'd asked him a question, and sat on his haunches, but didn't stand. Not without permission.

Wish sighed. "Get up, get your guns. Let's shoot some shit."

She led them towards the rifle range, tired again. What she'd said of her experience was true and she didn't like it. She hadn't *wanted* to kill all those people. It wasn't her fault she was good at it.

Sometimes at night she tried to count how many men might've died at her hands, and how many families were left ruined. She wondered how it balanced against animals that had to kill for their daily meals, and if there was any way at all it could make sense.

Continuing past the degrebus stables, she paused as a shape in her periphery caught her attention. A silhouette, to her right – a woman? When she looked properly, the figure was gone. She forced her eyes quickly ahead again. It had been a ragged figure, watching her. Familiar in a bad way, because it was probably a ghost. She had enough troubles without adding ghosts. This plateau wasn't big enough for all the ghosts that might haunt her.

Uneasily, she led the recruits in shooting practice through the morning, offering instructions on how sniper rifles differed from regular mumblers and how the scopes worked. They set up behind the estate, where she had targets positioned at a hundred, two hundred, five hundred yards away. She observed them firing, to see where they'd need the most instruction. A good way to teach, she thought; no one wanted to sit in a classroom listening to her drawl on. That would come later, after they'd established she was Fun. But her mind drifted more than usual as she tried to get these guys going. Her eyes wandered towards the estate, to the closest doorway, expecting to see the figure again. A girl. A friend. But .. . they were all lost, gone. Wish felt cold, an uncommon sensation in her great coat, fur-lined to fend off Rock Stable's winds.

Bix appeared at her side and said, in his gravelly tone, "Time for a break?"

Wish looked from him back to the estate. Disappointingly empty. She noticed the closest students' faces watching her. People mostly wore that expression when she'd done, or was about to do, something terrible. She'd only been staring at nothing though – apparently these days that unsettled people enough. She swallowed and instructed quietly, "Have them practise for an hour then tell them to study Major Heskeph's guide. I'll be . . . I'm . . ."

She gave up on finishing that sentence and walked away. Ignored the recruits muttering. She searched the windows and doorways of the buildings, almost willing the ghost to come back. There was movement – officers in an upstairs room. A pair of men came out of a side door laughing, carrying buckets of slop. They lost some cheer seeing her, so she smiled, which made them frown. Wish quickened her pace, heading into the house's west wing. She should lie down. Wash her face. Lose herself in a book. She had a small stash of adventure novels, full of buxom women, hidden treasures and unlikely escapes.

Wish's heart was just lifting at that thought when she entered her room and found the ghost waiting. She shrieked and stepped back, checking to see who'd heard. The hallway was empty, no one to scold her, and no one to help her as she double-checked the room.

The figure was still there. Remarkably solid for a ghost. As Wish fought to slow her heartbeat, she eyed the woman carefully – familiar, yes, but badly changed. She was wearing the old blue-grey scout light armour, muddied and torn and burnt black in patches. Her hair was a long tangled mess, swept over one side of her face, covering markings that Wish was happy were hidden. Wish closed the door behind her and whispered, "Four Skills? That's not really you, is it?"

The apparition was slouched in Wish's chair, one arm slung over the side and the other supporting herself on a tall rifle. One of her legs was tucked under her, the other stretched out. Straight and long because it could not bend. A shard of dull metal stuck out the bottom of the trouser leg, attached to an empty boot.

"Four Skills," Wish repeated, this time in pity and apology, as the woman gave her time to process it. She came closer, lifting her hands, wanting to make it better somehow. Just to touch her. She was real. She was actually here. And she was in a terrible state.

Skills raised her brow with half a weary smile. "Good to see you, Wild Wish. Hope you don't mind I let myself in."

"Mind?" Wish gaped. "You were down there, weren't you? You were –" She took another step closer, not sure now if she wanted to hug her or hit her, for the brief madness she'd felt stirring. "Why didn't you say hello?"

"Didn't want to distract you," Skills said. "And thought I'd take the load off in the meantime."

"What are you doing here?" Wish cried, then she let out a thrilled noise and launched herself at the seated woman. Wish grabbed her in a tight hug, pressing her face into Skills' shoulder. Skills tried to lightly pat her back, but winced. Wish backed off, looking at the leg, then the patch of face covered by hair. "What happened? Are you okay? Where are the others?"

"Yeah, we've got some catching up to do," Four Skills said and Wish didn't like her tone. "It's not all good. And it ends with a request."

"A request?"

Skills nodded. "I've got a job for you. An ugly one."

3

While the statistics for fatalities during the One War are incredible, calculated both through casualty records and assumptions about the missing, it is often overlooked that the numbers left injured and scarred, to live in permanent suffering, were at least equally high. For these poor souls, the trials of the war never ended.
Sickness and Sin: Medicine and Religion Through the Ages, Grunberg, p. 675

Once Wild Wish had sat on the bed, at Four Skills' insistence, her fellow sniper sank deeper into the chair and exhaled. Readying herself for something heavy. "What do you know about the Saints Mire?"

Wish frowned. This was a bad start. "Isn't that one of the few places in Boldarow that's as unpleasant as Low Slane? No one goes there but sad monks."

"And primitive tribes, yeah. And there are grescinds. Only place in Boldarow you'll find grescinds."

Wish stared. If this was Oksy talking, by now she'd have learnt the entire history of the grescind and six different ways to cook one, but Skills was more efficient with her words, leaving Wish ignorant over what a grescind was. But she had a hopeful thought: "Are the others there? You want me to go get them?"

Skills shook her head. "No. What's there is a job no one else wants. The sort the Blood Scouts were formed for. I want you to rebuild the platoon and do it."

"Rebuild it with the others? You know where they are, right?"

"That's not what I'm saying. This would be a . . . new start."

As Skills stared into Wish's eyes, she recognised this wasn't necessarily a good thing. Never mind the clear skirting of the promise of bringing back her friends, Wish had been warned off even thinking about such ideas before. She said, "General Easter told me it was over. No more Blood Scouts."

Skills grunted unhappily; apparently she'd had similar conversations. "They'll change their minds. Again. Especially if you take this on."

"But I'm a teacher now, didn't you see?" It came out like a joke, and Skills dutifully smiled. Not really amused. Wish added, more seriously, "I'm not a leader. We need Tate."

"Yeah, see" – the sniper shifted, cringing with the combined pain of moving and what she was about to say – "she's not coming back. Near as I'm aware, the chain of command points . . ." Skills tilted her rifle towards Wish, as a queen might anoint a knight.

Wish shook her head. "You can't know that –"

"Sorry, Wild. I found them. Sun Squad, out in Low Slane. Captain Tate, Spyke, the rest. None of them are coming back."

The bottom fell out of Wish's stomach. She'd had two months to imagine triumphant returns. A fresh call to arms. Heroes wading out of the fog of their damned mission. They couldn't be dead. Not Tate or Spyke, the toughest members of the platoon. She shook her head, about to deny it, but Four Skills moved on.

"We got to Reeve Abbey late ourselves. Couldn't track you far after that. I didn't know much of what happened until I found Emi here. She said you won us the Battle of Wick. Saved untold lives."

"I cost a few, too," Wish said, imagining how Emi might've put it. The dirt-minder mage, the sole scout she had kept in contact with, often lurked in Footward, the town at the base of this mountain, but they didn't see each other often. The military had continual use for a mage, even a female one they didn't trust, which didn't involve visiting a training camp for snipers and flying reptiles. When they did reunite, it was mostly because Emi had wandered off from an assignment, and though Wish appreciated the company she was often too worried about their superiors finding out to relax. Emi still made Wish feel uneasy herself, too.

"She said you were responsible for everything they gave Captain Brade credit for," Skills said. "Not just Wick, everything. You got them through Low Slane."

"Hardly. You know Fixit's dead? Pound? Maybe the others, too. I left Newk behind, Skills. I –"

"You did your best," Skills said. "And I'm hoping you will again now."

Wish bit her lip, hating this already. She was finally with another scout, the most competent of them all, and it came with a bucket of "everyone's gone except you". But they hadn't just had Tate – what about Sabre squad? She asked, "Where's Larkin?"

"Gone. Maybe alive, I don't know. We had trouble getting to Reeve Abbey, even more trouble getting back." She thumped her fake leg in its empty boot against the floor. "We got separated and I couldn't do much to help." That came out apologetic, guilty, and Wish gave her an unhappy look of understanding. "It's got to be you, Wild. You're a lieutenant, after all."

Wish scoffed. "That doesn't mean anything. They didn't even know what rank I was before; they just threw it at me. I wasn't even commissioned, I think? I was only promoted informally in the field!"

"They gave it to you because you earned it. And this." Skills looked out the window, acknowledging Rock Stable. A ridiculously secure estate with no threat of real violence; its name said it all. "I hate to take this from you. I hate to ask . . ."

"But you are," Wish said.

Skills sighed. "They split up those of us in Sabre Squad who got back. There's them and others like us out there. More every day, I bet. We're better together, you know that. We *need* the Blood Scouts. Captain Tate wouldn't let them ignore that – and you've got a reputation of your own. If you start with the Saints Mire, you can quickly build from there."

"Start *what* with Saints Mire? If there's no one there, what's it got to do with us?"

Skills slid a hand into her coat and pulled out a battered, brown sheath of paper and held it up, saying, "It's got as much to do with us as we want it to, thanks to this."

Wish unfolded the paper and read an unsteady scrawl of

desperate writing: *Send Blood Scouts to assist. Urgently.*

"What the fuck is this?" Wish said. Why was someone leaving hauntingly scratched notes about them? In the Saints Mire? She didn't know much about the region, but knew it was in Elmn, the southern theatre, a long way from their activities in the west.

"That," Skills said, "is our ticket to reviving the scouts. Let me go from the top. The Saints Mire has been strictly neutral since the beginning of the war. It's a logistical nightmare with little strategic value. Both the Comity and the Drail kept symbolic armies near the borders, to demonstrate neither was going in, until about three weeks ago, when the Drail crossed the border. There's been no official word from the Arrow Council and our own people don't want to escalate things without knowing more, in case this is just the Onwail commander getting itchy feet. But it's been complicated by a group of Comity partisans also entering the Mire without orders. Communication's been cut off in the west, leaving that message" – Skills pointed at the paper – "as the only word we've had from either side, sent from the partisans via the locals. Command came to me asking if I knew them."

"Maybe some of ours are with them?" Wish suggested.

"Unlikely. They're led by a Tynesian guy called Kin Kasidee. He's built himself a reputation as a risk-taker, with a company who throw themselves into things most commanders would shy from. He's a showman, followed by men out for adventure – irresponsible, not really our kind of crowd. But I suspect Kasidee, or someone in his ranks, knew Tate. She campaigned in the east before forming the Blood Scouts. My theory, which Command agrees on, is that Kasidee wants us to legitimise his fight against the Drail incursion. A small scout unit could confirm the situation, give a go-ahead, maybe provide assistance, and see the Drail turned back."

"All I'd need to do is travel through another hellscape like Low Slane and face enemies unknown? Got it."

"Like I said, it's ugly. But that note's an excuse for Command to revive the Blood Scouts. The Saints Mire is holy land, politically and literally a quagmire, which they'd rather not touch. You volunteer to lead a team and assess the situation, they'd be mad to refuse, with your experience and these partisans specifically after our help. All you'd strictly need to do is report on what's happening, then come back as the leader of a new scout platoon. From there, you take your pick of people to rebuild the Blood Scouts for the next assignment."

Wish followed her train of thought, realising it might mean more than just that: "I could request that we search for everyone who's still missing?"

"Maybe. Hopefully."

"But it's not that simple, is it? It's never that simple. I've got to fight again. Maybe die in some stupid horrible place?"

"The fight's what we came for, isn't it?" Skills said, a little shortly. She swallowed the brief emotion, mouth tight, and dropped her eyes to her missing leg. "I never wanted to sit out the war. Don't have much choice now, though. And if it wasn't this, it would be something else. They put you here to keep things quiet about Wick and Reeve Abbey, but just for a while. You're too skilled for them to ignore. But we can work with this. Set terms."

Wish hung her head. Skills was right, of course, and despite the horrors she'd endured, she hadn't intended to become a hermit up this mountain. When she lay awake remembering and imagining the worst, there were also thoughts of new things she might do if she returned to the fight. There was always that possibility, somewhere and somehow, that she might make a difference. End this war. Seeing Skills here, like this, with that possibility removed for herself, made that all the starker. Wish asked, "How'd you lose it?"

"Doesn't matter," Skills said, then reconsidered. "Animal trap. It was stupid. Travelling by night. I was supposed to be the hunter, wasn't I? But here we are."

"I'm sorry."

"Yeah." Skills' eyes hardened. "You can say no. You've done enough. But we could do for others what Tate did for us."

Wish hesitated, fixing on that *we*. "You'd come too?"

Skills smiled sadly. "No. That part of the war's over for me. I can take over your training here, though. And I've all but put a team together for you already. You'll have Emi, for starters."

"The others from Sabre Squad?"

"Only Scraper. Command let her escort me, on account of my injury. Otherwise, you get strangers. For now."

Wish tried to place Scraper, a Blood Scout she wasn't familiar with. Not a sniper, for sure.

"I found some ogres," Skills went on. "One who knew Oksy – came about while I was trying to find her."

"Ogres? In a scout platoon?" Wish said, then frowned. "Have you spoken to literally everyone else before me?"

"You're the last stop on a long journey," Skills said, without apology. "The closest anyone was to the Mire itself, geographically. And I wanted to come to you with a plan ready. That's all. But you *can* tell me to leave. I'll forget all about it, even join you here. It's up to you."

Wish hesitated, tempted by the easy way out, liking this new idea of her and Four Skills up here together. A friend at last. But if the operation was already in motion, with all this potential – if *she* still had potential, as Skills believed – then where would her idling mind go knowing someone else was doing her job? She said, "Emi's on board?"

"Yes. The ogres, too. And you'll have a handful of other soldiers."

"Ogres," Wish repeated, that idea alone escalating this. Widespread as the war was, she'd mostly dealt with humans, which put something of a cap on how terrible it could all get, until Low Slane and the things she'd seen there. "Does the Mire have giants? Deadly insects? Giant deadly insects? And what's a grescind?"

"Their forna's easily avoided," Skills said dismissively, then shifted again, with another grimace. Wish noted then how stiff she was, holding in more pain than she showed.

"Can I get you something? We've got real wine up here."

Skills shook her head. "Alcohol makes it worse. It's okay, I'm done. I know this is a massive ask. You can say no. Absolutely you can."

"Stop saying that," Wish sighed. "You know I'm not going to. *You* wouldn't say no. And you wouldn't have limped up here if there was a chance I would. Of course I'll take some random strangers into another bog and find new ways to die. Damn, Four, what else am I going to do?"

"Live out the war safely. Go home?"

"While we've got Blood Scouts, and people asking for Blood Scouts, fighting without me? Forget this place, the wine's not even good and the linen smells. Plus no one here wants to talk to me."

Skills almost looked amused. Almost.

But Wish instantly felt guilty and added, "You didn't find any sign of the others? No idea where Newk is?" She left off the implicit: *or if she's alive.*

"I didn't find bodies."

That was something, Wish supposed. She hummed. She'd been imagining months, if not years, of tedium up here. A lot of time thinking bad thoughts. She said, "Okay then. When are you going to introduce me to the other idiots you've roped into this?"

"Oh. The ogres are waiting for you in town. But I'm not going back down that hill."

Wish's gaze softened as she considered Skills' missing leg again. A cold, industrious chunk of metal in its place. She asked, "You'll still come to the farm, won't you? When all this is over?"

Skills smiled again, without answering. Was that an *of course?* Or just pity?

"You're the best of us," Wish added, sounding even more pathetic.

"If I ever was," Skills replied, "I'm not anymore. You're more than you know, Wild."

Wish held her gaze, holding in tears. Straining to stop herself from spewing out more: complaints, confessions, despair. Instead of letting it out and throwing woes at her broken friend's feet (foot), Wish held out a hand. Skills shook it and offered a smart, satisfied nod.

4

People's homes. Ordinary streets. Shops and churches. Quiet attics and dusty cellars. Empty warehouses, overgrown parks and the gardens of country estates. Farms, factories, sporting grounds and dockyards. These were our battlefields. Everywhere you might have once found people, you found the fight.
All This Aflame: Memoirs of a Soldier, Lindon, p. 13

The gunshots startled Little Goan from his porridge and his first fear was angering his mother. He'd sprayed oats across the table, from his spit and spoon. But Mother's eyes were afraid, too, and he flinched again as the gunfire continued. The bangs that had been new and unfamiliar a year ago were familiar now: men in Hoster's Farmstead occasionally practised with the foreign rifles they'd gathered, but not normally this early. And they were usually sparing with how many shots they fired.

As Goan processed that in typical Little Goan fashion – *slow but he gets there,* they said – the gunfire got closer, coming from different directions, and shouting joined it. Mother threw down the bowl she'd been scrubbing and flew around the table to take Goan by the shoulder.

"Gun, get the gun, Dinny!" Father shouted outside. His angry voice had a frightened edge, as unnatural as Mother's scared eyes.

"Stay here!" Mother hissed as she thrust Goan onto his knees, forcing him under the table. He winced at the sound of more gunshots, running footsteps nearby and someone grunting in pain. Mother ran through the entrance hall to the bedroom and Goan crawled out, itching to follow her, not to be left alone on the cold stone floor – but the front door burst open and Father stumbled in. He fell to his knees, gasping for air, and Goan shrieked. Father flung the door closed behind him and collapsed to one side, propping himself up on his elbows. His shirt was dark and wet around his chest, his chin streaked with blood, soaking through his thick moustache.

"Dinny!" He struggled to get the word out. Goan moved towards him, but Father caught his eye and shook his head. He had a wild animal look, like their marsh goat in the spring, when madness had taken it. Mother had said it was too dangerous to approach.

Mother skidded back into the entrance hall with Father's rifle in her hands. She didn't know how to hold it; the men had never taught her. She needed to grip the handle and to steady the barrel and to place a finger on the trigger. And she needed to point it forward, not across her chest like a stack of wood. She almost dropped it as she choked on an upset sound, crouching next to Father. She started repeating his name, trembling, as he tried to speak.

"Soldiers. In the fields. They're here."

Mother offered him the gun in shock, not seeing that Father was too weak to hold it. He could barely hold his head up and blood was spreading around his legs. He wheezed, long and hard, and lifted a hand to her face. He whispered, "I love you," and died.

Goan clamped his hands over his ears as Mother screamed, then she was up and holding the rifle properly, by instinct. She moved into the kitchen, to look out of the window, and ducked as more gunshots cracked outside. She told Goan, "Stay hidden. When it's safe, run to the Rosens."

The Rosens? They *hated* the Rosens, the big family who lived over the hill. Mr Rosen never respected their border, Father said. Stole more from their land than the damn rodents.

Men ran through their field and a shadow flitted across the window. Their angry shouts were loud enough to hear clearly, but Goan didn't understand their words. The Imperials, they called them – awful men with wicked technology who were damaging the Mire. Mother had said they would never come here, though. They had nothing to tempt men from big cities with mechanical engines, even though marsh wheat and goats and tweed were all anyone needed to live. Mother *promised*.

The footsteps thumped up to the house and Goan retreated under the table as more guns fired far away. A man huffed loudly and said what Goan was sure was a rude word. Mother, crouched by the wall, clutching the rifle tightly, bracing herself. She would protect him. Now Father was . . .

There was a loud bang from by the door. The man shouted then more gunshots followed and the kitchen window shattered. Goan covered his ears again and ducked low, fighting to keep in a scream. Father's gun hit the tiles as Mother slumped abruptly on top of him. Her eyes were open, staring Goan's way, but there was nothing in them. Blood seeped from a hole in the side of her head. A hole in the wall let sunlight in.

Goan shook all over, blubbering. Tears pooled into his eyes.

The door flung open and a soldier marched in, growling as he scanned from side to side, a dark man in mucky green clothes. He had a rifle raised and was grimacing like he wanted to use it. Goan shuffled back and the man's lips curled in a snarl. He muttered in his foreign language and stepped towards Goan – but just as he left the light of the doorway, a weapon thundered outside and the soldier flew sideways, struck by a magnificent force. Goan quickly palmed the tears off his face to see: the man was gone.

For a moment, there was silence. Just Goan's heavy breathing and his parents lifeless on the floor. Then footsteps came again. Another voice, more weird words. It was a lighter voice though. Female? Without logic, Goan hoped it was Mother herself, about to enter, alive again. But someone else strode in, a woman in a long flapping coat with a gun much wider than any rifle Goan had seen before. She walked with purpose, oversized boots clonking against the stone, and Goan tried to move but hit his head against the table with a yelp.

The woman looked his way, feet apart and gun ready. Her body was motionless as her eyes moved from Goan to Father and Mother, then back to him. Her coat was brown leather, layered around the shoulders and draping down to her shins, a once-white shirt underneath crossed with big belts of pouches and a great many metal cylinders that looked like bullets but were too big and flat.

She wore a scruffy flat cap over a mess of short but thick dark hair, sticking out all over like the straw of their scarecrow, and her face was shady around the eyes and dirty. She looked like someone who slept outside, Goan thought, but not like the Woodwings of Midwood or the Shadow Nomads. Her clothes were too strange, with that coat, those big laced boots and the gun – all from another world.

Then she smiled, a good and wide smile without malice, and Goan felt a crack in his fear. She glanced to the side, to where the soldier she had shot had flown, then called something outside in her language. She lowered her gun and walked into the kitchen. Goan scampered to one side and hit a table leg, watching the gap between her and the entrance. He couldn't get past.

She crouched, raising her free hand with an open palm, her skin dry and rough where it was visible through holes in her old fingerless glove. She said something, then paused and spoke again. Her voice changed slightly, a question of some sort. Goan shook his head: he didn't understand, and didn't want her here, or for any of this to be true. The woman smiled again and tried new, different words. Different languages. She had a gift of tongues. A great power. He wondered then, as she continued, if she wasn't a spirit come to save him. Unusual in appearance, not obviously holy, but . . . an angel?

"What about Mirian Garter?" she said, and Goan lit up at the familiar words.

He nodded enthusiastically. "Yes! You speak Mirian!"

"I do." The woman held his eyes, unblinking, and placed a hand on her chest. "Havikare. That's my name. You can call me Havik. And you are?"

Someone else walked into the house and Goan looked around her to see a tall and angular man with an incredibly long rifle and a tight leather vest. The woman, Havik, shot him a look and said something that sounded like an order, but the man merely stared into the kitchen. He had only one eye, the other covered by a thick patch. He regarded Goan's parents with distaste, drawing the boy's attention back to them. Dead. Both of them.

Havik's face bobbed in front of him, blocking the sight. "What's your name?"

"My . . . my . . ." Goan whimpered. *My parents.*

"Your name," Havik insisted, smiling again, and he was drawn back into her eyes. She had nice eyes, inviting. Nice teeth. White.

"Goan," he said. "Little Goan."

"Everything's going to be okay, Little Goan. You're safe now."

The one-eyed man huffed, as unfriendly as she was nice. He moved on into the house.

"We've stopped the bad men," Havik said. "Look at me, Goan, keep looking at me. The bad men are dead, but more might come. I need you to do something. Can you protect this farm?"

"P-protect?" Goan echoed. How could he be safe if his parents were dead? How could more men come?

"Yes. We need to keep moving. We're good people, understand. Have you heard of Kin Kasidee? He's a hero and we're his friends."

Goan jumped at the sound of drawers being opened and closed, the one-eyed man searching the house. "What's he doing?"

"No, that's not him," Havik said. "Kasidee is fighting the rest of the bad men right now. Helping people like you. Will you help me help them, too? We need food. Fresh clothing. Did your father like to drink? The special drinks that adults enjoy. They can cure us when we're ill. Help us fight."

The one-eyed man tramped into the kitchen with a big canvas bag, messily stuffed with clothes. He barely acknowledged their presence as he started opening the cupboards.

"Father's bag," Goan said, concern rising.

"Will you lend me these things?" Havik asked, gently. "Help us help others?"

Goan swallowed, and looked from her back to his Mother's lifeless face. His tears returned, shimmering thickly. He startled at the touch of the woman's hand, catching his chin.

"You're a very brave boy, Goan," she said, guiding his head back to focus on her. "I can see how brave you are. I need you to be brave a little longer, that's all. Lend us these supplies and stand guard until we come back. When the rest of your village is secure."

"Farmstead," Goan corrected.

"What's that?"

"It's a farmstead. Hoster's Farmstead. There's thirteen families, us and the Rosens and the Daragakes and then the Witlies and – and –"

"We'll make sure they're all safe," Havik said. He was shaking, still, and wanted to cry, realising their neighbours might all be hurt, like his parents. His best friend Mari, was she safe? But Havik's smile broadened and he could believe, somehow, it *was* okay. These people were tougher than the bad men.

"Over there." Goan interrupted the one-eyed man's search, pointing to the corner beyond the sink, where two crates were stacked under a cloth. "That's where my dad keeps his drink." The one-eyed man tore the cloth back. He frowned. Goan explained, "Under the potatoes. So Mr Rosen doesn't know how much he has."

The man set a few potatoes aside and paused. He nodded to Havik, then dragged the canvas bag over and started thrusting Father's bottles in. Goan cringed; Father would be furious.

"It'll be an incredible help," Havik said. "And now we can go." Goan's hand shot out before he knew it, grabbing her arm. They couldn't leave him. *She* couldn't. But she kept smiling as she peeled his fingers off and stood up. "You'll be fine."

"No, please!" Goan said, crawling out from the table, hands balling in protest. "Please stay! What should I do!"

The one-eyed man walked past without paying him any attention, bag over his shoulder, but Havik considered the boy and his kitchen. The man leaned outside, checking the field, then mumbled something and left.

"Do you know why they call your home the Shadow Sails?" Havik said. "The Prophet Sandway walked these very lands and it was here, right in these hills, that he met the Saint of Shadows. On this exact spot where we stand, perhaps Sandway and Shade reached their understanding. Some consider darkness to hold evils, but Shade also softens the harsh light. It blends extremes and takes us from one side to another. Do you know the Book of Bones, Little Goan? It says there can be no light without dark, no dark without light. Find your strength in the spirits that still dwell here."

Havik turned to Goan's parents and crouched again. She took Father's rifle and held it towards him. He accepted it, mind adrift trying to process her words.

"Be strong. Defend this house, while we're away. You are a brave man, Little Goan. I see the Saints' strength in you. Can you keep being brave? For me?"

The gun was heavy in Goan's hands, but the weight felt comforting. Havik's words circled around him, calmed him, and he nodded as he wiped away his last tears.

"Good. Watch the road. Let no one approach and we will return." Havik rustled a hand through his hair, then she left too, her gun propped against one shoulder. Goan stared into the empty hall, feeling a fresh loss, and avoided looking at his parents again. They lay in a terrible pile in the corner of his vision.

Shaking off the horror and fear, Goan left the kitchen to check outside. He gasped as he saw the body of the soldier who had broken in, crumpled in a deep corner of the hall with his body shredded as if mauled by a vicious animal, blood and bits all up the wall. Goan looked quickly away, out across the field, and saw dark shapes spread through their harvested field like discarded sacks. Bodies. Ten at least, most in the same green clothing as the man in the house.

Goan slid to the floor, against the door frame, and watched the horizon. Havik and her friend were gone, though he didn't know how they disappeared so quickly. But they'd be back. She had promised. He just needed to protect the farm until then. He steadied himself and the rifle and kept watch on the end of the road. No one else would get close. It was up to him to keep Father and Mother safe now.

The sun slowly continued to rise and birds returned to singing as a breeze blew through, flapping the dead men's clothing in the field. Goan fought to keep steady, watching, despite the weight of the gun pulling him down. His finger shivered against the trigger.

A head appeared over the horizon at last – a broad man in dark clothes, the enemy's green? Goan fired and the gun jerked from his grip, making him squeak. He looked up and saw the man had fallen.

For a second, Goan stared, disbelieving, as his heart pounded. He'd done it. Got one. Damn them. He *would* protect this farm. He snatched up the rifle and ran, slipped on the mud and kept going. He aimed down at the invading Imperial bastard soldier, ready to finish the job. The man wheezed and Goan froze in shock.

"Mr Rosen?"

5

*A soldier was forced to be many things, rapidly changing
even over the course of one day: a builder and mechanic;
cook and craftsman, their own doctor. It is no wonder then
that many sought to specialise, to consolidate their new
skills. To be a gunner, a pilot, a marksman or medic: these
opportunities allowed ordinary men to become
extraordinary.*

**The Death of Class: How the One War
Reshaped Society, Gables, p. 45**

After two months at Rock Stable, Wish had forgotten how fast the
war moved. Just as you got used to one place, or activity, or idea of
what it meant to exist, orders were given and all that was gone. Four
Skills' arrival rapidly revived Wish's itch to get moving and
complete a very specific task. She'd find Emi and the ogres with
Scraper in Footward, with the rest of her team waiting in western
Elmn, in the city of Hail Crossing. The Rock Stable major had
already agreed to the reassignment, and gave orders for Wish to be
fully equipped for her journey. As the last person to find out about
all this, Wish accepted that her part in it was preordained.

Quickly packing her bags with the few possessions she'd
accrued, dusting off her light armour and travelling cloak, she found
fresh excitement in the nerves. New lands, new challenges and new
people lay ahead. New people was the best part: if she could get in
and out of the Saints Mire quickly and reform the Blood Scouts,
then her whole purpose could shift to tracking down friendly faces,
new and old. She said her farewells to Four Skills, knowing when
they met again it would be to share in this lofty goal. The other girls
were out there waiting for her to round them up. Rue, Dakoda, and
dear Newk to start. The memory of her kiss resurfaced in Wish's

mind, one she'd avoided thinking too much about. She longed to gather them all in her arms and hurry them far from trouble. Back to her farm . . . It could be real again.

She smiled as she hiked her bag on one shoulder and walked towards her carriage to town. It was a small wooden wagon with tall wheels and faded blue paintwork, a frail mountain horse to pull it and a ropy man on the driving platform – all waiting at the gates of Rock Stable just for her.

"Lieutenant, ma'am?"

A voice pulled her rudely from her thoughts and she spun, saying, "What?"

It was the ringer with the thin moustache, standing alongside the recruit with blond curls. Startled by her tone, he now stumbled over whatever he'd been about to say. "I was going – I mean – sorry – ma'am." Moustache clicked his heels together in stiff attention. He nudged his companion and Blond Curls straightened up, too. "We heard you're shipping out on assignment. We wanted to ask –" He hesitated, then rushed it out. "We would like to come with you."

Wish stared for a moment before replying, "No you wouldn't."

"We came to be trained by you. If you're leaving, we want to come."

"What?" Wish repeated. This didn't connect with her fantasies of a moment ago. The new Blood Scouts didn't start with entertaining undisciplined men. She was thrown, too, by the dark-skinned recruit's voice, which she'd not properly considered earlier: he had the rough accent of a labourer out of Stanclif's capital, Vasseer, not the refined voice she expected from colonial ringers.

"We requested this station, ma'am," the blond one said, not meeting her eye. "We know what you've done."

"What I've done?" Wish's voice pitched higher. The trainees usually understood she was an accomplished sniper without knowing specifics. What did these ones know? Was it the mass murder on Green Rise? The violence at Reeve Abbey? The countless dead in Wick? The child she'd almost stabbed on the Cracked Trail? She didn't need this.

"Are you okay?" Moustache asked. "You look –"

"No, I've got somewhere to be," Wish said. She shook her head, turning to the waiting carriage. "You're taking me to Footward?"

"Ready when you are," the driver grunted.

"Ma'am?" Moustache said. "We want to be taught by the best."

"Four Skills is the best – she can teach you better than me. And you're *safe* here."

"If she's the best then why are they sending you and not her?"

Wish paused. There was an obvious answer, with Skills' leg and all, but it touched on her own doubts. Only a few hours had passed since all this was thrown in her lap, and she'd so far managed to avoid the critical question of what she had done to convince anyone she could lead anything. She looked past the carriage, past the edge of the plateau, to where the distant country was visible below. Far below. She flinched, seeing Loose falling to her death. Worse thoughts lay out there: an ambush that had killed Tate, much more competent than her. Fixit, broken by a monster, only there to take care of them. Killed under her command. This was a bad idea. How had she let Skills convince her?

Wish said, "You come with me, you're likely to end up dead."

"Most people in this war do," Moustache replied with surprising readiness. "I'd rather we died with the best than got lost in the shuffle with the rest."

Wish paused, dark doubts receding at the sheer silliness of his rhyme. She twisted back to him. "Did you practise that?"

"A little." He wore his cheeky smile. Newk smiled the same way – not a native of Stanclif like him, but with shared roots, somewhere in their blood. Maybe this was a sign. Or maybe Four Skills had arranged this, too, like she'd arranged everything else. Some flattery to encourage Wish along.

She took a breath. Well, if they were going to put this much effort into it, who was she to get in the way? The Scouts could use a few men to heft their equipment about, at any rate.

"Fine," she said. "Ask Skills, ask the major. If they let you come, and you can catch me up, it's your problem."

***

There were sounds of violence as the carriage arrived at Footward's Bottom Up Inn. It was a top-heavy tavern with metal-framed windows crowded by silhouettes of men drinking. No music was playing, and the typically clamorous conversation was reduced to only a few loud voices. Trouble inside.

Wish thanked the driver as she lugged her pack and rifle in through the entrance. The inn's crowd of uniformed soldiers and local miners hunched over tankards as they collectively focused on a very large man looming over a much smaller one; the latter was making all the noise. He had big shoulders and studded leather armour, especially thick around his arms, his shaved head lined with scars. Behind him stood four similarly dressed men, with leather belts holding tools, whips and batons.

"Go on, I can see the animal in ya," the man growled. "Show the rest of them."

He shoved the larger figure, who didn't shift.

"Show us what them big mitts are good for!" The smaller man encouraged his companions with mean laughter. "Better for something than spilling drinks?"

The larger man rose higher and Wish's eyes widened as she took him in. Stooping, he barely fit under the beamed ceiling, and he was almost twice the short man's broad width, with a double-sized head pitted with dark, angry wrinkles. An ogre. Surely one of *her* ogres, given their rarity. And Wish realised then he wasn't alone, with two more massive figures in the press of bodies of behind him.

"Like any animal – just takes the right attitude to put these war pigs in their place!" the insulting man shouted.

Wish stepped forward, but a hand caught her forearm and she turned sharply to find Emi beaming at her. The dirt-minder slid between the drinkers to come close to Wish and whispered, breath thick with alcohol, "You got here just in time. This is going to be *fun.*"

"Those ogres are with us," Wish said, almost as a question.

Emi nodded. "And that pack of beast trainers think they can handle them. The barkeep's taking bets."

"Last warning," the ogre said and his deep voice vibrated the floorboards under Wish's boots. He didn't elaborate, those two words and his black-eyed glare a complete threat.

The man laughed again. "Nah, mate. This is *your* last chance. Step out. Don't come back. Or do I give the fine people a show?"

The ogre shifted towards the beast trainer and the smaller man stepped back, hand flashing to his belt and the handles of his sheathed tools. If he was a beast trainer, with weapons designed to subdue large animals and the confidence to take on someone twice his size, this could get unpleasant.

"Ah, ah!" He hopped on his toes, and the ogre stretched up again, folding into the ceiling.

Madness, Wish thought – as if they didn't have enough trouble in this war. And after so many idle hours worrying, she had to deal with *this* as her reintroduction to the war? No. Wish was suddenly shouldering her way past complaining men, splashing beer. The beast trainer was making another cocky threat with the ogre growling like an engine revving to life. Then Wish's pack and rifle hit the floor with a thump that made the man turn, not quick enough to avoid her short blade coming for his throat. He croaked in surprise as the edge pressed into his neck, and went rigid with fear.

"What's your unit?" Wish heard herself say, and flashed a look to the man's companions, all half ready to draw weapons. "Who's in charge here?"

With everyone startled, probably as much by her gender as by her forcefulness, no one answered.

She raised her voice: "Is there no ranking officer here? I've got lieutenant, what are you?" She leant closer to the beast trainer, putting pressure on the knife, and he went up on his tip-toes with a hitched breath. She noticed Emi out of the corner of her eye, watching with glee amid the grubby crowd of confused men.

Wish glanced to the bar, to the barkeep, a man with long hair and a voluminous belly. "You. Why didn't you stop this?"

"Not my fight," he huffed.

"You're digging a grave, girly," the beast master snarled, though not daring to move.

"I said I'm a *lieutenant,*" Wish spat, her spittle hitting his eye. "What are you?"

The worry briefly hit him then, the question of rank worse than the threat of the knife. It was quickly replaced by disbelief, though, his lip curling, so Wish tightened her hold on his shirt and slid the knife up to tap his jawline.

"No," Wish said. "You had better not ask me to prove it."

"Ask her to prove it!" Emi called out unhelpfully, making her wince. But the beast trainer cracked, slightly twisting his head to shake it, to say he was done.

"Fine," Wish said. "Get out of here." She lowered the knife and the man slumped with relief. He glanced to his friends, who were looking anywhere but at her, scratching their heads in innocent theatre.

"Had enough anyway," the beast trainer said, rubbing his neck where the knife had produced a thin trail of blood. "Stinks of ogre in here."

He shoved his way towards the door, his unpleasant companions reluctantly joining him. That was good, Wish thought, ignoring her rapidly beating heart and the little doubts that were creeping in. Could've got herself hurt or looked ridiculous with everyone watching. But with no one else in charge here, she had done her duty and embodied her rank, at last; a good start for commanding ogres. But with the hubbub starting to return, she shouted with an afterthought: "Wait!" The bar went quiet again. The trainer turned back red-faced, almost out the door. "Apologise to this man."

The beast trainer glanced at the ogre, appalled. "That's no man."

"And I wasn't asking," Wish replied.

The man swallowed, lips tightening. She had maybe pushed her luck too far, now she didn't have a knife at his neck. He scanned her uniform, looking for signs of rank, but her gold lieutenant's patch was hidden under the great coat. He spat aside, shook his head, and Wish tightened her grip on the short blade. He grumbled, "Apologies. Must've been mistaken." With that, he pushed quickly out the door. The dam burst and chatter and movement resumed, men pressing towards the bar and filling the space around Wish. She was jostled with thanks or nods of respect and someone pressed her pack and rifle into her hands. A pint of ale was given to her with the words, "Nicely done, Lieutenant."

She drifted deeper into the room to where the ogres lurked, finding herself shaking slightly and nervous. But she'd done it. Wild Wish the officer, breaking up bar fights, showing the rabble who was in charge. Inspiring recruits, being given a command, maybe she was going to be okay. She found her smile as she drew up to the three huge ogres, their bodies an impassable wall of patchwork uniform and leather pouches.

"Lieutenant," said the lead one, who the man had been goading. His deep-set, scowling face wasn't welcoming.

Emi swept in from nowhere, an arm snaking over Wish's shoulders and squeezing her closer. She cringed in the mage's embrace. The mage said, "Wild Wish. Let me introduce you to Sergeant Caracker. He used to be a captain, until he got fed up with people telling him what to do."

Wish gave Emi a questioning look. All three of the ogres were now glaring at her. Not fans of authority, and here she was having just flaunted hers. Their general disapproval and her immortal nervousness about Emi rapidly sapped her confidence and she felt her face reddening.

It got worse as Emi continued: "But as you saw, Sergeant, you step out of line here and Wish *will* mess you up."

So much for a good start.

6

Though attitudes were outwardly shifting before the One War, most imperial societies still ranked "lesser" citizens according to criteria established over many thousands of years. So when such species joined the war effort, Urlians were immediately assigned menial, labour-intensive tasks and excluded from officer training. What success they did have in influencing tactics was diminished or outright hidden. Even when Prognane Sembler famously routed the Comity at the Battle of Villa Duke using tactics taken from the classic campaigns of Anyan Url, the Arrow Council went to great lengths to claim Sembler had been inspired by a dream rather than through reading his history books.
Don't Call Me Ogre: Rethinking Modern Urlian History, Blonc, p. 89

Wild Wish gathered her new team around a large circular table. The three ogres barely fit in the space, perching rather than sitting on their stools, about as comfortable as they might be in a child's playhouse. Even their oversized tankards, the sort that men bought as a challenge or a joke, looked small in their head-sized hands. They looked more unhappy with her than the tight conditions, though, going by their dark scowls. Emi introduced the other two as Runt, which may or may not have been ironic considering he was about the same size as the others (maybe slightly leaner?), and Ohno, who was female, though Wish had trouble spotting any discerningly feminine features. There was also a skinny human soldier in a Stanclif blue-grey uniform sitting next to Ohno, looking very small by comparison. He had an unkempt mop of ginger hair, and when Emi introduced him as Toothless he cheerily waved and said, "Hello!" No one explained why he was there.

Wish was more concerned about the way the ogres were staring at her, and had an urge to apologise without knowing what for. She asked, mostly just for something to say, "What was that guy's problem?"

"Same as ever," Caracker replied. "Humans trying to make themselves feel big."

"Because we make them feel small," Ohno added. She had dark hair braided close to her scalp, a bulky combat vest and very muscular bare arms. Wish scanned her slab-like body again for hints of curves, wondering if that vest hid double-sized breasts or just more muscle.

"But good thing we had an *officer* to put them in their place," Caracker said, thickly sarcastic, snapping her back to the moment.

She hadn't made the professional impression she'd hoped to, and that seemed fair enough now her mind had wandered to ogre boobs. Still, she said, "It worked, didn't it?"

"If you think pulling a knife to break up a fight is appropriate behaviour for a lieutenant."

"Um. I'm sorry, was he actually your friend or something?"

"Absolutely not. But there's a hell of a difference between knocking a man flat and cutting his throat, ain't there? Especially when we're dealing with people on the same side as us."

"I thought she showed great restraint," Emi offered. "Much less blood than usual."

Wish shot her a look, not sure if the mage was referring to something specific or merely being an arse. Runt made an irritated noise, his seat creaking under him. He told Caracker, "Not impressed so far, Sarge."

His voice was higher pitched than Caracker's, but still . . . big. He had a sweep of sandy blond hair and a flat nose, blue eyes not quite as deep and dark as Caracker's, and he wore a set of colourful ribbons tied to the chest strap of his vest. Since every soldier knew it was safest to be bland, to avoid drawing attention, Wish was dying to know what that was about. But his scowl also made him the nastiest looking of the three, and this wasn't the time to ask.

"Okay," she said. "Maybe I acted rashly. But what were you going to do?"

"Wait for him to pull his snap-baton then punch him," Caracker said, simply. "If it's self-defence, we can't get called out for being too aggressive or emotional."

"What's a snap-baton?"

"A sparking stick used to train pack beasts," Ohno said. "Even those idiots wouldn't have drawn an actual weapon in here, see."

Wish took a breath, feeling like she was on trial. All she'd done was threaten someone with a blade. But then, it wasn't the first time her instincts had taken her that close to stabbing someone unnecessarily. Maybe they had a point. Maybe it was a mistake leaving Rock Stable, where Sergeant Bix could mete out violence on her behalf. She said, "Okay. We've got off to a bad start. I'll do better. Can we start over?" She put a hand on her chest. "I'm Lieutenant Wild Wish and Four Skills said I could trust you to help us get through the Saints Mire."

"Yeah," Caracker said. "We already met."

"I know, but we're starting over –"

"No. Before this. You took a good soldier off my hands when we were fighting near Palicier. Price."

For a moment Wish thought he might be confusing her with Captain Tate, but then it hit her. She *had* encountered this ogre, maybe eight months ago, in the trenches. It was the day she met Oksy, when Captain Tate had taken Boot Squad to hunt a mage and uncovered a female sniper nearby. Oksy had arrived with this huge escort, a memory which brought back an earlier concern: "You were her commanding officer. What happened?"

"I disagreed with the colonel." Caracker's glare was stacked with a lifetime of resentment and a general warning to Wish. "Got shot eight times on his bad orders. When I finally said no more, they wanted to execute me. As a compromise, I fucked off. Reached an understanding with Command, making us available for special projects." He held up his palms to indicate their current situation. "You've got Price to thank for this one. She was a good sort. Said you were, too."

"You've spoken to her?" Wish exclaimed, eyes wide. "Where is she?"

"Dunno. Last saw her near the Step crossing, early summer. Had a few letters from her, but not since you all dived into Green Rise."

Wish's heart fell again. "Oh."

"She wrote about you. One to watch, she said. So when your other mate came asking questions, suggesting we join up, I entertained the idea."

"But neither of them mentioned you had a screw loose," Runt added.

"No?" Wish said, genuinely surprised. It was just typical, though: brilliant Oksy was always one-upping her with her shooting and her trivia, so it made malicious sense that she'd also only sing her praises while Wish was busy complaining about her. Always the better person. Something tightened around Wish's heart. She missed her.

"Now," Caracker said, "between Price's letters, your one-legged mate's proposals and this loon's jokes" – he pointed loosely at Emi, who winked – "we got to wonder how much of what we've heard is true."

"All I'm seeing is an uncertain little girl," Runt said.

It was Wish's turn to scowl, because, sceptical as they might be – dammit she had her own doubts about all this – Runt sounded as obnoxious as the beast trainer. But the other two were watching her with the same questioning gazes. Demanding she justify herself. Tempting as it was to merely cite rank, she doubted that would go down any better than drawing her knife again. She could convince them calmly. Had to. Four Skills had said she was more than she knew . . .

"I don't like to boast," Wish ventured, and paused. In a real Blood Scouts meeting, someone would've interrupted to contradict her. Instead, the ogre glowers worsened (though Toothless was happily smiling; with rather good teeth, she noticed). She continued, "But I am a good scout and a better sniper. You might've heard differently, but I *did* win us the Battle of Wick. And maybe Green Rise. And I kind of broke up the Dread Corps."

Caracker sat back on his complaining stool, folding his considerable arms. He wasn't convinced, and his companions' faces remained stony. This was why she didn't like to boast.

"She's also a delight to be around," Emi added.

"What's that mean, you broke up the Dread Corps?" Caracker said.

"Well, a lot of them were on a train we destroyed. We did a lot of damage with just a few of us. I'm sure I can do more with a full platoon."

"What full platoon?" Runt scoffed. "You're two bite-sized women. Hardly a leg's worth of muscle between you."

"Three," Emi corrected, and a little shard of hope caught Wish, that there was at least one more guaranteed ally here somewhere.

"Where is Scraper?" she asked.

"She took her dinner upstairs," Toothless said helpfully, pointing towards a door. "Too noisy for her down here." Wish had a fresh urge to ask who he was, but Caracker interrupted.

"How many more have we got meeting us in Hail?"

Four Skills hadn't said, had she? It *might* be a full platoon. Almost certainly not. There had been mention of a guide, though.

"I don't know," Wish admitted, and Runt scoffed again, convincing Wish that she really didn't like him. Defensively, she improvised, and found herself speeding up, to stop them criticising her: "With the generals making their big pushes before the winter sets in, we shouldn't expect huge numbers. But we don't need them – this a recon mission. Trust me, I led a team through Low Slane. Have you ever been? I wouldn't recommend it. And did I mention I'm a scout? I can move pretty well unseen through any kind of territory. Which, you know . . ." She gestured vaguely to encompass the fact that these three were more noticeable. "I'm kind of wondering if you're right for a scouting mission yourselves?"

"You what?" Runt shifted angrily, but Ohno wet his short fuse with a chuckle. Wish warmed at that, liking the woman of the group, at least. Obviously.

But the ogress said, "You've got no idea where we're going, do you?"

Wish's heart fell. "The Saints Mire? A land of sad monks and grescinds."

"A land of rocks and bogs. Home to some big beasts. Big because they have to be. They got horses an ogre can ride, because a regular horse would sink in the mud. We can walk through the same marshes you'd have to swim across."

"Ah."

"Alright, enough," Caracker said, finally showing mercy. "This ain't a pissing contest and she obviously needs more prep. I don't doubt you've got some skills, girl, but let's be clear: you want the command, you're gonna earn it. Otherwise, we'll handle things ourselves."

Wish stiffened at his words, her awkward smile dead. She was used to doubting herself, and to others doubting her, but he couldn't outright dismiss her rank. *Girl*. She was allowed to use that word, not him. A memory resurfaced of Captain Brade, the man who'd taken them for the death march to Low Slade, under her command. He would've let the monstrous scientist Doctor Vorhale live, and tried to set off an unthinkably terrible bomb. Both times he'd undermined Wish when she *knew* her way was better. When she was supposed to be in charge.

Caracker didn't blink and Wish wanted to let it go. He was a lot bigger than Brade. But Four Skills had trusted her with the future of the Blood Scouts. Four Skills believed in her. Oksy had written letters about her. She couldn't bow to another Brade, and this would define their operation moving forward.

She said, quietly, "I've already earned it. Just because I'm friendly, it doesn't mean I can't fight. Or lead." There was quiet, and the ogres didn't look moved, so she went on. "If you're coming, I *am* the lieutenant, and unless something crazy happens, like, I don't know, snakes eat my eyes, or Colonel Bedaggery himself commandeers the platoon, then either we're a team with me at the head or you're out."

She offered as stern a look as her soft face was capable of. Caracker was rock-like, basically a troll. He could reach across the table and crush her skull in one hand. But one corner of his mouth lifted, not a smile but some concession. Runt narrowed his eyes, less impressed and holding in something demeaning. He deferred to Caracker, though, and the lead ogre nodded. Satisfied, if not enough to say so.

Emi slapped Wish's shoulder and said, "Great. That was getting tense, wasn't it? But now we've all measured your dicks, we can have a few drinks and share our most embarrassing memories. Wish can start, she's got the most."

Tough as she wanted to appear, Wild Wish felt her cheeks flush. But the ogres raised their ales, drama over. She smiled again, at no one in particular. Not sure how she'd got through that and vaguely aware it was only the start. Was every minute of running a platoon going to be a battle of wills? Sniping was easier. She had an urge to leave and stood with a forced smile. "Right. Where's Scraper?"

"Oh sit down," Emi flapped a hand. "You do *not* want to disturb her. Have some food, have a drink, relax."

Wish remained standing, not sure she could relax. Or should. Captain Tate would've kept a healthy distance, wouldn't she? A quick briefing and then out. But the room was lively and the beer and food smelt good, now she paid attention. Ohno and Toothless, at least, seemed nice. She slowly sat back down.

"So," Caracker said. "We're dying to hear your plan for this mission."

"Oh," Wish replied slowly. "Great."

Somehow, the evening didn't devolve into complete disaster, and between fending off Emi's remarks and occasionally barbed questions from the ogres, Wish managed to enjoy a drink and dinner. It drifted by quickly before they turned in, an early rise ahead. Wish had her own room, tucked tightly into the tavern's eaves, and slept soundly. When a tentative knock came in the morning, she rose to find the final scout, Scraper, standing outside. Wish went from bleary-eyed distraction to smiling brightness and cheered "Hi!" when she saw her. She deflated at the reluctant expression on Scraper's face and the barely audible, nonsensical, "Yes, ma'am."

Scraper was a narrow-framed woman with lank black hair whose old blue-grey fatigues were worn to almost white. She turned to leave Wish without another word. Wish frowned. She vaguely recognised her from the Blood Scouts but suspected her shyness was why she wasn't more familiar. Not to worry; they'd get better acquainted on the journey.

There was a long train ride ahead, from Footward to their destination at Hail Crossing, so they hiked down to the single-platform station – their full crew and Toothless, who was apparently coming with them. A huffing steam engine was waiting, already packed with soldiers and busy with men tossing bags and crates about. As they went to board themselves, the humans in one carriage and ogres towards the rear, two soldiers stepped in her way. The recruits from Rock Stable proudly smiled as they announced they'd got leave to join her on this suicide mission. The moustached ringer, calling himself Private "Dalliance" Devan, said he'd brought cards and liquor for the ride and Wish, still not fully awake, dismissed him with a mumble. As they boarded and squeezed themselves onto a couple of benches, Dalliance struck up a conversation with Toothless, quickly explaining he was from Vasseer and wasn't it a great city? Toothless politely agreed. The blond-haired soldier, Private Fawset, was a lot quieter. Surrounded by a crowd of soldiers, he was probably realising – as Wish was – that they were reentering the war prematurely. Should've stayed at Rock Stable.

The train horn blared loudly and they trundled out of town. Wish tried to appreciate the comfortable transport – smoother and warmer than flying on a wyrling, and less effort than lugging a heavy backpack on foot – but it conjured unpleasant memories. The last train she'd ridden had been the Drail's immense Iron Barge, which she had personally derailed. She'd killed a lot of people and almost died herself. It was hard not to connect the trundle of wheels with the patter of gunfire; the chatter of the crowded men with the shouts of Dread soldiers who wanted her dead. She saw the ceiling coming down and a Drail inquisitor woman with murder in her eyes. The woman who'd looked like a pirate, who died oddly smiling. Wish had seen her face a lot in her mind. Wondered why the woman was there. Why she'd so resolutely wanted Wish dead, but was amused by her own failure.

She also wondered if they might've got on, in other circumstances. She doubted it. But the pirate woman had been one of the last people Wish had properly touched, grappling on the floor and over bodies. She'd seen few other women up close since then, bar Emi, Four Skills, and Rock Stable's matronly nurse. How much better things were before, when she'd marched in the company of dozens of women. So far, this Blood Scouts revival wasn't living up to her brief expectations, with three ogres, three men, and two women who weren't talking. Even Emi had gone quiet, huddled in her overlarge navy great coat, meditating. She looked more frog-like than ever, knees tucked up, head hunched in her neck, the wide features of her face forming thin, sealed lines. Wish had previously treasured the dirt-minder's periods of downtime, where she recharged or prepared herself, calm in contrast to her potential mania, but she wouldn't have minded a little of the old banter now. Scraper was equally unresponsive, not meditating but staring through the world, as though her glassy eyes took in something beyond the train. Wish suspected she might be revisiting dark memories but didn't ask. The few attempts she had made to engage her had been met with monosyllabic dismissal, and Wish understood why she hadn't remembered this scout from before.

Still, the views improved as the day wore on, and to Wish's surprise she found her mood improving too. When the sun dropped, the fields gave way to a broad coastline before the brilliant blue water of the Most Blessed Sea, an expanse dotted with the small-seeming shapes of ships.

"Is that Fort Barricode?" Private Dalliance asked, shifting along the bench so his leg knocked into Emi's and the dirt-minder opened her eyes with a look he ignored, at his own peril. Dalliance was pointing to an approaching cluster of wide, low buildings on the water, boathouses and factories, and towers specked with tell-tale barrels of large weapons. "I heard they got raided a few weeks ago. Surprised anything's still standing."

Wish looked closer. The buildings were dark from scorch marks. There were holes in the roofs.

"I think we retook it," Toothless said. "But they had to drive off a Mattin dreadnought. Hell of a battle, must've been."

Mutters of agreement went through the carriage, nearby soldiers joining in, sobering at the thought they were getting closer to the fighting. Wish wasn't sure what a Mattin dreadnought was, but she imagined it was one of the fiercer ships out there. She noted Toothless said *drove off* and not *destroyed*.

"Welcome back," Wish whispered to herself, the war all but upon them now. No turning back. She caught Emi's eye, seeing the dirt-minder had heard her. Emi smiled in her usual understanding way. A promise of trouble.

7

In the strange lands of the Saints Mire, it's hard to shake the pervading feeling that everything between the Blessed Sea and the Mocking Mountains is cursed. The mud will drag you down, the trees will tangle you up, even the grass may cut you with poisons. But the cautionary tales are a delight not to be taken too seriously! I do not believe, for example, that all who swim in the waters of the Black Lake are marked for death – but it rather adds to the fun of bathing there!

The Mire Most Easy with Mr Zambizee,
Zambizee, p. 14

Bodi Tarrant was the first to spot the scouts returning. He'd taken a double shift to be sure of it. Not that there was anything else worth doing in the Irregulars' camp, with Raltman demanding quiet while he hesitated over what to do about the enemy across the lake. Their position was secure, with three hundred soldiers hidden within the rock labyrinths of the Black Lake's southern shore, and they should've been enjoying the spoils of their recent victory, but the over-cautious lieutenant had their fires burning low, while Larrist pressured him into breaking camp altogether and running. It was fine, though – Havikare was coming back, and she'd sort it out. And next time, damn it, Bodi would make sure the advance party took him with them. He might've only been fifteen, but he'd been inked in the Pillared Asylum. He'd killed with his bare hands and travelled the continent and didn't belong with these second-rate nobodies.

Bodi skidded into the camp entrance, where the path was widest between boulders, and raised a hand in greeting. Havik and Lost One rode towards him, both on bloody massive trudge horses, with a small troop of scouts behind them and no sign of Kin Kasidee.

"Fuck's up here?" Lost One asked as they stopped a short distance from Bodi. He directed his one-eyed glare to the quiet camp.

"They got a concern," Bodi said, hurrying to take the bridle of Havik's horse. He had to stretch, with its head almost two feet above his own, but they were easy beasts to control. "Can I take her for you, Miss Eens? How was the journey?"

Havik smiled down at him and that gave him a buzz. He was thankful for the dark. She didn't answer, her attention drawn to other men emerging from camp. Raltman was at the front, a big bearded brute with a scar through his lower lip. Kasidee had left him in charge purely because he looked like a fucking animal. Beside him came Larrist, a scrawny prick who had none of Raltman's muscle but a lot more meanness in his weasel face.

"Welcome back, Commander. Were you successful?" Raltman asked.

"Very," Havik answered *him,* to Bodi's annoyance. She leaned over in her saddle, closer to Bodi, and he lowered his gaze deferentially. "And we intended to celebrate. But it feels like a funeral up here."

"We need to relocate," Larrist announced. "There's lights on the north shore. Trouble."

"Might be nothing," Raltman said. "Or it might be something we can handle well enough. Thought we might send some men over the water for a closer look, but were waiting until you got back."

Because he was a bloody simpleton with no initiative. Bodi cleared his throat, about to say *he* would've gone over there all on his own.

"How many lights?" Lost One said.

"Can't tell. But I reckon we put out a boat –"

"Over the Black Lake?" Havik interrupted. "Haven't I told you about that water? If the rumours of it having no bottom are false, you don't want to find out what *is* down there."

"Aye, but there's a rowboat. Thought if it floats alright that wouldn't cause a problem?"

"Then it's a good thing you waited. Alright, just show us." She vaulted off her horse. Bodi released the bridle and held up his hands to catch her, too late – she'd already thumped into the dust and started marching ahead. All this time waiting and he'd missed the chance to help her down. He skipped to keep up, leading the horse. Without looking back, she held a hand towards him and said, "The Wildchild, Bodi."

"Yes, yes!" he said, rushing back to unstrap her hefty gun from the saddle. The thing was a marvel and he was honoured to touch it, the triple barrels gleaming even at night. He jogged to catch up again, ordering another man, "Take care of the fucking horse."

As Bodi handed Havik her gun, Lost One climbed down more carefully, taking his time over collecting his equally impressive rifle. Raltman trotted to Havik's other side, like he wanted to say more, to apologise or whatever. Bodi spoke first: "I'm happy to volunteer and go by foot, Miss Eens. We could sneak round the shore and take the measure of these pricks easy enough."

"On the opposite side?" Havik said. "That's a couple hours trek at least – we can't leave it that long. When did you see them?"

"Er," Raltman said. "Maybe two hours ago. Not long after nightfall."

Havik glanced back with a rare look of surprise. Bloody incompetence waiting that long, wasn't it? But she said, "Right. You did well to keep the camp quiet, anyway."

Bodi reckoned she was bullshitting. A minor threat could've easily been put down before it grew; a major threat wanted retreating from, like Larrist said. Neither warranted *waiting*. But Havik's words made Raltman nod with relief. She knew how to keep things cool.

They strode through the camp's crags and caves, with the Irregulars they passed at attention, watching. Bodi held his head up, walking with the bosses where everyone could see. He said, "This way's quickest, Miss Eens. Did you have any trouble today?"

"Nothing serious," she replied, and he loved that because after a dozen brutal battles he was yet to uncover anything she considered "serious".

"Is Kasidee far behind?" Larrist asked, keeping up with long strides.

"He's not coming," Havik replied, and didn't explain.

They reached the lake's shore and huddled around the rocky outcrops overlooking the lake. It brought Bodi blessedly close to Havik as they checked the view. The Black Lake deserved its name, the dark water at night like looking over the edge of the world; Havik had told them stories of tentacled things down there, possibly alive for centuries unseen, waiting to snatch prey. Even the water was deadly; if you sank here, you weren't coming back up. No one had dared swim further than the hip-height shallows, and half the camp were afraid to even go in there. But now there were distant shapes visible on the far shore, demonstrating the lake's width. Small pricks of lights, like fallen stars.

An Irregular on watch held out a telescope which Havik took as Lost One moved past and lifted his rifle, using the scope.

"Small camp," the watchman reported. "We've spotted maybe a dozen total."

"Wouldn't think they'd light fires if they knew we were here," Lost One said.

"That's what I thought," Bodi quickly agreed. "We should get them before they figure it out, right?"

"How could they *not* know we're here?" Larrist protested, his frustration strengthened by prolonged attempts to convince Raltman the same.

Havik's brow knitted. She didn't like what she was seeing, though Bodi doubted the telescope offered much more insight than the naked eye. You had a few shimmering balls of light in the abyss with rough shapes around them – men hunched in rest or tending to camp duties. At least three fires, and the peaks of a couple tents. Mostly outlines.

"Definitely Drail uniform," Lost One said. "At least two goblins."

"Goblins?" Raltman echoed with surprise.

"Even better," Bodi put in. Goblins upset the average soldier – their cruelty was legendary – but they were weak and ill-disciplined. He'd stabbed one himself back in the Asylum. "No one sends goblins scouting. Not if they want to stay hidden."

"You've been hanging out with the wrong goblins," Havik murmured, and he flushed, idiot. "They can be world-class sneaks. These ones are either massively incompetent or baiting us, camping on the water's edge like that. You haven't seen movement elsewhere?"

Raltman shook his head, but with a worried expression. Like he'd forgotten to check.

"It's trouble either way, isn't it?" Larrist said, standing behind them. "Kasidee said they'd be at least another day out – they're much faster than we thought. They might've reached Guiltway already. We *have* to retreat to Sinner's Forest, to reassess."

Bodi gave him a sharp look. He wouldn't be talking that way, like he knew best, if Kasidee himself was here. Damn shouldn't talk that way to Havik.

"Yeah," Havik replied softly though. "We'd best break camp. But no one's retreating. We've established a route east and Kasidee's waiting for us. We *were* going to go at first light, but . . ." She waved a hand towards the distant lights, giving Bodi a look like this sort of nuisance was typical. He chuckled, but covered his mouth because no one else looked amused.

"If the Drail have already come this far –" Larrist complained.

Havik twisted around, her huge gun angling his way. "We didn't come this far to run scared at the first sign of trouble. Did we?" Larrist swallowed uncomfortably, and now Bodi struggled not to smile. She gave the lake another thoughtful look and added, "What do you think, Lost One – could you hit them from here?"

"One or two, definitely," the marksman said. "Once they start moving, that'd probably be it. It's too far, too dark."

If the man said he could take down one or two, he could probably kill ten. And with his cover, and the camp ready to go, Bodi saw an opportunity. He said, "In the time it takes to strike camp, I can get around the bank. See up close what we're dealing with. We oughta have a better idea where the Drail are at, right?"

"Would you shut up?" Larrist said. "Who invited this boy? Think logically, everyone. If they're on the lake, then they'll be at the river too. We have to move south if we want to keep our full caravan hidden. Kasidee would say the same if he was here, but if he's not coming I suppose *someone* has to say it for him."

Bodi saw Havik stiffen, a nerve touched, and he edged a hand towards his knife.

Larrist turned away, decided, and waved a hand overhead. "I'm calling it. Everyone hear me? Spread the order: we're breaking camp. *I'll* keep us alive."

There was a distant pop, then Lost One's rifle went off as Larrist's face exploded in a spray of blood. The crack of the gunshot echoed off the rocks as he crumpled dead. Bodi marvelled at the efficient kill. He *wanted* to do it and he thought Havik might threaten it, but that wasn't how they ran things in the Irregulars. Kasidee always said they could be savage but not savages. And for Lost One to shoot –

Those thoughts were broken by Havik yelling, "Sniper! Everyone down!"

They dived to the ground and Bodi found himself pressed alongside Havik, their shoulders touching. Another pop followed – a shot from across the lake – and a bullet chipped the rocks.

"Wasn't in the camp," Lost One snarled, prone over his rifle. "Saw the flash to the west."

Bodi lifted his head to see past the rocks but flattened himself again as another bullet struck stone. His heart was pounding, face wet, he realised, from Larrist's blood.

"Fuckers were waiting," Lost One said. "Watching us watch them."

Raltman swore loudly, swinging his rifle round and firing. A handful of other Irregulars joined in, blindly shooting into the night. A man was hit in the throat and thrown into the boulders. Bodi didn't have a gun worth using, just his little revolver. His eyes darted between the rocks instead, picking out an escape route. He could cover Havik, get her to safety.

"How far?" she demanded.

"Not close," Lost One said, motionless as Raltman's men sunk back into hiding. "The fuckers wanted our attention on that camp."

"We're packing up and moving out!" Havik shouted. "Everyone, head to the west path – secure the wagons!"

Bodi saw men were already scrambling through camp, though, heading the other way. If the enemy had known they were here all along, distracting them with those lights on the lake, then more of them had to be out there. Creeping round the shore exactly as he'd intended himself. They must've picked Larrist out as in charge, maybe got spooked that it looked like the Irregulars might start moving.

"They'll be coming," Bodi said, crawling away from the rock and drawing his gun. Another gunshot hit a boulder above him, making him flinch. He looked back to the others crouching and cowed.

Havik met his eye, following his thoughts, and said, "From the east. Hopefully. Our exit should be open."

"I'll take care of it – start moving and I'll secure a rear guard!" Bodi said with a smile. He rose in a crouch and darted between the rocks as another shot pinged by his thigh. He flinched into cover but continued, encouraged by Havik's voice.

"Go get them, Bodi! You lot, watch the shore for boats! Mind our flanks! *Move* dammit!"

The gunfire picked up, spreading along the edge of the lake, as more Irregulars joined in, either spotting enemies or just happy to pop off random shots. Bodi couldn't hear if the Drail were firing back in any great number. He ran through the east side of camp and relayed Havik's orders to everyone he passed. His companions whipped up their weapons and moved with grim-faced purpose. These were Bodi's people, quick to act, tough, not like cowardly Larrist, and they took instruction without question.

"Strike camp! Secure the wagons!" he shouted. "You lads – on me, watch the east flank!" He ran away from the shoreline to where the camp thinned and the rocks grew bigger and further apart. As he reached the edge of camp, looking out into the shadowy distance, someone fired from the rocks to his right, then another gun fired to his left, higher up.

"Contact!" someone yelled. "Drail coming in!"

"Give them hell!" Bodi shouted back. "Saints save the brave!"

He saw them then, shapes moving through the dark plain, low to the ground. Small, almost childlike. Bloody sneaky goblins, much too close to the camp. The grassland lit up in short bursts as the enemy returned fire and Bodi pressed himself into a rock. He took deep breaths. The texture of the gunfire suddenly became more chaotic, the goblin weapons banging like clumsily closed doors. Goblins, little fucking freak green things carrying guns way too big for them that flashed bright and disorderly. They screeched a grating war cry that sent a shiver down Bodi's spine. One of the nearby Irregulars swore and ran and Bodi yelled, "You fucking coward, they're just bloody goblins!"

To set an example, he turned to the enemy, lifting his pistol, ready to bring Havik some skulls. A shadow darted in from the side and a hot pain lanced his belly, knocking the strength from his legs. Bodi buckled but was held upright by something in his burning gut. He looked down into the wide sharp smile of a savage green man half his height, a jagged hunk of metal in its claw-like hands. The front edge was embedded in Bodi's stomach, and when the goblin wrenched it free everything spilt out.

Bodi choked as blood filled his mouth and the revolver slipped from his fingers. He fell onto his knees and the goblin scuttled past. How'd the little prick get so close? Men shouted in retreat, the gunfire drifting into camp as more goblins ran in. Bodi tried to hold his insides together, hot blood flowing through his weakening fingers. Impossible. He couldn't go out like this. Not to fucking goblins. He had to make Havik proud. He was gonna be all Kasidee said he could be.

Another shape rushed through the rocks and paused before him. Bodi focused on the goblin's crooked teeth as the freak grinned, aiming a chunky pistol at his chest. He spat on blood, trying to get some words out, at least a last defiant curse. He only managed a splutter as the goblin shot him.

8

So much that took so long to build was lost so quickly in the One War that only the greatest tragedies are now remembered. In any other conflict, the decimation of Rulet, the destruction of Wick, and the levelling of such architectural wonders as the Pantheon of Kalk, the Hail Crossing and Balnia's Tower of the Unwed might each have lived forever in notoriety. Instead, they are consigned to footnotes beneath much greater atrocities.
Architecture of the Imperial Age, Caryon, p. 135

As the train rolled around the Bulk Mountain foothills, craggy peaks to the right and the sea to the left, eager anticipation swept through the soldiers at the promise of their final destination, the marvel of Hail's Crossing. Men pressed to the windows at the far side of Wish's carriage in a big excited mob, but they were soon hit with shock rather than wonder, uttering curses or variations of, "What happened?"

Wish didn't need to see to know the answer. War had happened.

"And this is the safe part," Emi commented.

"Think that already passed," Wish replied.

Dalliance returned from the throng of bodies shaking his head. "Bloody monsters. It's a whole war of bloody monsters."

His tone invited them to ask what he'd seen, so Wish deliberately didn't bite. He sounded more like a Stanish labourer than ever, like her father's apprentice, Slovey. Whenever he saw her in the shop, Slovey dropped leading comments to trick her into showing an interest in him, always things like *what a morning, what a day, what a shame.*

"What'd they do?" Toothless asked, having not joined the shoving soldiers to look for himself.

"Blown the damn bridge, haven't they?" Dalliance fell into a rapid account of the Drail's obvious unnecessary force, typical of how malicious the enemy were. But this was nothing compared to a village he'd seen attacked in Farne, where they'd left a crater a hundred feet deep. He'd seen a child's arm sticking out of it. No body. "Bloody Drail animals – now this?"

Wish looked out the other window, preferring to watch the sea. Wide open, free, untouched by destruction. Except for the peak of what she suspected was a wrecked boat not far off the shore. Damn.

She couldn't avoid seeing Hail Crossing for long, anyway, as the railway curved around to bring them parallel to the city, and the men trotted from one side of the carriage to the other. The sea joined a wide river that flanked the far side of the built-up area, a fine array of arched rooftops and pillared doorways, many painted in light creams and yellows that gave a sense of general wealth. The city held dome-topped larger structures, churches and towers that rose up a central hill. A rich, painting-worthy sight, except for what lay beyond it. Rising gloriously past the hill was an immense bridge, built of pale stone and decorated with more pillars and arches. It was taller than everything else in view and wide as a city block, with buildings of its own in the walls, like an entire neighbourhood on a sky platform crossing the river. Except it didn't go far. While the skeleton of the bridge's greatness remained, with tall chunks of stone and brickwork standing in the water, it was a scattering of broken parts, half-submerged like another shipwreck. It must've taken a series of huge explosions, and indeed a particularly heartless attacker, to destroy such a grand bridge.

"Bloody animals," Dalliance repeated, shaking his head.

Wish agreed, but silently wondered if the Drail had even done it. It was the sort of thing she could imagine herself doing, even if mostly by accident.

They entered the city through arched tunnels that took the train to a central terminus, where the destruction was blocked out of sight. Instead, they found cobbled roads and colourful awnings over market stalls, people in bright civilian clothing mingling with some sense of everyday normalcy. Spread between them, the usual hallmarks of the military were fairly restrained, with only occasional sandbags reinforcing walls, wooden boards across windows and razor wire funnelling streets. Soldiers in blue-grey and sometimes khaki uniforms loitered around unarmed, laughing with the locals. Walking through the streets, Wish's troop stood out, not just because of the three hulking ogres or women in uniform; people's gazes lingered on her tall rifle and the ogres' unmistakably hefty guns. Soldiers and civilians alike seemed to regard the weapons like mud they were walking in on Hail Crossing's otherwise peaceful carpet.

"Is it just me . . ." Wish started.

"No," Emi replied. "We're a dark cloud on their day."

"Ogres usually are," Ohno said.

They asked for directions to Command and passed through a bustling market square untouched by fighting, to a charmingly white-washed, turreted town hall. More soldiers lingered here, smoking, trading rations, but with even fewer defences. When Wish went to enter, a burly soldier stepped into her way and joked, "What's this, an invasion force?"

"Lieutenant Wild Wish of the Blood Scouts," Wish said pointedly, sending the man's eye to her shoulder, for the stripes that weren't there. "Reporting to Lieutenant Colonel Nasim."

The soldier waited with an amused expression, expecting a punchline. Then he looked over her shoulder to the ogres, and Emi, and grew uncertain. "You're serious? Alright whatever, but only you. Don't need your whole platoon in here."

"And Emi," Wish said, mostly because she could.

She and the mage marched through an opulent hall of dark marble and pillars, and continued up grand stairs to a princely office with a great curved window overlooking the square and much of the city. This room, at least, evoked the war, with maps and typed documents scattered around and crates stacked against the walls. Lieutenant Colonel Nasim was talking to two subordinates, who he sent away when he spotted Wish. Though his soldiers gave her distrusting looks on their way out, Nasim pumped her hand in both of his, beaming. He was rotund, about her height but twice her weight, with a jolly face and a bushy grey moustache.

"Good to have you Lieutenant, and not a moment too soon," he said in a Stanish accent too polished to be native, wriggling his moustache. It was incredibly fluffy and Wish fought the urge to touch it. She found her hand unconsciously rising. "You must be the mage?"

"Emi," Emi agreed, then added, "and she prefers Wild Wish. Or just Wild."

Wish shot her a look but Nasim bowled merrily on. "Right you are, Wild Wish. I've heard good things. Your captain really sings your praises and we're eager to see you clear this whole mess up."

"My captain?" Wish's heart bounced into her throat. Tate had been in touch? Was she *here?* Four Skills had been mistaken –

"Yes, I've already sent for him," Nasim replied and her heart fell again. *Him?* Had they assigned someone else to lead this mission? "It's a hell of a thing. This posting has been a blessing until now; the very point was that there's no trouble here. I don't mind saying it: I fought in Camano myself, and this was my reward. Minimal staff expecting minimal fighting – a glorified watch post, if you will. I trusted that the Drail in Onwail had the same understanding."

"Was that made official?" Emi asked, as Wish's mind still questioned, *him?*

"More of a gentleman's agreement," Nasim said, plodding up to a huge map on the wall. "Are you familiar with the region? If not, let me give you a quick rundown. Actually, where are my manners, would either of you like a drink?"

"No thank you, sir," Wish hurried to say, before Emi could make an order. "About the captain . . ." She trailed off, not sure how exactly to say *who is he* with Nasim staring at her so pleasantly, an officer who hadn't appeared to question her credentials yet. Instead, she said, "Um. If you're going to brief us, shouldn't we wait for him to join us?"

Nasim laughed, genuinely, and didn't seem to realise neither Wish nor Emi joined in. "Very good. No, I dare say he knows the lay of the land quite well enough. So, see here – we're in the bottom pocket of the Most Blessed Sea, mountains either side of us, with the navy comfortably covering the coast from here up to the Broad

River." He trundled on as Wish looked to Emi for support in the mystery of the captain, and the mage merely mugged, amusing herself. Nasim described the mountain ranges flanking them, with the western front way north and wide of the sea and General Kettal and the Khib enduring the worst of the war further east. This little gap, he tapped the map, a small patch of land between the mountains and the sea, had been left alone. "Anyone coming south through the Mire would find us here to meet them, and anyone trekking north would have a hard time passing the Drail fortifications at Onwail. In between? No real military presence."

"Until now," Wish noted, distractedly.

"For the past year at least, yes. At the very start of the war, of course, when there were skirmishes along the front all the way from Eardung to Coakes; this area was no exception. There was a clash not far across the river, off to the east. Bloody catastrophe for everyone involved. The elements proved more deadly than either army. Estimated about a thousand men died in the Mire, between us, and I'd wager only a small fraction fell to bullets. Respecting the church and their cultural heritage was a convenient way for both sides to withdraw without outright saying the region wasn't worth the effort."

"Was it the grescinds?" Wish said.

"What now?" Nasim's brow raised with interest. "Oh no. They're a minor nuisance. It's the terrain. The Wet March is bad enough, sodden, soft – but get to Paradise Fails and it's hard to see where the coast ends and the land begins. Try marching a thousand men through that weighed down with guns and ammo and it's a recipe for a lot of drowned young lads."

"That's horrible."

"Most things are, these days," Nasim sighed. "But anyway, we gave up any hopes of it being a viable route to Drail territory. Hence, we've had rather peaceable understandings between Hail Crossing and Onwail."

"Until now," Wish repeated.

Nasim harrumphed, puffing his moustache magnificently. "So it would seem."

"What happened to the bridge?" Emi asked.

"Yes. That's another matter," Nasim said. "We had a couple of naval scuffles a month or so ago, with the blasted Drail trying to push into the river. Ludicrous idea – their warships couldn't fit through the bends – but I suspect they mostly just wanted to test their long-range cannons. It hasn't helped with sending a force in to investigate this latest bother, but we'd hardly be inclined to do so anyway."

"You've had some communication from across the river, though?" Wish said, recalling Four Skills' curious note. *Send Blood Scouts.* "Do you have anyone in the Mire at all?"

"A few men keeping watch, indeed. The priory of Hail is" – he puffed a laugh – "hale enough. No trouble there nor with the nuns at Saintshadow. No word from further north, though. They're old-fashioned, no wires or what have you, so either they use mounted messengers or signal fires, and the latter can only really show something's wrong. Otherwise the priories prefer to be isolated, so it's unclear what's happening."

"Excuse me," Wish said, picking up on probably the wrong detail from that: "There are nuns there, too? I thought it was just monks."

"No, no, there are ten priories in total, eight male and two female," Nasim said, as Emi gave Wish a sideways smile. The sort that suggested she knew Wish was thinking something lewd, even if Wish was not. Consciously, anyway. Nasim went on, "They're all rather dower as each other, I should say, so I don't expect to hear from them, but since the reports of troop movements I've reached out to all ten and only had word back from three. That doesn't mean anything in itself, yet – word travels slowly in the Mire – but we're quite sure there are soldiers moving in the north and west. Most likely securing themselves in the northern priories. They may eventually attack here; the only alternative is to squeeze an army through the mountains, which is horribly rough-going, crawling with nasty beasts, and easily defended in the west."

"Though that is, incidentally," a familiar, upper-class voice interrupted, a newcomer having slipped into the room unnoticed, "precisely the route Kin Kasidee took."

Wish spun to find Captain Brade leaning against the door frame. It iced her blood. Her companion to Low Slane, responsible for their deadly mission and the loss of her friends. The man who had wanted to set off a bomb that could've killed countless people. He wore burgundy pleated trousers and a brass-buttoned jacket and waistcoat. His jaw was smoothly shaved and his thin moustache neatly waxed. More handsomely presented than Wish had seen him before, yet still able to send a chill down her spine. Her immediate response slipped out unbidden: "Oh fuck off."

Nasim scowled so Wish quickly cleared her throat to try again.

"What are you doing here?"

Not much better. But while Nasim frowned, Brade smiled as he walked in. The last time she'd seen him, it had been after a long, cold truck journey between Wick and Lome, after which he had disappeared into his own machinations. A welcome departure, as far as she was concerned: they'd had very little to say to each other after arguing on the hellish Iron Barge.

"Please, don't say that no one told you I was here?" Brade sounded concerned. "I did discuss this with your charming friend."

"Four Skills." Wish said the name like a curse. She'd mentioned a guide, but not *this* one. Not a repeat of the disaster that had destroyed the Blood Scouts. Had Skills deliberately neglected to mention it?

"It may be," Emi mused, tapping her chin, "that you're considering punching this man, Wild. I suggest we not do that." The comment deepened Nasim's frown and earned a questioning look from Brade, as though *she* had said it.

"What?" Wish gaped. "I don't – I mean, I'm not –"

"Forgive her, sir," Brade said. "We've been through some things together, as you're aware. The fault is my own – I behaved rashly and I owe her a long-overdue apology."

Wish's shock compounded, his voice and face too smooth for the vileness she remembered.

"I see," Nasim said, not entirely convinced. "Well thank you for joining us, Captain. I was just explaining the lay of the land. A subject I'm sure you're more qualified to talk on."

"But why him?" Wish blurted out.

Nasim's kindly face folded in irritation. "I must say this is not behaviour I find becoming before a superior officer."

"Is he even a military officer?" Emi asked. "I always assumed his title was honorary."

Somehow this was blamed on Wish, too, as Nasim blurted, "Lieutenant Wild Wish, please!"

"I'm sorry, sir," she said. "It's just – is this whole mission your idea, Captain?"

"Absolutely not," Brade said. "I'm here as an adviser, not a commanding officer."

"Until it suits you," Wish replied.

"Young lady –" Nasim growled, her rank lost as his indignation rose.

Again, Brade intervened. "Sir, if you please. Wild Wish, I did not mean to surprise or upset you. This is absolutely your mission and the authority belongs to you. I would be honoured to join you, if you're willing to give me a chance to make up for our past grievances."

The lieutenant colonel made another huffing sound, evidently thrown by this reversal of apparent roles, and Wish found herself equally unsettled by Brade's humility. He had threatened her before, threatened the lives of thousands. He was cold, heartless, a brigand – she'd clung to that truth when revisiting how bad things had gone. Except in his striking blue eyes, and a face she knew would woo most girls, there appeared to be genuine regret. She said, "Why? Is there something in the Mire you want?"

The captain smiled. "Sharp as always. And I won't deny a fascination for this region, but no. I want the same as you: to help stabilise the Mire. I will stand aside if you say so. You have the measure of me and my worth. The decision is yours."

She held his gaze, wanting to tell him to go to hell, to disappear forever, to take all memory of the dark things she'd been through on his behalf far, far away. And she did, in fact, want to punch him. But as she was quiet, trying to keep reasonable, Lieutenant Colonel Nasim intervened again.

"You'll need someone who can speak Elmish," he pointed out, correctly assuming she could not. His tone shifted, less critical and more thoughtful. "Possibly some Garter, and, if you have much to do with the priories themselves, even Old Lomian. Should you encounter the tribes, I believe the Gaunt Lanterns speak a dialect all of their own. Captain Brade *is* one of our empire's most gifted linguists, and there are few people as well-travelled as this man."

Wish took in a deep breath and let it out. She unclenched her fist, but not her teeth. Purely from Nasim's practical stance, this would obviously be difficult to argue. "I guess we have no choice, do we? I assume you have a plan, Captain Brade?"

9

Stanclif's notoriously unstable colonial interest, the Raw Coast, found moderate calm during the One War, as large sections of the native Rae volunteered to fight alongside Stanclif, convinced, like half the world, that the Drail Empire were a bigger threat. These former enemies of the empire hoped that through joining the fight they might also gain greater recognition from their oppressors. Yet the Raw Coast was never quite at peace itself, nor comfortable taking orders from the Stanish, and Rae soldiers changed allegiance more frequently over the course of the war than anyone else.

A Fine & Baffling War, Flegherty, p. 62

Captain Brade's plan was about as ropy as Wild Wish expected. Having been given the quick rundown of the Saints Mire's generally disagreeable territory, with a particular focus on how brutal the bogs were (and it was mostly bogs), she was informed their best hope was to enter the region via boat, through the delightfully named Paradise Fails. Using the waterways of Paradise Fails, they could easily (as if) reach the equally delightfully named priory of Drowndeep (not one with nuns), before striking out across the land where it was possible to drown.

After considering practical details like how much ammunition and food they could take, Brade took Wish down the hall to meet their additional support, gathered in a separate suite. They were a huddle of cutthroats who looked too nasty for regular service, dressed in mucky black uniforms similar in colour to the enemy's Dread Corps, but padded with pockets and straps for infinite uses. They glowered as Brade gave their names: "Sergeant Macmiddan, Sergeant Graveguard, Corporal Latebite, Corporal Ptrangus and

Corporal Basing. All former Rebel Rawboys, so you know upfront."

Wish, who had been striving to remain professional in the face of working with Brade, dropped her jaw and gave him a heavily disapproving look. She whispered, "What the hell is this?"

Brade glanced at the huddled men and indicated she step back, out of earshot. Matching her volume, smiling for show, he said, "Contrary to popular belief, the Raw Coast produces some of the most effective fighters we have. Particularly well-versed in stealth combat. Of all people, I'd expect you to appreciate the merits of taking in those others might not fully appreciate."

"I don't care where they're *from,*" Wish hissed, though now she realised maybe she should. The Raw Coast *did* have a reputation. "They're all NCOs who look like they've fought half the war themselves. I feel like I'm the *least* qualified person to be running this operation."

"Oh they've earned much more than their ranks, trust me," Brade replied. "But under Imperial law, the highest rank any Rae recruit can attain is sergeant. You, however, have followed in your predecessor's footsteps to slip through such regulations, possibly because the concept of female officers was previously so unthinkable it never got regulated."

Wish wanted to argue that this felt like a set-up, and that she was not supposed to be here, telling men like that what to do. She wasn't Captain Tate, who had a long military history before she formed the original Blood Scouts. But Wish had lost her cool with Brade once today, and didn't like how calmly he maintained his own cool. She'd just have to manage. It was a good thing, she told herself. If these men were officers, they could take care of themselves and she could quietly slink around in the background.

"You *are* qualified, Wild Wish," Brade insisted in her quiet. "It takes more than strength to run a command, and I'm looking forward to seeing what you can do – all the more so with the right tools. They're some of the best scouts 4th Brigade had to offer."

"Yeah, great," Wish said, just to shut him up. She needed to move on before snapping at him, to be Practical Wish, Respectable

Wish. She scanned the soldiers again and noticed the bald-headed Graveguard had a medic's cross on his shoulder, just visible under a layer of grime. He was taller and slimmer than the others with a stoop and heavy lines on his face. She made an effort to remember his name, medics always worth knowing, but was quite sure she'd forget everyone else's in about two minutes. His sallow face fit the term "grave" at least. Through the side of her mouth she asked Brade, "Aren't Rawboys supposed to be cheerful?"

"Not the rebels," he said.

Wish sighed.

"We're looking forward to cutting some throats for you, boss," the round-featured Basing volunteered, apparently picking up on her hesitation, and the others agreed with broad accented muttering Wish could barely discern. They seemed serious, so she offered the grim squad a vaguely encouraging smile.

Following this introduction, they regrouped with Wish's ogres and sniper hopefuls downstairs and the two teams warily sized each other up before tramping down to the river to see the boat Brade had procured. It was as scrappy and untrustworthy as the Rawboys. He announced it as a Hostian steam-powered pleasure barge, as if that was a thing people were familiar with. They traipsed down stone steps to the boat, bobbing in the bay below the looming wreckage of the bridge. It looked like six other vessels had been bolted together, tall and pale at the front, a patchwork of metal panels in the middle and a wooden shack wobbling at the back. It had a great black chimney on one side and a jaggedly uneven paddle wheel on the other.

Wish wondered out loud, "Do we think it's more likely to fall over or fall apart?"

"Explode," Emi offered a third option. "With a chimney that size, the engine's too big for its bowels."

"Great."

"It's just the style," Brade said. *The Vice Trawler* has been serving this river for two decades – it's famous for its character, in certain circles."

"The Vice Trawler?" Wish echoed the name with shock, trying

to read it written on the rotten wooden hull. "In what circles exactly? Scavengers? Rust enthusiasts?"

"Don't judge its appearances." Brade smirked. "It's discreet and fast, the two most important things we need."

Wish caught herself before making another snarky comment, realising he was enjoying this, and she was supposed to hate him, not engage in banter.

Sergeant Caracker said, "It's got to float. That's the most important."

"Let's just get on and see," Wish said.

She clomped up a rickety gangplank, her pack and rifle almost toppling her off the side. She jumped onto a deck that looked as unstable as the exterior suggested. A couple of sailors moved to greet her, burly men in tatty shirts. One reached for her things and she snarled him off. The tallest of them, with a brick-like jaw and long silver hair in a ponytail, announced that she was welcome aboard *his* boat. His importance was confirmed by his once-purple velvet jacket and a flat cap with a dented medal at the centre. Brade shook the man's hand keenly and the pair continued across the deck, chatting fondly, either old friends or quick to recognise fellow captains of vice.

The boat creaked loudly as an ogre arrived behind Wish, and Ohno said, way above her ear, "No surprise he's familiar with Hostian steam-powered pleasure barges."

"He's an adventurer," Wish replied, watching Brade laugh with the sailors. "Expert linguist, explorer, third-best swordsman in the world."

"Third?" Ohno said.

"Yet you've got a problem with him," Caracker noted, stomping to her other side. Wish was aware of the rest of the platoon filtering by, Brade's sinister Rawboys included. Dalliance and Fawcet lingered, glancing her way as though hoping she'd offer them guidance. She suspected the boat wasn't big enough that she could speak freely anywhere without being overheard. But she was never great at keeping secrets anyway.

"Brade's able enough," she admitted, "but has his own priorities."

Caracker grunted. "Known more than a few like that."

Of course, the ogre had already had run-ins with superior officers, which was not something she should be encouraging. Wish made a vague sound of dismissal, allowing the ogres to move on, and found Emi watching her. She raised her eyebrows to ask *what* and the mage shrugged with her usual enigmatic smile. She slid closer and whispered, "Be careful or they'll think you like him."

"Huh? Gross!" Wish cried as the mage walked on.

Brade came back to her with the boat captain and explained she'd have the main cabin with Emi; he would have the officer's room and the ogres the cargo hold. The rest of them could bunk wherever they found space. Wish quickly added that Scraper would stay in her room, not wanting any woman alone with this rabble. Scraper, who appeared somewhat ghostily nearby, barely acknowledged the offer and wandered off inside, unbothered. They were then treated to a quick tour of the boat's rickety bowels, which were surprisingly complicated and included carpeted and wood-panelled rooms with soft gas lighting. Like a pleasure house, Wish realised, hiding in a dump.

In under an hour, mostly spent loading supplies, they were away, chugging up the river to leave the peaceful port of Hail Crossing behind. All too quickly, the normalcy was gone, and ahead sat the expansive waters of the Most Blessed Sea. The sun was falling and dusk provided an appropriate backdrop for distant flashes of gunfire. Or cannons, Wish realised, watching from the ship's bow. To be that far away and visible, with no sound reaching them, they had to be monstrous large weapons. Boats had quickly evolved during the One War, like everything else, but she had not yet seen the great dreadnoughts and floating fortresses that were fighting a very different war to the rest of them. She could imagine Oksy reeling off facts about them, though: cannons that could fire over mountains, hulls heavier than towns, nonsense like that. One such marvel had destroyed the Hail Crossing bridge, after all.

Captain Brade would know, too. And his sailor friends. They could tell her all about how this sea had an ever-shifting territorial dispute of its own, with armies of small and large boats meeting for enormous battles. Were they called armies at sea? Fleets? But he had gone below and she didn't want to ask. One sailor did try to spark conversation, suggesting the distant flashes were probably the Drail's Blessed Sea flagship, *Horrorcast,* but she affected disinterest.

Two of Brade's recruits quickly got ill, going green and leaning over the sides of the boat, while the others loitered about sharpening blades or playing cards. The ogres draped themselves either side of the main deck, not caring that the sailors had to keep jumping over their legs, while Scraper and Emi rested in the cabin. Dalliance and Fawcet wandered up to Wish, glancing about as if trying to act casual, and she demanded, "What?"

"Just wondering . . ." Dalliance was smirking as usual and glancing at her sidelong. Fawcet held back, not so confident about approaching, and she folded her arms, expecting another loaded question. "Well. We've got some time travelling. Maybe you could show us a few things?"

Wish felt her hackles rising, regretting again that Sergeant Bix wasn't here to keep their cheek in check – but before she blurted out something angry, she realised he wasn't suggesting something leud. They were both watching her hopefully, making an actual request. She cleared her throat to cover her misunderstanding. "Like, gun things?"

"Yeah," Dalliance replied eagerly.

"On a crowded boat? Bobbing up and down?" She managed not to laugh off the suggestion only because she could see they really expected something from her. As if she could give them simple tips that would turn them into expert killers. "Maybe later. If I get a minute."

Before they could ask when that minute might be, Wish left them to walk up the rear steps to where a ship's wheel sat astern of the cabins, the tall pilot guiding it as the chimney puffed and the paddle turned. He was alone, chewing on a big cigar.

"Want a turn?" he asked, nodding to the wheel.

Wish considered it. There was a certain temptation in manoeuvring a vessel of this size. A slip of her hand could send two dozen men falling over. She'd have the power of a giant. A little *too* tempting. She shook her head and leant against the rearmost barrier. "No, I just want some space."

He grinned around the big cigar and said no more. A discreet barge, Brade said, with staff used to judging what passengers wanted – or didn't.

The peace of bobbing up and down, just enjoying the unsteady ride, brought Wish back to her usual thoughts. The Blood Scouts had last all been together on a boat, crossing the Heaven's Eye Lake. A big hold of smelly, noisy girls. Had the others seen worse things than her own squad? Vile giant insects; flames and bullets and blades; deadly mistakes . . . Wish closed her eyes and saw Loose falling, flailing, screaming over a cliff. She swayed and almost stumbled, shooting out a hand to steady herself against the rail. There was a short drop into the churning water, and her pulse quickened at the realisation she could have fallen in.

"In the early days of the Holy Garter Empire," Brade said, loudly announcing his arrival, "some considered it an honour to drown in the Most Blessed Sea." He approached from the steps, giving the pilot a nod. Wish returned an unwelcoming look, but he continued anyway. "It's said there were Saint cults who marched into the water in droves for a holy death. Others sought to anoint the great sea creatures as vassals of the Saints, hoping to be devoured as a passage to a glorious afterlife. Perhaps some early seeds of the Venerate Flesh in there."

Wish rolled her head to the sky. If she had to hear random lectures, she longed to hear them in Oksy's voice, at least.

"From my research," Brade went on, "the deaths came first, the religious connotations later. The Most Blessed Sea could more accurately be called the Most Bloody; there have been countless battles waged here, dirtying the water with death and corruption. The creatures were bred to be deadly and people grew so afraid it became expensive to cross. When the Holy Garters blessed this sea and called it an honour to die here, they were really encouraging cheaper labour."

"Yet it's come full circle," Wish said, pointing to the flashes on the horizon. If she couldn't ignore his ramblings, she could at least disagree. "Pretty sure no one wants to be here anymore."

"No," Brade said. "It didn't take long for people to take the name as ironic. The Saints Mire's history is much the same – these blessed places are deadly, with holiness borne of hardship. The priories challenge their penitents in the same lands that tested the prophets. And they remain defensive over letting anyone in. I've never gained full access."

"It's a bog," Wish said. "Why do you *want* full access?"

"I am professionally curious," Brade said. "There are legends about what drew the prophets there or why the priories remain. Thousands of years of dark history lie in that sodden soil. To say nothing of the treasures, relics and learning that's locked in the vaults."

"You love it," Wish noted, hearing echoes of how he'd talked of Low Slane, the nightmare land he had dragged them into. "You're like a collector of terrors. An explorer of the worst." She paused, gripped by a sudden thought. "Is that why you pretend to like me?"

Brade leant closer than she'd have liked. "Wild Wish, I've never *pretended*. You're certainly no terror. You stopped me from making things worse, remember. I was mistaken, with Vorhale and Wick. I own that."

Wish raised an eyebrow. "I don't believe you."

"So be it. But I intend to win back your trust."

"Sure. As if there isn't already a dozen things you're hiding about where we're going."

"Hiding?" He laughed. "Ask me anything; I've nothing sinister planned."

"Okay. At what point in this hellish mission are you going to stop and ask me to do something I never signed up for?" she shot out at once, and wiped that smile off his face. He considered his answer at length.

"This isn't like before," he said. "If anything, I actually think we might have a shot at a peaceful resolution to this. In my experience, the Drail commander stationed at Onwail is, above all, a sensible man."

Wish screwed up her face. "In your experience? Fuck. You know him?"

"We've met a couple of times. Colonel Dedecus Atmoor. There was a ball at Swinbalny Hall where he engaged me with some interesting conversation regarding the lessons of Takata and Virane – a man well-read in military history."

Wish found her mouth hanging open. "Why were you at a *ball* with a Drail soldier?"

"A Drail *officer,*" Brade corrected. "This was before the war. Above a certain rank, everyone knows everyone else. Did you know Statesman Dowel is godfather to the Screaming Prince's niece? They're mostly a bitter, scheming lot, but I felt an affinity for Atmoor precisely because he did *not* fit that mould. He's a veteran of Camano and helped sway the Battle of the Basin, but evidently has little favour in the Arrow Council, probably because he doesn't play politics. He was sent to Coakes before being assigned Onwail, one place as bad as the other."

"Coakes is a great big wetland too," Wish said. "Maybe he proved himself capable in one big bog, so they sent him to clear up another?"

"Doubtful. He struck me as a . . . cautious man. Honourable. I can't imagine him invading neutral territory lightly, and think it may be possible to reason with him."

"Wow," Wish said. "Yeah, I wasn't expecting that. It might also be possible he's had a taste for the fight and couldn't resist. If I'm a commander posted by unoccupied territory, with nothing better to do, I'd probably invade it."

Brade smiled. "I suspect you would. Nevertheless, I'd like to fully understand the situation, if we're expected to kill him."

Wish paused. He was watching her reaction closely, laying that out so plainly. She said, "We're here to observe and report back."

"Please," Brade said. "You don't need me to tell you how Command think. If the demands of the mission shift, well . . . we can't let the Saints Mire falls into Drail hands. They could hold the international churches hostage with control of the relics there. Yet *we* would be damned if we're seen escalating a conflict in holy territory. The solution needs to be quiet and clean. I don't doubt that the Irregulars had precisely that in mind requesting help from the Blood Scouts specifically."

Wish hummed thoughtfully, not liking this and wanting to blame him, but knowing it should've been obvious. If she'd only taken a second to stop and think about this properly. She said, "Is that why you brought Rawboys?"

"I brought them for the same reason that you brought ogres," Brade replied. "We want the best on our team, even if Stanclif Command have a habit of overlooking people from certain backgrounds."

Wish nodded. "And you trust them not to cut our throats at night?"

"More or less."

She stared at him; it was another attempt at lightening the mood, reconnecting, which made her only the more resistant to talking to him. Averting her gaze, she changed the subject, "What about these partisans? Did you meet them at a garden party or something?"

"The Irregulars? No, but I've heard stories," he answered, smiling. "Kin Kasidee was a bank clerk in Tynes. Just happened to be in Garter when the war started and he got caught up in it. He found he had a penchant for fighting by leading some civilians clear of a battle in the town of Duggier, and has since attracted more than a few dispossessed civilians who keep diving into unlikely conflicts. Most famously, they overran a small fort in the Mattin mountains, Fort Simnon, and held it from attack for fifteen days, until the Khib army was able to relieve them."

Wish raised an eyebrow. She'd imagined the Irregulars being a small troop of sneaky spies, not actual fighters.

"Yeah," Brade said. "But their propensity for violence may be a problem here, if they're antagonising the Drail. As for their message, requesting Blood Scouts, I've found no connection between his company and your platoon, but I suspect they heard stories of your exploits and thought you were kindred spirits. I suppose that's part of what we're travelling into the unknown to find out. And I do look forward to working with you again."

On that cheery, complicating note he pushed off the barrier to walk away. Friendly as they'd ever been, no sign on his behalf that things were not okay. But Wish kept in mind, watching his back, that he had a ruthless streak that was sure to resurface. She wondered how much harder this mission would be if she were to push him overboard.

10

We have been given opportunities to bridge the divides of class, species and religion. Lords fight alongside peasants, holy men with infidels, united in the common goal of survival – not just our own, but that of our entire culture, our species. We may carry differences as stark as day and night, but we are all Drail on the battlefield, and in this unity we find strength. We find Purity – and we shall find success.

**Extract from the Letters of
Colonel D. Atmoor, Garter, 719**

Colonel Dedecus Atmoor stood over a bloodied corpse, rigid with disappointment.

This was not how he'd seen his morning going; he was comfortably quartered in Prosper Priory, on good terms with the high venerator, and he'd looked forward to a day of catching up on front-line dispatches. He had dozens of new ideas to transcribe and send, and was contemplating advising General Foul on the positioning of his Forest Raider battalions when this commotion drew him to the priory's central courtyard. Now, instead of providing crucial insights to turn the tide near Fever Forest, he was looking at a dead body.

His men – praise Purity how he hated to think of them as *his* – had not only failed to capture anyone alive, but they had thought it wise to deliver this body for his personal inspection. Lieutenant Ilscot, the wretched leader of Section 5, had deposited it on the flagons of Prosper Priory's courtyard, *inside* the walls, in full view of any passing monks. The man was grinning like a goblin – appropriately, as Atmoor suspected Section 3's leader, Wideskull Bleacher, had put him up to this. That suspicion kept him from exploding outright, much as he wanted to take Ilscot's throat and dash him against the stone walls. Atmoor was a big man, more than capable of it, which made it all the more important he be seen as reasonable.

He took his time staring at the body while his indignation simmered down. It was a young man – most of them were, sadly – whose clothing could scarcely be called a uniform. Torn cotton trousers and a shirt fit for a peasant, with the barest leather-panel armour strapped over his chest and the tips of his arms. The leather had a scorch mark where it had done precisely nothing to stop a bullet. His stomach had been torn open, gutted like a fish. The lad's face was also purple and swollen, where the skin and flesh remained. Had the goblins *bitten* him? Hopefully it'd happened after death, when they'd moved his body too roughly or violently extracted his teeth or jewellery. Neither Section 3 or 5 had much honour.

There was no benefit in reflecting on the shortcomings of the legion, but Atmoor allowed himself a regretful moment all the same. Ilscot and Bleacher had reached Guiltway Priory and the Black Lake with impressive speed, but had charged into battle rather than await further orders. With more competent, more *patient* soldiers, he could have fully routed the enemy at the Black Lake and secured the Mire. Instead, he was staring at an unpleasant body on consecrated ground. Perhaps the mistake was leaving the operation to his lieutenants instead of handling it himself. But he was a colonel, and should've been able to trust his subordinates whilst he focused on more important things – such as strengthening relations with the churches (which would require *more* work now). To say nothing of how he had his dispatches regarding the Drail's broader dilemmas to consider.

The problem was his hundreds of men were either too poorly trained, too poorly equipped or too poorly conditioned. Two sections of semi-retired veterans, two of soldiers generally unfit to serve elsewhere, either physically or mentally, and a goblin horde – managing them was like herding bees. Wideskull Bleacher was the most capable leader of the lot, but when it came to goblins, intelligent leaders were a bigger liability than dim-witted troops, which was precisely why this lot had been stationed in Onwail. The Arrow Council expected Atmoor to whip them into shape for the wider war, on top of everything else, but the bad soldiers were just bringing the few good ones he had down. That was evident enough here.

Ilscot, with his dead body, was standing alongside Atmoor's very best man, Carrow, who had fired the shot that sparked this whole fiasco. Perhaps Carrow's nervous ticks really were a problem, despite Atmoor's belief that he was still a fully capable sniper, but more likely Bleacher or Ilscot had encouraged the premature violence, with the same bravado that'd convinced them to bring a corpse into a priory. But 17th Division were not sending any better troops; Atmoor just needed to handle what he was given more effectively. If there were degrees of efficiency with which one could handle shit. They had, at least, scattered the enemy and killed a few.

Atmoor looked from the eager face of Ilscot to Carrow's expression of permanent worry. The former was a gaunt, crooked-toothed son of a bitch who belonged in a prison, the latter a tall, presentable man who couldn't stop the right side of his face from twitching. Measuring his tone, Atmoor said, "Why, exactly, am I looking at this body?"

"Significant ain't it, sir?" Ilscot grinned, showing off the gaps in his teeth. "That mark on him there."

Atmoor cocked his head to one side. Under the torn clothing and blood there were hints a faded tattoo on the dead man's arm. Young as he was, he must've been a child when he received that tattoo.

"Know your enemy and all that," Ilscot went on. "It's a Finnock sawbird. What they give captains in the Pillared Asylum up in Necostis. One of the worst gangs in there."

The vulgar man had a point, after all. It could've been told instead of shown, and the insight spoke to Ilscot's own background, but the detail offered a fresh idea of what they were dealing with. The Pillared Asylum was one of the vilest places in the world – at least before the war made almost everywhere equally terrible – harbouring notoriously wicked criminal gangs. It suggested that the quality of Atmoor's own soldiers was not the sole reason for them failing to crush the enemy. He said, "This Kasidee might be more formidable than I assumed."

"Exactly!" Ilscot clicked his tongue. "And look – I thought we might've bagged a commander, but not at his age, no matter the gold he had on him."

Atmoor gave him a look to convey, again, that he did not approve of grave-robbing, particularly not when they tore out teeth.

Ilscot squirmed, but continued. "He's a foot soldier, right? If they've got Finnock captains in the regular ranks, that crap about Kin Kasidee holding a fort might be true. I could believe fifty hardnuts like this might fight off three hundred Drail."

"Indeed, each of their men is probably worth a handful of ours," Atmoor said, which deflated Ilscot's enthusiasm. But encouragement worked better than scolding, so he went on, "Well observed, Lieutenant. Next time we'll take measures to account for their potential advantages." He turned his attention to Carrow. "Did you identify their leadership?"

"I s-s-s –" Carrow squeezed his eyes shut, straining to get the words out. Atmoor waited, deliberately impassive. If Ilscot said anything, he'd have him whipped; their marksman might've struggled to speak, or sleep, but he was more capable than most soldiers in this war. Carrow took a deep breath, then quickly forced himself on. "Saw the man I took to be Kasidee. Sorry, I was mis – mis – mis –"

"He got a captain!" Ilscot announced happily, slapping the stuttering sniper's shoulder. "Go on, tell him."

Carrow was less keen, it being unclear if Ilscot was genuinely pleased or trying to goad him into more talking. "Sh-sh-shot someone giving or-orders. Not – not –"

"It sent them running," Ilscot interrupted again. "They had themselves dug in deep, thinking they were safe. It'll be a while before they make camp like that again, I swear."

Not a good thing, considering it was harder to flank a moving enemy. But short of outright retreat, there were only so many places Kasidee could go next. Atmoor thought out loud, "They won't retreat. Kasidee came for a fight. Call everyone back from Guiltway and the Sails. Have Bleacher rein in the horde to join us, while Section 5 take the rear. It's time we moved on Carlwen. I'll personally lead the march."

Atmoor readied to dismiss the men, to get this body gone – a second too late. A man shouted and footsteps quickly approached. The group parted to see the priory keep's doors open and the flapping cloaked shape of High Venerator Ultemy racing towards them. Though a frail old man with turtle features, made comical by his attempts to keep his billowing clothes from tripping him, Ultemy exuded importance and commanded the greater part of the local region. The need to appease him was part of the reason Atmoor had stayed in Prosper for so long – and might be quickly undone, from the anger on his round, red face.

Ultemy approached snapping accusing words, as his chief aide, Brother Redfire, rushed to keep up and translate. Another problem with the old bishop: as virulent and vocal as he was, he only spoke Old Lomian, an ancient language that even a well-travelled scholar like Atmoor had little use for. Ultemy arrived with taut arms clawing the air, spitting things only Redfire understood.

"He asks why there is a dead body in our courtyard," Brother Redfire said, as affable and kind-faced as Ultemy was furious. The venerator shot his translator an unhappy look and continued more angrily, to compensate for Redfire's softness. Redfire remained faintly smiling, going on in his refined accent, "He'd like you to know it is a great offence to spill blood on the floor of a priory. It is written in the Book of Body that those who sully sanctified property shall be pierced by hooks and pulled apart by the Great Beasts. Worms will spill from their wounds."

"By the Saints," Atmoor muttered at the oddly specific proclamation.

"There's no blood spilt," Ilscot replied defensively. "He's lying on a canvas, right? We're not idiots."

Atmoor held up a hand to silence him. "Please apologise to the High Venerator for us. It will be removed this instant."

Ultemy barely caught a breath as Redfire spoke, then carried on snarling and snapping. Atmoor nodded to his men to take the body and Carrow and Ilscot bent to carry it themselves.

"He inquires," Brother Redfire said, "if there has been bad news from the east?"

Atmoor liked this monk, more than most of his own men. Though much shorter than him, Redfire was almost equally broad as Atmoor and carried his considerable weight like he knew how to use it, but had a gentle aura. It made his frequent comments of hell and damnation sound more poetic than horrific. His almost perfectly round shaved head, with an incredibly neat thin beard that encircled his mouth, was always welcoming and kindly, and his management of the cantankerous Ultemy was the main reason their Prosper advance had remained bloodless. Oh, for a legion of Redfires and Carrows.

"Good news, actually," Atmoor said. "I can confirm that Guiltway Priory is secure, though there was significant collateral damage." That was an understatement, as he understood it, but these monks were hardly about to check for themselves. "And we've driven the enemy away from the Black Lake. We'll be leaving a small contingency here as I move to Carlwen."

Ultemy only briefly listened to the translation before cursing in his ancient tongue, but Brother Redfire gave Atmoor's words more careful thought. The monk absently translated a few sentences while watching Carrow and Ilscot huff out through the priory doors.

"Do you expect much trouble at Carlwen?" Redfire asked, his own question and not whatever Ultemy was snarling.

"That depends on two things, I suppose. Whether they are ready to open their gates for us and whether the Comity Irregulars get there first."

Redfire nodded understanding, and relayed some of this to the venerator as Ultemy made more upset comments.

"It would go smoother, I imagine," Atmoor said, "if I had the company of a local liaison who I could trust. How beholden are you to this priory, Brother?"

Redfire raised an eyebrow, smiling faintly as Ultemy glared, awaiting translation. "In the interests of avoiding conflict, I might make an exception to travel from my post. If the High Venerator will allow it."

"In the interests of avoiding conflict . . ." Atmoor avoided smiling back. They had a long way to go, with scrappy fights to come and hardened criminals in the enemy's ranks. Criminals in his own ranks, at that. Damned if he was going to make this entire journey with nothing but incompetents. "I might insist upon it."

Wideskull Syrus Bleacher was deeply tempted to send his horde swarming through the fields of Shadow Sails after the filthy humans. His boys were happily scrounging through the abandoned lakeside camp, so it was no trouble to keep them from the hunt, but he was itching to follow through himself. Problem was, Colonel Atmoor would have other ideas, and he'd pushed his luck already. Any goblin could see how tense the man was underneath that forced calm. Typical pompous tall, always liked to appear in control of their emotions; made them all brittle. A good goblin leader knew fluidity was freeing. One day, Atmoor was going to snap.

The trick was teasing around the edges of his limits, though. Poking him just enough to keep things moving without going so far that he'd reassign the entire horde someplace worse. When Atmoor deigned to address the goblins directly, coming out of his letter-writing quietude, it was usually to remind them of that. Couldn't have a repeat of the worm-eye massacres that got the goblins sent here; they'd been lucky not to be summarily executed and all that.

So, while they might've only cut down a few Comity talls in the night, and were missing the opportunity for a proper hunt, Bleacher contented himself with soaking up the sun on a rock overlooking the water, pinching his way through a little blood-stained booklet one of his boys had found. There were a bunch of these pamphlets saying similar things, apparently, which was bloody typical tall behaviour: a rogue army of humans sharing little notebooks of their leader's profound (yuck) philosophies. Atmoor had no idea how similar he was to this bloody Kasidee.

The booklet Bleacher had was leather-bound but cheap, a bit small for goblin claws, written in ink, apparently copied by hand. He'd expected a diary or logbook, maybe prayers considering their location, but the journal was altogether more strange. No names, no titles, just vague passages of sprawling thoughts, preaching that it was good to (a) defy conventions and (b) fight stuff. Moderately goblin-like sentiments, in fairness.

A series of whistles announced company, and Bleacher set the little book aside to watch a human galloping through the grassland on horseback. Major Weles, head of Section 1, what an honour. He was easily recognisable by how damn stiff and upright he was, always trying to make up for the rest of the company's slackness with his own posture. He slowed as he passed the first ranks of goblin packs, variously sunning themselves, gambling or crafting idols from the scrap of their fallen enemies. The major couldn't hide his disgust at one group working up a death ward, a fairly tame cross of severed limbs. Weles was an old-school veteran, saggy and pale with age, perfectly unflinching in interacting with goblins thanks to his superior attitude, but also totally uninterested in the responsibility of actually telling anyone what to do.

"Chieftain Bleacher," Weles said, drawing his horse up to the rocks. A small pack of goblin thins trailed mischievously in his wake. "Glad to see you've secured the enemy camp."

Bleacher was good at translating pompous tall, and what the man meant was he was glad the horde hadn't all run off already. "It's *Wideskull,* you daft prick, how have you still not got that?"

Weles' affronted expression was delicious. He was technically second-in-command and shouldn't let anyone talk to him that way, much less a goblin, but they all knew Bleacher was a more accomplished soldier than any of them, and his eight hundred greenskins were *scary.* So, pushing down his disapproval, Weles said, "Yes. Well, I've got Colonel Atmoor's orders. You're to bring Section 3 in and join our approach to Carlwen."

"So soon?" Bleacher whistled. They could've bloody taken Carlwen a week ago. "Are we allowed to join the raiding party this time?"

"There won't *be* a raiding party, Purity willing," Weles said. "The aim is to peacefully secure the town against the Comity rebels."

"Be easier to track them through the fields." Bleacher pointed over the grasslands east of the Black Lake. "Come at them from behind, out in the open. They left an obvious trail."

"We're spread too thin and have already lost unacceptable numbers in the Shadow Sails. Atmoor wishes us to regroup."

Translation: the colonel wanted them on a tighter rein while he gave it all a bit more thought. Bleacher peeled his lips back to show off his toothiest grin. "And what do you think, Major? Is the colonel right to be cautious or just plain scared?"

Weles gave the question proper consideration, inspecting the rocks where goblin heads were bobbing about. The Irregulars had left a good amount of junk behind, between scattered campfires and discarded bivouacs, making the aftermath of the fight look worse than it had been. "How strong did you estimate their forces?"

"Strong enough," Bleacher admitted. "But damn those talls ran fast. I was expecting a fight, didn't reckon they'd flee outright, otherwise I would've gone after them instead of securing the camp." A sad symptom of Atmoor's influence. "But they're a mad bunch, I'd say." Bleacher held up the booklet he'd been reading, opened it to a random page and quoted, *"We are the wind. We are not confined. When we combine, and blow strong, we bring down towers.* Not unlike some of Wideskull Fagel's writs, that. You familiar with goblin writing?"

"I can't say that I am," Weles said.

"Well, this lot aren't normal talls." Bleacher tapped the book. "And what'd Atmoor think of Ilscot's report?"

Weles looked terribly weary, watching Bleacher's smile. He knew, exactly as the colonel would've known, that presenting bodies was classic goblin behaviour. "It was somewhat offensive to the church, but the message was received."

"War *is* offensive. Did Atty tell them off? Ilscot and his golden boy Carrow?"

"No. Not on this occasion."

Bleacher snorted. "Right. He's got a few dozen more final straws left, ain't he?"

"Chief – *Wideskull* Bleacher, can I confirm that the orders have been received and understood? We want a complete withdrawal from the Shadow Sails by dusk."

"Oh absolutely." Bleacher slapped a hand to his forehead in an exaggerated salute. "We didn't kill enough of them to make hanging around here worth our while anyway." He gnashed his teeth, earning a rare flinch from the major, and a bunch of nearby thins laughed. "You can tell the colonel, kindly, that we are *ready* for more, and I'd be honoured to join him in taking Carlwen."

Weles' expression said he wouldn't pass that on. They could predict the response anyway.

"Come on Major, lighten up." Bleacher pounced off his rock. He rolled his shoulders. "This could all be moving a lot faster, right?"

"The aim is success, at whatever speed that requires," Weles said, exactly as it might've been repeated from the lips of Atmoor himself. But Bleacher knew he didn't believe it. Everyone in Atmoor's legion would rather the goblins run riot and be done with it, all except Atmoor himself with his plans and schemes. That was alright though. Bleacher could be patient too. He was getting intrigued by the vicious thins they were up against, and they'd have a good fight soon enough.

11

Naval advancements across the Rocc enjoyed an equalisation during the war. The great warships and cruise liners were previously operating outside Boldarow's borders, exploring the wider world, so the conflict provided a boon for internal lakes and seas such as The Most Blessed Sea, which, before the influx of war machines, were operating at 6th-century speeds.

Engines, Chimney & Rails: How the Rocc was Industrialised, Yun, p. 54

Despite the swaying, the creaking and a rotten damp smell, Wild Wish slept well on *The Vice Trawler,* in no small part for the rare treat of sharing a room with Blood Scouts again. Yes, it was Emi, who lay a little too close on their shared bed, and Scraper, whose general silence was growing increasingly unnerving, but they were still her girls. What was left of a greater group and better times. Wish intended to soak it up while staring at the ceiling, but the boat's rocking and her companion's gentle breathing lulled her into sleep, and suddenly a bell was ringing and the sailors were shouting, announcing the new day.

"This breakfast had better be bloody good," Emi grumbled, struggling into her boots, already half-dressed. Wish gave a sleepy smile.

Scraper sat on the floor, frowning, and said, "That's not a wake-up call."

Then Wish was up, jumping into her own boots, throwing their packs aside to get at the gun. Her body took over, never mind it had been over two months since she'd seen action. It came back naturally with fast movement and loud orders: "With me, Emi – Scraper, get the others."

Scraper didn't respond, so Wish gave her a hard push as she passed, gun now ready. A brisk few steps took her onto the deck, and she squinted at the fast-moving sea air and the bright morning sun. The crew were running about tying down ropes, releasing others, barking commands and responses too gruff to decipher.

Wish ran to the side of the boat and shouted, "What have we got?"

There was a dark mass of land on the horizon to the right. Open, choppy sea spread far to the left. No immediate sign of a threat, but the boat banked as it turned.

"Got you, you bastard!" a sailor snarled, running past Wish. He had some kind of musket, almost as tall as he was and ringed with dented metal. He pulled back its big hammer, aiming up, and fired. Wish jumped at the gun's boom and its great puff of black smoke, and followed its trajectory up to the clouds. Bat-like shapes fluttered far above.

The sailor cursed, having missed, and fumbled at the musket to empty the breach and stuff in powder. It took Wish a second to draw her gaze from his efforts, the antique weapon barely making sense to her, but the continued shouting and swaying of the boat drew her back to the chase.

"Can't keep up much longer!" the captain yelled from the rear, working hard at the wheel, and Wish understood all she needed to. Whatever those flying creatures were, they were getting away, and they couldn't allow it.

Wish propped a foot on the gunwale, jammed the butt of her Long 0.48 against her shoulder and aimed through the scope. A small target, but a familiar one: she'd spent long enough around these noisy creatures at Rock Stable to know a degrebus. Like little gargoyle monkeys, with long barbed tails. She took a rough guess at the distance, the height hard to gauge, then fired. One of the creatures spun, not hit but surprised by her bullet. Close. She adjusted the scope, slid back the bolt and fired again. The degrebus at the centre of the pack exploded in a burst of torn flesh and dropped with its wings fluttering raggedly apart, like a bag torn in two.

Wish jammed the bolt back, adjusted, fired again.

Again.

A pause for the boat to stop its sway, then one more shot. The sky was empty.

She scanned the grey clouds methodically, as best she could with the boat's constant movement. No sign of more creatures. But oh, a slither of blue, the sun poking through. Lowering the gun for a wider view, she became aware of the quiet on the deck, with only lapping water, the chugging engine and squeaking woodwork where there had been so much shouting before. She dreaded looking around in case everyone, inexplicably, was dead.

But she twisted to the side and found the sailor with the musket frozen with a ramrod half in his gun, staring at her open-mouthed. The other sailors were caught in a tableau of interrupted action, ropes or tools half-raised, all similarly staring. Emi was by the cabin door with Captain Brade, both smirking, with two of Brade's Rawboys behind them, gawking.

"You wanted to stop them, right?" Wish asked, suddenly apprehensive.

"How the fuck you do that?" the musket man replied.

She realised this was the shock of men who'd seen witchcraft, never mind that she'd done what they wanted. She scanned the waves and spotted some degrebus remains, bobbing on the surface. *Scattered* over the surface, more accurately. Four creatures she'd blown apart.

"You wanted to stop them," she repeated, because it had to be true – she hadn't just senselessly killed an innocent pack of animals. Had she?

"Think I get it now," Caracker said from the front of the boat, where the huge man was ready with some kind of harpoon. As if they might've got close enough for him to spear the enemy. He dropped the weapon with a clang and padded heavily down the deck, breaking the stillness. "That was bloody impressive, Lieutenant."

He loomed, as ogres invariably did, and looked like he wanted to pat her companionably, but not when emphasising her rank. His eyes went instead to the men by Brade, the hard-faced veterans who were yet to ask what exactly gave her the right to lead them.

"Someone buy her a damn drink," the soldier by Brade agreed, the oldest of the Rawboys, solidly built with a square head of grey hair. The spell broken, the soldiers and sailors joined in with laughter and shouts at what they'd just seen. They gathered closer, recounting it to each other and those who were just emerging from below. She noticed Dalliance and Fawcet filtering out, listening to what had happened, looking deeply disappointed they'd missed it. People did start patting her on the arms then, congratulating her or asking how she did it. The musket man joked that he should throw his gun overboard and she smiled rather than agreed.

Slowly she extricated herself from the throng and shifted towards the back, picking out Caracker as he lurked by the cabin, as tall as its roof. She mouthed, "What happened?"

"Coming on starboard," the pilot called out, and the sailors moved to pluck the degrebus remains from the water.

"Chance encounter," Caracker said. "They flew in from the east so I reckon they were scouting at sea and returning to land, but spotted us. Wouldn't have been a problem if I wasn't on deck." The ogre was unmistakably wearing the patchwork armour of a soldier. Wish wondered why he hadn't used his huge gun, instead of fumbling about with a harpoon, but didn't get to ask.

"Got it!" a sailor shouted triumphantly and the crowd gathered closer as he took something from the sodden corpse. He drew a piece of paper from a metal tube the creature had been carrying, and announced, "It's gibberish. Coded."

Brade shoved through and took the paper. He studied it briefly, brow folding with concern that Wish recognised. He murmured agreement, coded, couldn't understand it, but he kept the paper and left the group to their celebrations.

"Bad news?" Wish asked, stepping into his path. His expression said he didn't want to share it. "You can crack codes, can't you?"

"Mm. It's an old code," he replied, voice quiet. He read from the paper, *"Y. HC to E24. RC."*

"HC as in *Horrorcast?"* Caracker further translated, recalling

the name of the dreaded Drail flagship.

"*Y* could be positive, confirming orders or a message received – assuming it's coded from Drail. *RC* wanting further confirmation," Brade said. "E24, possibly coordinates." He pointed to the sky, the direction they'd been heading. The land had drifted closer. "The only Drail stationed out here are those in the Mire; no other reason to fly this close to Comity territory. If the Drail have requested assistance from a warship, we might not have much time. Their navy could shell half the region."

Wish considered the great, empty sea. "Could we lay a trap? If their flagship is on the way . . ."

"There's a lot of water to cover," Brade pointed out, "and we don't have the means. But there is indeed value in knowing the *Horrorcast* might be in the area. Only, given the Mire is a communications quagmire, we'd have to send the *Trawler* back to relay that information to Command."

"Give up the mission?"

Brade shook his head. "Have them drop us earlier. The boat can't go much further anyway."

"Great," Wish murmured. They had apparently arrived, and would jump out sooner than planned, with the promise of a war machine at their back to complement whatever horrors waited ahead. "Suppose we're due some exercise. Who wants to tell the team?"

Though the landmass appeared solid at a distance, the closer they got the more apparent it became that the Saints Mire's shores weren't neatly formed. It was a landscape of lumpy mud, tangled weeds and rocky outcrops that gradually grew denser, with gaps that twinkled in the morning light to hint at bodies of water as far back as Wish could see. The spread of tree clusters, thin-trunked and twisted, gave the impression of only sporadically firm land.

The Vice Trawler crept into the widest water canal they could spot, and slowed further as the passage narrowed. The pilot said he'd hoped to find an actual river further north, but the banks and depth of their current canal were unreliable. He dropped anchor within jumping distance of a rocky landing point, partly concealed by messy reeds, and they began disembarking, a few at a time, using the boat's smaller rowboat.

Wild Wish stayed aboard to make sure everyone got down safely, taking a last opportunity to survey the world from a slightly higher vantage point. It was mostly flat, the expanse they would have to cross, holes and crags aside, with no sign of civilisation. The rough idea was to head east until they found more stable land, and a road to the nearest priory.

"Probably better to come in here, anyway," the boat pilot told her. "Less likely to be seen. The Drail might already have eyes on the river. And who knows what state you'll find the priory in."

"How far to walk?" Wish asked.

"Five, ten miles at most, with luck." The captain squinted at the horizon. "Should be able to pick out the towers from here. Well. You'll see them soon anyway."

That wasn't encouraging, given that they plainly could not see any towers.

"Just stay away from the water's edge," he went on. "Especially once you get inland a little. They're not just in the water, the grescinds – it's any ground looks like it might be unstable or too moist. Stick to the dry spots and you'll be fine."

"It's *all* water's edge out there," Wish noted.

The pilot considered this, then grumbled, "True enough. Keep your weapons loaded and aim for the eyes. Your captain probably has some better advice and all."

She gave him a mumbled thanks. Relying on Brade for anything felt dirty now, and all the worse because she knew it was true. He was alighting from the rowboat, joining her platoon on solid ground. Fairly solid ground. As he steadied himself, he spotted her watching and waved. She nodded back subtly, leaving it to chance whether he saw it or thought she was snubbing him. From the way his smile faltered, she suspected the latter, and quickly wanted to make amends. She *had* nodded – she didn't snub people. But he turned away. Too late.

The sight of the men spread before her calmed that worry, though, as different thoughts took over. They were her platoon. A small platoon maybe, at not quite twenty bodies, but a platoon all the same. Not necessarily people she would've chosen, or looked forward to wading into trouble with, yet they were mostly rugged and hard-looking men, there for her to command. They might potentially be companions and confidants of a sort. Friends, if she could figure out how to make friends of men.

"I'm glad we got to see you shooting back there," the boat pilot said, drawing her attention back. "Otherwise I might've been concerned. Ready?"

"Ready enough," she answered with the start of a smile. Time to get back to the fight, and action. It didn't feel *good* exactly, but there was a certain comfort in it all the same. The comfort of knowing she wasn't going to have much time to sit around worrying, at least.

"Good luck then. I hope you don't get eaten."

12

I must've met a thousand men during my tours. Some I came to know as brothers. Some, the bond felt even stronger. I could not confidently recall most of their names, though; the names that I took to heart were not what they might use outside the army. We were born anew in the fight, after all. Our titles reflected what we became.
    All This Aflame: Memoirs of a Soldier, Lindon, p. 34

Captain Brade gave them a basic introduction to the creature that had shaped the nature of eastern Saints Mire: grescinds were merciless predators that dragged smaller creatures into the bog, sometimes to eat and others seemingly just out of spite. What constituted smaller creatures? Most things. They were, in short, giant crabs. Big as pack beasts, maybe as big as a truck. And, he added, they often worked in groups. But for their fierceness, they were also reticent: they stuck to the water, submerged, and if the group followed the rocks, they could avoid startling any grescinds. All this Brade announced like a lecturer, well-versed in public speaking, often with a wry smile and occasional gestures of his hands. Animated and lively and open. Wild Wish couldn't recall him being so open with the old Blood Scouts, and wondered if it was because he was amongst men now. He was in better health than he had been at the start of their journey to Low Slane, though.

Once he'd given his little speech, Brade focused on leading them safely between the waterways, and no one took up the conversation in his stead. Tough act to follow. They trod in a tight formation of heavy breaths and clunking backpacks, over rocks and around sickly trees, retreating from anywhere their boots squelched. It felt tense for Wish, a walk with strangers, none of the comfortable ease of marching with her Blood Scouts. She wouldn't be able to stand hours of awkward silence before reaching the first priory, let alone for days to follow. They *had* to become friends.

Wish considered the soldier walking closest to her, one of the Rawboys who'd been ill on the boat. He was hook-nosed with short black hair and a wiry, stooped frame. Some of the colour had returned to him, but his skin was still vaguely green. Wish said, "You feeling better, sick boy?"

He slowed as his face contorted incredulously. "What'd you call me?" His accent was best described as broad: fast, slightly high-pitched and clipped in that uniquely Raw manner.

"Sick boy." Wish gestured back the way they'd come. "On account of all the, you know –" She mock-vomited and Private Dalliance, walking just behind, covered a laugh with a cough.

Sick Boy scowled. "My name's Artilli. Use it."

Wish felt an urge to hide in a hole. This had gone instantly wrong and there was a chance that if she kept talking he might hit her. He had very *shrewd* eyes, and a tight, tense posture. But she was still their commanding officer and wasn't allowed to be afraid of these men. Sergeant Bix would have knocked this man on his arse and spat in his eye. Why wasn't *he* here? Without him, she needed to stick to the friendly plan, and said, quietly, "I didn't mean to upset you. Nicknames just show we care."

"*Sick Boy* is insulting," the man said, but hearing his own hotness, he glanced past her, realising others were listening, including some ogres at the back, then added, snidely, "Sir."

"Alright," Wish said. The group overall had slowed down, even Brade looking back from ahead. "What do you prefer? All of you. We'll fight better, and faster, on familiar terms. You can call me Wild or Wish or whatever, I don't stand on rank. Now you go."

"I already told you it's Artilli," the Rawboy answered. "Artilli Ptrangus, that's my name."

"No one's remembering that, Sick Boy," another Rawboy called out, lightly – thankfully voicing exactly what Wish was thinking. That soldier's response was more the sing-song friendliness she'd been lead to believe was common on the Raw Coast.

Sick Boy – Ptrangus – reddened as a ripple of laughter went

through the others. "Shut up, Basing. You shat yourself two nights running back on White Hill."

"Yeah but I kept my lunch down on the boat, didn't I? Got a temper on him, though don't he, boss?" the other Rawboy, Basing, said. "Maybe you oughta call him Ptrangry."

"Are you kidding me? That's harder to say than my actual bloody name!"

"Much!" Basing laughed, as though that was the point.

"They call *me* Toothless," the ogres' lanky young charge volunteered, more helpfully. "That wasn't ever positive but it is what it is. I agree with the lieutenant, it came from a good place, at least. Meant the lads knew me."

"Because they was being ironical, I guess," Ptrangus sneered, unimpressed. "Look at your gnashers. Fucking pearly whites."

"It's because I'm a coward," Toothless said, chuckling at his own expense. Wish frowned, unsure if that was a joke too, considering he'd come in the company of ogres and was marching into the deadly unknown. "I thought scouting would mean avoiding the actual fighting. I like the idea of staying hidden. Problem is, I'm a bit dim as well as yellow. Didn't realise these sort of missions are actually more dangerous."

"Okay, this isn't encouraging," Wish said.

"Before anyone gets any ideas," another soldier piped up, the blond-haired trainee from Rock Stable. "Fawcet is just my name. It's an old Stanish name. Not anything funny. It's not because I tried to *force it* with some girl and it's not because I'm leaky in any way. I've heard it all."

"Well it fits," said the man who'd allegedly shat himself, "because you seem like a real drip."

A scatter of laughter went through the group. This was getting better.

"And Toothless is no coward," Caracker said from the rear. "I've seen him survive two charges on the front and he helped repel the Balnian cavalry at Palicier. Lad's just modest. I saw plenty supposedly better men break under much less."

That quietened the group again, now he'd brought up the war.

They tramped on with murmurs of appreciation that made Toothless look more abashed than his self-deprecation.

Dalliance tried to lighten things again by saying, "Well, I earned my bloody name. Been slapped on the wrist more than a few times since signing up, and I don't mind saying. We fight hard, we oughta be allowed to play hard."

This got a few chuckles.

"Perhaps we should have a song!" Emi suddenly perked up, having apparently been biding her time looking for an opening. Wish knew this would quickly escalate, but the mage burst into song before she could stop her, making up for a lack of tune with volume. *"Myyyy husband is a wader, he's only one foot –"*

"Ah!" a Rawboy cried out, shrill enough to send everyone's hands flying to their guns. It was a stocky soldier, Latebite, out to the left; he was hopping on one foot, the other boot dripping wet and draped in tangled weeds from where he'd slipped into the water. "Holy Cane, why's there no solid fucking ground here?"

"Step on the rocks," the older, grey-haired soldier advised. "It's not that hard."

"It *was* a damn rock, shitmouth, you think –"

"Everyone back!" Brade shouted, rushing back down the line with his sabre drawn. Wild Wish bumped into someone as she grabbed at her rifle bag, almost knocking both of them down. In another second, the water erupted where Latebite had tripped, a wide stony platform bursting up in a mess of vegetation. The men scrambled out of the way shouting and falling over one another, as Wish stared at a creature for which *giant crab* was painfully simplistic. Somewhere in its covering mess of tangled weeds, multiple limbs were moving, with jagged claws shifting forward. The flat rocky slab that formed its top was shell-like, but it looked more like a living island than a crab. It chattered as it rose, either a noise from deep in its mouth or the sound of it clicking and snapping in movement. And there were *body parts* – the monster was decorated by dead men, three or four at least speared around its carapace, in old clothes, withered but fleshy. Why were there bodies?

The grescind attacked before fully rising, jolting Wish into action. Something big and pointy shot out from its dangling mass and a soldier screamed as it caught him around the waist. Latebite was thrown in the other direction as another limb stuck out, then Caracker was there, as tall as the great creature, and he brought down a crude, foot-wide blade to hack off one of the snatching claws. With his other arm he raised his gun, wide as a beer keg. The creature struck back and his enormous shot went high as he tripped over the moss.

Wish wrestled with her rifle, something catching in the bag so she couldn't draw it, and cursed in anger. Someone else fired, and then half the platoon were shooting, bullets ineffectually pinging off the carapace. She yelled, "The eyes, aim for the eyes!" But she hadn't seen any eyes.

"Move, now!" Brade instructed, sliding to her side and hooking a hand under her elbow. At the same time, he parried a reaching limb with his sword, cutting off a segment that looked part bone and part tree. He shoved Wish and her feet fell into step, running, the rifle bag back over her shoulder. The captain shouted at the others, "Leave it, get clear!"

She saw what concerned him then, as a big shape moved to the left, another island-like platform rising from the water. Behind that, another. Wish shouted, "There's more! Run for the dry ground!"

There was a big crack and a large object whooshed up behind her. The first grescind was caught bodily by a giant hunk of flying rock that smacked it back into the water. Emi started laughing near the back of the group as its limbs thrashed about, splashing them all – the mage having used her power to throw the rock. But a soldier was caught in its claws and lifted flailing into the air, pulled with it. Wish recognised his hair, blond and flopping with his desperate fear: Private Fawcet. The creature made an awful pained screech as it struggled to keep upright and its claws closed, cutting the man in half with an awful crunch and a spray of blood.

"Keep your senses!" Caracker boomed, and Wish glanced at the platoon now sprinting behind her, the ogre captain grabbing Emi as she doubled over cackling from using her magic. He hefted her up under one arm, making her laugh even more, and he strode past the rear soldiers. Ohno, his ogre companion, drove a big booted foot into the centre of a smaller grescind trying to climb out of the water. It was forced back down, but Wish saw a terrible broiling sight beyond – the pools between rocks bubbling and pulsing with more craggy land masses coming to life, some the very platforms they had walked on.

She was yanked aside by a rough hand and forced into running again, in the middle of the crowd of men, most barely upright as they tripped and slid over the wet ground. The soldiers with guns ready fired to the sides as more grescind emerged, and the earth shook with the steps of the ogres catching up. Wish picked up speed, aiming for a slope ahead, to get clear of the water, but just as she fell into a rhythm her boot slid out from under her and she flopped forward to smack her chin on a rock. She bounced back, dazed, as men tramped past. Someone pulled her up, but her legs wouldn't carry her – then she was lifted airborne with the soldier alongside her. She shrieked and thrashed out, caught by one of the claws! But she was shaken hard and sternly told, "Quit it, I'm trying to help!"

That confused Wish enough to take heed of the ogre above her – Ohno. She was pinned under the big woman's arm, and they were moving fast, in large leaping bounds. Wish twisted about, to see behind: the area was alive with the movements of giant creatures, a dark, unreal mass. Ahead, the other two ogres were carrying as many men as they could – Emi particularly struggling in Caracker's grip. A handful more men sprinted just behind. Further back, there was a terrific scream from someone who had been left behind.

Wish held on to Ohno's arm, eyes wide.

How was it possible? Had they actually sent her somewhere worse than Low Slane?

13

The most diverse tales of military history undoubtedly belong to the light-foot soldiers, otherwise "shock-raiders" in Khibba, or "guerrilla" in Remmish. The scouts, bombers and spies of the imperial armies aspired increasingly to this style of fighting, but the real glory always lay in the accounts of displaced civilians, veterans and vigilantes. Often forgotten by history, those who operated outside the central armies, variously dubbed Irregulars, Displacers or the Melted, had a greater impact than we may ever accurately realise.

Light-feet: How Hiding Changed History, Prodder, p. 1

I'd happily do away with every one of our so-called light-foot partisans. For each partway-decent squad of civilians, I have a dozen companies of wayward, opportunistic bastard brigands.

Extract from the Letters of General Kettal, 722

Kasidee was upset that he'd missed the fight at the Black Lake, but he wouldn't let it show. He welcomed the straggling company with smiles and words of encouragement as they regrouped in a misty field in the Shadow Sails, under the watch of distant windmills that stood as crooked, broken giants on the horizon. He patted shoulders and nodded greetings as men and occasional women tramped past, a colourful crowd with arms and armour from a dozen nations, scarred or tattooed or just plain dirty. Kasidee used as many of their names as he knew, which was most of them, and saw sparks of appreciation in their tired eyes.

It was the least he could do after their night evading the Drail, while he'd been out here hoping to catch the next patrols to venture south of the river. He'd been waiting for action with some of his best men, stupidly unaware that the enemy weren't coming because they'd gone west to ambush his camp. He should've been at the lake. He would've put up a fight, in that defensible position.

Then, if he had done, more people might've died. The losses had been reportedly minimal and they miraculously got most of the supply chain clear, thanks to Havik taking charge.

Shaking another gunner by the hand, telling him he'd done a good job, Kasidee allowed himself a moment's distraction to look over the field to the trudge horses towards the front of the company, where Havik sat hunched and staring his way, impassive. He itched to get all these greetings out of the way so he could go see what she was thinking.

Havikare, his marvel of a lieutenant.

Kasidee had felt a dozen times blessed since this war began. He had been living a charmed, romantic dream, from that first day he'd grabbed a gun in Ulgaric. He'd meant only to defend himself against the Drail infantry who'd burst into his bank, but things had escalated. He had discovered a natural talent for fighting and revelled in the thrill of protecting his fellow clerks that day. He fell even more naturally into the leadership role that the Ulgaric townsfolk thrust upon him as they routed the small Drail force. In the space of a week, he went from being an unassuming teller, working to raise money only to satisfy his father, to partisan hero, with first a handful, then a dozen, then scores of displaced people looking to him for guidance. The Irregulars were born of hardship, but he'd be lying if he said he wasn't enjoying the ride. It was something most of them had in common. Sure, he'd seen awful things, lost friends, *done* some bad things, too – but this was *living*. This was more raw than anything he'd read in the Weagalian Claw novels or the Chronicles of Brade. Now, there would be storybooks written about *them*.

With their Annals expanding daily, they were even writing their own.

Kasidee had earned his position through action, and had never once had his leadership contested. Part of that, he felt, came from never asking to be here. He was serving them, not the other way around. Besides, once Raltman and his Choketown thugs pledged loyalty to him, tough bastards to a man, it would've taken a very brave man to complain. Now they also had medics and cooks, artillery and entertainers. Lost One single-handedly raised their fighting prowess to a world-class level, and they had performed some incredible feats in this mad war. All that had been a worthy success already – then Havikare had appeared.

They'd found the unusual, initially quiet woman walking alone down a dusty mountain road, almost dragging her oversized gun. Kasidee led by example to show her respect from the start, a female fighter he knew was special, and the rewards had been more than he could've imagined: she was a bookkeeper of another kind. A one-woman encyclopedia, familiar with everything from the complete Weagalian Claw romances to the most obscure Tikan mythology. And she *got* Kasidee, better than anyone. She saw how the Irregulars could be a spark of light in the One War's misery, and how far their Annals might reach. And though that interest never seemed to indicate anything really personal, to encourage him closer to her, she delivered ideas of where to find the greatest adventures, the greatest riches. She said, semi-seriously, that Kasidee himself might be the Weagalian Claw of the eighth century – a modern hero.

Except the Weagalian Claw would never have missed a fight while his company ran from the enemy.

Kasidee watched the last of his company arriving and called out, loudly, "It's alright Agneth, you've made it. Good to see you here and well."

A woman at the back found a smile at being recognised.

"We'll cut down those goblins yet," Kasidee went on, addressing this more widely. "It's a minor setback, but one that would've cost anyone else a lot more. So who's up for sticking it to them?" There were general murmurs of agreement before he called out again, more enthusiastically. "Everyone take a break, freshen up, eat if you haven't already. Then we'll make a push to camp at the woods. A double ration of rum for everyone this evening, how's that?"

The cheers picked up. Off the other side of the crowd, Raltman leant his booming voice, and that got the rest going. Someone, probably Brocken, had the standard up, a great tall flag. He swept it from side to side, catching a nice flourish in the morning breeze. Kasidee put his hands on his hips, giving them all a moment to soak it in. They were an incorrigible bunch, never stayed down for long, and he loved them for it. He'd just keep that niggle of doubt and regret inside, at least until they were out of the open.

Kasidee mounted up and rode back through the company, accepting fresh greetings from those who'd had a minute to rest. He reached the front, where the others were waiting on horseback. Lost One said, "We got enough rum for that?"

"Details, man, details," Kasidee laughed. He turned to Havik, finding her watching him with her head to one side, expression studious. He asked, "Happy?"

"Overjoyed," she said.

"What do we think about heading for Midwood? I'm still considering Carlwen. We could take the town if they're stretched out towards Black Lake."

Havik continued staring in that thoughtful way of hers. Kasidee didn't like how deferential he sounded, and how he found himself apprehensive over her answer. She would undermine him, he was sure, and he would accept it, because she knew more about this territory than anyone. He held her gaze, though, warning her to word it carefully. She turned aside, peering at the hazy horizon, and said, "No, your first instinct was right. We want to reach the woods and make for Midpeak. Carlwen might be closer, but it's a lot weaker. And culturally insignificant."

Kasidee nodded, following her gaze. It was sinister country ahead, across the Shadow Sails, with more twisted windmills and peaks of mountains in the distance. Somewhere above the mist, nestled in the clouds, was a monastic fortress reminiscent of Fort Simnon, the site of the Irregulars' most famous battle so far. If they got there quickly, the Drail would have a hard time following. They could repeat history at Midpeak – even if repetition was less captivating. He said, "Yeah. We can leave Carlwen to the green-coats. As long as the men are up for a longer journey. We can't push ourselves too far."

"Don't you worry about the men," Raltman assured. "They'll go as far as they need to."

"We'll have shelter in the woods," Havik added. "A chance to recuperate and for others to catch up."

"Indeed," Kasidee said, though he doubted those who hadn't made it out with the rush were coming back. "We'll pour drinks for the fallen. Remember them well."

The others murmured agreement. The losses, though few, were unfortunate. Larrist hadn't been well-liked, but he was brave in his way, steady in a fight and always willing to voice his opinion. He didn't like losing young Bodi either, though the lad reportedly died valiantly in the rear guard – he'd find a good write-up in the Annals. He'd been a keen storyteller himself (if prone to exaggeration), a prison runaway who'd crossed the continent. He'd also been one of their most eager youths who were utterly besotted with Kasidee and Havik.

His death might've been avoidable if Kasidee had been there to fight.

He sighed, some of that melancholy creeping up. Part of the game, though, wasn't it?

Kasidee turned away from his lieutenants and watched the company stirring, cooking stews and resting their legs. Impatience got the better of him, and he called for them to start marching.

The company fell into easy order again, without complaint, to filter out of the field and follow their mounted leaders. They rode in silence broken only by the thumping of their great horses' feet, two abreast on an unpaved road, with a few hundred men's feet tramping tiredly behind them. They continued through desolate land mostly carpeted in moss instead of grass, the houses stacked stone and wood. Its misty dimness fit Kasidee's sombre mood.

Nowhere much to rest here, no cover as good as they had at the Black Lake, and without promise for much better until they reached the Midwood. Of course, the woods carried dangers of their own, as home to one of the many savage tribes of the Mire. They'd need to be careful, keep hiding, as was the Irregulars' greatest strength. Sometimes Kasidee wished he could just put up a fight and push back the enemy in one fell swoop, though. Get that out the way and move openly . . .

"You're looking way too serious," Havik warned him, steering her horse alongside his.

"Just tired," he said.

"Then stop thinking so much and save energy."

Kasidee gave her a wry look and she winked. It was hard to stay brooding in his own head with those dark eyes drawing him out. He said, "Should we have stood and fought at Black Lake?"

Havik raised her brow questioningly.

"Their troops weren't as bad as we might've thought. Right?" He twisted in his saddle to aim this question at Lost One, the marksmen riding just behind, alongside Raltman. "We hardly lost anyone."

"They were weak," Lost One agreed. "From what I saw, not much discipline."

"Exactly as expected," Kasidee said. "Onwail is a dumping ground for the dregs of the Drail army. Goblins, ill men and the elderly. We might've turned them away even after an ambush."

"It all happened too fast," Raltman said.

"It wasn't our time," Havik said, more convincingly. "That wasn't a position we needed to hold and the fight wasn't on our terms. And our losses were limited *because* we retreated. We've got plenty of fights ahead, don't worry."

Kasidee accepted that, but looked over his shoulder again to his column of weary men. Whatever she said, it was a bad start.

"They had at least one able shooter," Lost One pointed out. "Took Larrist's head off at a good distance."

"They probably thought he was you," Havik said, meaning Kasidee.

"Got themselves a bad deal there," Raltman added. "Wanted a cock and got a prick."

They all snickered, even Lost One with his unpleasant laugh. Better to joke than dwell on the death. But it was a good point. If Kasidee *was* there, he might not have survived. The Drail had tried to play them at their own game, fighting dirty. Who was to say what else they had in reserve, behind the goblins? The patrols in the Shadow Sails were further south than he'd expected, and they weren't supposed to have reached the Black Lake. A retreat had been the *right* choice. It just felt too . . . timid. That wasn't what Kin Kasidee was about. Not anymore.

He remembered Bodi again, when the lad had happened upon their camp back in west Elmn. Kasidee had been cautious about taking him on – was cautious about *everyone* who insisted on fighting with him – but Bodi had said, "We might all die because of this war, but your way sounds more fun."

The memory brought a genuine smile to his face, possibly the first all morning, and that earned him a pleasant look from Havik. It was a shame to have lost the kid, but he got his adventure, didn't he? They all would, in the end.

The trees and mountains gradually came better into view. Forbidden lands, full of mysteries. They were approaching the legendary forest of Midwood, for fuck's sake. They said those who did not die there came back mad, and whatever they left behind haunted the woods. Malevolently. But if Kasidee was honest, the possibility of finding savage tribes and demonic secrets was a draw, not a danger. No one had the motivation or resources to properly civilise this land, and the tree-dwellers were almost certainly still there, hiding in trees a hundred feet tall. The Rocc's greatest adventurers hadn't properly braved this land, and here they were . . .

The trudge horses stomped and snorted to show their disdain for the woods. The men tramped to a stop as Kasidee slowed his horse, with uneasy murmurs and forced laughter. Dread pretty well emanated from this place, calling out *come in and die.*

Raltman's horse reared up and he angrily tried to steady it. Havik leant over to take the reins, offering calming words to the beast. She then focused her gaze on the woodland.

"We're being watched," she said. "If not by tribesmen then by the spirits themselves." She sounded serious but a smirk teased her lips, and Kasidee knew she felt the same way as him. The danger made it worthwhile.

The mist had barely parted, giving the giant trees an unwelcoming aura. The Mire itself had such strange, shrouded energy, it was no surprise the Prophets had come here to connect with the Saints. The priories still stood and the empires were afraid to fight here, but Kasidee was going to march through it, into history.

"What's the word you used?" he asked Havik. "That feeling like we're going somewhere different. Crossing over."

"Liminal," Havik reminded him.

That was it. The whole Mire was liminal, she'd said, where the border between real and spiritual was thin. The Irregulars shuffled through it now with a tired, half-dead gait, as if on a road to the afterlife itself. He'd have Brocken write that down, Kasidee thought. Never mind one abortive fight in the night. When they were done, the Annals of Kin Kasidee's Irregulars were going to be spectacular.

14

The world sees the Rae through a Stanish lens. Not that I discount some of the positive perceptions – we are a musical people, a lively people, good-humoured and generous. But we are a lot more than that, too. The Stains want you to think us harmless and fun. They want you to forget how hard we've fought. How dangerous we are.
Tog Mo Lamh – *Why We Rebel*, Coil, p. 16

Wish collapsed at the side of a road, out of energy and satisfied this was a sign of civilisation. *Road* was perhaps generous, but the path was wide and flat, stretching towards the hills, its mud rutted by wheels. The platoon gathered around her variously tossing down their packs and weapons, squatting or outright flopping down onto their backs, all panting for breath. The ogres continued ahead, not quite as depleted as everyone else, along with Captain Brade, who was apparently a lot fitter than everyone else.

"Those must be the priory towers." Caracker pointed and Wish considered the foggy distance. She tried to imagine a building not far down the road, but couldn't see anything bar the occasional gnarled tree.

"A few miles off, no more," Brade agreed. There was an unspoken hint that they should carry on, but Wish gave him a warning look. The men were exhausted, uniforms heavy with mud, water and sweat. One of the Rawboys groaned loudly, clutching a leg – Latebite. The medic, Graveguard, crouched by him bandaging the wound. Wish scanned the others – Ptrangus was holding his shoulder where he'd taken a knock and Scraper had a hand pressed to her chest, staunching some other wound. Emi sat in a pointy crouch with a wicked grin on her face, quiet but watching them all madly. Everyone had minor injuries, at least, having escaped the monsters only thanks to the ogres carrying them through the bog. The ogres appeared well, from the way they carried themselves, though Caracker's face was streaked with black blood.

"Are you hurt?" Wish asked, and he looked down from his great height with vague dismissal. She indicated her forehead and he put a meaty finger to his own, making himself wince.

"Just a cut."

"Until it's not. Sort it out."

Caracker appeared ready to argue, but Ohno came alongside him and said she'd help, taking bandages from one of her many pockets.

"How many did we lose?" Wish asked the group. "I saw them get Fawcet."

Dalliance released a long, upset groan. "No – no come on, it didn't –"

"Keep it together," Wish ordered. No energy for subtlety now. "Anyone else? If we left anyone behind that needs help, I want to know."

"I saw Basing take a blow," Latebite said, then hissed at the pain of Graveguard pressing his injury.

"It's not so bad," the medic murmured, either very callous or badly lying.

When Latebite calmed, he added, "No chance he survived."

Wish frowned, recalling Basing from the brief chatter before everything went to hell. "The guy who shat himself?"

"Be fair," Brade cautioned, "in those circumstances –"

"Before, I mean," Wish said. "By Bly." She pushed herself to her feet and swayed, her breath back but her legs aching. "Scraper, are you okay?"

"Scratch," the woman replied bluntly.

"As long as those things aren't poisonous. Are they, Captain?"

"No," Brade said. "But I wouldn't say they're clean, either. Sterilise your wounds thoroughly. Is that it then, two lost?"

Wish ran her eyes over the others: she still had Emi and Scraper, Dalliance if not Fawcet. Three healthy ogres and four Rawboys, with only one serious leg injury. Everyone except the mage looked worn and unhappy, but considering the size and number of those beasts it was a miracle so many of them had got out alive. Well, they had a little help – the unique experience of facing a grescind was followed by the unusual experience of being carried under Ohno's arm.

"We should've brought a whole platoon of ogres," Wish said.

"No such thing," Ohno replied as she wrapped a bandage around Caracker's head. "You'd be lucky to find more than five in one place. Even three is an achievement."

"And we ain't carrying you squirts the rest of the way," Runt said roughly, no less charitable for having saved their lives. "Thought you lot knew how to fight."

Caracker tried to say something as Brade's Rawboys stirred with irritation, but Ohno pulled the bandage tighter, keeping him occupied. The stout older Rawboy said, "Didn't see you taking down any of them damn sea monsters."

"I was gonna fight them all on my own while you ran, was I?"

"Did you see me run?" the soldier shouted, marching into the road. He was incredibly square, his bristly greying hair erect even after a spraying of water and mud. He was also apparently unafraid of a man twice his size. "We did more than you, you great damn ox."

"Oh, *now* you're brave, huh?" Runt replied.

Ptrangus moved surprisingly quickly then, from reclining to up and behind his friend in an instant, fists clenched. "We got a problem here?"

The ogre sneered at the pair of them.

Caracker pushed Ohno off. "Runt, stop."

"I'm just talking."

"And I'm telling you not to."

"Nah, let him talk," Ptrangus said. "An ogre's wit's always good for a laugh."

Brade raised an eyebrow to Wish, suggesting this was her responsibility. She rolled her eyes to the sky. She'd forgotten this part, how even in the Blood Scouts disagreements quickly flared, particularly after going through something awful. Though usually there weren't ogres and Rebel Rawboys involved. As the men flung barbs between them, pressing closer, muscles tensing, Wish willed Caracker to break it up, recalling how little he thought of her attempt to stop the bar fight. But he snarled at one of the Rawboys' jibes himself, and Ohno hovered behind him with a scowl. Wish took up her rifle bag and wearily started unpacking it.

A gun went off beyond the group while she was fiddling with the straps and Wish looked up with alarm. Brade stood with his revolver raised and an impatient expression. His hair was out of place, his fine shirt and jacket ruffled from their running, and for it all his gaze was fixed accusing on Wish, not the squabbling men.

"Handle your platoon," he told her, and the men's eyes tracked from him to her. The confusion of his focus popped their argument. What the hell? Wish glared, aggravation rising. These were *his* men being unruly. Ogres she'd never asked for. He wanted to distract them by digging at her? And now all their angry looks were directed her way.

"I can handle them," Emi said though, unsteadily getting to her feet. She almost fell over, waving her arms for balance, and laughed. Not quite recovered from tossing huge rocks about. Scraper appeared too, then, sliding up close to Wish with her eyes narrowed at the men, her hand on a knife hilt. The men took her in, then Emi; any of them who had missed how she'd dropped that rock on the monstrous grescind had at least heard the effects of her dirt-minding mania.

"Great," Brade said. "Why not escalate things further –"

"Don't." Emi sharply pointed at him. A couple of the men flinched. The smile on her face didn't help. "Unless I'm mistaken, Wild Wish hasn't given *any* of you permission to talk."

Brade's colour rose, completing the full house of upset men. Emi was no Sergeant Bix, with his quiet authority – yet no smart words or easy solutions came to Wish. She wanted to suggest they all just relax, but that was weak, and now she looked at the rifle in her hands she realised shooting in the air was no longer going to help. She bit her lower lip and tried to imagine Captain Tate in this situation. Or Sarge. They exuded easy authority the same way Bix did. She simply didn't *have* that.

"Okay. So. You're supposed to be Blood Scouts now?" Wish said. She knitted her brow. "You don't know what that means. We're elite. The best. We've killed giants. We do *not* argue like –" She paused, stopping herself saying *men*. She'd always imagined the scouts were more considerate than male soldiers. But she remembered how aggressive Rue could be. Her friends had come to blows a few times in Low Slane. She said instead, "Like children. Blood Scouts work together. We survive together." But that wasn't true either. Where was Rue now? Or any of them? What was left of the farm in her mind, and the girls laughing, lifting each other up? Her vision glazed over as she looked through the men, not seeing them anymore. She quietly told herself, "We pull our friends through. Stick together . . ."

The way her voice trailed off brought calm to the group, at least. She could feel something like pity replacing the anger. She sighed, staring at the ground between her boots. Tried to remind herself that they *weren't* gone. Rue and Oksy and Dakoda and Newk. She would find them. She took a breath and looked up again, met the men's eyes.

"Those were *grescinds,* understand?" she said. "Some of the worst shit out here – they could take down armies, and we survived it. Right, Captain?"

"Yes," Brade agreed, softer now. "If they'd been prepared, we wouldn't have stood a chance. Even with ogres."

"We deserve a pat on the back," Wish decided, and moved on quickly, now she had their attention. "It's okay to be upset, but not with each other. We made it through together. Got it?" She eyed Runt and Ptrangus in particular, waiting for responses.

Runt scowled but subtly nodded. The grey-haired veteran more readily mumbled an apology, and added, "Lost my cool, Lieutenant. Won't happen again."

"I appreciate that . . . sergeant," she guessed at his rank, in lieu of his name, but the hesitation made it clear she didn't remember that either.

"Macmiddan," he told her, charitably.

"Sure. And look, we're not far from our first stop. These monks can give us ale and wine like you haven't seen on the front line for months. You've earned it."

Brade shook his head, a promise too far.

Wish frowned. "Food? Beds?"

A nod.

"Okay. Can he walk?" she asked Graveguard, and the medic returned a sceptical look. Latebite was stretched on the ground, legs black with blood wherever they weren't bandaged. "Fine. Here's our first opportunity to prove the Blood Scouts spirit. Who wants to carry our wounded?"

The troop squelched along the muddy road in wet clothes. *Dry land* in this place was relative, and it took a lot of concentration to place each step on rocks or scant patches of grass instead of in sludge or puddles. The road turned around a hill and looked out towards their destination, revealing a less-than-hopeful sight. Drowndeep, their first sign of a settlement in the Mire, was about as appealing as its name suggested: the priory sat in a low-lying countryside of shallow hills carpeted with a patchwork weedy grass, the trees a skeletal array of leafless branches. It was tall, rising in a handful of towers, but its uneven heights and rickety angles made it look like a junkyard for great chunks of scrap metal. Even at a distance, the uneven patterns of its walls and edges, comprising metal panels, chains, spikes and blackened wood slats, betrayed a haphazard construction not unlike the boat they'd ridden in on. And with its empty windows and a surrounding of water and mud, it looked *cold*.

As they slowly approached the priory, a soldier crept closer to Wish. She could feel the hesitation in whatever he had to say, and kept her own eyes ahead to delay whatever the problem was. He cleared his throat nervously. Wish looked aside at Toothless, the self-professed coward – she had to bend her neck a little. She had been on the taller side of the old Blood Scouts, and realised now that she was shorter than all these men. Maybe she had an inch on Scraper, but probably not if the woman stood up straight. What

Toothless had in height, though, he gave up in nerves, biting his lip and hunching.

"Shit and buckets, what is it?" Wish said, earning a more pained expression from the young man.

"Um. I didn't want to say before."

"Is it going to become less of a problem if you keep it quiet?" Wish said, really hoping it might. Toothless scrunched his face tighter and shook his head. "Then let's hear it."

He told her, almost inaudibly, "I lost my rifle."

Wish stopped dead. "Seriously?"

Toothless nodded. It was hard to be mad at him when he looked like a struck puppy. Somewhat terrified. What did he think she would do, shoot him dead? Beat him with a cane? But her mind tripped over his claim. They'd been walking for twenty minutes, how did he just lose a rifle?

"Can you . . . find it?" she suggested.

"It was back in the bog. When those monsters attacked."

Well, that had been chaos, so not exactly a surprise. Just not something Wish had taken stock of yet. She frowned, eyes running from Toothless back over the rest of the men as they slowed down, realising something was up. They had set out from *The Vice Trawler* laden with supplies, and now she saw they were travelling much lighter than they should've been. One or two small packs a piece, diminished in size, instead of bags rising well above their shoulders strapped with weapons and tools. There were a few helmets missing, too.

"Did anyone else lose their gun?" Wish called out, making Toothless flinch – a couple of the Rawboys gave irritated curses, and she saw he particularly shrank from Caracker's gaze.

"Dropped my short blade," Dalliance admitted, sheepishly.

"I couldn't keep hold of my pack," Ptrangus said, with contrasting indifference, and Wish flashed him an angry look. Indeed, he had his mumbler rifle slung over one shoulder and no bag on the other.

"Anyone else lose side-arms, ammo, food?" Wish asked and met a chorus of shy responses that quickly revealed they had pretty much all dropped something. One or two of her own pouches had probably fallen off, too, she suspected.

"I lost my gun," Latebite spoke unhappily over the others, and they quietened. Ohno had been carrying him, and no one was under any illusions he'd be going much further anyway.

Wish turned to take in Drowndeep again, their supposed sanctuary. She hoped they had food and warming fires, both difficult to imagine from here. She strongly doubted they'd have a spare rifle. The troop were waiting for some kind of conclusion from her, not least Toothless, who looked worried she'd tell him to make a new weapon out of his breeches or something.

What would Captain Tate do? Besides effortlessly remind everyone things were under control. You always believed Tate would just handle it, keep the platoon in order. But Wish had that responsibility now and had no idea what lay ahead.

"We'll figure it out," she said. "Who knows, maybe we'll get through the rest of this without needing to fire a shot anyway."

She regretted the words even as she said them, knowing she'd probably just damned them to so much worse.

15

In the Mire, vibrant and varied tribalism harks back to cruder times. Each region carries its own mix of personalities and aesthetics, making Mirian culture worthy of an entire volume of its own – however, it would take a lifetime's work to penetrate each community. For my own part, I barely scratched the surface of the Little Tears and Wet Walkers who accepted me; it would take a hardy expedition to reach the caves of the Mock Mirians and I'm frankly not sure I'd get away from the Shore Stalkers or Gaunt Lanterns with my life!
The Eclectic Traveller, Winimpal, p. 265

The closer they got to Drowndeep, the more Wish's enthusiasm waned. A shanty village sat before it, on waterways that expanded either side of the priory. The sun winked through the grey clouds, reflecting off a lake surrounding the rickety structures, as the ground narrowed going into the village. The platoon walked between shacks tied together with thick twine and rusty chains, the walls either slick leather or driftwood. They were mostly single-occupancy huts, resembling an impoverished street market back in Stanclif, but worse, and a good number appeared to be empty. The locals watched their approach with folded arms, mostly burly men with inky tattoos decorating their veiny arms and bone jewellery strung like trophies around their wrists and necks. They wore vests and thick breeches of the same leather that made up their homes, and some had plate armour that appeared ceramic, until Wish recognised it as segments of shell. Together with the occasional tall harpoon and big hunks of meat and drying bones hanging along lines, it was apparent this was a village of hunters. Were the grescind their prey? They were undoubtedly dangerous and looked universally angry. Wish glanced at Captain Brade for reassurance.

"Mirian Shore Stalkers," he said. "A respectable enough people."

"Yeah?" Wish raised her eyebrows. He walked ahead, to show it was safe, but his usual casual smile and easy charm weren't there.

A bearded man emerged from the village and said something in gruff Garter; Wish knew about eight words of the language, but understood well enough that it was a demand to know what business they had here. Brade replied with a grave expression, gesturing towards the priory then back to their troop. The village leader grumbled and huffed, and said something that drew their audience's attention particularly to the ogres, who shifted, ready for trouble. If this lot hunted grescind, they might make sport of ogres.

"Emi," Wish said, "you following this?"

"It's about what you'd expect," Emi replied, gifted enough in languages herself, frowning at the exchange. "Man-talk, boasting. The captain just told them about our battle with the crabs."

The Shore Stalkers regarded Latebite and his injury with comments that sounded like disappointment. A guy with a stringy moustache spat in disgust and the bearded leader raised a clenched fist, then pointed roughly at Caracker and spoke angrily.

"He got a problem with us?" Runt growled.

Brade replied, lips tight, "Everything's fine, none of you move or speak."

"Captain," Wish said, "that doesn't sound fine."

"And whatever you do," he went on, "don't smile or laugh."

He continued, huffing along to match the village chief's tone, as Wish wondered what there was to laugh about. Then she felt a terrible urge to smile just to spite them. Her lips twitched and she strained to suppress it. The village chief stared at her sharply, as if sensing her thoughts. He snarled at Brade and Brade replied with something equally hostile, then the chief raised his fist again and it *was* kind of funny, these posturing tough men. But he extended a finger. Pointing right at her.

They were savages who wanted the woman. Of course. Wish froze, itching to grab her short blade. She wasn't going to fuck around getting her rifle out.

Then the man's finger pointed up, and he met Brade's eye again sternly. They held each other's gaze for a painfully long moment, then the tribe lifted their hands almost as one, raising fingers. Were they taking some kind of vote? Worshipping the sky? The hands fell again, and the village leader stared at Wish for a disturbing moment. Finally, he nodded.

Brade said something and Emi translated in a whisper, "He accepts his terms. But none of the shit they said before made much sense. Something about the moon and rising waters, a spear in the throat?"

"Whose throat?" Wish bleated.

The village leader stepped aside and held a hand up to indicate ahead.

"He'll take us to the priory entrance," Brade said, though with a grim expression.

"Captain," Wish started, but he subtly shook his head. The message was clear in his eyes: don't question it, don't look back. Wish passed the village leader and the other glowering men. The troop fell into step behind.

"Don't fucking like this," the grey-haired Rawboy, Macmiddan, muttered.

"Just be cool," Wish told him, though she felt anything but calm herself. She walked through the increasingly morbid village of strung bones and fierce hunters, towards the priory gates, only a hundred yards ahead. Drowndeep was hardly a promise of safety itself, even more unpleasant up close than from afar, its walls as ramshackle as the village. The entrance was a pair of big arched wooden doors studded with black iron, set into a base of roughly stacked stone and a rising two-towered gatehouse of warped wood and metal, with uneven spikes to prevent people climbing up. Similar spikes appeared scattered around the structure, right up some of the towers, and the windows had prison-like bars.

The village leader strode past Wish and knocked loudly, almost making her jump. He shouted to announce their presence, angrier then ever, then waited. The priory looked dead, hard to believe there was anyone inside, and Wish feared they'd be left out here with the hunters.

Then a bell sounded, deep in the building, with a dull, funereal clang. Again, again, like a death toll. Wish frowned at Brade but the captain stood with his hands behind his back, giving nothing away.

A rattling mechanism unlocked and the priory doors opened slightly to reveal a man in a rough black tunic tied with a chain at the waist, over trousers and chunky leather boots. His round eyes bulged at them, head a wrinkled bald ball, and it took him a surprised moment to take in the gathered soldiers. The village leader continued negotiations here, growling at the monk, who wore a deeply troubled expression. Finally, the monk agreed to something with a few curt words and the villager stepped back, creating space for them to continue.

"We can enter," Brade announced, and the monk stepped aside so Wish could go in.

"I don't like this place," Wish muttered and Brade made a dismissive sound that could've been agreement. The gateway opened up into a courtyard and they went in, following the monk. The priory worked like a castle, thick outer walls surrounding a central square, with iron balconies and jutting rooms hanging overhead. The largest square tower sat directly ahead, a keep that rose importantly to the rear of the priory. Supply crates and work benches littered the tight space and monks lingered near the fringes, watching with as much worry as the villagers had hostility. They were penned in like prisoners within the surrounding village of huntsmen. But dry stone slabs formed the floor, and braziers burned nearby, so it wasn't all bad.

The monk who'd opened the gates flitted about by Wish's side, watching to make sure everyone else made it inside, then he scuttled back to lock the gates before rejoining them. He asked something in Garter and Brade answered with a word Wish new, *Stanish,* then the monk finally cracked a smile and clasped his hands together. He said, in an unusual accent, "Good people of Stanclif, welcome to Drowndeep. My name is Brother Estekof and I am here to serve you. I trust your journey was well?"

"Well met, Brother, your hospitality is greatly appreciated," Brade replied, his smirk returning at last. "It's also greatly needed. We have a man injured by a grescind."

"Ah, bless our bones," Brother Estekof replied with genuine alarm, which spread to the other monks as they saw Ohno lowering Latebite. They reminded Wish of small animals with big nervous eyes and skittish movements. Their robes were all the same tunic and trouser combination, adorned with heavy animal-hide boots and chains. They were also all shaved bald, though some had similar tattoos to the villagers. Now she looked, the workbenches weren't dissimilar to the villagers' either, with animal parts hanging up and barrels open with viscous liquid. Estekof addressed his fellow monks, then insisted, "Brothers Meskle and Farlhay can tend to him. Please, they are excellent healers."

Two monks came to Ohno's side and one touched her elbow, pointing towards a doorway. Ohno looked to Caracker, who looked to Wish, who looked to Brade. He said, "It's alright. The penitents of Bonesun are keen students of the body."

Wish processed that as the men led Ohno away with Latebite. Bonesun was the old, less fashionable name for Sandway, Fourth Prophet of Cane. The most controversial of all the prophets, said to have dabbled in bone magic. Some took that to mean healing, others necromancy. Ohno crouched through a doorway far too small for her, and her parting look was one of concern. Graveguard gave Wish a similar look, and she nodded for him to follow. The rest of them stayed in the courtyard marvelling at the towering priory and its weird adornments. There were spikes inside, too, Wish realised – and cages hung with bones like the fetishes of a witch's shack. There were no complete skeletons but some of the bones were distinctly human, which raised immediate questions. Even if there was a totally innocent explanation for making trophies of their dead, it was spit in the eye of the Church of the Venerate Flesh, who religiously committed bodies to the earth.

"What the hell is this?" Wish whispered, realising once again how spectacularly she had failed to prepare for anything they might encounter here. When she'd thought of priories, she'd imaged pleasant stone buildings and kindly monks pruning orchards, coddling hens and carrying flagons of ale. Not a swampland penal colony.

"Drowndeep," Brade said, with contrasting awe. "Once called Bonstar, the Bastion of Sandway, where the Fourth Prophet wrote the Book of Bones. It's stood against the elements for over a thousand years and you're amongst only a handful of outsiders who've entered in that time."

"Did they eat the others who tried?" Emi asked.

"Did anyone else *want* to come?" Caracker put in.

"Not for a long time," Brade said. "Though it has been a hotly contested outpost on occasion." To Estekof, he said, "I regret the tidings that have forced us here, but hope we will be able to ensure the ongoing defence of your priories."

Because she was supposed to be in charge, Wish added, "We appreciate you letting us in."

"Pilgrims are always welcome," Estekof said. "Inside these walls, you will enjoy our hospitality and protection and prayers. Besides, we have been expecting more visitors. If you'll accompany me to the hall, you may rest while the penitents prepare your lodgings. I will gladly tell you of the Mire and our recent goings on."

"More visitors? Who else has been here?" Wish asked. This priory was at the arse-end of the country, in its useless swampy lakes, and she'd not expected complications this soon.

But Estekof smiled. "Why, Sister Sonseen of Saintshadow arrived only two days ago, with word from the east. I'm sure she would be delighted to entreat with you."

"Sister?" Wish said. "As in, a nun?"

"Yes, of the Ghutan Order. She's been on quite a journey herself. Come, come."

He moved towards another door and the troop followed, still taking in the unusual priory. Wish calmed at the thought of there being another woman in this pit, at least. She walked alongside Brade and said, "They let the monks and nuns mingle?"

"Not normally, though their customs of hospitality aren't gender-specific," he replied. "It's good for us, though. The sister may have news. And it probably helped us get in, that she came first."

Wish recalled the village and the tension of their arrival. The locked gates, the rough men and the excessive spikiness of Drowndeep's defences. She said, "Are we safe here, Captain?"

"Hmm?" The question surprised him, as they entered the corridors of the keep, dim candles doing little to allay the darkness. "Absolutely. The penitents have a strict code of charity, and they know we're here to protect the Saints Mire."

"What about the guys outside?"

"Oh. Well. You can imagine, the Shore Stalkers are about as dangerous as the creatures they hunt, but they are also bound to the priory. They wouldn't harm guests of the penitents."

"You were talking to them about me," Wish noted. "I didn't pick up much friendliness."

"Naturally. They have a style of speech that sounds aggressive, and respect hierarchies of strength and leadership. They wanted to know who was in charge. I answered honestly; they could've been more reverent of an ogre leader, but might've been tempted to challenge us. It's not something to worry about unless they level grievances against us."

"And if that happens?"

Brade paused. "Then any disputes would be settled between you and their leader."

"As in . . ."

"Trial by combat."

"*Any* disputes?"

The captain nodded. Wish swore under her breath.

Enjoying her discomfort, Brade leant in closer and said, "For what it's worth, I expect you could handle yourself. But let's try not to offend anyone. Just make sure everyone respects the customs presented to us and let's keep our opinions to ourselves."

"Mm. Sure," Wish replied unhappily, then attempted some levity, "I suppose that makes the nun off-limits."

Brade barked a laugh, the most genuine amusement she'd heard from him. She scowled, not sure it was *that* funny, but he said, "Brace yourself. Women who take up the chains of the Saints tend to be formidable. They call the Ghutan Order the Sisters of *Biting.*"

Wish's eyes bulged. What *was* this place?

16

Some say Carlwen, once Castorly, should be revered above all holy sites, as the priory dedicated to Bly Castor, chief amongst the prophets. Indeed, if he truly visited and wrote the Book of the Body within these walls, I would agree and give it its due. Unfortunately, I'm not convinced Castor ever set foot in the town, and without his connection it's a deeply uninspiring place. Second in tedium only to Prosper.
**The Mire Most Easy with Mr Zambizee,
Zambizee, p. 84**

Standing on a raised hillock just outside Carlwen, with a view of the fortified town, Colonel Atmoor took in his entire assembled force. It would usually be suicide for an officer of his calibre to stand exposed in such a position, but here he could see and be seen. Kasidee's Irregulars were on the run beyond the river, and he doubted the Carlwen guard even had bows and arrows, let alone guns.

He had wanted to settle down to his letters, after ruminating for most of the journey on the problem of General Macwest on the other side of the Most Blessed Sea. There were solutions to be found, he was sure, in using their Singnese calligars to plant subterranean explosives. With their close-quarter advantages, plenty of calligars were going to waste in the open terrain of Elmn that would be better used in Lomian tunnels – if one could coordinate the effort between Prognane Lightwind and General Olden. But those insights would have to wait, because the people of Carlwen refused to open their gates, leaving it necessary to negotiate with their chamberlain.

Carlwen itself was impressive. Prosper had been grand, but it was a glorified abbey. The priory here was interwoven with a working mill town, powered by great wheels on the river side, and it had a dramatic sense of style. Its encircling walls were crafted from blue brick so dark it was almost black, a stone mined from the Mocking Mountains. The foreboding effect was accentuated by the wall's absurd tall towers, curved and tightening to fine lines on the outward-facing edges and pointed tips. There were twelve of them spaced around the town, sleek and windowless – little use for defences, apart from appearing sharp at a distance. They created the impression of a giant creature's claws reaching up over the town ready to clamp down, which was intimidating if not practical.

It was a fine backdrop for Atmoor's army. His command tent was erected on a mound that took in Carlwen, the river behind it and the Midpeak mountains off in the distance, and the better part of his two thousand gathered soldiers were visible. Closest were the tents of his elite and orderly first section, whose discipline helped keep the adjacent second and fifth sections in reasonable order, with row after row of smartly presented soldiers awaiting command, flags gently swaying in the breeze. Section 2's Mattin mortar artillery was lined up neatly at the back; there was no mistaking the might of this force.

Granted, the sections spread into greater disorder further east, like a cushion spilling stuffing from a knife wound, as Ilscot's men and the adjoining goblins of Section 3 on their far side looked more like a travelling carnival. Still, there were a lot of them and their cavorting, with shouts and music and occasional fights breaking out, was sure to unsettle anyone watching. Atmoor could, after all, unleash either a coordinated and careful attack, or a more unhinged one. He had been tempted to invite Wideskull Bleacher here to drive that point home, but it would've started things on a bad foot.

Instead, Brother Redfire had facilitated a convivial meeting; the man's merry manner, when presented before the town gates, had made the offer of a sit-down seem like a friendly opportunity rather than an imposition. So here they were, and Atmoor watched Chamberlain Furvair as the holy man observed the threat. Furvair, the only properly elected leader in any of the priories, was an honourable man. He had agreed to meet with only a suited accountant and the captain of the guard for company, trusting that the Drail Empire wasn't likely to murder them or decimate the town unprovoked. The guard was an actual armoured knight: Guardian Wallace wore blue livery and a gold coat of arms embossed on his shining breastplate. Together with Chamberlain Furvair's important blue cloak and gold chain, the leaders of Carlwen clearly took themselves seriously.

Having let them wait long enough to fully observe his army, Atmoor took his seat at the table between Major Weles and Brother Redfire, opposite the chamberlain and his accountant. Guardian Wallace stood stiffly behind them.

"So, Chamberlain . . ." Atmoor said, inviting him to start.

"You'll not set foot in Carlwen," Furvair stated factually.

"Let's not start with absolutes, shall we?" Atmoor said. He gestured to the spread on the table his men had prepared: bread and meats, and a sizeable metal jug of moss wine brought down from Prosper. Furvair regarded it with forced displeasure, unable to hide his temptation. He gathered up his oversized sleeve and reached for a bread roll and placed it on his plate, but resisted eating. Some compromise.

"There's no need for this formality, Guardian," Atmoor said. "Please join us."

"I'm comfortable standing," Wallace replied, stiffening his posture instead. He had an expertly trimmed short beard. There likely wasn't much else to do here than take care of appearances, so Atmoor allowed him to keep himself on display.

"First, I have no interest in bringing all my troops into your walls," Atmoor said, gesturing to the town. Carlwen was one of the largest towns in the region, but housed perhaps ten thousand people at most, behind those three-storey walls and perimeter claws. Not big enough to accommodate an army, but possessing an especially tall building at the centre, with a crenellated top and an enormous banner. The main keep, or town hall, or the priory's heart, whatever they called it: that was where Atmoor saw himself. The high windows would provide a good view over much of the northern Mire. He continued, "My intention is to bring in only enough soldiers to man the battlements, with a proviso that more could be drawn inside only if the fight comes to your walls."

"A cunning way to say that once my gates are open to some, they are open to many," Furvair observed. His eyes were on the cheese.

"Please tuck in," Atmoor invited, and the chamberlain hesitated briefly, for show, before accepting. He broke open his bread roll and scooped up a big slice of cheese, then slapped a hunk of cured beef on top. Atmoor poured wine for everyone as Furvair ate greedily. "High Venerator Ultemy was very accommodating at Prosper."

"I don't doubt it," Furvair said, around a mouthful, "but High Venerator Ultemy seeks only to protect himself. I have a town of people to keep happy." He swallowed and hesitated over taking another bite. He wisely chose to speak first. "Prosper has always bowed to the powers of the north. First the Garters, now the Drail. The rest of us in the Mire prefer our independence. It's not merely a matter of the harm that could come to Carlwen, should you enter – it's a question of the message that it sends."

"I understand," Atmoor said. "We would all rather the Saints Mire remain neutral. I respect the history of this land and the importance of your religion as much as anyone."

"Colonel Atmoor kindly attended Veneration twice a day in Prosper," Brother Redfire noted helpfully. "He dined with the venerator on multiple occasions and discussed scripture. I assure you, Brother Furvair, that you will not find a better champion for the security of our land and our church than this man here."

It was a bit much. Redfire's enthusiasm was welcome, but Atmoor was unsure how believable it was. He'd shared two meals with Ultemy, attended mass twice *one* day, and endured rather than discussed their preaching about the old ways. Wallace looked rightly sceptical, but Furvair was too busy eating another roll to care.

"It's not just about the church," the chamberlain finally said. "Carlwen has a proud military history of its own, you know? The Carlwen Guard are the only people officially permitted to carry arms within our walls. This has not changed since the Graff Rebellion of 198."

"Yet these are regrettably exceptional circumstances," Atmoor said. "There are bandits in this land, Chamberlain, and our defence against them counts on your cooperation. Entire villages have been exterminated in the Shadow Sails. My own scouts have failed to return. The priory of Guiltway is in ruins. When these men cross the river here, violence will follow. I'm not here to wage war, I am here to prevent it."

"Yet you wish to occupy our territory," Furvair said. "Should these men come, I would give them the same answer I am giving you. Our streets are not for you. Not our food or our wine, and definitely not our women."

Atmoor smiled humorlessly. "Respectively, that might have meant more in the past. It's a mistake to think you can reason with these people, and even more so if you believe your knights can fight them." He looked to Wallace. "Your duty, beyond protecting tradition, must be to protect your people. They might not want us here now, but they will when the enemy arrives."

"*Your* enemy," Furvair corrected. "We do not consider them ours."

"You will if given the misfortune to meet them. The nature of war now is *not* respectful and these men have no honour. If they did, they would not be here at all."

"So you say," Guardian Wallace said. "Yet you've brought goblins to our door."

"Unlikely souls for salvation," Redfire chuckled, "but we are all creatures under the Saints, are we not?"

"I can guarantee Section 3 will not enter the town," Atmoor said, though he could not. Quite aside from the possibility that he would need to use all his troops however they could best be positioned, the goblins had ways of turning up where they weren't wanted.

Furvair eyed him warily. "Shall we cut to the meat of it," he said, appropriately spearing another slice of beef with a fork. He waved it Atmoor's way. "The town remains neutral, as does the church, and we will not tolerate a military presence. However, I might offer you the hospitality we would extend to any travellers looking for refuge. Lodgings and support for a time that we deem fit. For those few travellers we believe we *can* support."

"Why, that's good and generous." Brother Redfire clasped his chunky hands together. Atmoor waited, aware Furvair was taking a long path to simple demands.

The chamberlain gave the accountant a conferring look before saying, "We might take in a select few, carefully decided guests. And even then, with the strain it might put on our town, such hospitality would, I hope, encourage an appropriate donation from the Empire. With that considered, we might entertain your best officers."

Though he'd been expecting it, the colonel's neck bristled with irritation. Everywhere it was the same. Greed, even as they sat here in finery, Wallace's armour shining. He kept his voice from showing the nugget of anger as he said, "And what would you consider to be an appropriate donation?"

"It is *quite* an ask. There are matters of respect, decency. Supplies. Potential damages. And as a representative of the Drail Empire . . ."

Atmoor nodded. He had a small war chest for this, of course, taken from the coffers of Onwail. If he overextended, the Arrow Council might compensate him later. But he also had an army and their clear presence made light of playing this game. Why, he had sent a letter to General Salter not two weeks ago cautioning him on wasting energy on politics and finance when he might find simpler solutions to secure the towns in northern Farne. It already rankled him that he'd paid off High Venerator Ultemy at Prosper. And the words came out: "As a representative of the Drail Empire, I hold the security of our lands and people as most important. To divert finance from our global war effort towards an uncharitable cloister of monks does not sound responsible to me."

Furvair's face fell and Wallace's mouth tightened. Atmoor knew he should be gentler, but he did enjoy correcting men who thought themselves powerful.

"I could, as easily, take my men and leave you here. I could abandon the entire Mire, if that would be preferable to you. These priories contain people of Drail descent, however, and what churches of ours remain, throughout the Empire, revere them, so I don't think that would be responsible either. The most sensible course of action is, as I've proposed, to secure our position here, so we can turn back the invaders. Your more pensive, and frankly mercenary, suggestion is simply out of the question."

Furvair shifted in his seat. "Well. It is a question of the *cost –*"

"Indeed. You can accept our presence and work with us, or you can suffer as Guiltway did."

Guardian Wallace made a move to the sword at his hip, and Atmoor pushed off from the table, standing to his considerable height. He had a head on the knight, and a lot more weight. It also helped that two riflemen were standing nearby. Wallace snarled, "You threaten a Priory of the Prophets."

"I am not threatening you," Atmoor said. "I am making an offer of my own. Work with me and we will drive back the enemy. Work against me and your town will burn. Your reward is survival."

Furvair's skin had paled as he realised, at last, that his safety was not guaranteed. He murmured, "There must be terms. We cannot allow a full-scale occupation."

"No, Chamberlain," Atmoor said. "You cannot stop it. That's up to me."

He only needed to hold the man's eye for a moment before Furvair broke his gaze, mumbling in complaint, but conceding. Atmoor imagined this man had rarely if ever truly been challenged. A weaker spirit than Prosper's Ultemy, for sure. He imagined he also commanded great wealth within those walls. The sort of comforts that would give him a good chance to settle into his ruminations, after all.

17

The Saints Mire has much to teach us about how power may be established through language. With the rise of the Church of Venerate Flesh, the Mire and its constituent parts were deliberately renamed to weaken ties to its past. Such tactics were employed again by the Movement of Knowledge, when the region's modern titles were adopted in Imperial Stanish or Drail.

Consider Drowndeep: a priory never fully converted by the Church, nor Civilised, and instead ostracised and outcast by its labelling. Its very name invites avoidance, and as such its history, and secrets, are widely lost.

A Primer of Modern Thought, H. Minant, p. 93

The great hall of Drowndeep was unsurprisingly not the greatest, and Wild Wish was unsure it should even be called a hall. It did have a large stone hearth with a good-sized fire going, which made the room toasty, but part of the heat was due to how tightly packed in everyone was. Its floorboards creaked under their collected weight, there were no windows, and its sconces burned dimly, while a pair of tables took up most of the floor space. Wish's platoon perched precariously on benches and tabletops like schoolchildren. Brother Estekof promised them food was on the way, and bowls of water were passed around, then he fell into a lecture about the history of Drowndeep. Apparently, the price of the monks' hospitality was hearing a sermon.

Wild Wish zoned out shortly into his account of the swamp fort, so many tens of centuries old and with blessed foundations and a network of tunnels sunk fifty feet into solid rock. There was something about battles between the Holy Garters and Mirian tribes, and the rise of a cult of Bonesun, and the Book of Bones, but

Wish was more interested in what food they would serve. Not bone broth, she hoped. Swamp snails or something, she imagined. They were penitents, that word hadn't been lost on her: people who liked punishing themselves. The Church of the Venerate Flesh revered the body, which variously produced either indulgent or very strict sects, but the more puritanical Saint worshippers had always been particularly dramatic and judgemental. A "starve a fever" kind of mentality.

"Ah, Sister Sonseen, you received my message?" Estekof interrupted himself and Wish's eyes shot to the doorway, where a nun stared in at the soldiers.

"Hard to miss this lot, wasn't it?" Sister Sonseen replied in gruff Stanish. Her accent was from somewhere south, with long vowels and clipped consonants, perhaps Weagalian? Not so incongruous as Estekof's, at any rate. "Who's in charge here, then?"

Captain Brade stood up, straightening out his jacket, but Wish bolted up too, blurting out, "Lieutenant Wild Wish, ma'am, with the Blood Scouts, of General Macwest's 3rd Brigade." She paused. She had travelled a few days east, outside the western theatre now, and she recalled Brade's Rawboys had been folded in from 4th. She asked Emi, "Are we still in 3rd Brigade?"

The mage shrugged. Her gaze had been a bit distant since coming in from the bog, not quite back to normal after the grescind encounter. Or what passed for normal from Emi.

"And you're it, are you?" Sister Sonseen said.

"Huh?" Wish replied, and in the long look the nun gave her she found herself rapidly diminishing. Sonseen wore a tunic like Estekof's, with an extra thick chain around her waist, and her head had been shaved but had a layer of grey fuzz growing through. Their similarities ended there: her robes were crimson in contrast to the Drowndeep black, and she had a stern, stony face, a hard jaw and icy eyes. Her bare arms crossed over her chest were corded with muscle, skin leathery with age. Something warned Wish that this nun might be tougher than every person in the room.

"This is the extent of what the great Comity has sent to help us?"

Sonseen said. "I appreciate the ogres but I think we need a lot more of them."

"With your pardon, Sister," Brade said, "we're just here to establish exactly what it is you do need."

"Oh? My mistake then. When I was racing across this country as quickly as the Saints would carry me I didn't appreciate we had the luxury of all the time in the world. And you'll be forming a committee I suppose, to decide how best to respond to the imminent doom of the Saints Mire. How long do you estimate this to take, in terms of ancient and irreplaceable spiritual sites destroyed?"

The soldiers shifted with mixed tension and amusement at the nun's rapid scolding, and Wish enjoyed seeing the captain's smile broken. She liked this woman.

"And I'm sorry, *who* did you say was your lieutenant?" Sonseen turned on her and Wish stiffened.

"Um. Me?"

She heard at least one snigger behind her.

Sonseen had the crooked expression of someone sure a joke was being played on her, but not sure what. "Right. What's your plan of action, then?"

"We arrived to Paradise Fails this morning," Brade said. "We had a spot of bother with the grescinds and came straight here. You arrived two days ago, Brother Este –"

"I did, yes," Sonseen cut in, "and I've only stayed that long to rest my mount, ready to leave tomorrow. I'm bound for Midpeak next."

"If you're travelling the Mire, we would greatly appreciate your news," Brade said. "What can you tell us of the Drail incursion?"

Sonseen eyed him suspiciously, then addressed Wish, "I believe it best to do things properly. I'll address the superior officer, if it's all the same to you. If you can be serious for a moment, who exactly *is* in charge?"

"I am. Lieutenant Wild Wish of the Blood Scouts," Wish said, more meekly than before. "This is my platoon."

"This is?" Sonseen said. As in, *only this?*

Wish nodded. "And they can all hear what you have to say. It's fine."

The nun considered Wish again, then said, "It really is as bad as they say. So many men have died that we're relying on women to fight? Very well. But let's please not speak through your lackey, even if he may be more eloquent than you. I'd prefer the input of the decision-maker."

Wish couldn't help smirking as she caught Brade's darkening face in her peripheries. But no way could she carry this conversation on her own, so she said, "Thank you, Sister – though Captain Brade is the best travelled of our unit, so his input is as valuable as mine."

Sonseen's stern expression did not waver, if anything growing a little more disapproving. She said, "So be it. You will know there's been soldiers spotted in the east already. We were concerned about them coming to Saintshadow, so I set out to coordinate our defences with the other priories. I don't know if Saintshadow has remained untouched since my departure."

"Do you have arms?" Caracker interrupted, and the nun levelled him a fearsome gaze. The ogre was folded up at the back of the room along with Runt and Ohno. The three of them barely fit under the ceiling, like they'd been crammed into a box.

Wish waited, expecting another scolding from Sonseen, but she answered curtly, "We do, of a sort. Like all the priories, we have walls and battlements fit for archers and siege weapons, with some modern enough to accommodate gunpowder weaponry. In Saintshadow, we have five cannon and eighteen ball muskets."

A few men made surprised noises and Ptrangus whispered, "Fucking muskets?"

"Cannon cannons?" Wish asked.

"What does that mean?" Sonseen said.

"Like they had on pirate ships?"

"And on regular ships, yes. And battlefields. They might be outdated but they're not that unusual. What we don't have is men to man them, so I came here to petition the monks and their Shore Stalkers. We have another sister rallying men from the southern priories, though only Drowndeep has actual fighters, while Midpeak may have some able enough to learn."

"What kind of trouble are you expecting?" Brade asked. "Do you have details of what's happened elsewhere?"

"Nothing concrete," Sister Sonseen said. "Rumours have been reaching us of soldiers in the east and north, since almost a month ago – we do not travel a lot, though, so it's taken time to send our own sisters out to investigate, and those women had not returned when I left. We have had no recent contact from either Prosper or Sinner's Gate, which would not be unusual except that we actively requested responses."

"With signal fires?" Wish suggested, recalling Nasim's briefing on how backwards their communications were. Sonseen looked insulted.

"No, we sent carrier crows ahead of our mounted messengers. Some did not return, some came back with no messages. For whatever reason."

"Sinner's Gate as well as Prosper?" Brade clarified, with a frown, and Wish gave him a look requesting an explanation, his understanding of the Mire clearly better than hers. When Sonseen nodded, he added for the room's benefit, "Prosper's the entry-point in the north, and would've been the Drail's first stop. They're unlikely to have reached Sinner's Gate, though – it's in the mountains, towards the eastern entrance Kasidee's Irregulars would've used."

"Indeed," Sonseen agreed. "But we were always more concerned about Prosper – High Venerator Ultemy never misses a chance to spread his word across the Mire. Sinner's Gate, however, we hear little from at the best of times. Besides which, crows are unreliable. Any winged creature in the Mire is in danger of Mirian hunters."

"So you're visiting the priories by foot?" Wish said.

"Not walking," Sonseen scoffed, with a spark of amusement. "I have a beetle."

"Are the Mirian tribes that hostile?" Brade asked, before Wish could check what she meant by *beetle*. "I'd have thought they'd respect the priories' messengers."

"Quite. Your empires' violence is like a disease; when the war started, and soldiers first arrived last year, the germ spread. Villages armed themselves and began fighting in anticipation of more to come. And now the problem will worsen, with more soldiers marching in."

"Not if we can help it," Wish replied, but it sounded weak even to herself. She cleared her throat and moved on, "We received a message ourselves. Supposedly from the Irregulars. Do you know anything about that?"

Sonseen nodded. "Of course. It was delivered via Saintshadow. A tradesman travelling between the Sails and Folsfeed encountered a woman and two men on trudge horses, armed with guns. They asked him to deliver a note to the Comity. Don't bother asking who they were – they offered no other details, not even their names, apparently in something of a rush."

"Trudge horses?" Wish said, resisting asking first about the woman.

"A special breed big enough to walk the swamps," Brade told her. "But –"

"That's *all* we got," Sonseen preempted whatever he wanted to ask. "We didn't think much of it at the time – while the Mire has avoided fighting it has still seen occasional soldiers passing through. But the seriousness of all this became more apparent about a week ago when a message arrived from Midpeak to say they had seen a distress beacon from Guiltway. There has been no contact from the priory since. We fear it's been taken or destroyed, hence where we are now. I set out to secure our own priory and check the safety of others."

"Okay," Wish said. "So the Drail have started moving south, securing priories –"

"Taken or *destroyed,*" Sonseen repeated pointedly. "Considering what happened to Hail Crossing, we're as concerned about wanton destruction as occupation. Between your Civilisation and their Purity, the empires would happily level the Saints Mire. There's power here that has outlasted hundreds of civilisations and multiple religions. Those who understand that are afraid of this place. We are connected to the Saints, to the One God. Even unbelievers feel it."

Emi grunted in agreement and Wish met her eye. The mage shook her head, though, not wanting to get into whatever was on her mind. Without her reaction, Wish might've discounted Sonseen's words entirely, but now guessed there was something in it. Faith was a rare and old-fashioned thing – her medic Fixit had been a lone voice of belief in the former Blood Scouts. In Swelig, people only visited the Cane Saints chapel once a year in respect of the harvest, and that was more tradition than religion. The only really religious people Wish knew growing up were the Tookers, a family of Vens who generally just seemed disappointed with everyone. Wish wanted to dismiss all this with the same cheery distraction she would've reserved for Winny Tooker ("That's great, I hope it works out for you!") but instead she said, "Is there something specific we should know about here? Does the Mire contain its own magic, something the Drail want to harness or manipulate?"

"Good question," Sonseen said, encouraging Wish for just a second before crushing her. "That's only exactly what's been causing tribes and religions to fight over this land for ten thousand years." She went on more seriously, "This entire region is awash with relics and legends. You won't find a mile untouched by miracles – the legends recorded in the Books of the Prophets are a fraction of the whole. The possibilities of what any invaders hope to uncover are almost unlimited. The flaming giant-slaying swords of the Mock Mountains? Nael's elixir of youth in the Wet March? Scripts of necromancy?" Sonseen gestured to the walls around them, indicating Drowndeep and whatever dark secrets it contained. "However, I suspect the simplest explanation to be the most likely. The real power these men seek is to destroy any hint of ours. To exercise dominance over a place such as this, that has a lure of its own."

Wish quietly let that settle, the nun's passion having permeated the room with general unease. She said, "Well. How should we proceed? The attacks have been in the north, right? Near the border?"

"That's where Prosper is, yes, but Guiltway is east of there. It's remote and inaccessible – an unusual place to target. We've received no distress beacons from anyone else, even if it is likely Prosper has been overrun. The monks at Midpeak, who have a partial view over these lands, have reported no signs of trouble at Carlwen or Gauntstone, though both are strategic positions. Perhaps you can tell me, as a military woman, how to make sense of the invaders' movements?"

Wish tried to picture the layout of the Mire, with the rest of the room, including Brade, waiting on her answer. She recalled the eastern mountains ran all the way down to Penitent's Pass, where Kasidee's Irregulars were said to have come from – the only viable route towards the front line. She said, "If they want to use the Mire as a cut-through, it'd make sense to hug the mountains. They might be heading east and down. Prosper to Guiltway to Sinner's Gate, that's a route to the front line, isn't it?" She looked to Brade and he frowned. That would be a nope.

"It's logical if you carve a line from Prosper to the Gate, I agree," Sonseen said. "But there's no practical benefit in a detour to Guiltway. Neither the Gulwood nor the Black Lake would be easy for an army to navigate, while the Low Bile that separates Prosper and Carlwen offers some of the most solid, open land in the entire Mire. They targeted Guiltway in particular."

"Maybe just to do some damage," Macmiddan suggested, sounding like he knew all about doing damage as a goal in itself. As Rebel Rawboys would. "If it's weak and remote, safe to attack, they might've just wanted to send a message. Sounds like it'd be an easier target than the others. Hell, they might've just wanted to give some angry soldiers a place to let off steam."

Sonseen scowled, disapproving but not disagreeing. It made a grim kind of sense. Colonel Atmoor's army were delinquents, after all.

"To your point, Sister," Brade said, "if there was something they particularly wanted from Guiltway, what would that be?"

"I couldn't say," Sonseen replied. "The priory contains writings and artefacts of great importance, but each of the Ten do. The subject matter and origins are diverse, spread out – you'd find corresponding treasures in various vaults across the region."

"Then I guess we'll have to get out there to see what's happening for ourselves."

"Do you know where the message for us was received, at least?" Wish asked.

"On the road from Saintshadow to the Sails, as I said," Sonseen replied. "They were travelling north, so if those soldiers belonged to you, they should have reached the invaders' position already. You're likely to find everyone in the same place. But I'd suggest heading for Midpeak. If anyone can tell us more, they will. It's the most central, best connected and best defended of the priories, and their observatory takes in part of the Sails and Carlwen."

"Where you're heading yourself?" Wish checked. "We can provide you with a military escort for your help, Sister Sonseen."

It earned a laugh from the nun, but not a pleasant one. "I might prefer you didn't. The Mirian tribes are likely to get excited by the idea of challenging a group of foreign soldiers. I daresay it'd be in your interests to receive an escort from *me,* though. I leave at dawn, and if you're interested in coming then I have a condition. You will all attend Veneration this evening."

Ptrangus stifled a laugh and Emi gave an unhelpful coo, but Wish kept still. Only the most dedicated attended Veneration. She'd never been to one of the church's masses herself, and Fixit, for all her other attempts to save their souls, had never suggested it. But she definitely wanted more help from Sister Sonseen, and the ceremony would be harmless. Probably. Without looking to her sceptical soldiers' faces for their input, Wish said, "Okay, we can do that."

They were in the Mire, after all. It would be rude not to.

18

In the centuries that followed the Great Schism, the Ten Priories fluctuated between the Revery of the Saints and the Church of the Venerate Flesh, often combining rather than separating their disparate religious traditions. Unique Veneration practices have long been rumoured across the region, including extreme trust falls (Midpeak); baptism in deadly waters (Folsfeed); hunting trials (Sinner's Gate); rectification of the night beasts (Saintshadow – details unclear); banquets of the flesh (Prosper); and even, dubiously, blood sacrifice (Drowndeep).
Sickness and Sin: Medicine and Religion Through the Ages, Grunberg, p. 254

The Veneration ceremony would take place after nightfall, *when the darkness had fully descended,* so Brother Estekof announced, meaning the scouts had half a day to rest. The monks provided a wholesome meal of steamed fish (or something seafood adjacent) with baked vegetables and a lightly spiced gravy, accompanied by tankards of bitter alcohol fermented from the marsh plants, which Brade said was like beer but really, really wasn't.

"I hear they whip themselves with chains," Emi said matter-of-factually, sitting at the table with Wish, Scraper and Brade. The mage's spirits appeared to have fully returned now. *"Tuning* the body, they call it."

"Some do," Brade agreed, "but not many. For most penitents, 'tuning' means rigorous exercise and meditation. I was taught a few techniques myself by a monk in the Balnian mountains."

"Oh, fancy," Emi replied, with subtle mocking. "You could be exercising with friends in the Balnian mountains yet you chose to come here with us."

"Trust me, I *would* rather be there," Brade replied gamely.

Wish doubted his words. He was where he wanted to be. He'd shamelessly asked Estekof if he could have some time in their libraries, there apparently being catacombs of books somewhere under the keep, and his eyes lit up when the monk agreed. She said, "Drowndeep is so much more dramatic, though, isn't it?"

"It has a lovely ring to it," Emi said, stirring her vegetables. "I believe it references the travellers they murder who are never found."

"Not quite," Brother Estekof said, carrying the jug of alcohol to their table. "More wosel?" Wish didn't want more, no, but on the other hand, it was alcohol. She raised her mug and he poured, saying, "The priory's name is not as old as its foundations. Bonstar was only reborn Drowndeep after the Schism, in respect of the old ways."

"The old ways being murdering travellers?" Wish asked.

The monk chuckled, though she was serious. "There is a great well here, in the tunnels below us. A place where problems, doubts and, indeed, sometimes bodies, were ritualistically returned to the Mire. Though not through murder. Even now, we keep the sconces lit."

"The Well of All Remains?" Brade said. "I'd like to see that, if possible?" From his eagerness, he'd apparently not seen much of the Mire in his past adventures.

Estekof smiled enigmatically and poured some wosel for Scraper, who glowered distrustfully.

"So you do bury some things, do you?" Emi asked. Recalling the morbid bone decorations of the keep, the question encompassed exactly where the priory stood with the church, and the Vens' famous obsession with the disposal of bodies.

"Yes," Estekof answered. "Where some spiritual journeys reconnect with the Rocc through the Well of All Remains, others find power through remembrance. This priory sanctifies the dead as the faith takes us most fittingly – burial, display or more. We are not the Church of the Venerate Flesh, and were never beholden to the Revery. The teachings of the Prophet Bonesun are our speciality, but even they are practised with flexibility."

Wish was quite sure the implications of half of what he was saying were flying over her head, but it did bring to mind another detail from earlier that day. Like this weird priory, the giant crablike monsters had bodies hanging off them, many appearing fresh. She said, "The creatures in the bog were decorated with corpses, too."

"Ah." Estekof's face fell. "Such is the will of the Saints sometimes, too, sadly. The grescind are majestic in their own right, and not creatures we fully understand. They do not feast on all who they kill, but hold others like talismen. The mud here preserves."

Wish inwardly cringed. What had become of the two men they'd left behind, Fawcet and Basing? Was one of them now hanging from a spike on a creature's carapace? Forever, if the place's twisted earth prevented decay? She shared a look with Brade, wanting to ask what the hell they'd got themselves into, but kept quiet. The monk moved on, smilingly offering his rancid not-beer to the Rawboys. Those soldiers, at least, had fallen into easy calm. Graveguard had reported that Latebite would be okay, though he'd have to stay here, with the practicalities of extracting him from the Mire a problem left for another day. At the far end of their table sat Toothless and Private Dalliance, though, and Wish's heart fell again. Both looked defeated.

Shortly after, Brother Estekof announced their quarters were ready and the platoon filtered down the winding stairs and tight corridors of the priory to underground chambers better described as cells, with beds slabs carved into the stone walls. Better than sleeping on the ground outside, Wish supposed, but not much. She had a space to herself, but couldn't bring herself to rest, staring through the floor back to the grescind attack. The sight of Fawcet struggling before he was cut in two. His screams joined a shrill host of memories. Fixit's last cry, Rue's shriek. Loose on the cliff, *No* . . . Wish closed her eyes. Breathed slowly. Recalled instead Dalliance's face. His eyes had been glassy, face sallow.

She left her pack and gun to creep to the cell where Toothless and Dalliance were silently sitting, the former thumbing through a notebook while the latter stared blankly at a wall.

"You boys okay?" Wild Wish asked.

"Yes, ma'am," Toothless said, a worried smile questioning what he'd done wrong now.

"Dalliance?" she prompted. He looked up with surprise. "You good?"

"Yes, ma'am," he echoed.

"Want to talk about it?"

Dalliance considered this at length, then very slowly shook his head. Wish waited, not sure what to add. Toothless gave her an encouraging look, to say he'd look after the man, but she was the one responsible for them. She knew what he was going through.

She said, "I think it's best to . . ." She hesitated. "Remember that it's all making a difference. Even when it goes wrong. It adds up."

Dalliance frowned and she half expected him to tell her to piss off. He nodded.

"I'm . . ." Wish paused. There was, of course, only one thing to say. "I'm sorry."

"He never got a chance," Dalliance finally spoke, and his voice was weak, all that cockiness gone. "He was a great shot. He never got a chance."

Wish swallowed, the sound of his cracking voice hitting her hard. It was her turn to merely nod. She could offer a hug, she supposed, but that wasn't officer behaviour. Instead, she asked, "Where are you from, Dalliance?"

"Huh?"

"I had a ringer in the scouts before. She was amazing with a sword. Newk. She was . . . is . . ." Wish trailed off, not sure where she was going.

"I'm from the Tight Lines," Dalliance told her, though. The shady network of alleys that made up the Stanish capital's main slums. Exactly as he sounded. "Me and Fawcet came out together. Neither of us had been outside Vasseer before. Wish we still hadn't."

She cleared her throat awkwardly. What next, ask what plans his friends had made for marriage and settling down? She said sorry again and left.

Emi was blocking the way back to her room, leaning against a wall, smirking as usual.

"What?" Wish said.

"If you're done failing to make small talk," the mage said, "the ogres have something that *might* be maltique."

Wish's brow lifted. She'd got a few bottles of plum vodka from Hail Crossing, if it had survived the morning, but hadn't seen her homeland's best biscuity liquor for months. Emi nodded towards the tight stairs. Wish stepped back to let her lead the way.

"Is there any point me asking how *you* are?" Wish asked.

"You know I'm never not fine," Emi replied, showing off her reptile smile. If they ever had a personal conversation, it was only when Emi had keen insights into Wish's thinking, never the other way around. But Emi added, "I'm not the biggest fan of this place's energy."

"You don't trust the monks?" Wish whispered, because there were probably listening. In their nasty robes and this nasty keep . . .

"Not the *monks,* they're harmless," Emi replied. "The *place.* I wouldn't want to dirt-mind here."

Wish liked that idea even less. She'd never seen Emi hesitant about wielding her considerable magic. "What happened earlier?"

"I don't know." Emi leered back over her shoulder, face especially wicked in the dark of the tunnels. "Normally, earth-minding gives you a brief connection to *everything* around you, but here, it felt . . . chaotic. Unstable or too busy, I'm not sure. It left me *queasy.* There's old, old energy in the ground – echoes of unpleasant things. I'd have to touch it more firmly to better understand, and I think it might . . . affect me."

"Yeah," Wish replied, "let's not do that."

Determining to push that complication far from her mind, Wish continued out into the courtyard, where the ogres were gathered. There were no cells large enough for them, if they could even fit down the tunnels, so Caracker and Ohno were resting on piled animal hides with a little fire burning between them. Emi approached them like old friends, slapping hands, and said, "Our commander could use a drink. Where's Runt?"

"Stepped outside to do his business," Ohno said. Typical for ogres, Wish supposed, who could seldom benefit from the luxuries of indoor plumbing (or holes in cupboards, as this priory offered). But she didn't like that the most difficult of the ogres was roaming unchecked.

"He'll stay away from the villagers, won't he?" she said.

"If they stay away from him," Caracker replied. "Not having a lie down, Lieutenant? You took a few blows today yourself and we've got a trek ahead tomorrow."

"I'm fine," she replied, wary of the bloodied rag around his head. He gave her a look but didn't elaborate. Didn't she look fine? There were stains on her clothes but no major rips. Was it her frightened, despairing face?

"Nah, she just needs something stronger than that rancid weed-wine," Ohno said, reaching behind her. The ogre held up a bottle that looked tiny in her big hand, until Wish took it and saw it was chunkier than average.

Wish took a sip and fire flooded down her throat. She coughed in alarm and blinked back tears. "That's not maltique."

"No." Ohno smiled. "That's boulder whisky. Distilled by trunks for big bastards."

Wish swallowed hard, making sure she kept it down. Since joining the army, she'd developed a tolerance for various vodkas, but this was unlike anything she'd tried. She took another, more careful sip, and let it tingle on her tongue. Or rather, melt her tongue. Through the fire, its oily texture and rich flavour hinted at something sweeter, complex, but her mouth and throat complained. She said, hoarsely, "But . . . I'm not a big bastard."

"That," Emi said, holding out a hand for the bottle, "depends on how you see yourself."

Wish smiled. This was probably a bad idea, consuming intense alcohol in a place like this, when she was supposed to be leading a platoon. But after a terrible start to their journey and the promise that it wouldn't get much better, she'd earned a break. Why not. If Emi could brush shoulders with ogres under the mad monks' bone fetishes, then so could she. Lethal alcohol was better than the screams of ghosts, after all. She asked Ohno, "How much have you got?"

"Enough to share, I hope," a Raw voice interrupted, breaking Wish's almost-calm. The hostile one, of course – Ptrangus-not-Sick-Boy, coming out a door. "Thought I smelt boulder spirits. Don't let Macmiddan know, he'll have it all in twenty seconds. Just as well those lads would sleep through the Great Rift, they would." Uninvited, he folded himself onto the tiles stretching a hand towards Emi. The mage sipped the bottle and gave it to him. He took a big gulp and Wish put aside the intrusion (and insubordination?) in anticipation of his reaction. But he exhaled and said, "Solid vintage. I knew we had you bigguns along for a reason." He took another gulp and passed the bottle to Ohno. The ogre looked impressed.

"Are you some kind of half-troll?" Wish asked.

He smiled, lightly, a big turnaround from his earlier tension. "Just Rae. Our blood's half alcohol at birth. But good on you for trying it, Lieutenant – not sure I've ever seen a Stain keep down boulder before, let alone a female."

Wish frowned, the compliment wrapped in both a racial slur and misogyny. She noticed Caracker stiffening, about to put him in his place, so tried to keep things friendly. "Sorry about your friend today. About –"

"With respect, Lieutenant," Ptrangus cut in, "fuck that. Being sad won't change things. Better to celebrate what we still have, am I right big chief?" He aimed this at Caracker.

Cautiously taking a share of the whisky, the ogre replied, "Easy to say. But grief is part of our nature."

"Aye and you know what Basing would've said? Quit crying and start dancing."

"You won't be doing much dancing here," Ohno said, twirling a finger in the air, indicating the looming walls and bone cages hanging grimly above.

Ptrangus took it in for himself and a shard of darkness broke his facade. He said to Wish, "More's the pity. I could show you some moves, Lieutenant."

"No, thanks."

"Ah, don't be like that. I gotta apologise for earlier, don't I? I'm not a bad guy and I *do* respect command, understand, we just have our own way of showing it. We're not Stanish drones any more than these bigguns are. It'll count when it needs to."

"It *all* counts out here," Caracker rumbled. "You show disrespect when we're walking, how can we trust you when we're fighting?"

Ptrangus eyed him shrewdly, considering an answer. Ready to argue. Any second, Wish could imagine the gates opening and Runt returning and this lot picking up where they left off earlier. She was tired, just wanted it to *stop,* and groaned loudly, "Forget it. It's been half a day and it's already obvious we're unsuited to each other or this place. I don't want to hear any more arguing, if we're going to force our way through this. You pass him back the bottle, you take a swig, we forget it all and move on."

The men held each other's eyes, a moment where they might defy her will, choose trouble instead. Then the ogre did as she asked, handing the bottle to Ptrangus. He took another big gulp, sighed appreciation, and nodded.

"Good, done. Now me." She clapped and Ptrangus gave her the bottle. He smiled as she drank more than was safe – had to lead by example, after all – and she struggled to keep her whole body from contracting. Then she passed it to Emi.

"What it's worth," Ptrangus said. "I got nothing against ogres. Reckon we've some shared experience. Never take whatever us Rae say at face value. We speak like dickheads but we act like gentlemen." He stood, and swayed, unable to totally hide the effects of the whisky. With a self-effacing smile, he winked at Wish. "I'll go before that ignorant mate of yours comes back, anyway – you don't need two pricks out here. Shit and hell though, we'd all be better off dancing. Enjoy your drink, Lieutenant."

They murmured goodbyes as he wobbled back inside. It was progress, Wish supposed, connecting the group. Even if the cracks were readily apparent. Emi nudged her elbow and said, "Better not let them know you dance like an absolute *weirdo.*"

***

It was only when the Veneration began in earnest that Wish appreciated the mistake of drinking ogre-grade spirits in Drowndeep. They were gathered in the courtyard with the braziers flickering, a starry night above. The place was packed by Wish's soldiers, a dozen monks and a procession of Shore Stalkers. An elderly monk led the ceremony, frail as a skeleton yet loud and mad-eyed. A bell tolled from the keep's tallest tower as more monks gathered in windows and spread along the battlements, the humming robed men and tattooed hunters and crackling fires growing increasingly imposing.

All this in a place called Drowndeep, where they rejected the church to display the dead. Or threw people down a well?

The celebrant's opening words echoed off the walls in a distorted language that sounded inhuman. Wish's vision blurred and she wasn't sure if it was the boulder whisky or something in the smoke or the weed-wine. She focused on a bone structure, then a malevolent face, then the jagged ugly spikes above, and she cursed. She almost lost her footing, but a big hand held her up. Ohno looked down from the sky and Wish smiled. It had been a good afternoon, drinking, talking about nothing at all.

She just needed to keep still. Say nothing and stay upright for however long this old bastard coughed out his nonsense. Someone jangled a chain, spreading incense, and it stung her eyes. She saw Sister Sonseen in a corner, glaring meanly, knowingly. Then everything started moving. Feet shuffled towards the celebrant's raised position as he shouted, hands in the air, and the bells clanged louder. Wish moved with the flow, no way to resist it, and Ohno tightened her hand on her shoulder, almost carrying her. What was the communion here? Wish remembered Fixit talking of death ceremonies, of eating parts dead flesh. Sarge – Fixit had wanted them to prepare her flesh, when a giant had broken her and everything was going badly.

Someone approached the celebrant and his hands came down

sharply as he called out a blessing. They moved on and he did it again, again, the crowd in line to meet him, with Wish getting dangerously close.

"I don't want to eat people." Wish bucked to get free, but Ohno held her steady and whispered, "Not what it is."

"Then what? What are they doing?"

But they'd reached the front already and the celebrant was waiting, Brother Estekof to one side and Sister Sonseen there too. Wish twisted and saw her platoon behind her, letting her go first for whatever this was. She was the example. There was no sign of meat or strange knives, though. Just three robed people next to a fire, pulsing about, Wish unable to hold them still in her vision.

"What do I do?" she whispered to herself, but loud enough for everyone to hear.

"Just come forward," Estekof instructed. "Accept the blessing."

Wish swallowed. This wasn't a bad place, she told herself. Not bad people, however it looked. She stepped forward and fought to keep upright. The celebrant shouted skyward and suddenly he had a hand on her wrist and she shrieked and he shouted louder and for a moment they were two feral animals yelling into each other's faces as he squeezed hard and brought his other hand down fast over her forearm. Wish flinched and stepped back as she was released, heel slipping over the edge of the platform, and her arms windmilled before Ohno's hand found her again. She steadied herself to take in the damage done to her arm. Had he cut it, branded her, worse?

But Wish frowned at the exposed flesh of her forearm, bare and clean where the celebrant had pushed up her sleeve and apparently . . . stroked her with his open palm?

"What the fuck?" Wish uttered. Ohno pivoted her out of the way, to a sea of staring faces, many eerily smiling. Someone moved past them, Captain Brade? He held his arm already exposed, and the celebrant shouted again. Not as dramatically. Wish hurried off to shelter in the press of bodies, as the bells tolled again and the ceremony continued. More tattooed people were entering as others exited, a train of sinewy people coming to have their arms stroked as monks chanted and increasing numbers of bells clanged.

"What the fuck?" Wish repeated, and found Ohno was gone, the ogre awaiting her own blessing.

It was Brade at her side now, and he said, "You did well. They'll appreciate that."

"What?"

He winked. It was done though, so she went quiet, tried to keep still again. Her hips weren't steady and her arm tingled. Had the celebrant wiped it with something? A drug?

"What now?" she whispered.

"This'll go on for a while," Brade said, "then the closing prayers. Then the feast."

"More of a feast than that lunch?" Emi asked, sliding in next to them. She was grinning, a little madder than usual, or made to look it by the fires.

"I doubt it," Brade said. "They were trying to impress us at lunch."

"Fuck," Wish muttered. Safest to keep to small responses. "Shit."

"Bollocks," Emi volunteered helpfully.

The celebrant was shouting again, and the bells chorused in another dull round of clanging. A murmur built through the crowd as Wish breathed deeply. She rested back and found a wall to support her shoulders. Her eyes tracked up the wall opposite, where a cage hung two storeys up, stuffed with the skeletal remains of a creature she could not make out. It had a long, sharp skull, demonic. She was unable to look away as the celebrant screamed and a handful of Shore Stalkers roared in agreement.

Keep it together, Wish told herself. Brade's words came back to her, should she offend these angry people. *Trial by combat.* They were in a deadly, confusing kind of hell, and it was a bad place to be drunk. Yet somehow, as the screaming picked up, she couldn't help shouting too.

19

By the time of the Third Prophet, the Saints Mire was respected and forcibly preserved as a historic and holy place, and as such it is one the longest colonised regions in all of Boldarow. Through centuries of conquest from various religious orders, kingdoms and later empires, all eager for the boasting rights of controlling this famous region, indigenous populations were permitted to stay only so they might provide labour and supplies. Even then, only the human populations were considered worthy, with very few exceptions.

Empires of the Rocc, Xanthial, p. 82

Lost One had become a sharpshooter for two reasons: first, he was a damn good shot, and second, it was sedentary work. He wasn't meant for lugging around equipment or jumping at orders, splashing about in mud doing busywork. Who needed that, when he could pick a spot and wait to do more damage with a perfect shot than a hundred idiots could do in battle? He'd taken out Drail captains, turned away wyrling riders from Fort Simnon, got the Irregulars through hell all without a sweat. But as his main priority was typically gaining the high ground, entering the stupidly tall Midwood meant he couldn't avoid sweating. Everyone else was uneasy about the forest, dark and chirping with weird noises, spattered with colourful (definitely deadly) mushrooms and unusual structures high in the trees. Lost One was just unhappy at the sight of thick slat ladders nailed into the trees, climbing a hundred feet high or more. Ladders he *had* to climb to get the higher ground.

He reached the top of one totally out of breath, to kneel on a wooden platform that circled a tree trunk wider than a house. Well ahead of the others, being the best as he was, he took a minute to recover. Damn, his lungs were burning.

His escort of a couple of soldiers clambered up onto the platform behind him. When they greeted him, asked what he'd seen, Lost One ignored them, pretending to be concentrating on the view as he caught his breath. It was expansive. They hadn't come far into the woods, so this watch-post took in some of the fields they'd crossed and the river off to the north, where the walled town of Carlwen sat. Lost One used his rifle scope for a closer look at that, and didn't like what he saw. Whole lot of men the other side of the river. A long way off, but close enough that they could press down on them fast.

That was behind them, though. They had a mountain ahead, which he wasn't looking forward to any more than he'd wanted to climb this tree. He took another moment, then moved around the other side of the platform. There were four men up here now, the Irregulars' usual swarthy mix of muscle and metal teeth, two with rifles, one with a shotgun and the last with just an axe. What was the point in him?

As he'd already snubbed them, they kept mercifully quiet as Lost One scanned the route ahead. More creepy bullshit. The woodland had been unsettling enough at ground level with its monolithic trees and wide empty paths, everything so big it felt unreal. Lost One wouldn't have admitted it out loud, but the place itself did instil a sense of dread. The platforms ahead made it worse. From the ground, only the ladder and this platform had been clearly visible. Now he saw bridges and covered sections, crude but civilised. The more he looked, the more he saw: structures partly hidden by their branch-like nature and leafy covering, connected by uneven boardwalks.

Woodwings, that's who Havik said lived here, in the canopy. People who weren't quite human, said to be able to fly like Drak birdmen. Seemed unlikely to Lost One, considering Drak birdmen had been purged from the continent through slaughter and torture over the course of hundreds of years. No way anyone had tolerated a separate race of birdmen down in central Boldarow. But then,

Havik said giants and other monsters had survived in the Mire unchecked, too, and this pretty sophisticated network of walkways suggested Midwood's tribes were, at the very least, unusual.

Lost One saw no sign of life, though. The bigger dwellings, like huge knotty hornet nests, appeared empty, with no fires burning, no food or belongings around. And seeing as he'd made it this far, the area wasn't being guarded. But that didn't make it safe.

"I want more men up here," Lost One said, not looking back.

"How many?" one of the soldiers asked.

"Many as we can. These paths go a good distance through these trees, we need to make sure they're clear."

"Right you are." The soldier moved to the edge of the platform and inhaled to shout, but Lost One whirled around with his rifle raised.

"Are you fucking stupid? If we haven't been spotted already you're not giving us away."

The soldier gawked. He was a slightly older, overweight drunkard who'd plainly joined the Irregulars to avoid getting pressed into real service. "But –"

"Climb back down and tell them," Lost One snarled. "Quietly. Tell Havikare we've found her Woodwings."

The man nodded, gave the others a glance like he wanted to ask someone to join him or go instead, then went off to the ladder without another word. Idiot.

Lost One walked around the platform. Stairs were carved into the trunk here, curving up towards another platform above, where a bridge ran to the next tree. He tested the steps and climbed, watching for threats. Still no movement, except for the bastards huddling beneath him, not sure if they should follow. He hoped they'd stay behind. He reached the bridge and scanned the canopy again. If there was anyone up there, they were doing a damn good job staying hidden.

The bridge wasn't inviting: a fragile mess of crude planks held together by rough vines so it looked like a tangle of debris. It didn't have any sides, nothing to hold onto, but it was pulled taut, no dip in the middle. Lost One prodded it with a foot and found it sturdy.

As rigid as the platform, almost. He took another step and considered the sheer drop either side of him. A strong breeze could be fatal. But it'd take more than a little drop to unsettle him, so he strode on.

A soldier cleared his throat, one of the fools creeping up the stairs, and Lost One could sense he was about to ask for orders. Fuck that. He moved over the bridge, about fifteen metres across; it didn't sway, impressively crafted despite appearances. He reached the opposite platform and glanced back, two of the soldiers now on the other side staring in horror. He glanced down, seeing Irregulars milling about at the base of the trees. The guy he'd sent with the message was about a third of the way down, taking great care over each ladder rung. Someone was going to fall, Lost One was sure. They were too hesitant, afraid. It was the same everywhere: people scared to take a shot, aims unsteady from nerves, reactions slow from uncertainty. Doubt killed people more than anything. He considered instructing them to tie themselves together, or crawl if they were that worried, but it was their problem. He had his own work to do.

Lost One continued as the men made worried noises, bleating for guidance. He saw more structures ahead, stairs going higher, bridges latticed through the canopy. He moved up another set of steps, wanting the best vantage point possible. It took him around another trunk and out of view of the men. He crossed another narrow bridge, thinking over Havik's little lectures about the Saints Mire. She loved how untouched this land was, and that passion was infectious. Some of the men genuinely liked the idea of protecting this place's historical importance, and some were even religious, but most, including Kasidee himself, just understood this was the perfect opportunity for adventure. They *all* got to be legendary adventurers out here, like Quarious Ludermaine, Kasidee promised. Lost One wasn't bothered about that – he just liked the fact there wasn't much fighting out here. But he understood part of the attraction, seeing how damn weird and intricate this tree-top village was. The same time, though, next time he'd suggest Kasidee and Havik find someplace sunnier to adventure. Drier. With more women.

Next time. Next time.

Lost One reached his first Woodwing dwelling, if that's what it was, and entered slowly, keeping his body low and his gun up. The place stank like his old rat cages. Curling his nose, he trod over a soft surface, the boards padded with animal fur or bird fluff or whatever, he couldn't see. It was an actual nest, the thought came to him. People up here were sleeping in bird nests. He continued into the light the other end and looked down to a wider platform a few trees across, with raised planks around it, like benches. A communal area?

Above that spot he saw racks, hanging cloths, animal skins stretched out in the flecks of light that came in through the leaves. *That* was recent. He crouched and ran his scope over the other walkways and their human hornet nests. This was the work of a lot of people over a long time. Too big for them all to be hiding, but not entirely abandoned . . .

"Whoa, oh! Oh!" a man cried out fearfully and Lost One looked back. He was too far around the trees to see the first bridge, but that's where they were, the soldiers trying to follow. Another one laughed, though not fully enthusiastic. Someone had almost fallen and his companion was trying to pretend it was amusing. Their noise sent a cluster of birds through the branches, squawking. Lost One followed their flight – some kind of grey-tipped crow – then scanned back to a movement much closer, in the canopy-village.

His sights found a person leaning out from one of the nests, looking in the direction of the noises. Three trees back and about twenty feet below, but plainly in his eye-line. Just a shoulder, part of the head, padded with feather and fur, with a birdlike beak. It could've been a humanoid bird, to someone less observant, but he noticed a ridge in the curve of the beak – a wooden frame. Some kind of mask.

More chatter came from the Irregulars as they joked about the near-fall and Lost One inwardly cursed them. Others had joined them, a whole party of idiots in the trees. But it wasn't all bad: they'd draw attention away from him. The native crept out without any indication they knew he was above, and he frowned, not so sure about how human they were now. A woman, from the shape of her hips, legs plumply fleshy, but there was something strapped to her back, a mess of stacked wood and fabric bound by leather. It extended down over her arms like a cloak of fragmented wooden slats, concealing the limbs below, and rose up into that hood/helmet with the beak. He'd never seen a Drak birdman – few people had – but it looked like the woman was wearing a wooden device that mimicked one. She paused, taking in the Irregulars below.

One woman. Where was the rest of her tribe?

Lost One could not approach her easily from here, with a handful of bridges and ladders separating them. He wouldn't want to anyway; better to do it at a distance, the way he always did. He kept her head in his sights as she pulled back, keeping low herself. Then she glanced over her shoulder and made a high, shrill sound, as natural as the bird calls they'd been hearing since coming in here. It was matched a moment later by another bird sound. Lost One swung his rifle round and saw, the next tree up, fifteen feet higher, where the branches grew thickest and touched the sky, a second woman in a wooden bird costume was leaning out. She ducked away and he heard her call again, louder. He swung the gun back to the first woman but she had gone.

Fuck. He should've done this on his own. Couldn't warn the others now without risking his own position.

More movement: he looked up to a platform where arms poked out over the edge, at least three sets of arms raising bows. Well, something like arms: they were wrapped in wooden slats. Lost One could clip them, maybe, but it was a risk. He checked the supports under the platform, thick wooden beams, not something he could knock out with a few shots. Another bird call drew his eye back across the village and he saw them coming out in bigger numbers now. A handful of feathered people dashed over the walkways, with tall bows and quivers of ammo. They were savages wielding primitive weapons, those bird costumes crude and unnatural. He noticed their swaying arms, tucked in tight to their bodies, something weird about them, too short and no limbs properly on view beneath the cumbersome wooden armour. They were also mostly curved like women, small – children, or hunched with age.

These were the leftovers, the sorts of people they found everywhere in deserted towns and villages along the front. Everyone of fighting age had gone somewhere else, even out here in the Mire. But they took up their positions, drawing their bows ready, still dangerous in their way. Not interested in asking questions, just upset anyone at all was out here. Shame. It wouldn't be much of a challenge. Then, any gunshots here might draw the tribe's real fighters back from wherever they were. The sound would probably reach Colonel Atmoor's men and all. The Drail could bring their coward marksman from Black Lake for a rematch.

Lost One watched the women and children with their bows taut, arrows ready, and he took in a breath. He had to keep his position for now. Wait for the safe shots, make sure he had the full measure of the enemy. Maybe they wouldn't do it. Maybe they would watch as the soldiers passed through on lower platforms, understanding this was a stronger force, people who had a right – and more importantly the strength – to pass through here. Maybe if they weren't crazed savages.

Someone whistled and the bows let loose.

Lost One watched arrows sail through the branches, out of his view, and heard a series of thunks and the Irregulars' chatter cut off by gasps and a shout of pain. Then a scream as someone fell, descending fast to the forest floor. Lost One watched the Woodwings ducking into cover to notch more arrows. He spotted one darting across a bridge to another position, swift and efficient. Leftovers or not, these natives could fight. He watched them pop up to release another salvo of arrows, and he waited, studying their positions and movements.

Perhaps this would be a challenge after all, he considered, as the Irregulars returned fire and men began shouting from far below. The woods quickly filled with the sound of gunfire and the branches tore apart around him. A perfect furore to hide his own shots, unnoticed above it all.

Steadying his breath, Lost One picked out the most able bow woman and fired.

20

Record VI. The Strange Man of Wet March
232. The Strange Man felled trees with no tools.
233. The Strange Man fished in the Saint's Tears with no rod nor net; his bounty was plentiful over a period of five days and five nights, including flatfish foreign to the Mire.
234. Both the Little Tears and Wet Walkers reported hearing the Strange Man's laughter decades after his departure. Many fear Pittle Ride, where he camped and laughed every night.

Record of the Miracles, Sabaddan, p. 28

Drowndeep's miserable nature made it thankfully easier for Wild Wish to motivate herself to get up and leave. If the bed had been remotely comfortable, the room warmer and the general atmosphere a bit less haunting, she might have been tempted to hide in her cell until her headache passed and her body settled. Instead, a long march through swamp terrain was almost appealing, to get away from this place, if she ignored her aching joints and throbbing head. Her mouth was fuzzy and she had the heat of regret about half-remembered things she didn't want to ask about. The hell ceremony seemed easier to accept if she pretended it was mostly a bad dream. So much for being a responsible leader.

Bloody boulder whisky. Bloody ogres and bloody Emi.

The platoon were walking in twos and threes over gradually hardening land, with mountains growing in the distance. They had left Latebite behind, and most of the others were sombre enough to fit the environment: Emi and Ptrangus were quiet and presumably regretting the drink too, while the others' general scowls suggested they were also still reconciling Paradise Fails' unsettling atmosphere. No one was smirking the way the old Blood Scouts would've, terribly amused by Things Wild Wish Had Done. Instead, she'd endured looks of concern or pity. A monk had thrust a curative vial of something darkly gloopy into her hand, which she'd accepted into a pocket "for later", meaning never. Emi had snarled like an animal when the man offered the same to her. Sister Sonseen generally regarded Wish a bit like a gargoyle might. It was fine; she was avoiding looking in her direction anyway, it being too early to process the weirdness of the Werlus beetle.

"A species unique to the Werlus River," someone had explained cheerily when they had been preparing to leave. Apparently it was an honour to witness the horse-sized insect with its many segmented legs and arched, mottled black shell, a nun saddled in its thorax with chains tied around its considerable mandibles. It was a living nightmare, and recalled the almost-similar creatures that had torn apart Rock Squad in Low Slane, making the unpleasant start to the day even more unpleasant.

The sky cleared somewhat mid-morning, though, with sunlight vaguely pushing through the Saints Mire's perpetual grey haze, to improve the general atmosphere. Light fell in majestic swathes on the distant mountains, revealing immense craggy surfaces, partly overgrown with trees. The peaks were almost as tall as those at the Horns of Heaven, though perhaps they looked bigger for the contrast of there being little else in this flat bog. Even the road, Wish noted, would be easily lost if you wandered a few metres off course, where everything was uneven tall grass. And indeed, Sonseen warned them not to stray, as one wrong step could leave you stuck sinking in the bog.

"We rarely find the ones who sink," she noted ominously, and Wish didn't like the way she stared at her as she said it.

A distraction came in the form of a cluster of three enormous creatures about a hundred metres off the road, perched like big rocks in the vague shape of toads. Brade slowed them all down to look, with a little awe in his voice as he explained they were something that translated roughly to *stone gulpers*. Harmless, he promised, though each was as big as a shed with a wide, flat gash of a mouth clearly visible from afar. Big enough to gulp a person or two down whole. They sat completely motionless, seeming to stare at the platoon with quiet contemplation.

"They mostly eat small animals," Sonseen said from atop her beetle, the twin details of them eating any animals at all and the modifier *mostly* undermining Brade's claim of "harmless". "But they are incredibly patient, unmoving creatures. Their tongues only stretch a few body lengths; they'll give us no trouble if we don't get near."

Wish grunted, perfectly happy to go along with that. As they continued, Brade fell into step alongside her and she saw how the mere sight of the toads had brightened his face. He wanted to get closer, clearly, so she murmured, "You do not have permission to get eaten by a toad."

He smiled. "Did the monk's tincture help? I tried a batch last time I was here, but it was something thinner, a nettle sap syrup."

"This?" Wish said, taking out the vial she'd been given. The contents of the glass cylinder looked like something scraped from a sewage pipe. "The sight of it's pretty sobering, I guess."

"Oh, I recommend trying it. They know what they're doing, these monks – you'll feel a lot better."

Wish squinted distrustingly at him, uncorking the vial and taking a sniff. Her nostrils clenched against it and she quickly closed it again. Put it away. She'd have to feel a lot worse before braving that. To change the subject, she said, "I take it you're enjoying yourself out here. Did you find anything interesting in Drowndeep?"

"A fraction of what I'd like to have," Brade said. She'd barely seen him yesterday, aside from at the ceremony, as he'd disappeared into the bowels of the priory. As far as she remembered. "They have a fascinating collection of bone instruments in one of the underground chambers, you know? The prophet Bonesun was said to work strange magics with them, though the ones that survive have been stripped of their power."

"Still worth something though, I guess?" Wish suggested. "If they've got history, I guess a certain type of soldier might come out here hoping to loot a few things of value?"

Brade considered that for a moment before shaking his head.

"Not under Atmoor's watch, I should think. He doesn't strike me as someone who'd encourage looting. And besides, there's a limited number of people left who would actually assign such relics real value. Going by the accounts I read in their records, they were most likely props that only 'worked' as long as Bonesun himself weaved his own personal charm into them. Or whatever magic he actually had."

"Emi says this place is dangerous," Wish recalled. "Unusual."

"I don't doubt it," Brade agreed. "One of the most interesting books they had, and only a partial record, is Sabbadan's *Record of the Miracles,* which lists many legends of the Mire. Lightning storms of unusual colour, people who didn't appear to age, whispers of unknown languages. One account attributes the prophet Nael with healing ten men afflicted with an oozing sickness."

"Oozing?" Wish questioned and Brade smiled again to suggest he knew that would stoke the imagination in unwelcome ways. "Delightful. So if they're not merely here to nab some treasures for personal gain, did anything jump out at you as another obvious goal? There must be things out here that someone might believe could be used to vanquish enemies, win wars. I doubt they're here to learn how to heal oozing."

"Again, I wouldn't give the reality of them much credence, and I don't see Atmoor doing so either," Brade replied. "But if any of the worst legends *are* true, it's as Sister Sonseen said – you could take your pick of possibilities."

Wish mumbled, reaching the end of her ability to reason through this. He took the hint and let her walk in silence.

Soon, a watch tower came into view and Sister Sonseen slowed her beetle. She said, "It's empty," making that sound like a bad thing. Wish inwardly groaned – would it be too much to ask for a morning without trouble? But everyone was looking to her for orders.

Around a yawn, Wish said, "Alright, let's check it out."

The road bent towards the watch tower, which was a sparse wooden structure with multiple beams nailed together where parts had rotted through. It sat next to an equally dilapidated watchmen's hut and a pool of water that fed off a stream mostly hidden by rushes. The tower stood twenty feet high with a definitely unsafe ladder rising to a simple fenced platform. A flagpole rose above that, holding a sad old flag, too torn and grimy to represent anything recognisable. Wish rolled her neck as the platoon gathered, some of the men holding their rifles ready. Sonseen rode her massive bug around the back of the hut.

Brade drew his pistol and looked inside, then came out shaking his head. "It's been turned over. Crates emptied, blood on the bed."

"Bandits," Sonseen decided, steering her beetle to loom over them. Wish couldn't avoid looking at it now, with its soulless round head and uneven, neck-snipping mandibles. "There should be a village a short way north of here. They may have been targeted. You'll see from up there, I expect."

Then everyone was looking at Wish again, rather than the tower. She took a deep breath, the swamp air invigorating, if not pleasant. "Sure, I'll take a look." There was a murmur from the men as she dragged her boots over to the ladder and dropped her pack. It was a relief, at least, to be rid of the weight for a second. She held onto the rungs extra tight as she climbed, taking care to place her feet, and after a huge effort got about three feet off the ground. She took a breather, painfully aware of the quiet as everyone watched, and muttered, "It's okay, you can talk amongst yourselves."

No one said anything, but someone cleared his throat. She didn't look back, and kept climbing. As she got higher, the wood creaked and she was aware of the rungs rattling, not sure if it was her trembling off the alcohol or just the shitty tower being shitty. Either way, it made her speed up, and she reached the top with only one slip and a spatter of concerned comments. Wish dropped onto her knees and used her rifle scope to investigate the swamp: more tall grass and occasional patches of water. Oh, a bit of dry rock, that was a change. She swung the gun north and picked out the shapes of far-off huts, wooden and rickety, not unlike the Shore Stalkers' village. Birds swooped over them.

Wish felt the last of the alcoholic mugginess draining as her senses focused. There was no smoke, but the walls were burnt to low cinders and most of the huts' roofs completely gone. At one side of the village, sharp poles had been jammed crookedly into the ground, with bodies speared on them. Wish lowered her gun. She checked over her shoulder towards the priory, now barely in view on the horizon, then called down, "Does the road take us past the village?"

"It's not the route I would have chosen," Sister Sonseen answered, her commanding voice easily carrying up. "But if there's a problem, it's a short detour."

"I don't think there's much we can do," Wish replied. "Happy to hear a second opinion."

The tower shook as someone else tested the ladder, then climbed up. Captain Brade emerged, tentatively testing the boards. He drew out his wood and brass extending telescope and had a look for himself. Wish rested an elbow on her knee and closed her eyes.

"Arrows and spears," Brade said.

"Local bandits?" Wish looked at him wearily. "How many tribes are in this area?"

Brade's expression mirrored her own distaste. "It's possible there are nomads out here, or Gaunt Lanterns pressing down from the north. They're the nearest other tribe, a strong and violent community. It's unlikely that they'd have crossed the river, though – that's a clear territorial boundary."

"Between them and those hard-cases back at Drowndeep, right?" Wish said. "And those Stalkers don't strike me as the sort to tolerate trouble in their land." Meaning that if there was trouble, *they* would have caused it.

Brade considered this at length, before saying, "We can head over there and investigate, and return to the priory to assess things further, but I'd caution it's not our affair."

"We left a man back there," Wish reminded him.

"I have every faith in the priory's protection. I also believe the Mirian's wouldn't attack outsiders in this manner."

"Only their bloody neighbours? How long do you think they'd been living together, this close, before someone got the idea to do this shit?"

"You heard what Sister Sonseen said. It became more volatile out here in the shadow of the war. All the more reason to check the

Drail before things get worse."

"Those people have been skewered like kebabs. It can't get any worse for them."

"And we can't make things better. This may be part of our war, but it's not *our* part of it."

Wish scowled, feeling like she should get angry at him for once again coldly informing her how things were. Yet, maybe because of her hangover, or her greater overall tiredness with *everything,* she found herself grimly agreeing. The Stalkers deserved to be punished, but there was a bigger conflict to end before they could worry about the little things. The empires could bring peace to places like this once the war was done. Justice for that village wasn't getting them home and it wouldn't bring back anyone who'd died.

She screwed her eyes closed at her own callousness. How could she think like that. How was this massacre a *little thing.* But there was no question of turning back to pick a fight with those Shore Stalkers. After all, they'd want a personal duel . . . She shouted down, "We'll rest for ten. If that water is good, fill up, take a load off. Sister, if you want to take a closer look, your beetle can get there and back quickly. Otherwise, we continue as planned."

There was low chatter below that could've been relief at steering clear of trouble or disappointment for not learning more. It didn't matter. Without bothering to respond, Sister Sonseen steered her beetle off in the direction of the village. Wish watched her stiff-backed retreat, wondering exactly how awful the nun judged her to be.

Brade put his telescope away and dug about in a pocket. "If you won't drink the monk's tincture, try this." He held a couple of white pills in his palm. "They work quickly, and effectively, but it's best not to rely on them. They're rather addictive."

Wish stared at painkillers, realising a man of his station probably had access to things ordinary soldiers could only dream of. She'd heard of men being shot for raiding medic kits for morphine and was always saddened by the thought of that desperation. She wanted no more a part of that than she did of the sewage water elixir.

And besides, abandoning that slaughtered village, didn't she deserve to feel miserable? She said, "Keep it. I'll be fine by lunchtime." She went back to watching Sister Sonseen's beetle becoming smaller. "Better the men know who they're following, isn't it?"

Brade stared at the side of her head, the pills still out, before telling her, "It's not how you appear to them that concerns me. You put in a fearsome performance with the Veneration last night, after drinking with ogres, and just climbed a vulnerable scouting position without a second thought. I want you to take care of yourself."

Wish frowned, preferring not to look at him. If she'd been irresponsible, it was because it was easy, that's all. Not because she wasn't thinking straight. She'd *wanted* to drink, and she hadn't even considered this tower dangerous. But if it'd keep Brade happy, perhaps it would be better to clear her head. She glanced at the pills again, steady in his hand. Would the pills make her forget? Stop caring?

"I don't know," she whispered to herself.

Brade looked sad for her, which was worse than him continuing to try to convince her. He decided for her, then, and closed his hands, rescinding the offer. With his other hand, he patted her shoulder. "They're there when you need them, just say the word. Get some water in you, at least."

He went to climb down the ladder and Wish noted how he pressed himself low, more careful than her. She squinted across the horizon, towards the mountains. She shakily got to her feet and scanned the other way, towards Drowndeep. The distant towers were hazy and dark, and she hoped to never see them again, with their murderous hunters and mad monks. She took a breath, though, knowing she'd find something worse on the road ahead. There were ten priories in this place, after all, and that was just the first one. She moved to the ladder and noticed the men below looking up at her, even those idly chatting. She raised her hand for a weak wave and forced a smile. Did they, like Brade, think it brave that she'd climbed up here?

It'd actually be *easier,* she considered, if someone shot her now.

It would cure her headache, at least.

21

It's so easy to form bonds here, ones that I feel could last forever. We're men ███████████████ *and thus must find connections fast, to help each other* ████. *It is meaningful and good,* ██████. *It also makes it* ██████ ██████, *how quickly those bonds* ██████████████.

**Extract from the Letters of
Corporal T. Sander, Balnia, 719**

Sister Sonseen returned from her investigation with cracks showing. Her lips twitched. As they continued through the marshes, Wish felt sure that the nun blamed her, at least in part, for the horrors she had witnessed. No survivors, she'd said. Wish wanted to apologise, but she also knew Sonseen would not want to hear it, or wouldn't believe it. But it was behind them, along with the bog's mouldy smell and splashy paths, as the terrain got more rugged and stony, rising into the mountains' foothills. Aside from the harrowing vision of a massacred village, the day rolled out peacefully as the platoon kept marching. They spotted no other villages, nor any signs that anyone lived out here, which was better than finding bodies, but gave the countryside a haunted feeling. Paradise Fails, indeed, sounded about as fitting as Drowndeep. And it was doubtful things would get more encouraging as they left it, considering the ground was growing more rugged – though at least there were no signs of other unusual animals.

Wild Wish walked with Emi for a while, the mage morose and lost in deep thought. Getting into the afternoon, what Wish had taken for the mage's hangover (a bonus that meant she didn't have to worry about Emi causing trouble) started to seem stranger, especially as she recovered but the mage kept her gaze down-turned. At last, she asked, "Did you really not get on with that whisky or . . ."

Emi made a low rumbling noise, looking sideways at her. Then she shook herself out like a dog shedding water and straightened up, smiling broadly. "I didn't sleep well. The whisky helped, but only a little."

"That place's energy?"

"That place, this place. You know at least half of the prophets were powerful mages. But because they pretended not to be it all went unchecked. That's why this country is so screwy."

"Sure."

"Five hundred years ago, if *I'd* been here, I could've been considered a god."

"That is a terrifying thought," Wish answered automatically, bringing back Emi's typical leer. It didn't last, Emi's mouth turning down again. The mage muttered to herself and shook her head. Concerned, but without a solution, Wish sighed and left her alone, only for Sister Sonseen's beetle to twitch up alongside them, its head-height knees clicking past.

"Sister," Wish said, shifting her pack and rifle on her shoulder. "Can I say something?"

"I'm quite sure I've never controlled people's speech," Sonseen replied.

"I mean. Would you mind?"

Sonseen slowed the beetle. "What do you need, Lieutenant?"

"Nothing. It's not that. I want to say . . . Those people back there, the village. I'm sorry."

Sonseen's gaze deepened to a scowl. "And what, specifically, are you sorry about?"

"That I couldn't do more?" Wish reconsidered and added, "That it happened at all."

"Then trust that I am far more sorry than you." Sonseen huffed. "Your army has much to answer for, I don't dispute that. You being here today, though, has not created this problem. Those villagers are dead because of me, Lieutenant. The tribes must have taken my arrival as an indication of coming trouble and decided to act on old grievances. And the monks of Drowndeep cannot do anything, not when I've been petitioning them to ask the Stalkers for aid."

Wish frowned. "What would the priory do otherwise?"

"Our faith is still alive in this land," Sonseen said. "Even if your people destroyed it everywhere else. The Church has its influence – but it must be wielded carefully."

"And that village . . ." Wish hesitated. She had to ask. "It *was* the Shore Stalkers, right?"

"Oh definitely. The spears they left in the hearts of those children were distinct enough. The cuts from their knives . . ." It came out bitter, but Wish heard the words choke Sonseen. Thank Bly they hadn't gone closer. The nun collected herself and went on, "Yet we need them, I suppose. That is why they did it, knowing this cost must be borne by us if we're to survive your war. Especially as the Empire chose to send only a dozen people led by a young lady."

Wish went quiet, head down, and in that lull Emi chimed in, "How many magic users do you know of in the Mire?"

Sonseen gave the mage a look of distaste but answered. "Currently, there's a witlacer working as a healer in Carlwen and rumours of another in the Mocking Mountains, though we rarely see or hear from those who live there. The Mire has been historically unwelcoming of magic, however, as offensive to faith."

Emi's eyebrows rose, her smile back, and Wish could tell what she was thinking. It was a tale as old as records, that the church punished magic users to prevent seemingly ordinary people demonstrating power that could compete with their saints and prophets. But the mage said, "Well, then, the Empire's sent you more than you realise. I could handle a tribe myself. While this *young lady*" – she nudged Wish with an elbow – "handles me."

Sister Sonseen grumbled wordlessly, an indication that this news didn't please her, but she didn't complain. Wish was sure that Emi's wording was deliberately provocative – of both the nun and her. She wanted to say she had *no* intention of handling Emi, but knew that would only make things worse.

"When we've dealt with what lies ahead," Wish said instead, "I'll see about coming back and making sure this area is safe."

Sister Sonseen laughed, a hearty and genuine sound that made Wish frown. "Oh, Lieutenant. For the head of a troop of unbelievers, you have a lot of faith."

Wish smiled back, choosing to take it as a compliment, but Emi sniggered and she sensed it wasn't. But screw them – her headache was fading and muscles easing, and having said it now she realised it *could* be true. Everything didn't have to be terrible, and if she couldn't believe in them coming out of this better off, then what was the point? She kept that thought in mind as they tramped into the mountains, and she called for a lunch break at a clearing with a patch of grass and sheltering tall rocks. She distractedly watched the platoon as she nibbled at a ration brick with a texture halfway between a slab of meat and sawdust. The Rawboys and ogres talked lightly, with some laughs between them, and Ptrangus even offered her a companionable nod when she caught his eye. But they kept their voices low and reserved, more subdued than her old Blood Scouts had ever been. She yearned for her old friends, wherever they were. For her farm and a safe place that she could return them all to. It might have been waylaid, and ruined for many of them, but the longer she thought about Sonseen's laughter the more her attitude steeled. They'd get this job done, then the next, and the next, and soon she'd have her scouts back. And her dream.

It started here.

She watched Dalliance and Toothless eating more quietly than the others. Both had somewhat forced smiles, Dalliance's a shade of his initial flair and Toothless seeming still to be discovering his. Wish caught a waft of their conversation, something about a girl Dalliance met in Farne. Big breasts, of course, and something that made him chuckle to himself. Toothless joined in dutifully. It was good to see the men starting a new friendship, because that was how they got over the old ones. But they needed more of a distraction, her scouting hopefuls. She could offer them *something*. More than she did for Private Fawcet, anyway. Wish kicked off her rock chewing a mouthful of dust brick and made a messy job of swallowing it as she walked over. Toothless looked up worriedly.

"We've got some time," Wish said, then properly finished her mouthful and repeated it, so they could understand. "Before things go to shit again, I might as well teach you a few things. Grab your rifles, we'll set up a range."

"What, out here?" Dalliance said.

"Yeah, unless you have a quiet barn hidden somewhere I don't know about?" Wish shot back, channelling some of Sister Sonseen's energy. She could feel a few of the others watching, the nun included, and added, "Would you rather have a picnic or learn how to kill?"

Happier with that line, Wish shouldered her own gun and marched out of the clearing, through a few rocks, down to where she'd seen another clearing on the way up. A couple of worn trees. About halfway there, she reconsidered: they probably *would* rather have a picnic. Even if the food was crap and the conversation stilted. But she heard the movements of her men grabbing their guns. When she turned back to address them, she found not just Dalliance and Toothless, quickly finishing off their food, but the three Rawboys ambling just behind them, and even the ogres lurking further back.

"Um. I meant just my scouts."

"Ain't we all your scouts now?" Ptrangus grumbled, folding his arms.

"Respectfully, Lieutenant," Macmiddan said more reverently, "I wanna know how you shot them bats down."

Wish frowned. "That's not what I . . . I mean, you're welcome to listen, but . . ."

They spread out through the rocks, and she saw Emi and Brade sneaking in too. Dammit, she'd suddenly become the lunchtime entertainment.

Wish sighed and walked down to the edge of a stretch of grass, opposite a tree, which she pointed at. "That'll be the target. I guess we'll start with observation, move on from there. No, actually, I should start with the rifle itself. Right now, we've got two telescopic sights between the lot of us and I'm not letting anyone touch mine." She addressed Toothless. "You and Dalliance can share. But I wouldn't bother with a scope until you can all hit the mark with open sights, anyway. And the first thing, which I can't stress enough, is that your rifles should all be completely clean and in perfect working order. I shouldn't need to say that. Is anyone's not?"

The looks on their collected faces were about as confident as her new students at Rock Stable, a lot of experienced veterans reduced to uncertainty.

"None of you checked this morning?"

Silence.

"Oh well this is going to be fun. Everyone take out your bloody guns and clean them." There was some hesitation, so she added, "Then we'll talk about the importance of quick reflexes."

They hurriedly tried to catch up, fumbling their weapons.

"You joining us, Sergeant Caracker? This part applies to everyone."

With some satisfaction, Wild Wish found herself slipping into the role that had kept her sane for the previous two months, deflecting attention from her back onto the students. Seeing she actually knew about this, the men hung on her words, first thoroughly cleaning and inspecting their barrels then listening to a short introduction on gauging distance and keeping a gun steady. She tested them on the usual tips no one had spread through the ranks yet, like steadying their breath but not holding it, squeezing the trigger but not jerking it, and not releasing it too soon. Wish sent a couple of them to scout for anyone nearby, to be sure their shots wouldn't draw bandits or enemy combatants or whatever land-squid monsters might be out here, then she set up rocks on branches and boulders for targets. The men lined up and took their shots – doing well, all of them, possibly putting her tips to immediate use. From Ptrangus's smug grin, she suspected they were all pretty good to begin with, though.

The fun was interrupted when Sister Sonseen came to Wish's side and suggested they get moving. They were unlikely to reach Midpeak by nightfall, she said, and they wouldn't want to travel after dark. That cheerful thought drew them all out of the training, which had lasted what, an hour? A brief moment where they might have been anywhere, without a war to contend with, or the memory of speared villagers and giant crabs to eradicate.

Wish held onto that lightness as she resettled her pack and set out again. They marched up increasingly tough inclines, and she took the lead, cheering the men on behind her. The steep climb felt good, reminding her she could do it – hadn't got totally soft lounging in Rock Stable. After following the winding road through the afternoon, trusting Sister Sonseen's sense of direction past any forks, and particularly where they reached a peak only to go back downhill, they finally followed a cliff edge curve to the eastern side of Midpeak itself. The view took in a panorama of lower mountains and far-off marshes, and in between was a spread of huge trees below. The Midwood, Sonseen told them – a place best avoided. Thankfully, they didn't need to enter.

They came off the road at a plateau, where they set up tents in gaps between the rocks. The platoon kept their fires low and chat quiet, though drinks were passed around and some of the men rolled dice. Wish sat guard, watching the night sky, where crowded stars poked through occasional breaks in the blankets of cloud, and she felt uplifted despite the day's bad start. How big and distant the night sky was here. And maybe, just maybe, her friends were out there under these same stars.

Toothless came to her, smiling awkwardly, and offered a steaming mug of chocolate drink which she took gratefully. He thanked her for the training and retreated into the shadows. The rest of them left her alone, even Emi, though Wish heard her laughing with Brade's men, no doubt cheating them at dice. The mage had recovered her humour, at last. Maybe she *had* just been hungover as well, not wanting to admit it. Or maybe she needed to put Paradise Fails behind them. This place wasn't so bad, or strange, or dangerous after all. Wish took in deep breaths of the mountain air.

She took herself back through camp and told the men to enjoy themselves but she was turning in. As she climbed into her tent, she heard the others packing up, voices lowering, following her example, and it made her smile. Just like back in Eardung.

Scraper crawled into the tent to join her and muttered something Wish didn't hear, then she slid into her sleeping bag and seemed instantly to sleep. The girl must have been physically absent for part of the day, Wish was sure, because she could've sworn she hadn't seen her within the group and barely even remembered she was with them. Then she felt bad, because she'd barely remembered her in the old Blood Scouts either. She'd make more effort to notice her tomorrow. She'd connect better with all of them. The New Blood Scouts were going to work, after all.

She rested her head and slept, peacefully.

A deep and long sleep, interrupted only by an explosion.

22

Artillery developed so fast during this period that new weapons were rapidly retired. The most incredible cannons of a year ago, even a week ago, became an embarrassment and a liability, and it wasn't uncommon for ordinary soldiers and civilians to scavenge ordinance that could have swayed entire battles in wars past.
Great Guns of the One War, Finisis, p. 43

Sergeant Mac Carrow, 1st Section Marksman in Atmoor's Legion, 17th Division, crouched by the tracks in the dirt, drawing a mental picture of the extent of the enemy's force. His men had reached the forest's edge by dusk, the able 2nd Section backed by the swarming mass of 3rd, but he'd decided long before arriving that they would camp here for the night. The woodland was ripe for ambush and naturally hostile, considering the sounds of violence they'd already heard. Savages killing savages; with any luck they'd wipe each other out and save him the trouble.

Yet the darkness and dense foliage ahead did offer an inviting respite. Carrow could go in alone, scouting ahead of the company's unruly soldiers and goblins. He might find some peace in the shadows. He wasn't supposed to be a leader; sniping was quiet work, private. Anywhere else on the front line, he could have been anonymous, instead of here, where Colonel Atmoor's misguided respect made him someone the others looked up to, even with his low rank. He wished the colonel would stop trying to support him.

"What are you thinking?" Major Weles asked, twirling his moustache as he stood behind Carrow. "There as many of them as we thought?"

"M-m-maybe. Maybe a few more." Carrow stood. There were deep tracks where heavy wagons had churned the ground amid the footprints of many men. Their numbers were a good thing. A force that large would move slowly and, if their goal was Midpeak, from this direction there would only be one road suitable for their supply train. Carrow had studied the map repeatedly, but unfolded it again, old but neatly pressed and more accurate than the army-issued interpretation of the Mire. Rather than try to explain his thoughts, which always took too long and drew either pitying or mocking looks, Carrow pointed and said, "Here. Th-th-th–" He stopped. Couldn't even get this out. Took a breath and thought of home. Mistway Park. He exhaled. "Th-th–"

"That's where they're going," Weles finished for him and Carrow glared.

They need that road, he'd wanted to say.

Weles reached for the map but Carrow drew it back. He hadn't kept it clean by letting slobs finger it. Returning a glower, the major asked, "How long?"

"That-that-that –" Carrow stuttered, looking to the woods. Recalling the gunfire they'd heard. He shook his head violently to clear it, but that made his lip twitch. With an angry growl, he blurted out, "They're not far ahead. The shots were close. They won't – won't – won't –"

"They haven't got there yet, sure, I get it," Weles huffed. He was staring into the woods too, irritation stemming less from Carrow's stutter than the concern of going in. His nerves, and distraction, stilled some of Carrow's, so his words flowed a little more freely.

"They'll probably make camp and start their ascent in the morning," he said, quickly pushing it out. "We should do the s-same. Move around the perimeter, to close some d-d-distance. Don't risk the woods until dawn."

Weles gave him a sideways look, uncertain either at the plan or the short barrage of ordinary speech from the sniper. Carrow tried to keep his expression steady, but his cheek twitched, the right eye blinking rapidly.

"Why not send the goblins in now? Get the buggers while they sleep," the major suggested. Despite his higher rank and general pity for Carrow, Weles was deferential. Even if they mocked him behind his back, most of the legion respected Carrow's instincts. Mostly because Atmoor insisted on keeping Carrow close, trusting that he was still fully effective and able. Even when Carrow wasn't sure himself. Weles believed, like Atmoor, that under Carrow's broken nerves was a professional soldier. A man who could've been great if he had come through Camano whole. But he had been blessed with a gift for shooting, and preferred putting that to use than trying to talk. His nerves were calmer with a finger on the trigger, the scope narrowing his mind. He just needed to get through these occasional strategic meetings to get back to it.

"Mm-mm." Carrow shook his head. "H-have Hollery move the 2nd Section. Shell the road. Force them to turn back."

Weles frowned. "Shell the road?"

Carrow pointed to two spots on the map. "Put – put Hollery here and his Top Overs sh-sh-should reach the r-road. At dawn."

"They'd damage the mountain itself. The priory at the top . . ."

"Small s-s-sacrifice. Much worse if they – if they reach Midpeak." Carrow held his gaze, to seal the orders.

"They'll flee south then? Away from us?"

Carrow shook his head. The south was impassable, with the woods and mountains thickening there; it would be a huge diversion to get through that way.

Weles narrowed his eyes and thankfully drew the correct conclusion: "It would drive them north, to the next best route? Ilscot's lot could pen them in while we send the goblins in from the rear." Carrow's plan obviously implied that, but it worked just as well if the major heard it from his own mouth, as if it was his idea. "With any luck, we'll be done with this rabble by mid-morning."

"I'll h-h-head in myself to be s-s-sure," Carrow added, regarding the woodland. "Now."

"You think that's necessary?" Weles asked, obviously concerned he'd have to manage the plan on his own.

"Need to k-k- – need to k-k-kill K-Kasidee," Carrow reminded him. Remove the head, that was the ultimate goal. For this insurgence to be properly stopped, the traitor Kin Kasidee had to die, and if anyone could confirm a kill like that, it was him. This time he would hit the right damn soldier.

"If that's what you want." Weles shrugged. "Looks damn creepy in there. But Bleacher will come in not far behind you anyway, I guess. Good luck."

And that was that. Carrow took only the most necessary supplies and set out with barely another word. It felt immediately colder as he crunched over leaves, entering a truer dark than the night outside. There was a psychic coldness to it, the chill of these foreign woods. But it was private, too. Calming – especially with his hands resting on his gun.

He crept between giant trees, and marvelled at the glow of mushrooms as they came to life in answer to the falling sun. Bulbous clusters of thick fungus ran around the tree roots and climbed in scabby patches over the bark, with some standing tall on bendy stalks and others frilly like the cuff of a gown. They lit up like hazy gas lanterns, bright blue, red, dots of luminous purple. He wondered why they glowed, if there was magic at work, a property that regular mushrooms lacked. Probably poisonous.

Those thoughts were scattered by the sight of a dead body.

Another man with tattoos, like the one Ilscot had recovered from the Black Lake, though this one was deformed by the impact of a high fall. An arrow had broken off in what was left of his neck. Carrow craned his head up, and spent a while staring at the canopy, picking out irregularities. An arm hung over the edge of the branch. Above that were platforms, a bridge, a ladder. He continued walking and found more bodies, some armed in the fashion of Comity rebels, others in furs, leather and feathers. Women, with the flesh of their legs, arms, and even bellies exposed.

Not exactly women, though. Their arms were encased in wooden devices that wrapped around and dug into their flesh. Big, complicated frames of hinged blocks and scrappy canvas. Crude, man-made wings, but fused with their shoulders and withered arms, embedded and partly tangled with flesh where the body had healed over their inception. Carrow wasn't sure what was worse: the nature of the warped people that would force these contraptions onto their women, and force them to fight, or the people who would shoot down such primitive women. Savages fighting savages.

But then, Carrow wondered if it was this place, or the whole Rocc, at this point. When he closed his eyes he still saw the horrors of Camano, and when he opened them, realities such as this were no better. Onwail had sheltered them from it for a short while only. It would find him wherever he went. And it came as no surprise, producing no nervous twitch, when he heard more gunfire ahead.

Kin Kasidee pressed himself against a tree trunk, a rattler short rifle in one hand and his sabre in the other. He flinched at the thunk of an arrow hitting the tree, then laughed. His heart was racing and he'd been chilled by the screams of men falling terrible heights, but damn if this absurd place wasn't something else. Crazy bird-howling people with bows and arrows trying to hunt them like rodents, amid twisted tree houses and luminescent fungi. He bent out of cover and fired into the branches.

"Saints' be damned, you feathered freaks!" he shouted. "We're not your enemy!"

It made no difference; the bird-people didn't want to talk, and neither did his company. That chance had vanished when they ineffectually ambushed the Irregulars. The tribe had been caught unawares and chose violence; it seemed the Woodwings hadn't been monitoring the forest border well, probably distracted by Atmoor's men in the north, and they'd only gradually appeared in haphazard groups to fight. His men were spread through the base of the massive trees with rifles booming in a tremendous salvo, lighting up in brief flashes and producing a cover of gun smoke. One man dashed from beside a covered wagon and an arrow pierced down through his head, out the eye. He fell metres away, breaking Kasidee's smile.

"Back the hell off or we'll burn this forest down!" he yelled. The branches above were bending and breaking and leaves erupted with leaping bodies, but it was too dark now to easily spot their attackers. Surely the natives couldn't see, either, with most of their arrows randomly piercing the ground. They were simply showering the convoy, a not unreasonable strategy considering the couple of hundred Irregulars made a fairly easy target.

Kasidee's ears pricked at the distinct sound of Lost One's rifle, a deeper boom than the more basic weapons most of them had, and there was a crash of foliage as one of the savages plummeted from above. Then a great wet splat.

There were dozens of them hooting and flapping about, using exactly the sort of tactics he himself did: a small, lesser-armed unit could dominate through speed and confusion. If they couldn't see them, they couldn't kill them, and they were wasting ammo and men. But Kasidee wasn't sending anyone else up the ladders after the earlier fiasco. He scanned their bulky wagons now scattered through the forest path and spotted the frame of the F-Apparat, their sole piece of artillery. Useless and inappropriate in this territory, but perhaps it would make more of an impression than their guns.

"The Apparat!" Kasidee shouted, picking out two nearby soldiers. "Ready it!" They gaped in confusion, then jumped as a flurry of arrows hit their tree. Kasidee pointed urgently. "We'll put a hole in the sky! *Move!*"

The pair ran in low crouches, avoiding a couple more badly aimed arrows, to slide down by the Apparat. They tore back the cloth covering and worked together to heave it from the support frame. Too weak – the weapon needed four people or more to shift. Kasidee shouted to others nearby and more ran out to help as their comrades gave covering fire. Another blast from Lost One's gun brought a grunt from above. The cannon got caught and the men's frustrations rose – then an arrow took one in the chest. He fell down gasping, trying to shout, but his lung was done. The other men backed off, about to break.

Gritting his teeth, Kasidee sprinted out himself, skipping aside as arrows sliced past him. One passed his face with a sting, narrowly missing a death-shot, and he dived amongst the men to lever the cannon's catch off. He yelled and the men heaved again, this time wheeling the Apparat onto the ground with a great thump. Two men clawed at the cache crates to retrieve a shell, two feet long, as Kasidee helped open the chamber and wind the mechanism. They thrust the shell in and ran, leaving Kasidee and the remaining team to pull the gun back, tilting it as high as it would go. The top angle was still low, not designed to fire straight up, where the enemy were – and one of the fleeing loaders was hit repeatedly in the back before he reached cover.

"Fling it back and fire on my command!" Kasidee shouted, getting his shoulder under the barrel. Two others joined him and together they used all their weight to upturn the gun. As it reached near vertical he shouted, "Clear! Fire!"

They all dived out of the way as the last man hit the trigger and the Apparat boomed. It eclipsed all the gunshots and screaming with its incredible power. Kasidee fell on his side and rolled over to watch the shell tear through the canopy. It ripped a hole in the sky and climbed towards the stars before exploding in smoke-thick fire. For a moment, the forest was lit in stark white, from the clawing branches and the scrambling feathered natives down the trees to the bodies on the ground and frightened faces of men. As it fell dark again, the Woodwings fled in all directions. It took a moment to sink in that it was over, before a general cheer swept through the company, followed by a few gunshots of celebration.

"Save your fucking ammo!" Raltman shouted, shoving through the foliage, fuming from the fight. Then Havik's voice rose above the others as she emerged, speaking another language, quietening what was left of the cheering.

Kasidee peeled himself up from the ground and approached her voice, glancing back to the F-Apparat. Its rear carriage was dented and sunken into the ground. He ordered, "Dig that out, make sure it's working," then went around a tree to find Havik with a hand to her mouth to amplify her shout, glaring accusingly up.

"What're you saying?" Kasidee asked.

She glanced sideways at him, not looking pleased, and his smile faded. "Asking them to parley. Warning them we've got a shared enemy coming."

She shouted up again, trying a few different phrases and languages. The company were slowly shifting out of cover now, watching with worry they'd done something wrong. But with many of their mates face-down in the dirt, and with the raised emotions of battle, a few were scowling at her attempts at diplomacy, too. It hadn't helped earlier and wasn't likely to help now.

"Havik, they're gone," Kasidee said. "For now."

She gave him another angry look, then stomped off into the dark. "Havik!"

She didn't turn back and he didn't have the energy to deal with that, so turned his attention to the broader company. A quick sigh, and a shrug that revived a few smiles, then he gave quick instructions: they'd go a little further then set up camp. First thing in the morning, they'd get out of these trees and race to the comforts of Midpeak.

Kasidee dreaded to think how late it was when he managed to settle down, the adrenaline fading at last, and he was stirred all too soon by a soldier saying the sun wouldn't be long in rising. Crawling out of his bivouac, Kasidee squinted up at the dark trees above, thinking there was no way to tell night from day here, though the fact that he could make out the branches said otherwise.

He resumed issuing orders between yawns, to get them moving before the Woodwings returned. Soon, the company was marching again, as if they'd barely been interrupted by battle or sleep, only to be brought to a stop by a tremendous boom. The trees shuddered and the birds took flight as loud curses ran down the line. Then came the crack and quake of an explosion with everyone ducking low and darting for cover. Kasidee stood stock still, alongside his horse, following the path of the sound. It was close, but not enough to harm them. Not aimed at them.

Another boom followed and as the company gathered themselves, worry mixed with relieved laughter. The shot burst against the ground ahead.

"Fuck me, they're shelling the mountain," Raltman said.

"The pass," Lost One added. He looked to Kasidee and Kasidee nodded ahead, sending the marksman off to investigate. At a third blast, the men swore more vocally, stirring with uneasy energy.

"Keep it down," Kasidee said, and they quietened as he met Havik's eye. She'd not spoken to him after the battle, her face troubled. He knew that look. The Woodwing attacks sat badly with her; she prided herself on understanding this place, and her inability to connect with the tribe here was a personal failing. But this wasn't a Weagalian Claw adventure or a Brade romance – such savages rarely respected outsiders. The natives simply wanted them dead, and now the Drail were joining in. He said, "They'll be coming in."

"Yes," Havik replied. "We'll have them at our rear with an avalanche ahead, and the tribes still hovering above."

"We're not clearing an avalanche," Kasidee said, that at least seeming obvious. "We have to get out of here." He recalled the lay of the land. If the route ahead was cut off, there wasn't much choice . . . "We can make for Gauntstone and leave Midpeak for later."

Havik barked a nasty laugh. "We *need* Midpeak. They'll secure it for themselves if we're not quick enough."

"And they'll kill us all if I try and take a company up a mountainside they're busy bombing," Kasidee said, a little testily. "We need to survive these woods first, worry about the rest later."

Havik glared with fire in her eyes, her frustration from the night stoked anew. He had to keep control, before her doubt could spread to others, tired and afraid as they were. She was right, that was the problem: Midpeak would only get harder to reach if they didn't head there now. And if the Drail had guns powerful enough to reach the mountain, they'd have the northern passages watched, too. Except . . . guns that big could create quite an explosion. Thinking out loud, he suggested, "If we hug the mountain and stay hidden long enough, a small team could get around them unseen. Reach their artillery and create a distraction."

"Get right into their ranks?" Raltman questioned. "That ain't easy. Or safe."

"Neither's staying here to die," Kasidee replied. "They'll be coming in after us, soon." He met Havik's eye and found her scowling but thoughtful.

"We should've sought out the Woodwings," she said. "I could've convinced them to help."

"After we killed their women and kids?" Raltman said, a font of doubt.

Kasidee considered it, though. "Maybe they will anyway. The Apparet turned them away well enough, but they're gonna be no less happy to see goblins in here than they were to see us. Things are going to get crazy" – he found his own spirits improving at the thought – "so we can get a few guys clear."

"Huh." Havik nodded. Hope. "You're right. A small team could get up the mountain, too. Yeah. You lot get out of here and I'll head for Midpeak myself."

Kasidee gaped, but knew her well enough not to argue. If she said she could do it, she would. He merely said, "You and how many men?"

They were interrupted as Lost One came running back into camp, face grim. He met Kasidee's eye and shook his head, the situation as bad as they thought.

"Any way through?" Kasidee asked.

"There's no road left. Not that we can use."

"Then it's settled," Havik decided. "Head for Gauntstone, bomb those bastards – I'll find a different path up to Midpeak and we can regroup later."

"Just like that?" Raltman scoffed, disbelieving. It finally got a hint of a smile from her.

"Just like that."

"Alright," Kasidee sighed, then fell back on their mantra. *"Saints save the brave.* Raltman, Lost One, you boys take a squad and watch Havik. Make sure nothing happens to her. We'll be at Gauntstone when you're done. It's time to step everything up."

The Saints Mire overall, and this woodland in particular, was *crawling* with unhinged talls, and Wideskull Bleacher loved it. Bless these lunatic birdmen and the brash Irregulars, he'd barely waited a day before Atmoor was willing to unleash the goblins again. No one else was going to race through the forest, after all, and the colonel probably sensed that it'd be hard to hold them back with gunfire on the horizon and the gates of bloody Carlwen closed to goblins anyway. Not that the horde would've chosen lounging in a pompous town over a good ruck.

It'd been a fast and fierce morning, in the sort of terrain that suited goblins best: too random and closed in for any pretence of positioning and tactics like Atmoor usually tossed about. Just a simple order to spread out and fuck things up. And the birdmen were putting up a solid fight, hard to see high in the trees, feral in their attacks. Not particularly dangerous, with those arrows and spears, but spirited. Bleacher enjoyed the drumbeat of gunshots, the serenade of war cries, the scents of blood and smoke. He strode behind the first wave of goblins with pistol and blade, as befit a leader, springing into action every time a sneaky tall swooped out of the trees. His face wet with blood and pulse racing, he only regretted that the fight was sporadic, not as many tribespeople as their collective noise suggested. A few hundred total, maybe, spread through the entire woods. Most were likely dead already, the others retreating.

As the sounds faded and grew more distant, the violence replaced with laughter and cheers, Bleacher slowed down, sniffing at the air for some clue to their actual targets. A couple of scouts had run in with suggestions of Kasidee's trail, the ruts of wagon wheels and a few spots where the humans had fought each other, but the birdmen caused too much distraction to quickly follow. There was no hurry, though. The further the Irregulars ran, the longer the goblins' leash became.

They *needed* this, after so many months stewing idly in Onwail. Centuries of working together, goblin mercenaries fighting alongside human armies, and those pricks still didn't get how they worked. You chose a target and trusted to the swarm. It appeared random to outsiders, but goblins had their codes: they'd kill the warriors, or any with warrior potential (if in doubt, toss them a blade and see what they did with it); burn the supplies that couldn't be requisitioned; break the structures that could be used against you. Get around bigger targets to hit weak spots, avoid grouping to present a big target yourself. Simple principles that allowed a thousand goblins to operate as one chaotic unit – and prevented the resurgence of the likes of these partisans they were chasing now. And it wasn't like they were *more* ruthless than everyone else. The Drail green-coats had levelled whole towns. The Stains had at least a dozen massacres on their ledger. Yet the goblin assaults in Coakes, early in the war, had shocked a few people back in the carpeted halls of Arrow City, and seen big groups like Bleacher's wasted on guard duty.

Not here, though. To drive home the importance of their efforts, Bleacher had read more of Kasidee's leaflets and impressed on Atmoor just how wild this lot were. Fighters after his own heart. However cautious Atmoor wanted to be, they were dealing with loons, in a land of loons, and Bleacher's remedy was the best and simplest. Besides, as long as the colonel was hiding in a town that wouldn't give Bleacher the time of day, the goblins were gonna do what goblins did . . .

23

Large-scale fighting is rarely decided by how many are killed, but rather by how effectively the most strategic positions are held. Sometimes, a man with a good vantage point and a stable rifle can do more harm than an earth-minder capable of levelling a town.

Sniping in Farne, Heskeph, p. 12

Wild Wish watched the mountainside explode from a tall cliff edge. She clung onto the rocks and glared at the ground as it shook, threatening to break. They were maybe fifty feet higher than the impact, and half a mile away, but she felt the mountain tremble under the attack. Her platoon cursed as another shell hit, and they watched the slopes creaking, expecting chunks of the earth to fall apart.

"Blessed be the Saints," Sister Sonseen said. "What weapons have you brought to our land?"

Wish was curious about that herself, peering in the direction the blasts had come from. They stopped firing and the quaking calmed, the mountain settling without a collapse, though chunks of rock shifted and slid where the black cloud remained. Far beyond the trees, where there lay grassland and the shimmer of a river, she could just make out the black dots of gathered military forces. She took up her rifle and scoped out the artillery. Three big-bore guns, the sort that took a whole bunch of men to load and fire.

Caracker came forward and asked for Brade's telescope to look for himself. He squinted hard, and Wish wondered if ogres' eyesight was better or worse than regular people's. He said, "That's a team of Vranker 160s. Top Overs. Don't think that's what we heard at night."

The first blast, the one that had woken them, seemed a distant memory now. Wish had set out in the dark to investigate, with the others soon following, high above the fighting. There hadn't been more trouble since, though, the dauntingly massive forest dormant enough that the platoon were able to return to camp and sleep. Wish hadn't; she had kept watching, waiting, until the platoon stirred again, packed up and joined her, ready to keep marching. They'd walked about ten minutes in the predawn before the new explosions stopped them.

"Why the hell they shooting at a mountain?" Ptrangus demanded, as offended as if the Drail were attacking ducklings.

"That's the road to Midpeak," Sister Sonseen said.

"The Irregulars must be in the woods," Brade said, "with the Drail trying to cut them off. I'd say we've found our armies."

Wish scanned the mountainside, no sign of people on the trail. She searched down through the trees, then spotted something sticking out where branches met the cliffs. She pointed and asked, "What's that?"

Caracker took a look before passing the telescope back to Brade, who said, "A bridge?"

"In the trees?" Sister Sonseen said. "That'd be the Woodwings. They live in the canopy."

"So there's a way down?" Wish said. "We could get to the Irregulars."

"I wouldn't recommend it. The Woodwings are fiercely territorial – no one travels safely through the Midwood. And by the looks of it, they're the least danger in Midwood this morning."

"If the Irregulars are still down there, they'll be running," Brade said. "We don't want to get caught up in the chase. But the Drail clearly thought they were heading for Midpeak – if any get through, we'll find them there."

"Regardless," Sister Sonseen put in, "my destination remains the priory."

Wish considered it. They were a half-day's hike from Midpeak, which remained hidden in the tall reaches of the mountain tops. A fortified priory certainly sounded better than a woodland teeming with violence. But on the other hand, if Kin Kasidee was running, they might need help – and considering the size of the Drail's force, this might be their last chance to catch up to them. She said, "I think it's worth a closer look before we pull back."

"Those walkways ain't built for us," Caracker pointed out, squinting towards the distant bridge. She couldn't argue with that: it looked narrow and unsafe even for a human.

"Okay," Wish thought out loud, "we're not aiming to sway whatever's going on down there. You're right, Captain, Midpeak is still our best hope of understanding the overall situation, and possibly connecting with Kasidee, but I still want a closer look here. I think you should escort Sister Sonseen to the priory, and talk with whoever's in charge there. Start thinking about what we can do to defend the site if the Drail push in."

"Defend it?" Runt scoffed disbelief. "Against those numbers? Them guns?"

"I'm not saying we're staying," Wish replied, ignoring his attitude. "But we'll establish whether there's anything we *can* do. I'll be right behind you; it shouldn't take long to get down in the trees, scout it out and come back. I assume the priory itself will be easy to find?"

"The routes are clear," Sister Sonseen confirmed. "Follow any of these wider paths up, they all lead to Midpeak."

"You're not suggesting going on your own?" Brade said. "Wild Wish, I appreciate you're new to delegating, but we have men who can scout for you. Hell, if anyone goes, I should – I at least might communicate with the Woodwing tribe."

"Yeah," Wish said, but she already knew what she wanted. Not to risk anyone else, and to see things for herself. "But I'm not planning to make contact with locals, just to see what's going on. I can do that quickest alone." That met a general rush of dissent, as the men variously expressed she was ridiculous, so she added, "I *believe* I'm our most experienced scout here."

The Rawboys made disbelieving noises, and Macmiddan grumbled, "Respectfully, boss, some of us probably been doing this sort of thing since before you were born."

"I've infiltrated more countries than most of you have heard of," Brade said, frankly. "Go to Midpeak, Lieutenant. Keep your command."

That finally steeled her resolve; she couldn't give Brade his way. "This isn't a debate. If it'll make you all feel better" – she looked sideways – "I'll take Emi with me."

"Why only two people?" Ptrangus put in.

"I can go." Toothless raised a hand quickly, though sounding like he'd surprised himself.

"You don't even have a gun," Wish said.

"I can borrow one. I can spot for you. Lieutenant, I'm ready."

"Do you want a medic, at least?" Graveguard said, *everyone* getting their bit in.

"No, enough –" A shrill sound made Wish pause, and she looked towards the woodland. It grew in volume, not one single noise but a lot of nasty voices joining force in a collected, shrieking battle cry. She hadn't heard that grating, chalkboard screech often, but she knew exactly what it was.

"Goblins," Ohno said it out loud.

"Lot of them," Caracker grumbled.

"Might be best no one go at all," Dalliance said, and Wish saw the general unease across the group. Toothless didn't press his volunteering further, and the Rawboys were collectively frowning. A patter of distant gunshots started, deep in the trees, as the unhinged noise of the collected goblins rose. Wild Wish took a breath, watching the canopy as if she could see through to the men fighting below, whatever slaughter had begun. The last time she had encountered goblins, they had been roused from the ruins of the mill where she'd failed to shoot a hawk giant. Two of her friends had died. But the fighting was distant enough, still, and she didn't need to get close, just to get an idea of who else was down there.

"Emi," she said quietly. The mage's words to Sonseen came back to her: the mage alone could probably handle anything this land had to offer. If Wish wanted minimal company, this was the way. "You and me. Two's enough; we want to go unseen."

"It's a date," the mage replied.

"Are you –" Brade started up again, but Wish cut him off: "Yes."

She passed off her pack and took only her rifle, inviting no more questions even if she could see Brade still wanted to complain. The

Rawboys regarded her oddly, but looked ready to sit out the prospect of goblins, which was fine. She only had a brief pause, noticing Scraper hovering at the rear of the group, looking small alongside Ohno, with a fixed expression. Wish considered inviting her, to make her feel included, but this wasn't a time for niceties. She tightened her helmet and wished the men good luck, though she was the one who'd need it. Sister Sonseen regarded her from her beetle steed and nodded, hand raised in either a reluctant blessing or a dismissal. Not wasting any more time, Wish jogged a little extra blood into her limbs and set out. She and Emi strode down the mountainside, hopping like goats over the rocks, as the sounds of gunfire and goblin screams rose. It was hard to tell if the goblins were celebrating or in pain, horrible either way.

By the time the pair of scouts reached the bridge, the sounds had quietened, though occasional shots and goblin yells continued. Wish tried to push it from her mind as she considered the trees ahead. Though the forest was a fraction of Eardung's size, the trees themselves were as huge and ominous as those there; she wondered if these ones were even *bigger*. It felt that way, looking down the immense height of the cliff, and up close it was evident the locals' uneven plank bridge was built with nothing to hold onto.

"I'll test it," Emi volunteered, and the mage hopped past and trotted sure-footed over the planks. Wish cringed just watching, but the bridge held and Emi waved back with an encouraging grin.

"Easy for you," Wish muttered, "your mindless feet can stick to anything." She took a deep breath and stepped out, cringing again as her boot landed. Sturdy as it was, she swayed from the dizzying view, and almost stepped right back.

"Don't look down," Emi advised, and Wish nodded. Sensible. But she had to look down, or she'd walk over the edge. She flitted her gaze from the bridge back up to Emi, and, mostly focusing on the mage, darted out over the boards. By the time Wish reached the other side, she was letting out an anguished, "Ahhh!" sound, and Emi laughed as she caught her in her arms and they fell back against the supporting tree.

Wish breathed deeply, letting Emi hold her up, then quickly

stepped out of her embrace, dusting herself off. "Thanks."

"You are *always* welcome, Wild." Emi leered, eyes intense, and Wish was torn between gratitude and the feeling that it might've been better to bring literally *anyone* else. But at least the mage's mood had improved since Drowndeep.

They'd ended up on a platform encircling the trunk and leading off over two similar bridges. There was a series of similar platforms and carved stairs going deeper into the woods. Wish pricked her ears to a gunshot and said, "Guess that's our route." She took the next bridge with little more confidence, and the next, as Emi crossed them breezily. Then they paused to scan the canopy for signs of movement, listening for gunfire, and Wish asked quietly, "You're feeling better, right?"

Emi's eyes had their typical wide, mad stare, and she showed teeth as she nodded. "Oh yeah. It's not so bad here."

A little pocket of goblin shrieks came from somewhere below, bouncing off the trees, dauntingly close. More gunshots followed. Between the dark forest and the feral sounds, this didn't feel much better than Drowndeep.

"It's still *bad,*" Emi amended. "We shouldn't be in these woods. Or anywhere near these priories. But it's not *as* bad. The mountain, these woods, they haven't got as much . . . sickness as that marsh."

"Sickness?" Wish echoed, and the mage nodded again, smile broadening. Like the idea of an ill land was something to be marvelled at. "Is it going to cause us trouble?"

"Not from here, I think. Not if we don't . . . interfere. But I'm not sure we could anyway. You know touched metal? Where materials are warded against magic? To prevent manipulation. It feels a bit like that, out here, but in a messy, primitive way. Halfway protected from magic, halfway corrupted by it. It's old and kind of unstable."

"Great. Because we need more problems."

"It's not an *extra* problem," Emi pointed out. "It's part of why anyone would come here. Honestly, I'm surprised the Arbitration never shut this whole country down. I bet you something in the energy around Guiltway would explain why the Drail went there on a tangent."

Wish frowned, somewhat impressed that Emi remembered such a detail, given her limited input before, but not liking the thought there could be genuine weirdness behind all this. "Well, hopefully soon we'll be able to just ask someone."

They continued on a route she estimated to be broadly north, cliffs on their left so they could easily find their way back. The Irregulars would be pressed in this direction, most likely. Crossing more walkways and going through small nest-like structures, Wish grew curious about how elaborate the Woodwings' network was. It was a sniper's paradise, and would give them a good vantage over the goblins if they happened to cross paths. Unless the goblins had climbed the trees. Were they known to be keen climbers or upset by heights? She twisted back to ask Emi, and a gunshot cracked through the canopy, the tree bark exploding by her head.

Wish fell with a yelp, pushing herself flat on the platform. Emi grunted as another shot followed and the mage was thrown back into the tree. Wish's eyes widened as the mage slammed into the trunk and bounced forwards – she reached up a feeble hand, too slow to grab her leg. She watched Emi flop over the edge of the platform.

"No!" Wish screamed, so loud her throat scorched.

Emi fell rigidly, coat flapping against the wind, a sickly high drop and nothing between her and the forest floor. Wish rolled back as another bullet tore into the platform. Gritting her teeth with mad fury, she scrambled onto her belly to get around the trunk, into cover, then up to her knees. She ran in a crouch, lifting her gun. More shots followed, from different directions. She circled the huge tree trunk, coming around the other side with her rifle up, eye at the scope. The shooting had stopped but she saw a telltale sway of a distant branch. No one there. Had he repositioned?

Rapid movement drew her eye down and at ground level she saw a group dressed in mucky Drail green scampering out between the trees. Goblins with chunky rifles, chattering and laughing. She followed their trajectory to a body in the mud: Emi, flat on her face. She didn't look broken or bloody, but she wasn't moving. That fall would've popped a normal person, but surely the mage had softened it somehow. Surely she was alive.

The goblins were scurrying towards her.

Wish picked out the lead one, head in her sights, and snarled as she pulled the trigger.

Her finger slipped off, without firing, as a hand clamped over her mouth and pulled her back. She tried to shout into a gloved palm and bucked about as an arm wrapped under her chest, holding tight. Dragged back behind the tree, she couldn't find space to elbow or headbutt, so she kicked. The goblins below screeched and laughed as they descended on Emi – *defenceless* Emi. The mage made a noise, a movement – she was alive! But the goblins were swamping her, she couldn't fight. Wish tried to scream, but her assailant held her tight.

A voice whispered urgently in her ear, "Quiet, keep quiet."

It was husky, low, but unmistakably a woman, and that surprise cut through Wish's panic. She tried to twist around as the goblins cackled. There was a terrible thump. Emi was still. No way she was fighting, or half the woodland would be coming down. Wish threw back all her weight, sending her and the woman holding her onto the boards. The woman's grip didn't loosen, only got tighter, and two strong legs wound forward, entwining Wish's. She found herself completely pinned, unable to move, and the woman hissed, "There's a hundred of them down there. Keep. Fucking. Quiet."

The threat stilled Wish again and she heard more movement. The patter of feet clomping carelessly through the leaves. Many, many feet, getting closer, passing under them. Mad, fiendish cackles surrounded Emi. Wish felt the woman's grip shift. The hand under her chest rubbed her, a comforting gesture. Tears ran from her eyes as she tried to speak, to reason with this woman. She couldn't abandon Emi. Not Emi. The toughest of them all. The hand muffled her attempt to say so.

"She's gone," the woman whispered. "But you're alive. Let's keep you alive. Are you calm? Going to be quiet?"

Wish stiffened. If the woman released her, she could jump up and shoot them all. She could kill a hundred goblins; she'd killed more men in the past. They *couldn't have Emi*.

"No," the woman decided, and her grip tightened again. Wish twitched, testing the woman's limbs, absolutely no give. They lay there together, Wish on top of her, feeling her heat and the rise of her chest as the woman breathed in her ear. The goblins swarmed on for a painfully long time, pattering underneath with a rising gabble of noise, before finally thinning out. As the urgency and adrenaline faded from Wish, replaced by despair, she shuddered against the woman, and again the woman's hand stroked her in comfort. The fingers pressed into Wish's cheek squeezed reassuringly, and she became stiffly aware of how this person was pressed into her. Her unclean, sweaty smell. A feeling stirred deep in Wish, unwelcome and obscene, as she recognised this woman's hip was pressed tight against her arse, their legs entangled.

"It's okay," the woman whispered, softly. "They're gone, mostly. But it'll only take one to bring the lot of them back. Please. You *have* to be quiet. For me."

Wish's mind fractured, part of her wanting to smash back and fight, to demand who the *hell* this woman was and why she should do anything for her when she had just left her friend to the worst kind of death. Another part wanted to obey, though. Didn't want to upset this woman who, wrapped so tightly about her, might have just saved her life.

"You're Blood Scouts, aren't you?" the woman said. "You came for me?"

Wish was motionless. The clamber of goblins had gone – Emi was gone – and all she had left was this confusing embrace. Seeming to sense her defeat, the woman finally released her hand and Wish took in a breath to fill her lungs. She didn't move or shout, but asked quietly, "Who are you?"

"Havikare Eens," the woman replied. "Havik. I'm going to let you up. Can you keep calm?"

"I am calm."

"Can you *keep* calm?"

Wish swallowed. Could she? If there was only the slightest chance she could get Emi back . . . But she caught herself. Stop. She had to stop. She said, quietly, "I can keep calm."

"Okay."

The woman's legs relaxed, and unwrapped from her own, and the arm slid off her chest. Wish dived forward, grabbed her rifle off the boards and spun back ready to fire.

24

Do not speak to me of coincidence. We live in a world where witlacers can bridge flesh and mind, and the mindless can spread their will through the earth, and you expect me to believe that great people and events collide by mere chance – that there is not some deeper pattern that pulls us all together? No, my friend, you are the one who is naive!

Exhuming Murro: a Tragedy in
Four Acts, Qalter, p. 43

It was her smile that stopped Wish. Genuine and *pleasant,* it showed off white teeth, reached her eyes, and seemed totally inappropriate. Havik remained down in a crouch opposite Wish's own squat, her hands, in worn fingerless gloves, raised and empty.

"Easy," she said. "Easy."

She had a mess of black hair longer at the back, falling crookedly over her eyes, and a rounded, smooth face with a squared jaw and button nose. Her grimy white top stuck sweatily over a full chest, and her long, draping coat, patched in places, was complimented by thick belts of massive bullets.

Wish held on tight to her rifle, needing to do something but not sure what. If this had been a man, some random soldier, she could've shot him and charged on. But this was a woman who'd held her close and whispered in her ear and looked like . . . that. She glanced over the edge of the platform to the fall. No one below, now, only mud and leaves. No sign of Emi.

"Where are the rest of you?" the woman asked, and Wish frowned.

"Where are the rest of *you?*" she threw back.

The boards creaked to her left as a man said, "One right here."

"Stop, whoa, hold up!" Havik cried, raising her hands higher, directing one towards the man as Wish flicked her rifle to him. He was a beast, thick with muscle and lined with tattoos, scarred face partly hidden by a beard, mean eyes narrow. He had a stubby gun with a cartridge sticking out the side. "She's a friend. We're friends." Havik addressed this at Wish. "We're on the same side."

"You're the Irregulars?" Wish checked, and Havik smiled again, nodding.

The man said something gruffly in Drail. Then, guessing she didn't understand, he repeated it in clipped Stanish: "Lower the gun."

"You first."

"It's fine, Raltman," Havik said. "That's enough."

The thug, Raltman, hesitated, keeping his eyes on Wish, but he did lower his weapon, and raised one hand to show peace. Wish kept her rifle raised.

"You can trust us," Havik told her. "I know things got ugly, but –"

"You let goblins loose on my friend," Wish snarled. "Fucking goblins."

"They did not kill her," Raltman said. "The fall did not, too."

Wish felt her chest expand, released from a great pressure. "You saw? She's alive?"

"Maybe. She was breathing."

"Oh thank Bly." Wish lowered her gun with relief. Emi, dammit, she was alive. But captured. She looked up again sharply. "Where are they taking her? I need to stop them."

"Not on your own," Havik warned. The woman didn't seem to blink, Wish realised, taking her in, and it gave her a slight tingle. She'd found the Irregulars. A woman. She'd been pressed hard against her.

"My platoon are already heading to Midpeak," Wish said. "Where are yours?"

"Making a run north," Havik said. "What's in Midpeak?"

"We hoped you might be. Or that they'd know something."

"It was our intention. And if you'd like some company up that mountain now . . ."

"I'm not leaving Emi behind. I'll bring her back alone if I have to."

The thug scoffed a laugh, but Havik gave him a scolding look. "Fuck off, Raltman. Round up the others." He scowled at her, but she clicked her tongue and he moved away, down the platform's steps. Havik showed Wish her smile again. "We won't catch up to our full company now and you won't catch up to yours – and we can't go after those goblins without an army. If we take shelter at the priory, we can form a plan from there. Your friend's a mage, though, right? She'll be okay."

Wish frowned. "How did you know?"

"Normal people don't survive falls like that. The goblins won't hurt her, not too much; they're superstitious. If she doesn't do anything stupid, they'll keep her safe for now. Probably take her to their commander."

"Where's he?" Wish asked, not hugely reassured with the requirement of Emi restraining herself.

"Carlwen. The town across the river. Behind a few thousand troops. Your platoon – are you the captain of the Blood Scouts?"

Wish nodded, not bothering to correct the rank. "Are you the one who sent for us?"

Havik's smile broadened. "I can't believe you came. I'm honoured."

There was something terribly disarming about her, the warmth of that smile. Wish was straining to keep tense and move after Emi regardless her warnings, but felt a pull from her. She said, "Who are you? How do you know about us?"

"I'm no one. Just a partisan. But I've been following your activities, what I could learn from the rumours. It's inspiring. It's true that you swung the Battle of Green Rise?"

"You know about *that?*" Wish felt her cheeks flush, that brutal morning hardly something she wanted to remember, nor to be remembered for. She saw men popping into mist under the hammering of machine-gun fire. Loose falling. Emi falling now, her own scream added to the noise. *No.* Wish closed her eyes and took a deep breath, but opened them again at the sound of Havik moving closer. The other woman still had her hands up, eyes keen and friendly.

"Hey," she said, reaching slowly towards Wish. "Hey. You're alright."

Wish flinched as Havik touched her shoulder, squeezed it. Her hand stayed there.

"You're good. You're so much younger than I expected."

"I'm . . ." Wish started, but the response she used to sound tough in front of the Rock Stable students didn't come. She swallowed and said, "I don't need an army. I can get to Emi –"

"Listen." Havik came closer, so their knees touched. Wish's heart leapt. "There's a sniper out there. Even if you *could* get around the goblins, we can't stay."

"A sniper," Wish echoed. "He shot Emi?"

"Yeah. We have one too, but the best we've managed so far is to keep him moving. For now. Do you have a way out of here?"

Wish held her gaze, then looked aside. "Emi . . ." Havik squeezed her shoulder again, drawing her gaze back. There was deep sympathy in her eyes.

"If you want to save her, we've got to save ourselves first. Okay?"

Finally, Wish let her shoulders slump. There was no hope in charging after a whole army. She was an idiot, shouldn't have come here at all, definitely not alone – as her men had said. But this woman was here with her, with soldiers of her own. Touching her shoulder. Wish nodded and stood. "That way. There's a bridge to the mountainside."

"Great." Havik twisted to scoop up a cap from the boards, which she shook out and put on, then she grabbed a gun Wish hadn't noticed before. It was as long as her 0.48 rifle but not like anything she recognised, with a blocky barrel comprising three wide tubes and a thick, carved wooden handle. There were words etched along the barrels, in ornate writing that she couldn't read, darkened by dirt. Wish noted the bullet belts again – the sheer size of the ammunition.

Havik paused, realising she was staring, but indicated they move on. Wild Wish took the lead, creeping across the platform and scanning the return route. She considered the first bridge warily, its height all the more daunting after Emi's fall.

"We've been crawling across some," Havik said. "Four points of contact, more stable."

Wish shook her head. Damned if she was going to spend longer here than necessary. She fixed her eyes ahead and raced over the bridge. She reached the far platform and took a few extra steps to slow, then stopped, breathing deeply. When she looked back, Havik was strolling across the perilous bridge, big gun propped against her shoulder, with a delighted expression, amused by Wish's dash? She felt her cheeks warming again and moved on.

Descending the next steps, Wish startled on seeing a group of men waiting, staggered around the platform and the nearest two trees, headed by Raltman. They were each about as ugly and menacing as him, with various shades of tattoos and cheap firearms. They watched Wish warily but kept quiet. Havik stayed close, armouring her against them, and Wish continued. She'd figure all this out once they were clear of these damn woods.

A couple more bridge dashes, a few more stairs, and Wish was relieved to see the cliff with its bridge ahead. The allure of open daylight fell on the far plateau. She ran across the last bridge, giving a relieved whoop as she reached the hard ground on the other side, then turned back hoping for another smile from Havik. Instead, she saw the gang of men with hard expressions. For whatever reason, they looked unimpressed by her enthusiasm.

Havik walked after Wish and they waited as the men mustered the courage to follow. None came as quickly as Wish, though one tried, dashing with a defiant shout that died about two thirds across, before he hesitantly staggered the rest of the way. Raltman came last, down on his knees, shakily snarling at the view below. Had they crossed all the bridges this way? Wish hadn't been paying attention. When Raltman reached them, everyone safe, his scowl said that if anyone said a word about it, they'd face his wrath.

Wish took in the mountain above, the cliffs climbing towards a cloudy peak not visible from this angle. They'd have to follow the trail back and find her scouts' footsteps to guide the rest of the way. How quickly could they catch up, mount a rescue for Emi? What could they actually do? Dreading a hopeless answer, Wish focused on keeping moving and said, "We're heading up. A long way. When you're all ready."

She eyed the group, the men recovering their breath from the tree ordeal, and as she did the sound of boots on the bridge drew her attention to a final soldier joining them, a tall guy with a sharp jaw and one narrow, accusing eye, steeped in shadow that could've been tiredness or filth. The other eye was hidden behind a ragged patch. He came off the bridge looking down at the height with general disdain, and strode straight past the men towards Havik, no words of greeting. He said something negative in Garter. Havik dismissed him with a wordless smile, then they both looked to Wish.

From the way everyone else quietly stared, the newcomer was plainly important, so she asked, "Are you Kasidee?"

The man sneered and turned back to Havik, not deigning to reply, which stirred new concern in Wish. So far, Havik aside, the Irregulars weren't the friendliest or most trustworthy-looking bunch.

"This is Lost One," Havik said brightly. "He's our marksman. But our Drail friend slipped away. Again." Behind her cheery tone, her eyes betrayed irritation, and the sniper, Lost One, sulked back with an unpleasant look of his own. Wish noticed his rifle slung over one shoulder, possibly the longest one she'd ever seen, its barrel dark metal with an unpolished wood frame and a narrow scope that ran half the length of the gun.

"What is that?" Wish asked. "How strong is the scope?"

The marksmen followed her gaze and frowned, not especially wanting to answer. He replied in heavily accented Stanish, "Coaerm 0.44 Automatic. I can shoot a pigeon at half a mile." His tone told her he considered that enough to prevent further questions. Never mind why he would *want* to shoot a pigeon from so far away. Or at all. She was especially unsure about this Irregular now. These men were as rough and ready as any she'd met, dressed in their hodgepodge of tatty canvas and leathers, like a collection of escaped convicts.

"I prefer to get close," Havik said, more amiably, shifting up next to Wish almost as proof. "Most of us do, in fact. We operate best from the shadows. *This*" – she held up her hefty gun, with an *I-saw-you-staring* smile – "is a four-gauge Camanese Stop Gun. The Coaerm Wildchild – at least that's what it translates to. *Deknonypa* in Camanese. It barely needs to be aimed."

Wish's heart lifted – in contrast to the surly sniper, was this a sign? She said, "That's me."

Havik raised her brow. "I'd imagine you're the opposite, with that rifle."

"I mean the name," Wish explained. "I'm Wild Wish. That is – I mean – it's what I go by." Very smooth.

"Ah." Havik looked amused again.

Now they were out of immediate danger, Wish felt her awkwardness rising, and the company of these unruly men wasn't helping. Stupid. She couldn't slip into old ineffectiveness here. Emi needed her. She cleared her throat and turned her back on them. "Right. Anyway. We're heading up. A long way. Anyone can't keep up . . . that's your problem."

Then she sped off, to set a pace that would put her ahead of their questioning looks and the memory of the wretched forest. Ahead of Havik and her distracting smile, and the possibility of blushes that would give the thugs any reason to think she was weak.

Midpeak couldn't come quickly enough.

25

The demographics of the front line hinterlands underwent irrevocable shifts during these years, with troop movements and communities displaced by the conflict. Criminals and the mentally unstable were released into military ranks or escaped when their jails and jailers became caught up in the war. An entire Garter village was discovered to be populated by escaped convicts and a Mattin valley was condemned by the Arbitration due to the influence of the travelling witlacer, Dwerdin, one of many corrupt militia leaders who emerged in the confusion.

Empires of the Rocc, Xanthial, p. 672

Kasidee looked out from the rocks with a handful of his veterans, a plain of uneven grassland separating the tree line from the River Carlus, which in turn separated them from a company of hundreds of uniformed riflemen and a scattering of artillery units. The distance was negligible for those weapons: if the Irregulars were spotted, they'd be slaughtered. There was no retreating into the woods, though, with the din of gunfire they'd heard pressing in from the east, goblins clashing more ferociously with the Woodwings than he had. The Drail here were over-cautious though: by not crossing the river, they wouldn't have great visibility of a narrow route of big rocks and occasional trees along the base of the cliffs. Not quite enough to hide the Irregulars outright, but with a little help . . .

"The moment they're distracted," Kasidee said, "I want every man moving faster than he's ever moved before. Stay out of sight, get clear of the woods Hug the rocks, move so we can be sure they won't see us. Then north, past their flank. We're avoiding them, understand? Do *not* engage."

There was a murmur of agreement and a couple men hurried back to relay the orders. The Irregulars were well-practised in being discreet when they needed to be, even dragging some six or eight wagons of supplies and the F-Apparat. The trudge horses would be the hardest thing to hide. Kasidee had ordered them dismounted to pull loads or be walked, but he needed to make sure no one was looking, at least for long enough to give them a head start. There was only a section of Drail out there, after all, not Atmoor's whole force: if they could establish a better position, the Irregulars could turn them away.

"What about Havikare?" a sergeant asked: Colen, a man crooked in appearance and manner, with one eye bigger than the other. "Ain't we waiting for her?" It was said with concern, and notable that he mentioned her and not the others, though Raltman and Lost One were absent too. Colen was big with long, thick arms and an eagle tattoo up his neck, and even if Kasidee hadn't made an effort to learn names, he would've recalled this man as belonging to the criminals they'd picked up in their chaotic crossing of the Vantac Split. One of countless hard men who had been drawn in by Kasidee's promise of freedom and adventure, and quickly developed protective loyalty over Havikare. It was partly that she was a woman, and the defence of her honour (ha!) appealed to many of the Irregulars – but mostly they loved how she told stories. She had a gift for it, beguiling any who would listen with tales of ancient legends, epic adventures from centuries past, and wonders of the wider world. She spoke of all this folding in Kasidee's tales, too: how they defended Fort Simnon, or his duel with a Dread Corps squad in Castle Grand. Events she wasn't there for but knew just how to frame.

Kasidee wanted her with them now, too, but he couldn't show doubt. He knew better than to question her ideas or try to steer her. And he fully believed it when he said, "She'll catch us up. She's got her own tasks to complete, and we've got the harder part of it."

Colen grunted unhappily. "I can take five men back, make sure she's okay."

"She already *has* an escort. No. Get your men ready, we're about to do the impossible. Any of those Drail bastards survive the war, they'll be telling their grandkids how we moved like ghosts around them."

Colen was about to say something else, as the other men moved off, but a bang came from the horizon. Kasidee looked to the enemy line, jaw setting as another bang followed and two balls of black smoke and broken dirt erupted behind the Drail soldiers. Then gunshots, puffs of smoke. It was too soon, but he couldn't fault his volunteers for their enthusiasm: five of their scouts had headed out with no fuss, and he doubted they'd be coming back. The sight of the enemy panicking was warming. A neat answer to their rude awakening that morning. The Drail line broke immediately, men scattering in all directions but circling towards the attack – reversing their position. A man on horseback sped down the flank, waving a hand about as he shouted orders – far away as he was, Kasidee could see the officer was incompetent from his body language alone. The men weren't paying much attention to him in their confusion.

"Should we move?" Colen asked.

"Wait." Kasidee watched as the Drail ranks split and the horseman tried to reform them. He was directing them away from the river, sending crowds running towards the drifting smoke. Another explosion erupted further back, and their pace increased, more shots were fired. Kasidee held out, making sure the soldiers were turned away. "Go. *Quietly.*"

The sergeant dashed back to pass the order along. Kasidee watched the Drail commander slowly regaining control, speeding up his men's retreat. If they'd been a little closer themselves, able to easily cross the river here, the Irregulars could've routed these fools without having to hide. But they'd have their chance later.

Rough as the last two days had been, Kasidee felt his luck was turning again. It always did. His mother used to joke that he was Saints Blessed for his ability to pluck success from failure, and here again was proof as his company marched towards what must've once been a monastery. One of the forgotten churches, left to ruin, most likely because it sat in untamed swampland where the ground was increasingly liquid and everything smelt vaguely rotten. It was perfect for a couple hundred vagabond soldiers needing shelter.

Kasidee rode at the head of the Irregulars, mounted again, with a handful of gruff sergeants on the trudge horses they could spare. The horses made light work of terrain that was sucking at the men's boots, and were dragging the wagons sloppily over roads too muddy to let the wheels turn. Havik would've had something to say about the ruins, dramatically towering with broken arches and pillars, but without her the men rode in silence, ignorant of its history. They found a lengthy cloister building with three remaining walls and part of a roof, and the fragments of a tall cathedral, one wall showing a carved Blade of Cane. Crudely fashioned, incredibly old. The Irregulars filtered out through the ruins, setting up fires and tents, carefully hidden behind walls with an eye to the east. They had men spread through the swamp keeping watch further out, but it paid to be cautious.

Kasidee settled down for a mug of warm broth, trying to decide whether to credit their own stealth or the enemy's ineptitude for the success of their escape from Midwood. It was definitely one for the records, and he called out for it to be submitted to the ledgers. The glorious flight of the Irregulars, right under an army's noses. Then, from the sounds of the racket in the woods, the bulk of Colonel Atmoor's men had been coming up behind them anyway. The details didn't entirely matter now.

Sitting on a broken stone wall, with Colen and a few others similarly enjoying their broths in quiet thought (well, quiet at least, he wasn't sure how much these men thought), he considered the next steps. The path to Gauntstone would be wide open, considering the Drail were overstretched back towards Carlwen. But absent of Havik and her insistence on the importance of the priories, he allowed himself thoughts of the border. He could march to Onwail itself and lay siege to the empire. Invade and secure actual enemy territory. It was fanciful thinking. Scrappy, directionless fighting that would end in retreat or calamity. No, they'd keep up this dance, with increasing confidence considering the weak hand Colonel Atmoor had shown so far. From Gauntstone, they could circle back towards Midpeak. Never mind penetrating the Drail empire, he'd be the man who secured the Mire, and with the unlikeliest of troops.

Kasidee took in his disparate force of thuggish soldiers, men who'd be turned away from decent jobs – refused entry to public buildings, even – because of their appearances. They looked tired but healthy. A solid number with a good stash of supplies, their standard resting tall and intact (if grubby) against a wall, next to the F-Apparet pridefully wiped down and on show like a totem. He asked Colen, "Do we know how many men we lost?"

The man looked up, surprised from his broth, and swallowed.

"It is Colen, isn't it? We picked you up in Enderwen," Kasidee added.

"That's right, sir, thank you, sir." Colen frowned, thinking, then answered the original question, "Last count, think it was near twenty-four yesterday, along with the fifteen or so at the lake." And they'd only lost one wagon to the mud, most of its supplies easily redistributed. Over two hundred bodies still here. Kasidee could do great things with those numbers. But Colen went on, "Then there's the lads still out there from the bombing. And Havik. Me and some of the lads . . ."

Kasidee could imagine the rest. They weren't any happier than him that she'd branched out alone. But at least he was confident that on this occasion they'd had the brunt of the action. He sighed. "We'll find her if we need to. But not yet. Trust me, I didn't enjoy running either, but look where it's taken us. The Drail are spinning in circles, probably lost half their men in those woods." He pointed sharply at Colen. "In no small part, I'll have you know, thanks to me suggesting Havik talk those savages around."

"She talked to them?" Colen said. "That was her – she got them flying freaks on side?"

Kasidee smiled and flat-out lied. "Absolutely, I know she did. I only wish I'd sent her to do it sooner." He paused, hearing his own words. They'd been stalking through these lands for weeks now, popping in and out of sight, and he himself had left the company numerous times on small-scale sorties. But it was reaching a head, and Havik was distracted at best, so it was time to remove any hesitation. It would be smoother from here. He put down his mug, took in a breath and stood up. He raised his voice. "Listen up, all of you. We touched greatness, today, I want you all to realise that. Comparable to when we pushed back the Drail at Fever Forest or blew the factory at Great Barne. Not all of you were here for those, so I'm glad you were with me today. By the time we're done here, even Fort Simnon will look like child's play."

The crowded company quietened, shifting to give their full attention. He hopped onto the broken wall, putting himself on display, and turned to take in as many men as he could. What a force they were, not just ordinary people but the worst of the forgotten and downtrodden, in ill-fitting clothes, few able to read, yet tough, heroic. Legends, under him. They couldn't be further from his old banking office, pushing numbers and enduring stuffy meetings about *nothing* of consequence. Here he was a true leader, ready to brave the world and inspire people who'd been meant for the gutter.

"Listen up!" he repeated, much louder. "I know some of you are worried about Havik and the others! I know you're fed up with being on the back-foot, biding our time! And if you're not still hurting from the cowards' attack at Black Lake you're hurting from the cowards in the Midwood. Well, we've run our circuit round the Drail and I'd say we're about ready to strike back, wouldn't you?"

A cheer went through the crowd. Colen got to his feet alongside Kasidee, watching carefully. Kasidee focused properly on him to continue.

"Trust that Havik's taking care of what I asked her to. The Drail will be on our trail again soon – but we're not far off securing Gauntstone. I don't know about the rest of you, but it feels to me like time for another fight. What do you say?"

That brought an even heartier cheer, fists and mugs swinging over heads. Colen nodded, appreciatively, and Kasidee smiled. He raised his hands.

"Soon, we fight! Where's the ledger already, Brocken? We've successes to record and a plan to map out! The Irregulars march on! Saints save the brave, and you've seen nothing" – he pointed sharply up – "nothing, I promise you all, compared to what's still to come!"

Colen joined in the shouting, his fists clenched and veins popping up over his neck, down his arms. It looked as angry as it was celebratory. Kasidee watched the company work itself into a frenzy, bumping chests and banging pans, brandishing guns overhead. Swearing, lots of them just swearing. Anyone for miles around would hear them, most likely, but it'd be mad to come closer. Kasidee marvelled at the passion he could instil, the power of these people, and how much more potential they had yet. Yes, they were meant for better things than sneak attacks, better things than a raid across the enemy border. Not for the first time, he silently thanked Havik for falling into his lap and bringing him the promise of the Mire.

In these dark lands and against a force ten times his size, they would find *glory*. How could he not believe? The world would remember Kin Kasidee.

26

Our next generation of rifles were supposed to make everything easier. Better guns so you can kill people from further away with less effort. So I find myself questioning, once again, how in hell I end up still walking hundreds of miles and hiking up mountains and through bogs and all while carrying hundred-pound sacks of crap? At what point in the advancement of these bloody weapons do we get to rest our damn legs?

**Extract from the Letters of
Major K. Tyne (Unedited), Elmn, 720**

After about an hour of hard clambering, Wild Wish realised they were not going to reach Midpeak priory soon. In the shadow of increasingly severe rock faces, it wasn't possible to see the building itself, and as they hiked on, and on, Wish wondered if they were even going in the right direction. No one was complaining, though, somehow trusting she knew what she was doing, and she had other things to worry about, like *had she killed bloody Emi,* so just kept moving.

Eventually, someone called out from further back that they saw a quicker way. If they were willing to climb, Havik translated from the sniper Lost One, it seemed they could cut off a good portion of the road. Assuming the climb took them back to the same road. Wish was happy for someone else to take responsibility but the climb, up thirty feet of near-vertical rocky outcrops, wasn't an easy prospect. The toughest bit was at the start, where the tallest rocks offered little to hold onto.

Havik moved past her and threaded her fingers together, saying, "I'll give you a boost."

Wish stared at her cupped hands. "My boots are dirty."

"So am I," Havik replied a little too readily and Wish almost blanched. Where she'd normally assume she'd misheard, or taken it the wrong way, there was something naughty in Havik's eye. Wish swallowed and nodded, best to ignore it. She steadied her rifle, planted her foot and launched herself up by shoving on Havik's shoulders. The shorter woman hoisted her with a good boost of strength and Wish overshot the top of the rock, grazing her elbows and rolling up with minimal grace. She twisted back to offer a hand but found Raltman already taking Havik's place, hands ready to give her a boost. Wish moved out of the way and checked the rest of the climb. An easier mess of footholds and platforms from here. She continued up, scraping her hands and knees to move quicker, to seem able.

Wish reached the summit with a lot of huffing and a few slips, and crawled onto another stretch of gritty road. It was flat and well-trodden, but narrower than the one they'd left below. It kept rising, curving around another bend, so she figured they were okay to continue. She turned in time to see Havik following, and crouched to lend her a hand, pulling her to her feet. Havik pushed a shoulder into her side to steady herself and winked.

What was *that?*

Wish hurriedly stepped away, muttering, "Saved some time, I guess." She began walking, aware that Havik wasn't following, but was staring at her.

"Do you want some water?"

Wish turned to find she had a water skin out, cap off, and was sipping from it herself. She held it towards Wish and it seemed rude to say no. Wish took a sip, lips touching where hers had. Havik plainly watched. This felt wrong. There was something going on here and Wish didn't like it. Or, she did like it, but didn't like *that,* with Emi maybe dead and them possibly lost and a bunch of unpleasant guys having replaced her actual platoon. The attention of a woman and the niggling excitement was too much right now. She hadn't been touched so closely, even considered someone else's touch since –

"Newk," Wish whispered, earning a frown from Havik.

Any elaboration was cut off by Lost One reaching the road and glaring accusingly at the pair of them, followed quickly by another of the men. As they dusted themselves off, Wish backed up, mind tripping over itself. Newk felt like a lifetime ago, in another world. A great, powerful woman who'd *kissed* her. And comforted her. Last seen with her head split open. But had Newk ever looked at her the way Havik was? There was a question that had haunted Wish for months – was Newk just trying to make things easier for both of them? Playing a game. Wish shook the thought off.

No. Newk was amazing. She would get her back.

Havik was a stranger. Possibly playing a different game, just teasing.

Wish waited for the soldiers to gather themselves, with more water shared around and grumbles at the exertion, then she quietly suggested they move on, and walked ahead. This time, Havik strode up alongside her, saying, "If my estimate's right, we shouldn't be far off the Slide."

Wish frowned, hearing the capital in that name. "What's the Slide?"

"An incline to Midpeak on the southern side. Another climb that'll save us some road."

"How do you know that? Have you been here before?"

"No, I've read a lot. I studied maps, too. I've been fascinated by the Mire for a long time. It's got a magic all of its own. Did you know in Fendarin's time, when the Prophet Sandway was denounced by the Empire of Three Moons and marked for execution, it's said giants stood shoulder to shoulder blocking the Penitent Pass and the imperial troops turned back without a fight? They were frightened as much by the idea of these giants being organised, in defence of a man, as by the danger itself."

Wish didn't entirely follow the anecdote as her mind settled on the phrase *a magic of its own,* recalling Emi's concerns. Before the mage had been shot. She blurted out a question that she should've asked much earlier "What are you actually doing here?"

Havik regarded her gently for a moment and answered as if it was obvious. "Fighting for the Mire. To defend that magic.

Someone had to."

"But why? I mean how – how did this start? What made the Drail invade?"

"It was only a matter of time before one side or another came in here."

"Alright, then why not report it to Command, get help?"

"We've never operated that way. We're doing our bit where we see ourselves fitting best. You more than anyone must appreciate a small, unregulated troop can be more effective than mobilising an entire army. And there's nowhere more important we could be."

Wish eyed her sideways. "Are you religious?"

"No." Havik smiled. "My interest here is academic. I'm a scholar. Or was. Kind of." Her brow knitted, then she admitted, "I was a librarian. An assistant librarian, actually. I love books. History, culture, religion. These things all collide out here. I kind of . . . I have a big imagination, I suppose. In everything I read, the Mire seemed like somewhere that big, special things happened." Her face folded with thought, a little unsure, or shy, and Wish felt a fresh pang of sympathy. This woman had dreams like her? But Havik continued, "When I watched my library burn, with all those books gone, I knew nowhere was safe. And if I could protect anywhere, I wanted to protect the Mire."

Wish slowed down, not sure what to say. "They attacked your home?"

"Yes. We lost everything. Everyone in this company has. We're all strays, collected between Garter and Elmn, or further afield."

Wish thought of her own home, in Swelig, a perfect idyll to return to. It would never be touched by this distant, devastating war. For all the death and destruction she'd seen, it was always, at least, separated from her home. She said, "I'm sorry. I'm fighting to get back my village. A farm, actually."

"You have a farm?" Havik sounded impressed.

"Um. I will. It's something I . . . imagine for myself," Wish replied, borrowing on Havik's honesty about her bookish background. She resisted the instinct to say she could come. Too soon. "So do you all love the Saints Mire this much?"

Havik laughed and it was wonderfully hearty. It made Wish smile, even if she'd said something daft to cause it. The woman shook her head. "No. The Irregulars were fighting long before they found me. But Kin Kasidee appreciates a noble cause – when I told him what I knew of the Mire, he couldn't come quickly enough. They all understood."

"But the Drail have an actual army here, don't they? How do you expect to stop them?"

"A little bit at a time." Havik shrugged. "We've been branching out through the region, testing the waters. There are secret paths and traps that can help us fight, with the right understanding. We've visited some of the priories already, and our next goal was Midpeak. I hoped to meet the Archvenerator Turbulence the Sixth and discuss their defences."

"Turbulence the Sick?"

"*Sixth,*" Havik corrected, again showing her sly smile. "Not like the famous Sick Brigade."

Wish smiled back at the reference to her old station, a little sadly. It'd been a while since she'd thought of her platoon's place in the army, she realised. Marching to support General Easter's expansive campaign. "Yeah. It's . . . strange to meet someone who knows about us."

"I prefer *special,*" Havik said. "I know we can work together. I look forward to it. Between the Irregulars and the Blood Scouts, we'll reveal the Mire's potential, I swear."

Wish raised an eyebrow at that wording. *Potential.* Havik nudged her with an elbow, sending her slightly out of step. Crazy familiar, playful, for a soldier.

"I can't wait to meet your girls," Havik went on. "How many people have you got?"

"Oh. About that. We're not . . . Firstly, this is a reconnaissance mission. No one knew what you were doing out here. What kind of response was appropriate. There was just –" Wish stopped, going back through some of what Havik had said. How hopefully she'd first addressed her, knowing they were Blood Scouts. Sister Sonseen's account of the strange soldier woman who'd sent a message. "That note. Was it you?"

Havik gave her another endearingly shy look, head tilted forward. She nodded. "I am so honoured that you came."

Wish was smiling again. "I only hope I don't disappoint. But if you think the Mire is so important, why did you ask for us and not, like, a full brigade?"

"We're alike, aren't we?" Havik replied. "We have the right tools here to do this on our own, but if I could have *anyone* help us to pull this off, I wanted you and your girls."

Wish felt a weird tingle, this all getting stranger. Or, as Havik said, perhaps more special? She privately entertained the idea that this wasn't just a chance encounter; this woman was maybe interested in her specifically – Havik had known who she was. And if that was the case, and she had high hopes, Wish needed to be straight. She said, "Okay, I appreciate your confidence. But we're not here to fight, exactly. And there aren't . . . I mean, I don't have so many girls. Not at the moment. It's men, mostly. And not many of them. A few ogres."

"Ogres?" Havik whistled loudly. "Wild Wish, you are everything I hoped you would be."

Wish glanced sideways again, again flushing, not sure how to take that and not trusting her own thrill at the words. That her body was excited made her mind uneasy. You didn't just meet excitable, interested women in the woods who saved your life and smiled at you like you meant something. Not during a war and especially not in a place called the Mire, where people were getting chopped in half by giant crabs and maybe drinking blood and getting shot out of trees.

"Wait till you meet Kasidee," Havik said. "Never mind our numbers, we're going to do great things."

Wish let that lie, trying to tell herself it was okay. Havik had every right to be optimistic, and she was only worried because things were always typically bad. They'd join forces with Kasidee, after dealing with the whole Emi problem. And after visiting this elusive mountain priory. Parking the more distant problems, Wish said, "Did you call this archvenerator *Turbulence?*"

"Yeah," Havik said. "Have you met these people? They're dramatic."

Wish thought back to Estekof and the Veneration. All that shouting and the bone cages. She sighed deeply. What a place.

"There it is." Havik pointed as the road bent. The mountain opened up ahead, a small dip before a great imposing rise of rocky crags that climbed into the sky. Towards the top, where the rocks became grassy, it slanted steeply up towards the base of a wall, which faded into a mist of white cloud. "The Slide. We get up that and you'll hit the priory. Or we follow the road around through another few miles of switchbacks."

Wish stared, the climb appearing formidable but not quite sheer. "Okay."

They continued and the rocks seemed to grow, though, glaring impassably down.

"What about you?" Havik asked as they walked. "Are you a believer?"

"Me?" Wish replied distractedly, unable to keep from looking up. Why was it so *high?* "No. I'm from Stanclif."

"There are still religions in Stanclif, aren't there?"

"Not many." Wish knew precious few religious people. The Tookers and Fixit. One a family of misfits, the other dead. "And they're mostly Vens. I'm not sure I've ever met someone who actually believes in the Cane Saints." The memory of last night came back. Those mad shouting villagers and the venerator.

"You didn't come here with an interest in the Mire at all, then?"

Wish almost laughed, but caught herself, because she realised Havik was serious. "No. Sorry, all I really knew was this place is worth avoiding. That's proved true enough."

"Oh it's mad, but it's exciting, isn't it?" Havik replied, giving Wish a moment of pause. *Exciting* was not the best word for this damp and deadly place. It was hard to deny the bright look on Havik's face, though.

With the cliff close enough now to form a distraction, Wish jogged ahead and scanned the rocks, big where the road cut through, rising maybe fifteen feet up. She put her back against one and laced her fingers, saying, "I'll boost you."

Havik paused, regarding Wish curiously for long enough that the brutish Irregulars started to catch up, similarly staring as though unsure what she was doing. Havik said, "I don't think that'll do it."

Wish looked up, the edge above clearly out of reach. Raltman paced to one side, indicating the rocks with a grunt, and she saw the cliff broke to a more manageable incline about twenty feet further on, a place they could scramble up without a boost. Wish watched the men going towards it, one of them shaking his head at her, leaving Havik behind to smirk at her still-knitted fingers. The woman moved closer and quietly said, "Another time," then went after her men. Wish dropped her hands, fresh mortification setting in. Did they think she'd just been eager to have Havik step on her? Had she been?

She couldn't dwell on it, with the troop getting away, and she found herself hurrying to the back as they hefted themselves up. Havik was just ahead of her now. There were easy hand and footholds to climb, a good foot or more of space at each step, but it was steep, little better than using a ladder, forcing Wish's focus onto the ground just ahead of her. Not the backs of Havik's legs. Definitely not her behind (hidden by the chunky folds of her big coat).

By the time they reached the top, most of the men were out of breath, and Wish had a good fiery ache going in her arms and legs. But as they crawled out over the rocks onto the grass, she saw it wasn't over: the next stretch rose almost as steeply, with grass instead of clear steps or supporting rocks, so they had to ascend in a crouch, hands low. The scramble spun Wish's head more than the simpler rock climbing or even crossing the tall tree bridges, for the unsettling feeling that it'd be deceptively easy to slip here, with a sure slide over the cliff. To fall as Emi had. As Loose had, thrust off Green Rise . . . *No.*

"Almost there," Havik promised, her voice an anchor, and Wish grimaced thankfully, though the woman wasn't looking back. She'd just sensed her concern. Definitely some strange connection going on here.

Then, the men began disappearing up ahead as they dived over the slope's summit, and Wish sped up, to be done with it. She *did* slip, a boot gone from under her, but dived forward and pushed herself on with a hand grappling through mud, to come up over the edge of the incline and onto a flat surface. She fell on her hands and knees and took in deep, relieved breaths. Havik strolled up and looked down with a benevolent smile framed against the sky. Then she walked off towards the priory.

Wish sat back to catch her breath, taking in what lay ahead.

Midpeak, the greatest priory in the Mire, was visible at last in all its glory. Or at least, some of its glory: now they were close, an imposing wall took up most of their view. It rose like another cliff, towards battlements with crenellations and slit-windows, built for war. An immense buttress jutted out a short way along the wall. It looked impenetrable.

"The entrance should be this way," Havik called out, already heading there, and Wish watched as she drifted into the cloud like a fading ghost. It was unreal, all of this – the high climb to a fortified palace, the disorientating grassy slope and the thuggish tattooed men who'd accompanied them here. Most of all, this mystical woman Wish was drawn after. The Irregulars followed her like obedient dogs, barely acknowledging the incredible priory, and Wish pushed to her feet, too. Only Lost One lingered at the back, eyeing Wish with distaste. She gave him a smile.

"It's not you," he told her, killing her smile.

"Huh?"

The one-eyed man, as creepy before this cloud-castle as Havik appeared magical, kept staring miserably. He added, in his thick, surly accent, "She makes everyone feel special." And with that vote of confidence, he curled his nose at Wish and walked after the others.

Wish stayed a moment more, and realised for the first time how cold it was up here.

27

Midpeak, you will be delighted to hear, is every bit as impressive and imposing as it promised to be. It was a rare honour to be permitted entry, and one I wish I could describe in more detail, but alas –! Should you ever get the opportunity, I do recommend visiting.

The Mire Most Easy with Mr Zambizee,
Zambizee, p. 38

Like Zambizee before me, I wish I could tell you more of Midpeak, but my sparsity of detail is due to being turned away. I hold that disgrace of a traveller, and whatever irresponsible impression he made, at least partially responsible for this priory's particular reticence.

Legends of the Ten Priories, Brade, p. 165

They were within the cloud now, but it seemed to have thinned, partly blocking out the sky and distant views – the enormous drops – and gradually revealing the incredible building they needed to skirt. Wild Wish got only a limited idea of it, walking alongside the formidable wall, until the ground widened to let them wander further out, to see how the priory rose in parts above the wall. It was a castle, really, with a perimeter wall that jutted in and out, up and down, following the complex contours of the mountaintop. At every corner was a turret, which varied in size, though all were tall, round and peaked with ornate metal animals on top. There were no signs of movement or life within, except for the fluttering of an occasional flag on the battlements or rooftops – their markings unclear, like banners of old laundry.

Finally, Wish's troop reached the gates, where two great turrets flanked a pair of arched iron doors, studded with spikes, all framed with thick stone carvings of swirling patterns with occasional grotesque faces that might've been human, demon or something in between. Crude, mostly, but hand-crafted and detailed. The place was dark and quiet and Wish had to squint at the covered walkway above the doors to try and spot anyone inside. There were shadows that could've been people. As Havik and her men slowed down, Wish sped up to reach the front.

"Hello!" she called up. "I'm Lieutenant Wild Wish of the Stanclif Army. Has my platoon arrived?"

There was movement at last, men ducking away then reappearing, and finally one man leant out from the darkness. Captain Brade, hands on the battlements. "Good Castor, Wild Wish, you found the Irregulars?"

"Some of them. And not without complications. Can you open up already?"

"Of course." Brade ducked away and more hurried and secretive movement followed across the battlements. There was rapid discussion, barely audible and probably in another archaic Mire language. Apparently Brade was having to convince the monks. Wish scanned her companions. She probably wouldn't open the gates of a magical mountaintop palace to them either. She caught Havik's eye, though, and the woman smiled conspiratorially. Well. She wouldn't open up to *most* of them.

There was a great clunking of locks disengaging and gears moving, and the doors swung outwards with a groan. The Irregulars moved out of the way, looking into the entrance. Wish walked ahead with the happy thought that Midpeak was about as opposite to Drowndeep as a priory could be: just inside, there were stone houses framed in timber, with slanted tiled roofs and oak doors, varying in size and apparent function, with craft signs hanging above entrances – a blacksmith's anvil, a book, a cobbler's boot. The ground was paved and the road rose between low walls to another level of houses, then another, concentric rings that led to a turreted keep whose tip disappeared into cloud. There were occasional monks in blue robes lingering in doorways or the entrances to alleys, young and old, men and women, pale-skinned and thin but clean. It was an actual town, alive and prospering, sturdy and dry. Also, though, strangely quiet and still.

Brade came out from a doorway with a couple of monks behind him. Behind them were Sister Sonseen and Private Dalliance, the rest of the platoon absent. Brade said, "They've put us up in the East Billings. Happy to take us in if we stay out of the way, though it took a little negotiating. Lieutenant Evans, meet Venerator Fold, right-hand to the chap in charge, Archvenerator Turbulence."

The monk beside Brade gave her a slight nod. He was bald and turtle-like in both the shape of his head and hunched shoulders and the leatheriness of his skin. His beady eyes pierced her.

"Okay," Wish replied uncertainly. As well as the monk's odd quietness, she noted Brade's rare use of her actual name, these more serious and serene types probably less enamoured by wordplay. "Well, I'd like to introduce you to Havikare Eens, one of the captains of Kasidee's Irregulars." She threw the woman a look, realising she hadn't officially established she was an officer, but from Havik's smirk and her men's general deference, she guessed it was true. For an extra accolade, Wish added, "She's got a Coaerm Wildchild."

"So I see," Brade said, before she could regret the random comment. "A rare weapon; they stopped making them in '94 or so, I believe?"

"A lot of our arms are antiques," Havik said. "We work out of necessity rather than industry."

Wish didn't like the interested look Brade gave her, apparently impressed by her eloquence. Maybe her accent. He held out a hand. "Captain Rikard Brade, of the Farwell Brades."

"Oh I know," Havik said, shaking enthusiastically. "I recognise you from prints." She gave Wish a sly look. "You didn't tell me you were travelling with another celebrity. Captain, it's an honour, I've read all your books."

"Really?" Brade sounded more amused than impressed, not believing her.

"*A Walk Through Tribastan* was my favourite. It'd be hard to imagine the Arlini people accepting you as one of their own if it wasn't too outrageous to be invented."

Brade's expression shifted, definitely impressed now, but cautious – the same way he'd used to look at Wish. Like she was an exotic curiosity that he wanted to study. Havik's smile was a little too encouraging, so Wish cut in, "There's just a small group of the Irregulars here. The main force has already moved north."

"I see," Brade said, and drew his lingering gaze from Havik to the others. Considerably less impressive, though Wish appreciated that Lost One gave him a nasty look. If he was jealous of Havik's attention on her, he was going to be livid over this little display from Brade. The captain frowned, enthusiasm waning. He asked, "Where's Emi?"

"Yeah," Wish said. "She . . . I lost her. She fell. There were goblins. A sniper. I'm not sure if she made it but they got her. They got Emi, Captain. We need to get her back."

"They got Emi," Brade echoed in disbelief. Dalliance swore behind him. "How?"

Wish had spent enough time with Brade to recognise the darkness brewing under his outward calm. She needed to deal with this carefully. Havik intervened, though: "There was nothing we could do. Their sharpshooter's been hounding us for days. He took out one of my lieutenants in our camp. And the forest was overrun. If Wild Wish hadn't shown up, we couldn't have found a way out."

Brade looked from Wish to her, sceptical. "Even so. This is a serious problem."

"Obviously," Wish said, sharply. "Hence *we need to get her back*. The fighting's stopped for now, they'll be complacent, with Kasidee on the run. We can slip through their ranks. As soon as I've rested up, addressed the men, I intend to take everyone down there."

"Your intentions aren't really the issue, are they?" Brade replied, basically a growl. "The clouds are starting to part, we have an excellent vantage point here and it's plain how outmatched the Irregulars are. Colonel Atmoor has an army, we have barely a platoon, and you let them take a *mage.*"

Wish went quiet. Not just a mage, but her friend.

"This has gone from bad to so much worse," Brade went on.

"However much the army under-utilise Emi, she's still one of our strongest assets – Command would sooner sacrifice armaments, land even, than mages. Hell, they only let us have her because this was considered a low-risk assignment."

Wild Wish held her tongue, muscles tensing. She might've argued, if not for their audience of passive monks and watchful Irregulars. She was in command, after all, and needed to appear it. But then, he wasn't saying anything she didn't already know herself. Emi was more than a mage and a friend – more even than their most valuable weapon. She was the last real link back to the Blood Scouts. And she might already be dead. Because of her. Yet she'd already spent half the day climbing a mountain getting distracted by Havik.

Brade took a breath, ran a hand over his slick hair and shook his head, Wish's quietness and the general Midpeak atmosphere working to keep the lid on his own nerves. He said, "There are protocols for this. I mean, it's that serious an issue we have military edicts. At all costs, we're not supposed to let the enemy take our mages alive, you understand?"

"I do," Wish said, for all the darker meaning that conveyed. It wasn't just that they should do everything they could to save Emi. They might torture, interrogate, even turn her. Wish couldn't imagine Emi ever breaking, but they might do untold damage in their attempts, not just to her but to the world around them. The military edicts, those protocols Wish hadn't even considered to this moment, said it would've been better if she'd shot Emi herself when those goblins appeared.

"Given the chance, she'll fight her own way out," Brade went on. "But do you think she's the sort to take her own life rather than let them take it?"

Wish tried to picture it. It was hard to imagine Emi ever doing anything particularly responsible, or taking anything particularly seriously, even a threat to her own person. "I expect they'll have their hands full if she gets her strength up, but I couldn't predict what she'd do."

"Yeah," Brade agreed, then shook his head again, the whole

thing a mess. "Okay. Let's regroup, we'll circle back to it shortly. What about the rest? Have we established where the Irregulars stand, at least?"

Wish shared a look with Havik, whose raised brow invited her to answer for them. "They came in to defend the Mire."

"You had intelligence over Atmoor's movements?" Brade asked Havik, and under his scrutiny Wish realised she still wasn't sure of that answer herself.

"We had good reason to come," Havik answered readily. "The priories are at risk. They bombed the mountainside this morning, didn't they? It's lucky Midpeak is still standing."

"It will keep standing," Venerator Fold spoke for the first time, too proud of his priory not to. "The artisans of Sostar understood earthquakes and the hellfire of volcanoes. If any structure can repel those unholy guns, this one can."

"If any structure can," Havik echoed ominously.

"What was the plan?" Brade asked. "At best you've provoked the Drail to greater violence, without any apparent recourse. I'm quite sure at this point no one asked for your help?"

"By the time they did, it would have been too late. These priories have immense cultural value. It's not just the buildings and people – they hold artefacts from civilisations passed. Signs of the Saints, mementos of the prophets. Our aim was to get to these *before* they got damaged."

"Or stolen," Wish put in, recalling her earlier discussions with Brade. "It's possible they're here to loot, to horde treasure or use these items for themselves."

"You think an army would go rogue to steal religious relics for their own gain?" Havik said, with a curious look that almost made Wish blush. "Astute. Some of the stuff out here must be worth a fortune, to say nothing of what the legends claim they're capable of."

"But as I've said," Brade said, "it seems unlikely as Atmoor's intention. He's a practical man of high standing who I wouldn't expect to be concerned with wealth, much less magic. Though it might be less complicated and easier to manage if their goals do somehow turn out to be as mundane as theft and not something more . . . esoteric."

Wish frowned. That was a more generous response than she'd received before for such suggestions.

"Either way, I suppose they saw an open opportunity," Havikare said. "A land of ancient treasures, none well protected."

"Well, the monks have their own ideas there." Brade addressed Wish. "Midpeak itself is safe from invasion, more or less, from what I've gathered. At least as far as needing any help we, or even the Irregulars, might offer. They were incredibly reluctant to let us in. They're equipped for a siege of months themselves, and the monks are trained in firearms. They secured rifles and ammunition discarded during the incursions here last year. The venerators say they're ready for a fight."

"That's great," Havik replied, smiling broadly. "Then the place is even more valuable than we thought. I'd love to see it. Are they going to venture out across the Mire in deadly prayer groups?"

"Chance would be a fine thing," Brade said, his efficiency interrupted by a game smirk. Was *he* flirting? But no, the captain flashed Wild Wish another look that betrayed his underlying frustration. "You better come up to the observatory, meet the archvenerator, and we'll see what we can see. If you care to join us, Ms Eens, your men can recuperate with ours. Private, can you take them?"

Dalliance mumbled compliance and sent a sympathetic look Wish's way. Worried, even. She nodded to say it was okay. Everything would be okay. The sour-faced Irregulars wandered off with him, Lost One looking like he'd rather join the officers' talk but not deigning to request it. Brade marched towards the central keep, his stride urgent and making Wish and Havik skip to keep up. They passed rows of pleasant houses and shops, the streets spotless and windows clean. No sign that the bombing that had quaked the mountain had done any damage at all up here, making the place appear genuinely blessed. It was a priory built to last, unreal, almost a retreat from the reality out there. A nice, safe, slightly surreal place, as far removed from Drowndeep as possible. Wish was certain she didn't belong here.

"Welcome to Midpeak, anyway," Brade called over his shoulder. "For what it's worth, you're now amongst a handful of foreigners to have ever set foot in here. Such are the changes the war has brought. Last time I came, nothing would convince them to let me in."

"Of course," Havik said, "as you wrote in your *Legends* series. Since we're here now, do you think you'll get access to the vaults?"

Brade gave her another impressed look, and Wish gave her a less happy one.

"Well," he said, eyes ahead again, "It won't hurt to ask. But I'm getting increasingly hesitant to believe any good's going to come from us being here."

28

Respect positioning over numbers; visibility and timing over strength of arms; an understanding of the land above all. The folly of a great many of our generals lies in failing to appreciate the value of strategy over vainglorious details. If you'll indulge me, I have laid out my thoughts on exactly what we should be doing along the front . . .

**Extract from the Letters of
Colonel D. Atmoor, Garter, 719**

"You see," Colonel Atmoor said to Brother Redfire, standing alongside him on the battlements of Carlwen, where they had a panoramic view of the central Mire. They were watching the distant climax of the chaos on his western flank, as Ilscot finally got his troops back in line. Black smoke drifted vaguely over their heads, still thickest around the guns that had been destroyed. If Atmoor had been there, he could have rallied the men to secure Kasidee's escape routes. Likewise, he regretted not being in Midwood itself, as he'd watched the flashes of gunfire between the great trees, the specific texture of the fighting hidden but clearly ill-disciplined. But he couldn't hold his men's hands on the field any more than he could lead a goblin charge through the forest, and now here he was with his formerly excellent hold on the woods breached. He said, "You judged me harshly for attacking the mountain pass, yet it seems we didn't go far enough. We should've shelled the western ground routes, too."

Brother Redfire's typical smile was gone, and indeed hadn't been present for most of the morning, the affable monk having been exposed at last to real fighting. At this distance, none of the blood and gore was visible, even the deathly screams too distant to really register, but it wasn't hard to imagine that every spark of gunfire potentially signalled another life lost.

"Still, we'll not lose faith, hmm?" Atmoor said, tapping Redfire lightly on the shoulder. To a runner, he offered quick instructions: Sections 2 and 5 to maintain positions as 1 swept around to secure the west flank, while 4 would remain closer at hand. The goblins were filtering slowly back from the woods, spread out, and Atmoor had no illusions about reorganising them effectively until at least the evening.

"You're not giving chase, then?" Redfire asked, hopeful of them ending the violence.

"Either they'll be moving faster than my main force can keep up with," Atmoor explained, "or they'll be waiting in positions that put us at a disadvantage. No. We have a defensible spot here, clear visibility, space to manoeuvre. Trust me when I say this is where we belong, and we are safe here."

Redfire tried and failed to look cheery again, but as if to undermine Atmoor directly, the chittering of goblins grew louder as the first of Section 3's rabble got closer, moving in packs that showed no sense of military order. They were pushing each other, laughing as they squabbled, dragging their too-large rifles and bags of spoils like brigands.

Atmoor took in a deep breath and let it out. There was no telling what the goblins had got up to in the woods, though he hoped they'd put a dent in Kasidee's troops. He expected, more likely, that they had spent the morning fighting the tribes. Violent, dangerous tree-dwellers, by all accounts, who might warrant the full force of Drail Purity overall but were currently an unwelcome distraction. Yet Atmoor's brow knitted as he saw a particularly lively set of goblins dragging a heavy load between four of them, with the singularly decorated uniform of Wideskull Syrus Bleacher at their head. Seeing Atmoor watching them, the goblin commander hopped up and down, waving his gun overhead and shouting excitedly. If they wanted to show off another dead young man, Atmoor was going to scream.

The colonel grunted dismissals to his aides and hustled off the battlements, concerned that Bleacher would try to enter town with his prize, regardless of their agreements. He hurried down the steps and out a side gate, calling for his men to signal the goblins to stay put. As he came out onto the path he saw the little troop jumping excitedly, laughing in their horrible birdlike fashion. They had altogether too much energy, the four-foot greenskins, which often came out in clawing and gnashing, and Atmoor loathed walking among them – even someone of his rank might fall prey to an instinctive, unseen bite. But he had to set an example, and strode with his head high. That inspired Brother Redfire into trotting behind him, equally brave.

Bleacher snapped at his men, flapping a claw for calm, and he grinned wickedly at Atmoor's approach. It was, of course, impossible for a goblin not to grin wickedly: their mouths stretched almost as wide as their oblong heads, lined with shark-like teeth, their too-big eyes always glimmering with predatory focus. Bleacher was the best-presented of all the goblins in Section 3, in his wide hat and scuffed Drail officer's uniform, both far too big for him, threaded together from multiple jackets and pants that had likely belonged to dead humans. The right side of his torso shone with an array of stolen medals that a regular soldier might be shot for, but no officer of the Purification would dare challenge him.

Atmoor grunted as he saw that there was indeed a body between the goblins, partly concealed in a blanket they'd used to drag it on. He thumped up to Bleacher saying, "We discussed this, didn't we? If this is something I *have* to see, I would've come to you somewhere discreet."

"She's still breathing," Redfire said, pressing closer. The goblins scattered like a school of fish, then closed back in with biting teeth, making the monk flinch. He stood his ground, arms hunched but body coiled to push back.

"Back off, the lot of you," Atmoor snapped, loud enough that the goblins retreated again, with looks that promised violence rather than deference. Bleacher made a clicking noise, communicating in their own limited language, and the goblins skulked further away. Atmoor said, "What do you mean *she?*"

He was looking at a soldier in an expansive greatcoat, filthy with mud and blood, tall enough to be a man but with slim, shoulder-length dark hair. Redfire crouched and turned the body over to reveal her face: not especially pretty, with somewhat goblin-like features herself, in the big eyes and wide mouth, but indeed it was unmistakably a woman. There were scratches across her face and her coat and clothes had been ripped by claws, but her main wound appeared to be a big black splodge high on her chest. Redfire proceeded gingerly, putting his big fingers on her neck to check her pulse, then pulling back her coat to inspect the sticky chest. Her jacket and trousers were the faded blue-grey of Stanclif.

"You sealed the wound well enough," Redfire said to Bleacher, "but she'll need help. This barely missed her heart, I think – her lung could be badly damaged."

Atmoor frowned, sensing already that the soldier's gender was not the only thing special about this woman. Not with the simple fact that she was still alive after such a wound. He said, "I'm impressed you brought her back in such a condition, Wideskull."

"We're not savages," Bleacher drawled, with the typical accompanying goblin spittle. He leaned on his rifle. "Case it ain't already obvious, this one's got magic. What a gift, right? They say she fell from the sky. Handed to us, already out for the count. But thank Sharptooth Hissle, he reckoned on her value and made sure the lads didn't rip her to shreds."

Atmoor gave an appreciative glance to the hideous sergeant, a wart-ridden goblin lurking nearby with nothing in his appearance or clothing to suggest he was any more respectable than the others. Hissle giggled and a bubble of snot erupted from his nostril.

"Good man," Atmoor murmured, choosing instead to focus on the prisoner. "What's the nature of her magic?"

"Sort that can slow a bullet and protect her from a deadly fall," Bleacher replied drily.

"A witlacer could heal themself," Brother Redfire said, "but that kind of protection would indicate an earth-minder, don't you think?"

"Yes," Atmoor agreed. "She'll live?"

"With a bit of help. I can petition Chamberlain Furvair for the assistance of his best people. We should act fast, though. Provided of course . . ." Redfire trailed off, the implication clear enough, and voiced without judgement. *Provided they wanted to keep her alive.*

"Under the Treaty of Tynes," Atmoor said, "outside battle, it would be considered a crime not to assist a combatant in need of aid."

"She's no combatant though, is she?" Bleacher said. "Not in the treaty's meaning. It protects them that take oaths and follow military rule. But they're a dangerous lot out there, subversive, sneaky fucks. Criminals, not soldiers."

There was truth in that, though it galled Atmoor to hear it come from a goblin: he always suspected the vicious greenskins were well-versed in military law precisely so they knew exactly what they could get away with. Yet Bleacher's point carried an unintended weight, which Atmoor voiced: "Assuming she's who you think she is, Wideskull. If Kasidee's Irregulars had an earth-minder in their ranks, this isn't how I would expect to find out."

The goblin's face contorted as he muddled through that, and Redfire looked up with growing concern. Bleacher said, "Reckon they've found some friends?"

"Perhaps," Atmoor replied. The possibility of Comity reinforcements has been a long time coming, after all. It couldn't be a large force – there'd have been *some* indication of that – but they wouldn't send a mage on her own, would they? The colonel saw his caution was well warranted, and any further move on Midpeak or the southern Mire was out of the question for now. He said, "Get her all the help she needs, Brother Redfire, but first gather whatever touched metals Carlwen has to offer and secure her. Make sure no part of her has contact with untouched material, understand? I want to know as soon as she wakes. It's a marvel you came this far without her stirring, Wideskull."

"Eh, we know how to deal with mages, Colonel," Bleacher sneered. "You want my men should go with the good monk, keep an eye on her?"

"I do not," Atmoor replied, quite sure the goblin's repeated attempts to get into the town were done just to annoy him. "I want you to draw Section 3 out of the woods, with a mind to protecting Carlwen from the southern approach. Defer to Carrow on where to position yourselves. If anyone else comes through Midwood, we're to see them from a long way off."

Some of the humour left Bleacher, his more sinister resting face setting in. "These cowards have been doing nothing but running since we got here. If my boys stick to their tracks, we'll catch them up again, more reliably than waiting for them to turn back and come to us."

"It's not the Irregulars I'm concerned about right now. It's whoever brought *her* out here. They'll *certainly* come for her, and we'll be ready for them."

29

At the top of the world, I saw all creation,
As promised by the Saints:
Within Clouds the Rock becomes clear.
The Scrolls of Venzus, translated by Birganio, 52:3

Completing one more tough climb after two days of them, Wish's legs felt impossibly heavy. She determined not to show weakness with Havik behind her, but reached the top of the keep thinking she might flop over and roll back down at any second. They finally entered a large circular room with a domed ceiling and panoramic windows, and it was all she could do not to immediately sit on the floor.

An immense brass telescope sat at the centre on a system of gears, so big it had its own seat, beneath a wooden ceiling split in the middle, yawning slightly to let in the blue sky. There were papers and smaller floor-mounted telescopes scattered everywhere, the observatory a feverish lair of looking devices. At one window sat an elderly man in a wooden wheelchair, looking distantly out, with a younger monk standing like a statue at his side.

Brade announced, "Archvenerator Turbulence the Sixth, our lieutenant has arrived."

The old man twisted in his chair and offered a crooked-toothed smile. Wish paused at the sight of his face. Where his eyes and forehead should've been was a lattice of horrific scarring, the top of his head apparently having melted at some long-ago time. He shakily stood from the chair, leaning on a rickety cane, and replied to Brade first in the indecipherable mess of Old Lomian before shifting to reasonably fluent Stanish. "Greetings, young ladies."

Wish frowned at Brade, unsure how this eyeless bishop could've guessed they were young ladies. Plural. Did he have special senses? Could he *smell* her?

"The sky has opened," Turbulence went on. "This is a rare opportunity. Come." He moved closer to the window and Wish had an urge to rush to his side and hold him up. The monk behind him was stoic, suggesting no help was needed. Unless he was just incredibly callous. Brade gestured Wish forward and she approached with Havik alongside her.

They all looked outside and Wish caught her breath. For a moment, she could've believed the whole Rocc was there beneath them: a tremendous vista of the Saints Mire sat clear in the afternoon sun. To the right were the treetops of the expansive Midwood, before plains of grass either side of a winding river. A fortified town beyond that, circular and punctuated by weirdly curved, pointy towers. To the left, past lower mountains and rocky outcrops, spread a green, mostly empty landscape, before another distant settlement, with a horizon of trees and more hazy mountains. And amid the grandeur of an entire world within view, people moved smaller than ants. A broad phalanx gathered north of the river, with sporadic groups spread between them and the trees. More by the fortified town. The entirety of Colonel Atmoor's force, as plain as pieces on a game board.

"They are fewer than two thousand," Archvenerator Turbulence reported, softly. "Perhaps as much as a third of that are abominable species. Low creatures."

"Goblins," Wild Wish translated.

"Atmoor's in there." Brade pointed at the town. "Carlwen. They've made a command post of it. If Emi's been taken anywhere, it'll be straight to him."

"Then that's where we need to go," Wish said, drifting closer to the window.

"Please, the optiglass," Turbulence said, indicating a standing telescope. She put her eye to it and found the landscape magnified many times more than her rifle could manage. She swept it over the fields to find Carlwen, and had to look past the telescope then back to convince herself it wasn't an illusion. Through the telescope, that far-off block of buildings was a clear image of battlements, with little knights in shining armour up the top, flanked by Drail riflemen in green coats, and a series of turning wheels on the river. The peaked ears of goblins were visible outside.

"Wow," Wish said.

"Makes you feel like a god," Havik said, though she stood back with her hands in her coat pockets. "You can see all the way to Gauntstone. Kasidee should be out there." She pointed to the settlement in the distant left. Wish redirected her telescope to try and pick out the elusive Irregulars. What she found instead was a wasteland of marshes dotted with occasional crumbling ruins. Ancient, she imagined, not recently raided, but as desolate as Paradise Fails. She couldn't see anyone out there, and continued until she spotted the priory. Though not as clear as Carlwen, she could at least make out rooftops and chimney smoke – it must've been incredibly far away.

"Atmoor's forces are sticking close to the river," Brade said. "If Kasidee broke through, they haven't given chase."

"They're camped in a fort," Havik said. "Why chase us when they can dig in?"

"I'd imagine they want to come here."

Turbulence chuckled. "No one has taken Midpeak in a thousand years. Their guns may shake the mountains, but they will not defy the Saints' protection."

"Respectfully," Wish said, "the Saints might not be familiar with modern artillery." She swept the telescope back over the woods, to the walled town. The troops were spread out, and despite their sheer numbers her confidence rose. "Atmoor's got no order out there – look at them. A small force could slip by the ones outside. If we got in, cut the head off his command, the rest would fall apart." She levelled a look at Brade. "Retake that town, *get Emi back,* and we can scatter his army."

"You can't hold a town with a dozen men," he replied.

"But we could with three hundred." Wish turned to Havik. "Couldn't we?"

Havik was already smiling. "In theory, but we'd need some help. You have munitions here, supplies, that I could take to our men?" She directed this at the blind venerator.

Turbulence considered the question, motionless, before saying, "Midpeak has opened its gates to the Stanclif Empire as a courtesy in the direst of times, but the Church of Venerate Flesh, and the Scholars of the Saints, transcend empires. The One God does not take sides."

"Really?" Havik replied. "The entire history of the Holy Garter Empire says otherwise, likewise the Saints Crusades, the Ringed Legions. The Veneration of Farne, the Orders of the Arrow, the Azrian Mission – your church has backed a few fights in the past."

Though Brade looked aghast at her rapid schooling, Wish found herself warming at Havik's confidence. She was *smart*. The old man's cracked lips twitched with delight, too. "Impressive. Yet each of those events came with much deliberation from the Holy Seats. Do you know, too, how the dynasty of the Holy Garter Empire came to receive its blessing?"

"Yes, but we don't have time for a council of nine archvenerators right now," Havik said. "We only need to ready ourselves here, rest, and take what supplies we can – that you can spare. You've got an unholy horde ransacking the Mire and Wild Wish is ready to deal them a decisive blow to restore peace. Will you help me help her?"

Turbulence tilted his head, seeming to look through his grim scarring at Wild Wish, judging her worth. The moment stretched out and he noisily smacked his gums. He murmured, "This one. So young. So pure."

A laugh almost exploded from Wish's lips and she quickly covered her mouth. She shook her head and said, "Sorry, Archvenerator."

"I see your truth, dear daughter of the flesh," Turbulence replied without offence. His scarred brow knotted slightly, as he studied her without seeing. He held a trembling finger up towards his own head. "You're hurt."

Wish chilled at the sense that he was reading her mind, where the real damage was. She swallowed and began to shake her head again, to insist that she was fine, really. The darkness inside was a temporary thing and she would soon get back on track. Save Emi and the Mire and leave this twisted place. Find her friends, get them out of this war and back to Stanclif. To her farm . . . But her temple grew warm, and itched, and she raised a finger to it. Touched blood. She scowled at her red fingertip – a seeping cut from earlier, that was what the blind bishop saw? She shot Brade a look, mouthing, "What the fuck?"

"The powers of this world are not always obvious," Turbulence explained. "We find faith in the fantastic. The flesh respected, the flesh combined." He gestured over his shoulder with a trembling hand, to the motionless monk who was staring creepily into space. "Nideon lends me his sight. We move beyond boundaries together, so it was written in the Book of the Body. And we, too, must connect." He held his gnarled hand forward, inviting her touch.

Wish swallowed. Civilised as Midpeak appeared on the outside, it suddenly felt about as weird as Drowndeep, in its own way. She had zero desire to touch the spotty, wrinkled skin proffered. But she had done worse in the fighting of this war. She took his hand, limply, and her vision immediately flooded white. Wish stepped back, startled, cursing as something jolted through her. She blinked rapidly, the room coming back with Brade and Havik watching with concern. Turbulence looked pleased with himself, holding in a laugh. She wanted to punch him for the dirty trick, old and frail or not.

"What the hell?" Wish demanded, as the bishop turned back to the window. "How did you do that? *What* did you do?"

"I took a better look at you," he said. "We do not need eyes to see, nor speech to communicate. Will you be quiet with me for a moment more? Stay and appreciate what this observatory really reveals."

"Um," Wish said, much more interested in leaving, "we don't have time. Those people are as likely to bomb this castle as try to take it, and they've got my friend –"

"If you cannot take one minute for prayer," the bishop interrupted, "you need an hour. If you cannot find an hour, you need a day."

Wish looked to Brade with exasperation and he gave her a slight shake of his head. She needed to play along. She took a breath and said, "I can take a minute. What do you want me to do?"

"Stay. Satisfy the curiosity of an old man, and we will court Cane's favour, and not tempt Readinot, to see how we can help each other."

That sounded about as cryptic and unpleasant as Wish might've imagined, but she slumped in concession. Hopefully she could just let him ramble a while and they'd be done. At the least, she supposed she could sit down. Brade patted her arm with a nod, his expression saying she could handle this. He trusted her. And he was going to leave her to it.

An hour later, following a lot more standing in silence with her mind increasingly wandering, aches rising through her tired legs and niggling little wounds, Archvenerator Turbulence finally gave a heaving sigh and dismissed Wild Wish. He had not said a word since the others left her with him and his creepy aide. She wished she could tell what was going on in the archvenerator's head, as he occasionally shifted position and finally sat back in his chair, but he gave nothing away. Probably, he was just making her wait because she'd been impatient, so she decided not to speak and make it worse. She'd just wait, and wait, and wait. At least she had a beautiful view. Though she couldn't help recalling that however green and expansive it was from afar, it was cold and soggy up close. Smelly.

But damn she was tired, and Emi was in trouble, and Havik had gone. She liked Havik, she had decided. A woman in charge of tough men and able to talk back to a bishop. And interested in her. However messed up the rest of these circumstances were . . . . It brought a little smile, which she tried to suppress in case Turbulence judged her for it.

As the hour stretched on, Wish plotted how to move forward. Brade could get them to Carlwen, and Havik and the Irregulars could reinforce them. Wish would do the dirty work of killing anyone who got in the way and she would personally drag Emi out. A plan perfect in its simplicity.

At Turbulence's words, "That's enough. You may go," she practically ran down the stairs to get away, and skidded into the room where her men were gathered. The arched hall of Midpeak's East Billings building resembled the eaves of a church with its tall windows, pillars and wooden benches. There were no decorations, just sconces, so it was possibly a lecture theatre or a prayer room — but whatever its usual function, the combined squeeze of weary Blood Scouts and Irregulars made it a temporary barracks. Everyone was there, Havik and Brade included, all waiting for her.

Barely stopping for a breath, Wish blurted out her plan. Her platoon and a handful of Turbulence's best-trained monks (warrior monks!) would navigate Midwood to subtly exit in the unguarded east, then make their way north, cross the river and reach Carlwen, while Havik took her men and supplies to rally Kasidee and encircle the town from the north-west. They'd skirt Atmoor's main force by a wide margin in both directions, sneak into Carlwen and confront the colonel himself. At the least, they could damage Atmoor's command (kill him) and save Emi. At best, they might take Carlwen itself and leave the Drail force scattered. Handily, the plan provided a confident solution to the terrible news that she'd lost Emi before anyone could berate her about it.

In the ensuing silence, she saw a lot of doubt on her men's faces, as they realised this was no longer a simple reconnaissance mission. The three ogres' stern looks from the rear, where they stood with arms folded, were particularly unnerving.

It was the weaselly Rawboy Ptrangus who spoke up first. "What if she's already dead?"

"Then we need to confirm that," Brade said. "We cannot walk away from the possibility of the enemy having captured one of our mages. And as we *are* in a position to push the Drail back ourselves, we have both an obligation and an opportunity here."

"Just this lot, against thousands of them?" Runt said, apparently not including himself.

"Our company are excellent fighters," Havik said. "Each worth plenty of Drail. We've faced worse odds."

"Aye, but they're not here, are they?"

"We'll also have warrior monks in support," Wish added, liking how that sounded. Holy and ordained. Even if she hadn't run it by anyone yet. The ogre opened his mouth to speak again, so she quickly went on, "And two thousand men is nothing in this war. Two well-placed machine guns could cut them down in minutes. With the higher ground, the right positions, and whatever armaments we capture, we'll take them." The men grumbled, not quite satisfied, but Wish was feeling elated by her own promises. "We're doing this. We're saving Emi and we're securing this damn Mire. Boo. Rah."

That didn't bring about a cheer, but it did end the discussion with nods and muttering. As if her boorah was a dismissal, her platoon drifted in one direction while the Irregulars drifted in the other, regarding each other with little fondness. Wish sat back against a table and her neglected legs screamed in relief. She couldn't go to Havik now, and the woman gave a brief wink from across the room before turning to her men.

"You should get some rest," Brade said, at her side. "It's been a long day."

"Oh? I hadn't noticed. Thanks for leaving me alone with the old loon, by the way."

"I imagine he didn't so much as speak to you, did he?"

Of course Brade had a better grasp of what was going on up that tower than her. Wish narrowed her eyes to implore an explanation, too weary for words.

"Archvenerator Turbulence is famous for his miracles. A living embodiment of the power of faith, they say – with eyeless sight, psychic knowledge and such. The claims are likely either greatly exaggerated or illicitly produced. I can't say for sure, but I'd imagine either Turbulence or Brother Nideon is an accomplished mage, combining the will and parsing schools. They might not even know it themselves, if they truly believe in the power of the flesh, but the bottom line is they somehow share senses. I expect he got a good feel for your intentions in the time you spent there, however pointless it felt for you."

Wish squirmed slightly, not liking the idea the bishop might've actually been reading her. *Why?* The Mire was sucking more from her spirit than she'd willingly granted.

"He hasn't sent us away," Brade went on, "which means he's satisfied with whatever he got from you. Believe it or not, Wild Wish, I think you've done enough just by being here. I can take care of the rest for now, if you'd like to sleep. I've already got access to some maps and hope to attend their libraries to learn a little more about the surrounding regions."

Wish offered a narrow smile, one instinct telling her to say no, purely because it was him. But part of what made the captain so irritating, she realised, was that as well as being potentially duplicitous he was also very competent.

"It's fine," he said. "Your plan is solid. Bar one small thing. The warrior monks."

Wish scowled. "What about them?"

"Even if Midpeak were willing to spare men, they might've learnt to fire rifles but none of them will be familiar with combat. It would be better to keep our operation tight. Professional."

Wish kept scowling. She hated how much sense he kept making. But she was too damned tired and let it out with a grim exhale. "Yeah. Okay. Why did I even get this command, Captain? You could've had it all along."

Brade smiled. "I'd have hoped you know me better than that by now. I work best alone, in subterfuge, as I expect I shall do again when we're done here. You have more propensity for . . . working with others."

"But I want to run a farm, not decide how everyone dies."

"Ah, it's all part of the education," Brade said. She was unsure if he was joking, and didn't get to ask, as a shadow fell over them, Caracker looming large.

"Can I have a word?" the ogre said, about as subtly as an ogre was able. Wish looked past his considerable thigh, appreciating he'd left troublesome Runt behind, and the rest of the men were pretty well spread out, not close enough to hear.

"Sure," she said. "Which part of the plan's bothering you? Other than all of it."

"You trust them?" Caracker asked.

Wish frowned, following his slight nod to Havik and her men. Pretty, vibrant, smart Havik, who had held her close to avoid sniper fire. Eyes bright as she talked with her filthy troops. The one-eyed marksman caught Wish looking and glowered.

"I'm still not exactly clear," the ogre went on, "on how this lot ended up out here."

Wish paused, realising this was a detail she'd hoped would somewhat just drift away, after Havik hadn't exactly answered her or Brade directly. She said, quietly, "Havik has a lot of respect for the Mire. I understand it was her who persuaded Kasidee it was worth protecting."

Caracker's forehead creased. "Before or after the Drail crossed the border?"

"Does it matter now?" Wish said, without thinking. She glanced to Brade, trusting he'd be practical about it. "Considering where we're at?"

"Not right now," Brade replied, though his level tone said he shared the concern.

"Okay, yes, they're not exactly the best-presented bunch. Or friendliest. But neither are we? I trust Havik, at least. She knows what she's doing, and they respect her." Wish met Brade's eye again. "You like her, don't you?"

He gave a sympathetic look, confirming her phrasing sounded childish. "I'm not sure about *liking* her. I agree that she's in control and is intelligent."

"But . . ."

"I'm wary of flatterers. The Saints know I've used the technique enough myself."

Wish raised her brow, having not even considered Havik's enthusiasm might've been feigned. The captain hadn't seemed to doubt it earlier.

"More importantly, she's not Kasidee," Caracker added. "We don't know what he's up to or if they're even properly in league. They've been separated, after all."

Wish kept her eyes on Brade for his input and he shrugged,

roughly agreeing. She said, "You said it was a good plan."

"Yes," he replied. "It's as good as we'll get. But Sergeant Caracker is right to be wary. Maybe let's proceed with the idea that Kasidee's help would be a bonus, but not one we can guarantee?"

"Like fucking Reeve Abbey all over again," Wish huffed. "We go in alone thinking maybe we'll have backup, maybe we won't?"

"I have another suggestion," Caracker said.

"By Bly, I hope so."

"If you want to get into Carlwen unseen, it might be more use if I escort the Irregulars instead of joining you. We can connect with Kasidee in person and make sure of their help. Or I'll find a way to get word to you if it's not gonna work out. They're petitioning for supplies from the monks, so I'm sure they could use help carrying whatever they scavenge."

Wish didn't like much of that: not the idea of losing her ogres, or the suggestion that Kasidee would need extra persuasion, or even the way Caracker said *scavenge*. And as well as him, a sergeant she was sure she could count on in a fight, it would also mean dismissing Ohno, the most sympathetic of her new recruits . . . But it made sense. A way to plug her leaky plan. And damned if she had the energy to find an alternative. She said, "Sure. Let's do that – put it to Havik. Alright. Anything else we've got drastically wrong?"

Brade made a thoughtful sound.

"That was rhetorical, Captain. I'd like to fall asleep now."

30

In these nineteen months of unremitting battle, the mental condition has advanced to the degree that none in medical science can now deny it. The damaged mind is apparent wherever there is fighting, which is to say it can be found everywhere and with everyone. It was there before, in past wars, but discarded as weakness of character, ignorable on the smaller scale. None can say these men who suffer now were weak, yet I see it daily, how hurt they are. This is a disease for which we have no cure.

The Journals of Doctor Wreale, Wreale, p. 68

Gunfire burst starkly through Wild Wish's senses. She flew out of bed, skidding across the stone floor and banging a knee as she swept past her clothes to grab her rifle. She wrestled it out of the bag with one ear listening for more. The echoing cracks of a rapid barrage. How had they got in? Midpeak was supposed to be safe, able to see anyone coming a long way off. No time to think, she jammed in a cartridge and checked the chamber, slid the bolt back, the Long 0.48 ready before she was. Hopping on one foot, trying to get her trousers on, she flinched at another gunshot. In the hallway – were the Drail flooding the priory, murdering monks?

With her jacket barely on and her feet half in her boots, Wish shouldered the door open and almost fell. Hands shaking on her gun, she aimed one way then the other, down a long, unlit passage. No people. She frowned, could've sworn they were just here, but must've missed them – turned and ran for the door outside. She eyed the unopened doors either side of her, rooms silent. How had they missed the gunfire? Were they already outside? Wish tried the battlements door handle and it stuck, the rattle accompanied by more bangs that made her duck, eyes wide. *Outside.* Wish kicked her way out, the door giving way to brisk night air that caught her breath. She kept low, eyeing the battlements the living quarters adjoined. A tiled path stretched along a perimeter wall, with head-height merlons and waist-high crenellations looking out to the distant dark. Empty as the corridor, no guards and no lights, the priory fully asleep. Wish rushed to the wall and looked down on a narrow street of tiled roofs, beyond which the mountain fell away to a dark landscape of silhouetted bumps that could've been other mountains or just rocks, with smeared with shrubs or far-off trees.

Nothing was moving, not even the breeze. The silence drew Wish's attention to her own strained breath, her chest rising and falling, and she felt sweat chilling on her hands. She furrowed her brow, listening for the bastards, but as her eyes tracked the other way, up the sheer wall of the priory's central keep, she found only more darkness. Stillness. Then the creak of a hinge, and she whipped her gun around to the doorway she'd exited from. Shadows of bodies inside flinched in surprise. The woman at the front held up her hands, a plea for calm.

Wild Wish froze, startled to see Havikare regarding her with concern, eyes alight in the dark. They stood staring at each other, the dead of the night heavily apparent. Havik's face questioned what Wish was doing, the answer obvious: *I don't know*.

But Wish said, "I thought I heard something." *Was sure I heard something.*

Havik slowly lowered her hands. She turned to whoever else had stirred and whispered to them, told them it was okay, then stepped out and gently closed the door behind her. Wish lowered her rifle, not blinking as Havik came closer. She was dressed in her bulky coat and boots, but with only thin white leggings over her legs, and no hat to cover her sleep-tussled hedge of dark hair.

"Gunshots," Wish said, doubtfully. "There was fighting."

Havik nodded, moving around Wish to the wall, making a show of checking their surroundings. Satisfied all was quiet, so very quiet, she sat on the crenellation and raised her eyebrows to Wish, inviting her to join her. Wish carefully did, resting her rifle next to them, as she tried to recall what had brought her here. She'd been so sure of the shots. An explosion, even, a burst of light. But there was nothing. No smell of gun smoke or shouts or even movement. She thought back further. It had been daylight when she lay down to rest, just for a little while. She asked, quietly, "What time is it?"

"A time only ghosts are awake," Havik said.

They let that linger between them for a moment, appreciating that whatever Wish had heard was a dream at best. But it was more than that. As bad as the conscious memories, when they came unbidden. Worse, in a way, for it wasn't as tangible.

"How long . . ." Wish paused again. "I missed dinner?"

"And then some. But don't worry, everything's in order. You've got a good team in there, and the monks are cooperating. More than I expected they would, to your credit."

"Me? I don't think I've done much good here. Sorry for waking you. I . . . Sometimes, I just –"

"You've got no need to apologise to me or anyone else. There'll be new words for the way this war's damaged people by the time it's done. They should've paid more attention in the Camano War, or the War of Unification before that. But it's a sign you care. That's lucky, in a way – not everyone keeps hold of that."

Wish snorted a light laugh. "Lucky. I'd prefer to let go."

"No. You don't believe that." Havik was smiling, too, but clearly meant it.

Wish appreciated then that they were sitting close together, overlooking the Mire's nighttime expanse, with a sea of stars above. She twisted one knee up on the wall, awed by how many lights filled the sky. Every one of them was a possibility of new worlds, with none of this one's violence. But when she looked down again, she found Havik's starlit face and saw this life wasn't so bad. Havik brought her foot up to rest by her knee, getting comfortable too. Toe pointing in not far from Wish's crotch.

"Um." Wish stared at Havik's scuffed boot. It was wide, thick with padding around the ankle, but loosely open, laces a mess. She couldn't help asking, "What kind of boot is that? You don't have stamps?"

"What kind of boot?" Havik echoed, amused. "One with laces

and thick soles? I don't know. I got these from the Kopice market years ago. Yours are stamps? Think they're better?"

"No, I just – I was only curious. My dad's a cobbler. We do so much marching, I always tried to keep an eye on our footwear."

"Well if you're offering" – Havik arched her boot, tilted her head to one side – "I could find a hole or two for you to patch up." But she laughed, and prodded Wish's knee with her toe. "Or you can focus on taking care of yourself. Have you spoken to anyone about the things you see?"

Wish frowned. Part of her wanted to deny it, because Havik was reaching. She didn't *see* anything. Not anything real, anyway. Instead, she said, "Spoken to who? An officer, a medic?"

"Anyone. There are things that can help. First, you know it's not your fault?"

"What? Huh. That's . . . you don't know that."

Then Havik's hand was on Wish's knee, eyes holding hers. Wish stiffened as Havik said, "I do. I understand people pretty well. But from the first I heard of you, I knew you were special. Someone I had to meet." She glanced at the door. "We're not here by chance, Captain. Even now. When you didn't come back this afternoon, I made sure to get quarters close to yours in case you woke. We'll be gone by dawn, me and your ogres – thank you for that, by the way – and I've been eager to talk to you. People like you and me, we've found our place in this war, haven't we? We can cope better than most. But you feel guilty about that. Do you enjoy it sometimes, too? The adventure, the opportunity?"

"Um," Wish said, uneasy both at how accurately Havik seemed to be reading her, and how damning the assessment sounded. But close and touching as they were, she couldn't deny there had been thrills.

"You've done incredible things. You shouldn't focus on the regrets."

"A lot of people have died . . ."

"And a lot more will. *Millions* more. They're going to die with or without you, but you're making a difference. Besides, who wouldn't rather *you* kill them than some bloated man-pig?"

"That's . . ." A muddle of words came to Wish. *Sweet, nice, weird?* She fell short of how to interpret it and Havik went on.

"You wanted something, joining the army, didn't you? Excitement, the power, the purpose."

"Maybe," Wish admitted, "but not the rest. I've lost so much already. Hurt so many people. I can't stop thinking about it."

"Then don't. Look it in the face. Revel in it. All those lives crushed under your boots – a woman, out here, doing all that? You're a *goddess.* "

"Havik," Wish said carefully, seeing she was now grinning. Like it was a joke, but not quite. That last part at least was only semi-serious. Smirking herself, trying to keep this light, she said, "Can I ask. Are you mad?"

Havik laughed, gently. "The world's mad, Wild Wish. We've *got* to be."

"Alright. Okay. But I don't enjoy killing people. Kind of the opposite."

"Maybe not, but you have a talent and the times, the state of the world, demands it." Havik leant closer, that hand still on Wish's knee, the other coming up to her chest. Wish backed up and hit the merlon, nowhere to retreat. Havik rested her palm just above Wish's left breast, and sent her heartbeat racing again. "In here. You're so strong. I wanted to be like you."

"No." Wish shook her head, knowing she should push Havik off, get out from this, but at the same time absorbing her warmth. Drinking it down. "I'm a mess. A fat deadly mess."

"Well you're definitely not fat." Havik laughed again, removing both hands. "You're beautiful. In my opinion, for what it's worth."

Quite a lot, Wish silently told herself. Going by her body's reaction, anyway. Except this woman didn't know her, oddly familiar as she felt. They'd only walked up a mountain together and been squeezed in a tight embrace to avoid sniper fire. Wish said, "You're just trying to make me feel better."

"Obviously," Havik said. "But not *just.* I want you to appreciate yourself the way I do."

"You don't know me," Wish said out loud. Hard to believe that she was out here under the stars with someone so invested in her. And if this wasn't flirting, it was damn close. But she needed to be truthful. "Look, I do *not* want to be a killer. I ran away from my village because it sounded like fun, sure. Glorious war. It wasn't so great when I landed in the trenches, but the Blood Scouts turned things around. Then I was fighting to stop all this, so I could bring them home. I want to go home, to somewhere I can love and protect the people close to me." She paused, the faces of her fellow scouts coming back to her. Their jokes and smiles. Back when she actually *had* people close to her. She added, voice cracking, "Some of them are still alive. I'll find them."

Havik watched her with studious eyes, far too thoughtful. She didn't say anything.

Wish averted her gaze. "I know it sounds silly. A stupid dream. But they're survivors, Oksy, Rue, Dakoda. Four Skills. Newk. I have a –" She cut off, uncertain again. "You should know. I had a girlfriend, kind of."

"Where is she?" Havik asked without faltering.

"I don't know. The last time I saw her . . ." Wish trailed off, not wanting to revisit that thought, but there it was. Newk unconscious, her head split open by a damn grekkel. "I'm sure she's alive. I don't know. Maybe *girlfriend* is too strong. We kissed. I don't know if she was really interested in me or just . . . grateful? Being kind?"

"She was definitely interested in you," Havik promised, putting her hand on Wish's leg again. "But you know nothing's guaranteed, nothing lasts. We must take what we can while we can."

Wish frowned. "Havik. I can't. Right now, I mean, it's – I've never even –"

"Me neither," Havik interrupted, and that threw Wish.

"What?"

"I'll be honest, too. I don't care about most people. Most of the time, there's just nothing there. The few men in Kopice who *did* show an interest in me were vile. The rest . . . I found friends in books, and only in books. In my imagination, thinking what if the whole world was different? What if men were not in charge, and we weren't expected to please them, or all be the same? Can you imagine the world upside down – if spidroms told you what to do, or the empires gave us money instead of only took it? I thought of those things because the people around me, my town, my life, it all felt so . . . hollow." Her eyes lowered, unmistakably, to Wish's lips, and she chewed at her own lower lip. "But you . . ."

Wish was seized by a new panic. Was she going to kiss her? Did she want her to, out here, in the Mire? What about Newk? But Havik looked away again, sighing.

"This war forced me to abandon my books and face the real world. I watched Kopice burn, from the hills. But I heard of Kasidee's Irregulars, who were dancing in the face of these imperial monsters, and I set out to find them. I heard of *you* and your adventures, even more incredible than Kasidee – like something from my books. I have fought following *your* example. And imagine. I've actually got to meet you?" Her smile became sheepish. "To touch you, even."

"You are mad," Wish said, with amused disbelief. "What could you have heard about me? How? I shot a bunch of guys from a distance – who hasn't, now?"

"You killed more than a bunch," Havik replied. "And with a whole platoon of women? *And* you've lived up to all I imagined by coming here. We're in the middle of something important, in the Mire, and no one else realises, but *you* came."

Wish shifted, losing some humour at this misstep; she definitely hadn't chosen to come, and barely even understood why Havik thought this place was important. "I . . ."

"You're going to obliterate the Drail," Havik went on. "Do what the Comity has failed to. We'll find each other when this is done, won't we? We'll reunite and do more together. You and me. Maybe . . ."

There was a flash of that look again. Maybe *what?* Wish's cheeks warmed. Smiling. A quiet voice reminded her that Caracker doubted this woman. Brade called her a *flatterer.* And the one-eyed sniper said *she makes everyone feel special . . .* But there was a big difference, wasn't there, between flattery and the things Havik was saying? There was a connection here. Still, Wish said, trying to sound humorous, "I bet you say that to all the girls."

Havik raised an eyebrow. She answered with shattering frankness, "What girls?"

"Um. I mean."

"I've never wanted to know anyone like I want to know you."

They held each other's eyes, that word *know* carrying more weight than ever before. Wish replied quietly, "I think I'd like that."

But again Havik turned away, frowning. Instant regret? Had Wish misunderstood? Was that a bad response? *How?* No. She was looking to the horizon. There was a twinkle like a star too low. Another. Flashes, far away, at ground level. Gunfire. Real gunfire this time. Was there the distant tap of a shot, just audible? Had Wish actually heard something before?

"Where is that?" she asked.

"Gauntstone," Havik said. "Where Kasidee was headed, the other side of the Low Bile. Nothing we can do about it now."

"Low Bile," Wish said. "They named this whole country for nightmares."

"Names that were earned." Between the view and her deepening thoughts, Havik's tone grew grave. "Bile for the acids of the bog, sails where saints harnessed the wind, shadows against the balance of light, and the marches where armies clashed. None so true as the place where paradise fails."

Wish frowned at the side of her head. "Are you a poet, too?"

Havik smiled, drawn back to her. "Just a librarian. That was a quote from the Book of So, more or less. Whatever else you think of the Final Prophet, the man knew how to use words."

Wish hummed in agreement, because she didn't have many thoughts about the prophets one way or the other. Then they were quiet, watching the tiny lights of distant killing. Whether the Irregulars were under fire or had found a way to route the Drail, it didn't matter. It was a tiny, private show, just for them, and Wish reached out hesitantly to touch Havik's hand. The woman didn't flinch away, so she relaxed her grip into it. Her skin was a little rough. *Strong.*

"We'll have some trouble ahead," Havik murmured, more focused on the fighting than her touch. "You should get your sleep.

I'm sorry, I shouldn't be so . . . forthright. Distracting. Try not to take anything I say too seriously. But I do hope we'll reunite soon. In the meantime, be kind to yourself, Wild Wish."

Wish would, she told herself, though her heart was back-flipping now. Equal parts thrilled at Havik's words and panicked that she hadn't actually meant them. But it was impossible, in the most unlikely of places at the worst of times, that she had found something, someone, that felt good. So she smiled lightly, too, gave Havik's hand another gentle squeeze and whispered, "Sure."

31

The inhumane practices of capturing and isolating earth-minders, which continued well into the 7th century, are telling in their consistency. The same methods of torture that were used on followers of Fin Baston were employed for prisoners during the One War, four hundred years later, with the same unjust results.

We the Mindless: a Brief History of Ostracised Magic, Lombardo, p. 152

Colonel Atmoor was doing his morning stretches when a soldier knocked urgently. He was dreading news from the west after the night had been interrupted by the reports of fighting in Gauntstone. They could see the gunfire from Carlwen, but he had no idea if it was Kasidee's Irregulars attacking the priory for sport or if his troops had caught up to them on their own initiative. He was still awaiting word from Ilscot, believing either possibility equally likely, and while he despaired at the possible insubordination, part of him secretly hoped his men had indeed shown some cunning to put an end to things. But as he threw on his pressed jacket and straightened himself out, he sensed the messenger's knock wouldn't bring good news.

He opened his door to a red-faced young man who blurted out, "She's awake, sir! The mage is awake!"

Perhaps not such bad news after all.

Atmoor followed the soldier to the mage's cell, a guest room in the town's keep, chosen for its sturdy walls and heavy, lockable door. It had been grandly furnished before they removed everything, leaving only a feather mattress on the floor. Even that was risky. He could see the fear knotted in his escort's shoulders, but if there was going to be trouble, it would've happened by now.

The soldier readied his rifle before entering the room, giving a backward glance to Atmoor, who nodded for him to proceed.

Inside, a sergeant stood on the far side of the room also holding a rifle, keeping a good distance from the mage. The mage was sitting on her mattress, eyes brightly awake, dressed in a thick tunic with bandaging around her shoulder. Atmoor was taken again by her strange appearance, her somewhat reptilian features, with that wide mouth, all the more striking now she was awake, more alive, smiling nastily. Not unlike the goblins indeed, only she was twice their height and had smaller, fiercely intelligent eyes.

"Wait outside and shut the door," Atmoor instructed, and the nervous soldier exited, worriedly watching the mage. To the sergeant, a more hard-faced man, he said, "You can lower the gun. We're just going to talk."

The rank and file had little to do with magic-wielders, besides seeing the odd healer – certainly not the mindless, who were carefully policed in Drail territories. He had more experience, though. Her gaze was chilling, and being a woman she might be more volatile than most, but she was a mage all the same, bound by certain codes. Much like officers, she would understand as well as him that her safety was guaranteed and there was little to be gained by causing trouble. Besides, her wrists and ankles were shackled in bulky touched metal rings connected by a thick chain, anchored in two places to the floor. The Carlwen guards insisted the shackles would nullify her powers, hard as it was to believe any restraints could truly hold back the mindless.

Atmoor said, in Stanish, "You speak our tongue, I'm sure, but we'll talk in yours to be polite, shall we?" The mage stared hard without speaking, without blinking. "You do speak Stanish, I imagine? Do you understand me?"

She raised her eyebrows. Trying to unsettle him.

Atmoor moved on. "Let's get straight to it. We've established from your uniform, such as it was, that you're not with Kasidee's Irregulars – more fortune for you, because I extend greater hospitality to enemy combatants than I would to those criminals."

"You don't have criminals in your army?" she spoke at last, light and jocular.

"Hmm," Atmoor said. Ilscot's untrustworthy face came to mind. "There's a difference between reformed soldiers and renegades."

"That's a nice word, *renegade*. It fits your whole empire," the mage replied, her wicked grin stretching as she sat back. She was enjoying this, despite being mortally wounded and captured, and Atmoor compensated with a more severe expression.

"I'm giving you the benefit of the doubt because I don't see Stanclif supporting Kasidee directly, especially not with a mage. Nor do I see him having had access to you until now. So shall we start with your name, rank and unit of command. Then you can tell me where the rest of your men are."

"You speak very well for a Drail dogsbody," the mage mused. "I bet you got invited to all the parties." She affected a more refined accent. "Ballroom galas and whatnot. Dining on tiny eggs."

Atmoor studied her for a moment. In her disapproval, he sensed an angle that he might use. "I've moved in higher social circles, yes. It hasn't always agreed with me, hence I find myself here. Considering it's where we *both* find ourselves, perhaps you've fallen from grace with Stanclif Command yourself?"

"Oh no, they *love* me." The mage leered, her eyes bulging. She still hadn't blinked. "And they tell us if we're ever captured to *never* talk."

"Yet you're talking," Atmoor said. "And I'm sure you recognise these are exceptional circumstances. Can you start by confirming that at least? Has Kasidee earned the backing of Stanclif Command?"

The mage considered the question, her smile drooping. "You first. Where am I and what are *you* doing here?"

"Very well. You were shot by my people and brought here for care."

"Care?" She laughed.

"It was a miracle you survived, even as a mage. And doubly lucky that they have some very capable healers here in Carlwen. That is where you are, by the way, in the chamberlain's keep."

"What kind of healers?"

"Excuse me?"

"What *kind* of healers? A gifted surgeon, a hedge witch – someone put hands on me?" She was plainly avoiding the most obvious answer, a good deal of her humour gone.

Atmoor answered slowly, "A layman, not one of my own, but a respected member of the church. The council's own witlacer, a flesh –"

The mage spat as viciously as one trying to remove poison, then fell into a series of curses, picking at her bandages with disgust. Her movements, rattling the chains, made the watching sergeant tense, hands twisting on his rifle, but Atmoor gave him a look to warn him off.

"Tainted," the mage said, glowering at Atmoor. "You should've let me die. You've cursed me."

"No more so than applying any medication. As a magic-user, I'd expect you to know –"

"As a magic-user, you should expect me to have *standards*," she hissed, and he watched her fingers go taunt, ready to try something. Atmoor fought to keep steady himself, not to further provoke her or worry the soldier into panicking. Surely she wasn't this upset by the centuries-old rivalry between the magic schools? Hadn't they buried those conflicts long ago? The mage rattled her chains again and snapped, "Send me this witlacer. Cut off his head and let no one speak of this again."

"You're alive because of him," Atmoor replied firmly, realising she was serious. But this was personal, a childish grievance with no substance here. Typical of the mindless. "And, I might add, thanks to the mercy of goblins. Have some decorum – I understood that Stanish mages were trained to be of a certain class."

"Do I look like a regular fucking mage to you?" she snarled, bearing her teeth, and the colonel felt a chill the likes of which he hadn't in three wars and countless battles. He held her manic gaze, trying to let her temper cool. If he'd woken up a prisoner, he supposed he would be angry too. The mage breathed deeply and hissed again, until her hard stare softened. She snapped her head to one side and said, "Should've known. No one gets away from the Mire clean."

"On that we can agree," Atmoor said. "Shall we start again? My name is Colonel Atmoor, though I suspect you already know that. By the Treaty of Tynes, and on my personal honour, I *will* protect you. I can guarantee you safe passage back to Onwail and protection while we confer with your superiors. I expect there are conversations to be had that might even see you sent home as part of a prisoner exchange. Not everyone in my position would be so generous. In fact, most would prefer to summarily execute captured mages. Lucky for you, I don't often agree with my brash counterparts, to your benefit and to my eternal chagrin."

"Chagrin," the mage echoed, her sinister smile returning. "I can see how you and Captain Brade might have got on."

"Captain Brade?" Atmoor paused. "Rikard Brade? You know him?"

The mage rocked back on her elbows again, managing to make the poor conditions appear luxurious. "Sure, and he's coming for you. We've got powerful mages, expert swordsmen, and snipers who" – she tapped her wound – "don't miss the heart. Oh, our snipers are the best."

Atmoor felt uneasiness climb through him, sure that beneath her goading manner there was truth in this. Rikard Brade was nobility, a highly able spy and explorer, and it was perfectly believable that he'd jump at the chance to venture into the Saints Mire. He enjoyed challenges that others stringently avoided. And if he was involved, then Stanclif Command were more serious about this territory than the Arrow Council. Atmoor said, "How many of you?"

"Enough."

"And you came to reinforce the Irregulars?" Atmoor could imagine it plainly enough. No one had wanted to fight for this land, but now it had started they would throw all they had into it. That was the story of the whole war, wasn't it? Except Stanclif clearly better appreciated the Mire's value than the Drail. With this news, things would quickly escalate. Hell, they already had. Atmoor shook his head. "I came to secure this land, not to see it laid to waste."

"With a few hundred goblins and cannons blowing chunks out of the mountain?"

"With the means available to me. Who's your commander? Where are you positioned?"

"Everywhere," the mage promised.

"Would you stop that?" Atmoor snapped, monetarily breaking his cool. "There's no way you've brought in a force comparable to my own or we would've heard about it. And you won't have anything like the naval support I can call upon. *Have* called upon. All you're going to do is aggravate things further."

"Oh well. You shouldn't have invaded neutral territory, I suppose?"

"Damn you, this is no invasion, I am merely doing my duty. If you tell me where your commander is, I will see to resolving this without excessive damage."

"Do you really expect that to work?" the mage laughed. "And they call me mindless."

"I know Captain Brade," Atmoor snarled, stepping closer to her, clenching a fist. He took a breath at the surprised look on her face but she remained amused by his temper. "Despite what you may have been told, I respect this land. My mother was a devout Ven, for crying out loud. I want to stop Kasidee, not spark a fresh war."

The mage kept smiling, staring unblinkingly, but considered his words. She said, "I almost believe that part. But you poked the bear, didn't you? What were you expecting?"

"I *expected* to take care of the Comity's trash. To do what your superiors seem incapable of." Again, his words gave the mage pause, and he saw in her thoughtful expression that there was something going unsaid here. Somehow, they were talking at cross-purposes; both believing they were in the right, but perhaps for different reasons. As the truth slowly sunk in for him, the mage frowned, no doubt realising it too. He said, "You thought I started this? You didn't know that Kin Kasidee was here first?"

The mage hesitated, then shrugged. "If he was or wasn't, you still look like invaders to me."

She was right enough. The Comity were unlikely to let his

incursion here go unanswered, nor forgive the inevitable slaughter of the Irregulars. It had been wishful thinking that he might resolve the matter unnoticed. But there was hope here, a crack of light. He *could* mitigate this. He said, "We must slow down. If you tell me where to find your people, I'll reach out – diplomatically."

"Sure, do you want their names and ranks and sleeping habits too? Maybe the home addresses of Stanclif Command while I'm at it."

"Can you be serious? I am not trying to trick you. At least tell me some way that we can get their attention. I need to talk to Captain Brade."

"You *need* to watch your back." The mage leered again. "You won't see them coming. And when they set me free, I'm going to bring this whole town down." Her smile faded and he saw she was serious. "You know I can do it. And I will. With your dirty goblins and a fucking" – she spat again – "witlacer. It's a bit late for diplomacy, isn't it?"

Atmoor let out a big breath. He should've known better than to expect rational discourse from one of the mindless, but she'd given him something, at least. It would do for now, and he quietly excused himself. "Very well, I will see to it myself."

As he turned his back on the mage and strode out, she called after him in a sing-song voice, "Wild Wish is gonna get you!"

He had no interest in unpacking those cryptic words. He didn't need to break her, if such a thing would even be possible. He could guess well enough where her people would come from – already had, in fact. He had Carrow managing the southern defence, and if anyone was going to see them coming, he would. Atmoor merely had to plan for a chance at parley instead of battle. If he could reel his people in in time. Addressing the nervous soldier standing outside the door, he said, "Get word to Bleacher and Weles to meet me at once. Send our best men to find Sergeant Carrow and tell him to stand down and report in."

The soldier nodded and scampered off.

The problem though, was that Carrow *was* his best man. His less capable troops would need to race to get orders to him before he could do his job.

32

When a keg breaks, do not complain, just drink.

Coulard Idiom

Wild Wish could barely suppress a smile for her mixed, dreamy memories of the night. The nighttime rendezvous was too short, and she regretted finding Havik and Caracker already gone in the morning, but over a hearty breakfast she happily learnt Brade had done a good job of organising the others, all ready to go. They could get this done quickly and find a way back to Havik. Maybe fold her into the Blood Scouts and set out to do even greater things together. The others would like her: smart enough to give Oksy a run for her money; rugged enough for Rue; could probably talk to Newk in her own language . . .

The lightness in Wish's step was interrupted on the way out of the priory, her troop tiredly following, as she found Sister Sonseen waiting by the open gates. The nun had her arms folded against the morning chill and wore a grim expression. A group of monks were busying themselves opening crates, gun barrels noticeable inside. Wish understood she would be taking them back to reinforce her own priory later. *Warrior monks.*

"Blessings of the body upon you," Sonseen said, unenthusiastically. "May your journey be quick and safe."

"Thanks," Wish said. "What are you doing up so early? We're not travelling together, are we?" She turned to Brade, coming to join her.

"No," Sonseen said. "I just wanted to see you off and make sure you're aware what happened overnight. There was trouble in Gauntstone."

"I saw," Wish said, and on Brade's glare realised how that sounded. "I was going to discuss it with you." Except she hadn't intended to, not with any urgency. Battles interrupted the night all the time at the front, and only now did it strike her that it was more noteworthy here.

"How bad was it?" Brade asked Sonseen, not her. Of course, the monks had that incredible observatory – why didn't *they* raise an alarm?

"Bad," Sonseen said. "The fighting started outside the walls and parts of Gauntstone were burning, but the mists grew too thick to say much more. They haven't parted this morning."

"Well, if Kasidee secured himself before Atmoor caught up to him, they should've been able to defend the priory. Atmoor couldn't have sent more than an expeditionary force, from what we saw of how his armies were established last night."

"Is Havik heading into trouble?" Wish asked. They'd seen the fighting themselves, it didn't look like a huge battle, and Havik knew in advance, but even so . . .

"The archvenerator intends to find out," Sonseen said. "It seems you made a good impression on him yesterday, Lieutenant, and whatever doubts he had, Midpeak will act. I shall stay long enough to help coordinate what we can with the other priorities from here. After all, if we are forced to defend Saintshadow, then it will already be too late."

Wish smiled weakly, feeling she should be pleased that the monks were mobilising, but also a little guilty at this falling on their inappropriate shoulders. Had her presence corrupted Turbulence, through whatever magical connection he put out? Like a spreading disease: you've met Wild Wish, now you've got violence on you!

"I hoped to send a message to Gauntstone with your unusual friend," Sonseen went on, "but they were gone long before sunrise. The archvenerator will send Venerator Fold to Gauntstone too, with their best men, to help. We have no idea what state the priory will be in."

"Let's hope Kasidee's already dealt with it," Brade said.

Sonseen hummed, unconvinced, but nodded. "Yes, well. I don't mean to keep you, or darken your day. The forest is quiet, from what I understand. As long as the Woodwings don't trouble you, it should be a smooth journey. Next time we meet, I hope it will be with gladder tidings."

"I'm sure it will be," Wish replied brightly, and watched as a nearby monk timidly lifted a rifle, like he was worried it might snap. They were old guns, most likely Elmish, not models she was familiar with. It should've been disconcerting, and Sister Sonseen wasn't in the best spirits, but Wish still intended this to be a good day. Things would turn around by nightfall. Today they'd solve the Saints Mire, tomorrow the world.

Wild Wish tramped breezily between the titanic trees. The trunks and canopy were large enough that Midwood had an open feel to it, with morning light filtering in, and despite it being the site of Emi's potential death and a day's worth of fighting, it was good to be out in nature after the desolate bog and mountain. And when they did find the first signs of violence, with blood and occasional body parts dirtying the trees, there were no bodies, either the surviving Woodwings or the Drail goblins having cleared up after themselves.

Wish felt relatively sure they'd be able to get Emi back alive and she could perhaps put a bullet in Colonel Atmoor and break up this nonsense fighting. Sneaking in places and shooting people was something she understood. She also felt buoyed by Havik's words. And touch. The woman from the wilderness was interested in her (romantically? Really?) and was more certain of Wish's worth than she was herself. She would do this not just for Emi. Wish would punch a hole in the Drail's defences and Havik would swoop in to break the rest apart. Kin Kasidee might lead the company, but it'd be Havik's charge . . . Wish regretted she'd slept so long yesterday. The ogres and even Brade got to spend more time with Havik than she did.

In a brief lull crossing the treetop structures, as Ptrangus slipped on a bridge and kicked up a subsequent storm of inventive curses amid Rawboys laughter, she asked Brade, "Did you talk to Havik much? Learn more about the Irregulars, or . . ." *Her.*

"Kasidee?" Brade misunderstood. Deliberately? "Yeah, she told me a little. She's enthusiastic, I'll give her that. If you want my impression . . ." He trailed off, irritatingly.

"You still don't trust her?"

"It's not that. Don't take this the wrong way, but Kin Kasidee and his Irregulars seem to be dangerously romantic. He's trying to create his own legend. Havik made it clear he reads a lot, and they encourage storytelling in the company. She asked me a few times about myths of this land that even I'm hazy on the details of. They see the wealth of lost culture out here and they're actively hunting for a righteous fight. Most people have learnt better from this war, already."

Wish frowned. "Why would I take that the wrong way?"

"Because they're dreamers," he replied sombrely, not needing to add *like you*.

"And what, that makes them fools?"

He looked from Wish over to the men struggling over the high bridge. Toothless wobbled across with frightened noises, tightly clutching a rifle gifted by the monks of Midpeak, determined not to lose this one. Brade said, "You know how to apply yourself within the reality of this conflict, Wild Wish. You get things done. From the very fact that they're here, of all places, I'm not sure how serious the Irregulars are."

"Right," Wish replied shortly. Of course he'd find a way to dampen the fire. He couldn't appreciate that imagination also brought passion and hope. Happy to end this conversation, seeing the others were across, Wish walked out onto the thin bridge herself. She felt Brade's concern weigh on top of her own, crossing a fall that would easily be deadly, and moved quickly to get away from it. On the other side, she said, "Pick up the pace guys, we're not that high up."

Continuing, she reconsidered Havik's strange way of talking about the fight. About power and them being good at this. Enjoying it? Okay. She wasn't totally normal, but who was? It brought back a thought of Newk, determined to sever the heads of three hundred enemies in revenge for her village's slaughter. They were alike, weren't they? And a little guilt resurfaced for Wish. She'd left Newk about as far behind enemy lines as possible.

"You see that?" Private Dalliance cut into her thoughts, shifting up alongside her and pointing down to the forest floor. "What the fuck?"

"Shit," Wish said and waved at everyone to get down. Thinking time was over.

With hushed whispers and gestures, she got them spreading out over the tree structures, to check the surroundings. There was no sign of life or movement, her troop confirmed. Satisfied no one was watching, they descended a roughly carved ladder to ground level and regrouped at Dalliance's horrible discovery. Toothless gagged and the others made various noises of upset, but Wish came in close, unable to look away.

It was a goblin death ward. She'd heard stories of them: they created patterns meant to celebrate tribes' heritages, supposedly keeping enemies at bay. This one used the body of a Woodwing warrior, clear enough from the remains of his primitive, limited clothing of crude leather, twine and feathers. Also, the broken artificial wings that had been nailed into the tree astride him. The carcass had been picked apart, bound and nailed to the tree trunk above head height. There was barely any skin left, a scant indication of fingers and toes, ribbons made from muscles and a shredded face that would haunt Wish. There was an oddly compelling art to it, though, with the breakages and erratic angles that conveyed an oddly specific symbolism. Like an old rune in corpse form.

It weirdly conjured the memory of a summer morning for Wish. A market day in Swelig with everyone shopping and nattering. A stall at the end of the village, mostly out of sight, where two goblins in absurd three-piece suits were meekly handing out leaflets. One of them had a moustache, which stuck with Wish because she didn't know goblins could grow facial hair. They thrust a leaflet at her as she passed, with a jagged smile that made her yelp.

"Tempered Goblins Association," the moustached little greenskin said, as Wish quickened her pace to get away. "We're not all monsters!"

The name had only made her think of goblins with tempers. They were moved along, never to return to Swelig, but she later heard reports of the TGA from the cities, where goblin rights activists had been protesting, joining debates. She came to understand they'd meant *tempered* to mean *limited*. A small but growing number of goblins, not a common species in Stanclif overall, were trying to convince the world they weren't vile savages.

Looking at the death ward, Wish recalled the leaflet saying that goblins were rarely violent. She muttered to herself, "Lying little shits."

"Who?" Brade asked. He considered the display with tall Graveguard, the pair of them staring like academics at an art gallery.

"If ever you needed evidence of what we're fighting for," Macmiddan grunted. He had one hand resting his rifle against a shoulder, the other clenched in a big fist.

"Bloody had the tools on them, didn't they?" Ptrangus said. "Hammers and nails. Binds. Carried that shit out into a battle counting on a chance to do something like this later."

"Pack goblins, aren't they?" Macmiddan said. "Always hopping about with sacks full of tools and trophies. Hoarding, thieving, butchering –"

"They're called pack goblins because they move in packs," Brade said. "Like pack beasts, hounds and trolls. And this does not look like the work of pack goblins. They have limited cultural intelligence. This was done by harkers. It's a guardian symbol of Wideskull Flagel, if I'm right."

"Cultural intelligence?" Macmiddan countered. "You telling me this is a sign of goblin sophistication?"

"Somewhat, yes."

"Not for nothing, but this took a skilled hand," Graveguard murmured appreciatively.

Macmiddan grunted again, as if this made it worse. "Permission to take it down, Lieutenant? Don't care if it's one group of savages tearing into another, doesn't feel right leaving it here."

"Be easier to burn the damn tree," Ptrangus said.

The immense trunk, six paces in diameter, was about as tall as the highest buildings Wish had ever seen. She couldn't imagine it burning, and said, "If you're prepared to touch this mess, you're welcome to remove it. But I don't think we should hang around."

"Wasn't planning on it," Macmiddan said, and approached the tree, drawing a knife.

No one volunteered to join him as he cut the first straps, though Graveguard said, "Do you see the way these wing contraptions are fused with their skin?"

As Brade replied with something about the now-absent Woodwings' unique traditions, Wish scanned the ground for tracks. The leaves, branches and mud had been disturbed by plenty of feet sweeping through here, including their own, but it was plain that a good-sized group had come and gone in the easterly direction. She said, "The enemy may still be close. Spread out, stick to cover, keep low, watch each other's backs. I'll take point."

"With?" Brade put in, as an unpleasant squelch came from Macmiddan's efforts. Wish had no desire for company, not after Emi. They'd all be safer with her on her own. The way Brade stared said he knew what she was thinking, though, and it wasn't going to fly.

"I can spot for you," Toothless raised a hand, as if in class, all but hiding behind a tree to avoid the view of the death ward. Well. If he was that desperate to come, at least he was endorsed by ogres.

Wish sighed. "Alright. Let's move."

They managed another two hours of uneventful creeping. Wish suppressed thoughts of Havik to search for the enemy's trail in the mud and broken branches. Toothless generally kept silent, ten paces or more back, occasionally leap-frogging when they needed to cross open space. The woods went on and on, barely changing from one enormous tree to another, except for occasional signs of Woodwing communities far above, with no people to speak of. Then someone whistled at the right flank and Wish took cover, peering through her scope. Private Dalliance was leaning around a tree, waving for her to come closer. Wish nodded to Toothless to cover her and hurried back.

"Bodies," Dalliance reported. "Back this way."

Wish followed him down a slope to a rocky creek with a small stream running through. There were two dead goblins and one human strewn across the rocks. Dead for some time, by their colour and the dried blood on the rocks – one goblin peppered with arrows and the other cut open by a sword. The man, another scantly clad Woodwing, had a large chunk missing from his side. It looked like a small skirmish that had occurred away from the main fighting, unnoticed, hence the untouched remains. Scraper was standing guard, rifle low and face steely.

Dalliance prodded the closer goblin, the pin-cushion for arrows. "He's a green-coat alright, if that needed confirming."

Wish considered the uniform on the small figure, messily stitched where the green fabric had been torn apart and reformed from a much bigger person's clothes. There was something painfully childlike about it, recalling boys pretending to be soldiers, and despite the horror of the death ward, Wish felt a sadness rising in her. The inhuman creature looked more animal than man, peaceful and innocent in death, despite its sharp teeth and claws.

"Think there's more nearby?" Dalliance asked quietly.

"The opposite," Wish said. "These bodies were untouched; they haven't come here."

"Look at this thing." Dalliance crouched, picking up the goblin's rifle. It was as tall as the goblin and block-like, its square barrel four inches wide, its trigger encircled by a fist-sized ring, overlarge to compensate for clumsy goblin claws. "Bloody heavy. These small bastards must be strong as you like."

"Bag gun," Scraper said, and Dalliance looked up for more.

She didn't explain, but Wish knew what she meant, so completed the thought: "Cheap Balnian guns designed to fire whatever you can stuff in the containers. Usually packed with bags of scrap, hence the name. They're weak and inaccurate; the gunpowder fires the mechanism like a catapult rather than directly propelling a bullet.

But still deadly at close range." She nodded to the big hole in the Woodwing.

"Without meaning offence," Dalliance said, with a smile that was sure to precede something better left unsaid, "but you ladies are about as scary as you are intriguing, you know?"

Wish shrugged. She was surprised herself at the level of knowledge she had for such things now. But it paid to know about all guns, seeing as she might not always have the Long 0.48 handy. And on the plus side, at least Dalliance had got some cheer back since Paradise Fails.

"They died a while ago, anyway," Wish said. "We're safe to carry on."

Scraper took that as a cue to lead the way, and the scout slung her rifle over a shoulder to climb the rocks. Dalliance was still considering the bag gun, and said, "Mind if I keep hold of this? It's really something."

"You want to lug two guns around, that's your business," Wish said. "As long as it doesn't get in the way of –"

A far-off squawk cut through the creek.

Wish looked up to Scraper, halfway up the rocks with a wide-eyed, questioning expression. The noise came again: a call for attention. Not human. She looked at the bodies again. Of course, just because these goblins hadn't been found didn't mean no one was looking.

She nodded to Scraper to take a look and the scout quickly glided up the rest of her cliff face. She poked a head over, then ducked down again, holding up two fingers.

The voice came again, closer, now speaking a language that didn't sound entirely Drail. Wish went the other way, readying her rifle and climbing up the creek. She hurried over rocks until she reached a tree near the top and peered around. She saw Toothless, pressed against a tree of his own, rifle clutched to his chest. She caught his eye, nodded to tell him things were under control. Then to the other side, there was Scraper, crouched behind a rock with her gun ready.

At a rustle of leaves, Wish peeked out of cover and saw the

goblin, closer than expected – thirty feet away at most, skulking between the trees. The surprise almost made her gasp, the squat thing short but stocky, its wide head and overlarge, crooked mouth folded with leathery green flesh, yellow eyes searching. It had similar baggy clothing to the dead ones, and the same massive bag gun, as cumbersome as a pile of lumber in its arms. Wish rested her finger on her trigger. But if she fired, it might bring a whole army running. She caught Scraper's eye, the other scout looking her way, and raised a finger to her lips.

Scraper narrowed her eyes, nodded, then darted away between the rocks. Wish stared at the absent space she'd left. Was that somehow unclear? The first direct order she had ever issued to the woman and the response was running off to do her own thing?

The leaves crunched again and Wish gave the goblin another glance, a couple paces closer. With no other movement nearby, she was thankful the rest of her platoon were further back, waiting for her cue. She lowered her gun and slid a hand to her short blade. A few more steps and she heard the creature grumbling. A little closer and he'd come around her position. She slid the sword out, slowly and quietly.

A voice called from further back, hurried and aggravated, in that sinister hiss of theirs, and the goblin snapped something feral back. At the sound of more crunching footsteps, Wish leant out to see the greenskin ready to retreat. Then Scraper launched out from the trees beside it, somehow barely arms' length away, one hand cocked up over her head flashing a large butcher's knife as the other reached towards the goblin. Her arm wrapped around its neck before it could cry out. She fell down dragging the greenskin with her, stabbing viciously. The goblin struggled, wide and strong enough to almost throw her off despite her height advantage, but Scraper held on like a rodeo-rider and swept the blade back with a slick splatter of blood. Then she was up in a crouch, dragging the body quickly into the undergrowth, its gun left behind, all in the time it had taken for Wish to take a breath.

But however quickly Scraper had moved, it wasn't enough: far beyond the goblin murder, Wish saw a second greenskin, eyes bulging in witness. Too far away to tackle. There was nothing for it, Wish skidded out from the tree and whipped up her rifle, calling out in a hushed snarl, "Stop!"

The goblin gawked for a second, dropped its huge rifle and ran. Wish swore and sprinted after it, swapping her rifle and short blade between her hands. She picked it out leaping between trees, gaining distance despite her longer legs. She tried to double her speed. There was light ahead – open space – and she slowed before she reached it, seeing the goblin pull away. Wish skidded up next to a tree trunk, the edge of the forest, and watched the goblin charging up a grassy hill, towards a distant cluster of farm buildings.

Scraper tore up next to Wish, rifle raised, but Wish made a noise at her to stop. The scout gave her an angry look, wired from the kill and wearing the warpaint of blood, as Dalliance came huffing up on the other side. Wish quickly said, "Don't shoot – everyone's gonna know where we are. The little bastard isn't raising an alarm yet. He's scared shitless."

"But . . ." Dalliance said, not adding more as he caught his breath.

Wish watched the goblin, so fast it was almost out of range now. She said, "Send word back, everyone shift south, take cover. We need to get away and spread out. We can't be far from our exit."

Scraper nodded and left, but Dalliance hesitated. He gave the goblin one more look, now barely a dot in the long grass. That it wasn't screaming for help was a good sign, and Wish added, "Go ahead, I'll hold the rear."

"Lieutenant –"

A gunshot cut him off, and Wish snapped her head around to see the mist of the goblin's head erupting over the grass as it collapsed. The bang echoed over the field like a thunderclap, though its origin had been clear enough. Another fifty yards up the tree line, Toothless was down on one knee, rifle steady against his shoulder. An incredible shot at that distance. And an incredibly unwelcome announcement of their presence.

"Fuck," Wish said. "Get out of here. *Now!*"

Dalliance startled into action and ran after Scraper, his two guns rattling, and Wish ducked to watch for signs of an enemy response. Toothless lowered his rifle, turning her way. He gave her a thin smile, proud of the shot and oblivious to the trouble he might have caused. Wish held up a hand for him to stay put while she scanned the field. As long as they were still, any approaching enemies wouldn't see them. And there, beyond Toothless, she saw the first signs of the enemy: a group of huddling goblins ran snarling out of the trees, scattering into the grass without caution. As they spread out, Wish watched for a gap in their concentration, then waved Toothless back. He nodded understanding, the pride now replaced with concern, and he rose to move. The same moment, another gunshot blasted from across the field and his head snapped back, body collapsing.

Wish stared rigidly at the space Toothless had occupied, the young gone in the undergrowth. She slowly pulled her eyes away across the grass, past the goblins as they hopped up and down with a mixture of confused anger and jubilation. She saw the farm buildings on the hill. Where an enemy sniper was apparently waiting.

A sniper with exceptional aim.

33

Nine times out of ten, the element of surprise will decide a duel. Who sees who first. This is why we must excel at hiding, spotting, and patience above all. To doubt our chosen position and move too soon is fatal. Still, an ability to shoot with absolute perfection, and an element of luck, is also desirable.

Sniping in Farne, Heskeph, p. 18

He hadn't been watching before, Wish told herself, as if that simple fact was something to hold onto. If the sniper had seen them earlier, he would have shot her. Scraper and Dalliance too. He had been ready quickly after the gunshot though, finding Toothless in a wide tree line. He didn't know she was there, yet, but he'd spot her if she made the slightest mistake.

She stayed very, very still. Just able to keep an eye on the high farm buildings, from the shelter of a tree that she hoped cast thick enough shadow that she was mostly hidden. She watched half the goblins scuttling up the hill, two noticing their dead comrade and two excitedly approaching the farm. With any luck, they'd expose the sniper's position. But the others, another three more, were jogging towards Toothless's body. Wish split her attention, wanting to stop them as much as she wanted to spot the sniper. The image of the dead Woodwing resurfaced in her mind; she couldn't let them do that to one of her men.

The goblins up the hill disappeared between the buildings, their laughter and cheers filtering over the field, then they went quiet, no sign of where they'd gone. The ones reaching the tree line got noisier, gathering around Toothless. They prodded at him and one picked up his rifle, hoisting it overhead. He'd only had it for a morning. He'd been so relieved to be rearmed, and was itching to prove himself . . . Another goblin lifted a limp arm, tearing at it to remove his wristwatch, and Wish's muscles tightened with her urge to gun them down. It would be easy, with their big heads. But it would get her killed and it wouldn't bring Toothless back. He had died instantly, from that shot – she was sure enough of that.

With the greatest care, Wish slid down to her belly and placed her short blade on the ground, taking her rifle in both hands and quietly removing the scope cover. She shimmied back as slowly as possible while the goblins chittered over the body of her man. She tried to ignore them – her focus had to be on the sniper. There was no chance of moving with him up there. He might have even had a view towards the others, ready to pick them off if they left the woods.

She scanned the farm buildings through her scope: a barn, two single-storey cottages and the main house with a silo to the rear. All closely packed together, wooden with arched, thatched roofs. The windows at ground level were barely visible at this angle, leaving the gangway around the silo, maybe thirty feet high, or the two top floors of the main building, as vantage points. There were two windows, one open a crack and the other open wide, darkness inside. Above them, a third circular window, closed, but near an empty hole in the wood panels, broken from disrepair. Or possibly on purpose, for a good view out. There was also tall grass around the bases of the buildings, and between them, where someone could lie, sneaky if they thought your attention was drawn further up.

No. These people were watching half a forest; he'd want the highest ground, for the best view. But not the silo: its gangway was too exposed. She saw no bulky shadows there, no one lying in wait. The second-storey windows would be her choice. There were two, to provide confusion and alternative positioning. You could set up away from the open window, almost invisible in the shadow while having an excellent view.

Then again, that hole in the attic was small enough to conceal a sniper shifting from side to side. She trained the spot in her sights and looked over the rifle, judging the distance. The two goblins in the field were jumping around their fallen comrade, as amused by his death as the others were about Toothless. Another one had returned from the farm buildings and was peering out over the field, a little more serious. Back along the tree line, the goblins got louder as they argued over something of Toothless's, and there was a brief scuffle, something tearing. Wish blocked them from her mind, adjusting her sights, and watched the hole in the attic. The sniper would be prone, his head directly in line of the opening.

But she had to be sure. She'd only have one shot. If she chose wrong, he'd pick her out quicker than she could adjust her aim. The goblins would be coming for her.

Wish lay waiting. Slowing her breath, stilling her chest. She watched the darkness, finger on her trigger.

A goblin snarled with particular ferocity, and was pushed or stumbled loudly through branches, in Wish's direction. She flinched at the sound, as if it was about to fall directly on her, then tensed fully to force herself still. Quickly, she scoped the attic again, and saw movement.

Carrow had not slept. He would not for at least another day, he suspected; he doubted the Stanclif forces would remain hidden longer than that. It was still hard to believe that he'd clipped a mage in the woods. It was a long shot, and obscured, and he'd thought it to be a straggling Irregular until the goblins reported otherwise. If he'd known, he would've been more careful to eliminate the mage's companions, instead of retreating from Kasidee's rear guard. But it was an achievement nonetheless. He might be recommended for a medal for taking down a mage. They might give him a serious reassignment, at last.

In the meantime, he was left responsible for organising the Drail line for maximum cover of the woods, to return to Carlwen when a satisfactory watch was in place. He'd attended to the former and disregarded the latter. There wouldn't be a satisfactory watch without him, and what was he going to do in Carlwen anyway, drink hot cocoa and watch the sun set?

Carrow knew the maps well, and there were only two ways any sensible scout was leaving those trees. Kin Kasidee had already taken the first option, fleeing north-west, and that was Ilscot's problem now. Whether Stanclif sent an army or just a couple of assassins, they'd want to leave the woods near the village of Nufan, and circle up towards Carlwen from there. It was a village overlooked by a hill that took in half of Midwood's eastern frontier. Short of Stanclif sending a full armoured platoon, no one would leave those trees unchecked by him.

Dusk had fallen to night and Carrow kept his careful vigil. He had a blanket for warmth, biscuits and cold soup for sustenance. He scoped the trees more carefully in the dark, picking out small animals, the swaying of branches in the wind. Night turned to morning. He took the briefest breaks to stretch his muscles and relieve himself in a metal bucket, always with one eye out the window. He saw goblins move through the fields, filtering in and out of the trees with zero discretion. There were gunshots deeper in the words but little more; either minor run-ins with remaining Woodwings or, more likely, just goblins fucking around.

Towards lunchtime, Carrow's body protested, growing numb from a need to rest, but he remained focused, knowing the time was coming. Within hours. Half a day at most. He'd enjoy Carlwen's comforts in the evening, when he'd stopped the enemy advance.

More goblins shifted along the trees, even noisier than before, and he watched them with disdain, their caution falling exactly when it should've been highest. But they would provide a distraction. And sure as day followed night, the action came.

A goblin ran from the trees, up towards his position. No gun. A terrified, weak-willed thing. There didn't appear to be anyone following, until a gun flashed in the trees and the goblin fell. Carrow quickly targeted its source and fired without thinking, rifle already adjusted for the tree line. There was a moment's stillness as he observed the man's body – and the rifle fallen by him. The man was a skilled marksman, to have got the goblin from there. First a mage, now an accomplished sniper. There would be more. He swept his gun across the trees as the goblins burst out squealing. The little mob should've been enough to inspire a skirmish, if anyone was following the sniper, but the trees appeared empty again.

Then two goblins started blundering up to his position. A day of waiting and they were going to ruin it all. He hesitated against ordering them off or abandoning his post – needed to keep watching the trees. When he was confident they were in earshot he tried to shout, without moving, "S-s-s –"

It wouldn't come. He jammed his teeth together in frustration. One of the goblins thumped on a wall, calling up, "Who's here? Who we got? Show yourself!"

"Stop!" Carrow burst out, with more venom that was necessary. His cheeks burnt with the effort, but his voice carried loud enough to stall the goblins. Quickly, he continued, "Take cover and k-k – k-keep low! Quiet!"

The goblins cursed loudly, angry at being told what to do.

"It's C-C-Carrow!" he shouted, and that silenced them. One continued walking between the buildings, searching about as if to spot him, while the other hung back. He tried to ignore them, eyes on the trees again.

Snipers didn't work alone. There had to be at least one other enemy out there. And he hadn't seen anyone falling back. He just needed to spot them. The sun was above the trees, creating stark shadow, not ideal, but it meant most movement would be obvious. He ran his scope over the tree trunks, rocks too small to hide behind, bushes too dense. Midwood was not great shelter, with its large trees leaving wide paths between them. And the goblins were fluttering about, nasty enough to unsettle anyone. He imagined a sniper trying to pick out his spot. Not the silo, not the ground level. Surely the attic hole. A good spot, where he had indeed lain for part of the night.

Not now, though. The south window was his current position of choice, secure in a chair with the rifle resting over an upturned desk. Far enough back to be confident no one would see him.

The hall door opened below and a goblin plodded heavily into the building. It called up, "Sergeant you in here? Got orders from Atmoor."

"Sh-sh-sh –" Carrow tried to talk through the side of his mouth. He clenched his teeth again and let it go. The goblin thumped about, checking the downstairs rooms, as if he would hide there.

"Probably pointless now," the goblin said. "Seeing as Alfri's caught a bullet. Reckon we oughta slaughter them all."

What was he talking about? Carrow grimaced, straining to focus. A full day of quiet and when trouble came there had to be a goblin throwing his concentration. His eyelids felt heavy suddenly and he wished he could blink this away. But he had to secure the battle line, make it clear no one was leaving those trees . . .

"You see any more of them?" the goblin asked, plodding heavily up the stairs.

"F-f-fuck," Carrow growled to himself. Then a sudden movement in the trees caught the corner of his eye, the goblins down there fighting. Another movement in response, not far from them – there he was, the enemy – so close, the bastard! Carrow rapidly adjusted his aim and centred the cross hair on his face.

Her face.

He hesitated, mind abuzz. Imperial Stanclif, champion of Civilisation, were arming women? She was young. Didn't belong here. Pretty –

Wild Wish's sights found the movement, an unmistakable shape in the shadow, a head behind it, and she fired. She watched only long enough to see him fall. Her heart thumped – she'd made the shot, redirected, but almost hadn't – *she'd been watching the wrong place* – and she quickly redirected to the goblins squawking at the sound of her gunshot.

She rolled onto her back and kicked through the dirt, away from the trio lumbering towards her. She pushed up to a crouch as they exploded onto her position, spread in a wide line. The first one was close enough she barely had to aim, tilting her rifle up from the hip. The shot erupted through its forehead with a burst of skull and brain. As she jammed her bolt back for another shot the next goblin pounced around from the side, lifting its bag gun. She dived aside. The weapon boomed through the woods, sounding like a fistful of cutlery being hurled into the trees. Wish landed hard on her shoulder and rolled as the third goblin came screaming through the air, gun swinging like a club. She just avoided it, so the weapon crashed into the ground, metal bending. She kept rolling as it followed through, trying to stomp on her, and with her third roll, she brought the rifle around and fired up through its belly. The goblin was propelled back, bottom knocked out so it landed on its face, screeching, and she quickly pushed up, chambering her next bullet.

The other goblin had its bag gun aimed at her face, and its mouth spread in a vile, victorious grin. Wish saw the barrel of death, knowing this was it, and flinched at the gunshot. The goblin was thrown aside as a bullet tore through its temple, ripping out an eye and spraying blood over Wish's face. Past its falling body she saw the other goblins racing down the hill with their guns raised, roaring battle cries, but a salvo of gunfire followed. The shots were erratic and spread out, the leading goblin cut down by two or three, the next one clipped in the shoulder and sent spiralling through the grass. The last charging goblin was peppered by shots but managed to turn, and ran back a few paces before it was hit and fell. One more goblin, up by the farm buildings, ducked into cover.

A man took rough grip of Wish's arm and pulled her to her feet. She banged into a solid chest and felt his breath on her face as a Raw accent asked, "Are you hurt, Lieutenant? Can you walk?"

"I'm fine," Wish said, barely able to focus as the man all but dragged her clear of the mess of goblin bodies. The woodland and field were painted with bloody innards. She glanced back and said, "Toothless –"

"Nothing to be done," the man grunted. Macmiddan, she realised. Dalliance and Scraper were at the tree edge, guns aimed. Brade and Ptrangus were further along.

"I told you all to go," Wish said, as they retreated, converging on her. Far off, she thought she heard shouting.

"Well," Ptrangus huffed, "are we Blood Scouts now or not?"

34

It was here that I saw Shade.
Here They spoke to me and I learnt of the Shadows.
There can be no light without dark. No dark without light.
The Book of Bones, Sandway,
translated by Birganio, 82:13

As Wish's platoon hurried out of the woods, to an abandoned plot of old huts, she was vaguely aware of making quiet repeated promises that no more of them would die. They couldn't – they weren't yet a platoon, not by a long way, barely a squad, and she'd had enough of losing them. Enough of feeling like she couldn't protect them. They just had to cut the head off this monster. Get to Colonel Atmoor, save Emi. As the men caught their breath in an empty barn, she paced, snarling threats, until Captain Brade stepped into her path and said, "You're scaring them."

Wish paused, scanning those who were left. The three Rawboys looked tired and angry. Dalliance, leaning against the wall with his arms folded, had the same empty gaze from when Fawcet had got chopped in half. And Scraper, who'd kicked all this off, really, was blood-stained like she'd showered in it, standing with dark, unaffected eyes. Without knowing exactly what Brade was referring to, Wish fixed her mood on the lone true Blood Scout she had left, tempted to scold her. Blame her. But it wasn't Scraper's fault Toothless took a bullet. It wasn't Toothless's fault, either. It was a good shot and his intentions were sound. It was just war. Damned war. Forcing her tension out through clenched teeth, Wish said, "Alright. We lost a good man, but we'll mourn later. Do our job first."

"If they're this far south," Macmiddan said, "our route might be compromised."

"No," Wish answered before working out why. "That was one squad. If they had more nearby we'd already know it. But we've got to move before they get a chance to cut us off."

"That was half a dozen goblins," Ptrangus pointed out. "There's a thousand more."

"Yeah, I'd like to keep ahead of them, wouldn't you?" Wish said, and grabbed her rifle, her pack. "Let's get to the river before nightfall."

The men grumbled, but not loud enough to mean anything. Wish watched them readying themselves. Brade gave her a look that said he wanted to ask how she was really doing, the usual, and she gave him a look warning against it. He moved to the front and announced that he'd lead. He'd studied the maps and had a keen eye for trouble, so he said, and the troop believed him. Wish held back as they left the barn, until it was just her and Scraper staring outside. The blood-stained woman was watching Wish with caution, unsure if she was going to be told off. Or maybe if she should preemptively attack? It wasn't the time for this; Wish needed to divert.

"You did well," she said, unconvincingly. Then she latched onto an odd detail from the start of all this. "Why've you got a butcher's knife?"

Scraper continued staring, disconcertingly quiet. She reached around to the back of her belt. The scout drew her knife and Wish just managed to keep from flinching. The thing was even bigger and cruder up close than it had looked bleeding that goblin. It had been wiped clean, just about, and Scraper held it out.

Wish frowned. "Keep it. I don't care if it's regulation, it's just *odd.*"

Impassively, Scraper ignored the comment and waved the knife towards Wish's own belt. The empty sheath where her short blade should've been, left back there with the dead goblins.

"Oh. Thanks. No, you keep it. It's not my . . . style."

Scraper said, "We'll have more throats to cut."

It was Wish's turn to keep quiet. The woman had a sinister way about her, a sinister voice. Her wording, carefully chosen, wasn't quite right. Too general.

To cement this unnerving impression, Scraper pushed the knife forward again and said, "Please. I have more."

They made slow progress up through the rural region Brade referred to as the Saint Sails. There wasn't much cover, besides hedges and occasional clusters of farmhouses, or villages they needed to avoid for fear of people. The scouts moved smoothly though, hopping over each other's positions with an efficiency that rebuilt Wish's confidence. The Rawboys' experience started to show as they covered their tracks, subtly avoiding surfaces that would leave footprints, or deliberately creating distractions, breaking branches and carving paths in the wrong directions. They were quiet and operated without instruction. At one point Ptrangus slipped away for twenty minutes and returned with a building smoking on the horizon. As they crested the next hill, Wish saw a distant goblin squad rushing towards the burning hut, the extreme diversion apparently successful.

She was aware that they weren't far ahead of the enemy at any time, and Brade kept adapting their route as the squad noticed movements at their flanks. Their progress was good and Wish tried to recall Havik's encouragement, recognising the thrill of avoiding capture. A job well done. Then, as they were passing a burnt-out farm, while she crouched by a broken wall with half the group moving ahead, Dalliance came bumbling up from behind. Barely keeping his voice down, he said, "Trouble! Trouble!"

Swearing, Wish skirted around the other side of the wall and readied her rifle, just as a big object came clambering into view, pecked at by a rabble of small pursuers. The insect was immediately familiar and gave Wish a chill – Sister Sonseen, entirely out of place, was riding fast through the farm, with a handful of goblins waving their guns about, shouting at her to stop. She turned her mount in a clearing and the goblins swept out around her, with more hopping over broken bits of building. Surrounded, Sonseen tried to calm the insect by tugging at the reins. The goblins snatched up to try and take the straps for themselves, shouting conflicting orders.

Wish clutched her rifle, ready to shoot, but there were a dozen of them, more behind, with her squad already too far ahead to return unnoticed.

The goblins were trying to stop the insect though, not attacking, and Sister Sonseen exuded calm as she responded with her usual stern voice, one hand raised for clemency. They held back, apparently recognising her robes, seeing she was a civilian to capture rather than kill. The exchange that followed was in Garter, the goblins calming as one took charge, wearing a fine green officer's jacket several sizes too large. He spoke with a grin and his goblins bobbed about with chuckles, whatever he was saying laced with bad humour. Sonseen sneered and replied bluntly. She looked like a woman inconvenienced rather than at risk of being torn apart, but Wish recalled the death ward and felt enough fear for both of them.

Then their eyes met, Sonseen looking over the goblin heads as she turned on her restless insect. It lasted only a second, as the nun looked away again not to draw attention, but Wish saw the warning in her look. Sonseen quickly guided her mount around and gestured ahead, inviting the goblins to lead her away. They fell into ranks around her, following the insect out of the clearing, the opposite direction to the scouts, and the officer puffed himself up proudly, capture successful.

Wish knitted her brow, ready to gun them down and save the nun, but the retreat happened too fast. Sonseen had done this deliberately, unafraid of being taken. Somehow, Wish felt that was the point – a demonstration that she was safe. Why? What was she doing here? She wanted to contact the other priories, she'd said, but surely not Carlwen – and if she had, why take this route? She must have been following the scouts.

"Should we go after her?" Dalliance suggested as the goblins and the mounted nun passed out of view through the farm.

"No," Wish said. "They're not going to hurt a nun. We'll find her in Carlwen, too." She sounded more confident than she felt.

***

In the late afternoon, as it grew darker, a column of crooked towers came into view, with great canvas windmills fanning from the tips, unusually warped and dark, like half-melted candles. Brade explained they were the last vestiges of the extensive, ancient turbines that gave the Shadow Sails its name. Some were crumpled with rotten supports, but even the sturdy ones were deliberately twisted in their design, having been built according to visions recorded by the twin prophets, Tusk and Nael. Wish questioned what exactly qualified the saints to design buildings and Ptrangus said, "Not much, apparently."

"Some think they double as totems," Brade said. "But the prophets left their mark in the Mire in countless ways, with cryptic symbols and practices that centuries of scholars have never really unravelled. They may have been forms of worship or merely eccentricities. At their most effective, the prophets' relics likely tapped into the dual schools of magic for unique results. What if those windmills, for example, were designed to form a conduit between earth energies, configured in such a way that could make the turbines turn faster?"

"Do they?" Graveguard asked.

"I don't know. They might just be badly designed, that's the point."

The soldiers sniggered.

"How *ancient* are they?" Wish asked.

"Before Castor, at least," Brade said. "Seven hundred years, maybe more."

"Then I guess they did something right, if they're still standing."

"Or they're broken in just the right way to keep upright," Dalliance suggested.

The men chuckled again. Wish appreciated the levity. These windmills were a rare clue back to why they were here, if it was for anything: this place was special in ways they didn't even know. They'd protect it, as Havik intended. She strolled on, keeping the crooked windmills in view as the men led the way, and she reconsidered Dalliance words. *Broken in just the right way.* She liked that. Like a young woman who didn't belong in a war, and had picked up entirely inappropriate skills and responsibilities. *We've found our place,* Havik had said. Worth it, if she managed to kill others before they killed her and those she cared about.

Mostly.

Wish kept her smile until they reached a village littered with bodies. A road joined low-lying wooden houses separated by unkempt fields. The corpses were spread between them at regular intervals, so that the squad were able to keep a clear distance but unable to look anywhere without seeing death. Days old, picked at by birds and animals, there was a mix of murdered peasants and gunned-down Drail soldiers. Men, this time, not goblins. That made three populations of locals lost to fighting that had nothing to do with them, counting the village near Drowndeep, the Woodwings and these farmers.

"Least someone gave as good as they got," Macmiddan murmured.

"Possibly the Irregulars," Brade said. "But I don't see why Atmoor's men would've attacked this village."

"They're all pricks, aren't they?" Ptrangus said. "Goblins, men, privates and officers. Green-coats think they got a right to abuse anyone that's not Drail."

"They don't have a monopoly on brutality," Brade countered.

"You what?" The Rawboy mugged confusion, as if Brade spoke too eloquently to understand.

Wild Wish was only vaguely listening, watching for survivors. The enemy must've been driven off or they would've done something about the bodies and collected the guns. But had the village been completely massacred first, to leave this mess?

As they left the main road and tramped into a field, she noticed a distant farmhouse, and a movement in a window. In an instant, she was down on one knee with her scope on the window and her men scrambling to take cover. Dalliance called out, "What is it? Who's there?"

Macmiddan snapped at him for quiet as the others took positions aiming in all directions. Wish was gripped with an irrational spark of fear that the sniper had returned. Her shot in the dark hadn't killed him and he was there with all of them out in the open. She only just kept from squeezing the trigger. It couldn't be him. They'd be dead already if it was.

Whatever she had seen, if it hadn't been imagined, the person had ducked out of sight. She took a breath and rose slightly. Everything was still. With more bodies between them and the house, maybe it was just wishful thinking that there was something left alive here.

"Might be nothing," she said. "I'm taking a look."

"I'm with you," Brade said, his pistol up and ready. She nodded and they bent low to rush towards the farmhouse, the others covering them from behind. Wish kept her eye on the windows, but realised the door was wide open, the house as empty as the rest of the village. She got there first, pressing herself in at one side of the door as Brade braced himself against the other. With another brief nod, they both stepped inside, guns ready.

Wish almost gagged at the amount of blood.

There were legs, and bits of arms, perhaps a fragment of head, but most of the man (if it was only one) was spread across the rear walls of the hallway, his torso popped like a fleshy balloon. The sight broke Brade's typical calm where the goblin death ward hadn't, and he swore as he put a fist to his mouth. The blood was dry, almost black where it had sunk into the walls and furniture, innards wrinkled. There were tiny movements of insects Wish didn't dare look at closely.

Momentarily pushing this sight into a dark corner of her mind, hopefully never to be revisited, Wish stepped into the building and swept her rifle first through the doorway to the left, then to the right. More blood, and smears across the floor, but no other bodies. A husk of bread sat on a kitchen counter.

"There is someone here," she whispered. Brade crept past her, an eye on the stairs beyond the gore, and she rejoined him to follow his gaze. Small footprints in the blood.

"By Bly," he muttered, then raised his voice, announcing something in one of the local dialects. Wish watched his face, not sure they should be so brash. He called out again, tone friendly. A shadow came around the top of the stairs and Wish raised her gun. Brade's hand pushed the barrel down, the captain more ready than her. A young boy poked his head out, a rifle shaking in his hands. He was filthy with old mud, possibly blood, and his big eyes shone white with fear.

He replied in the same language, voice quaking like his hands, and Wish didn't need to understand the words to know their meaning: this was his house, and he'd shoot them if they weren't careful. He wasn't scared. Honest.

Brade responded patiently. He indicated the bloody mess and the world outside. The boy, with tearful eyes, lowered his gun and spoke in a voice that now made no pretence of bravery. Wish heard the name *Kin Kasidee.* A question. Brade shook his head. The child considered this carefully, looking between them, then he dropped his rifle and ran down the stairs. Wish lifted her rifle, but was too close to aim before he reached her. Then the boy's arms were wrapped around her waist and he was sobbing into her stomach, as she stiffly stood staring over him to Brade. He looked concerned.

"Kasidee was here," he said. "They killed the green-coats alright. Saved this boy."

"If he was saved why's he so . . . like this?" Wish said, keeping her elbows high as the boy clung tight. He was frail and vulnerable, and she could feel the desperation in his clutch.

"It's safe to assume he saw this happen. And . . . they left him here."

Wish considered the carnage again. The carnage outside. The fact that this child was left alone after seeing some awful things – at least partly involving Kin Kasidee. Something about that sat uncomfortably. This, she supposed, was what Brade meant when he said the Irregulars weren't serious. The sort of soldiers that left a hell of a mess behind.

"What should we do with him?" Wish asked, quietly, and the boy finally peeled himself away from her, sensing she was talking about him. Or finally realising she was hard as a plank.

He smeared a forearm over his snotty nose and mumbled a question that ended with "Havikare?"

"What the fuck?" Wish snapped accusingly, making him jump, so his foot landed in a bit of the remnant guts and he slipped with a shriek. Brade caught him, saving him from a much messier fall, and quickly offered assurances. The boy glanced sideways at Wish in fear, before hurriedly trying to explain.

"He's confused," Brade translated. "Shaken up. He asked if you were her. He met her." The captain gave a deliberate look to the eviscerated body, his point clear enough. They were looking at the effects of a Camanese Stop Gun.

"So she saved him," Wish whispered, a hopeful thought caught up in an uglier one. Havik had also left him here. Wish met Brade's eye, not sure what else to think. Her immediate instinct was to put it very quickly behind them. Get on with the job. *Don't* think.

Wish's squad crept tiredly into the night, the highs and lows of the day at last drifting towards numbness. She kept her mind as blank as she could make it. The seeds of doubts that Caracker had sowed in Midpeak were spreading. Now there was an abandoned child, a massacre and the weirdness of Sister Sonseen racing after them . . . Wish strained to focus. Save Emi, stop Atmoor, tackle the Irregulars question later. There'd be reasonable explanations which they could laugh off and seal with a hug. After all, when Wish took the child with them, to beyond the nearby ruined settlements, was that really any more responsible than leaving him behind? People got hurt around her.

At one point, Dalliance had to hold a hand over the frightened boy's mouth as they all hunkered under hedges, watching a pack of goblins skittering past. Their yellow eyes and teeth were especially frightening in the half-light, and it felt like only a matter of time before they'd stumble upon the scouts by chance. They were travelling through open land at unsafe speeds, with the enemy just out of sight, after all. The scouts couldn't pass the boy off quickly enough, and Wish happily left it to Dalliance and Ptrangus to race away to the east to find some slightly less dangerous place to leave him. When the pair returned, childless, she accepted their assurances that he was safe without asking for details.

Darkness shielded the final approach to Carlwen, the countryside crawling with more Drail. A final ridge brought them a hundred metres from a host of green-coat soldiers billeted with tents and campfires. A makeshift watch tower had been erected at the edge of the river, likely enjoying an annoyingly panoramic, unobstructed view, which the esoteric and impractical town walls with their scythe-shaped turrets would've lacked.

While Wish scanned the soldiers on the ground and those on the wall, looking for a way past, Brade lay close beside her with his telescope.

"So," Brade said, with nothing to follow.

"Yeah," Wish replied. She had got through tightly guarded lines in the past, crawling along trenches, navigating sewers and tunnels, and in one case descending a cliff on a rope. Usually, someone else – mostly Captain Tate – had provided her with a plan. Wish was there to do the killing, not the scheming, and she saw now that her idea of getting close to Atmoor lacked a few final details. She remembered Reeve Abbey, when they'd rushed in with disastrous results. How was she supposed to do better here?

"Their main entrance is to the north," Brade said. "They must have supplies coming and going. If we were able to disguise ourselves as merchants . . ."

"That town is locked tight," Wish replied. "If they let anyone in at all, we're not going unnoticed. Maybe the guards will thin out later, though. They can't stay up all night."

Brade gave her a look that, fairly, said her idea was as useless as his.

Wish bit her lip. "We need a big distraction. Havik should've reached the Irregulars by now. If they draw the Drail's attention, we could slip in, get Atmoor with his back turned."

"Except Kasidee will want *us* to create an opening," Brade

pointed out. Then he added a thought she had very much wanted to avoid: *"If* he comes."

There it was. The doubt made real, hard and unpleasant. It was stewing in Wish too, damn Brade and Caracker. Damn the random reappearance of Sister Sonseen and that massacred farm. None of it alone was enough to warrant too much concern but all together it was building up. She murmured, "Even if they're not entirely on the level, you said yourself they're looking for a fight."

"I'm not sure of the nature of it, though. And Kasidee won't attack the Drail without an opening." Brade paused. "You spoke to Havik. What impression of them did *you* get?"

Wish baulked at the direct question, because her immediate responses would definitely sound unprofessional. *Oddly alluring. Attractively smart.* She thought back to Havik's motivations, though, and how much she respected the Saints Mire and its history. That sounded serious. Though also, now she thought of it, somewhat murky on the specifics. Havik wasn't religious and her thugs definitely didn't look pious. An academic interest was unlikely to have them throwing their lives away on brave assaults. Then a darker detail came to mind, one that might've better explained her will to fight. Wish said, "Her town was burnt down. Everyone she knew was killed."

"Mm. Most partisans have seen that sort of suffering. Did she say where?"

"Kopice," Wish said. He gave her one of his deeper scowls. "What? Somewhere you actually haven't heard of?"

"Oh, I've heard of it. The massacre of Kopice was one of the most damning events in the opening stages of the war. Hundreds of civilians dead. Stanclif Command went to great lengths to keep it quiet."

"Huh. They usually love throwing stories of Drail atrocities at us."

"Exactly," Brade said. "They don't want anyone hearing so much about *our* atrocities."

Now Wish shared his frown. This definitely felt like a Bad Sign.

"It was early on," Brade continued. "The battle lines were still being drawn and those on the front were jumpy. Our officers thought Kopice was crawling with Drail spies, or insurgents or whatever, and things got out of hand. The accounts vary but the worst is most likely true. They killed everyone rather than risk the town hiding the enemy."

Wish's eyes widened. Why hadn't Havik mentioned *their* side had done it? Why hadn't she joined up with the Drail, instead of the Comity? She fumbled out an explanation without thinking it through, "Havik hated the people in her town."

"What else did she say?" Brade pressed.

"Only that it burnt."

As Brade's expression grew sterner, Wish had an urge to defend Havik. She was clever, believed in their cause, could probably see how much worse the Drail were than the Comity. Like the Rebel Rawboys. But he said, "Captain Tate was there."

Anything Wish could've or would've said evaporated. That little detail, just a few words, iced her veins. She gave it all the response she could: "What?"

"I don't know the details or how much of a hand she had in it, but I'm sure she was involved, there at Kopice."

"Maybe she tried to help? To stop it?"

"How well did you know Captain Tate?" Brade asked, in a manner that suggested *he* probably knew her better. As if the idea of Tate being a voice of peace was naive at best. "No. This is . . ."

"Bad," Wish admitted. Havik had wanted the Blood Scouts here. Havik was enamoured by the idea of them. Havik, who made her smile, comforted her, and *liked her* – she even protected her from that sniper. Havik, who kept calling Wish *Captain.* Did she think *she* was Captain Tate, involved in the massacre of her home town? Wish whispered, "What the hell's going on?"

"I don't know," Brade said. "But we need to tread very carefully. What else did she tell you? Anything at all?"

Wish shook her head quickly. "No. Only good things. Positive things. She wanted to work together! They're here to fight for the Mire, aren't they? Kasidee's fighting the Drail – what's it got to do with *me?"*

"I don't know," Brade repeated. "That's the problem. And we can't easily handle *that* without answering it." He pointed towards the impenetrable town and the collected strength of its occupying forces. They'd travelled days through hell, lost some good young men, and *Emi,* and they now sat before a few thousand enemies with no clear way through. And Wish couldn't help asking herself again, who would leave a child in the mess of that massacred farm?

"I . . ." Wish thought quickly, reconsidered, and realised she had to be strong. Havik and the Irregulars were a distraction – the Drail were still the enemy, and they still had Emi. Maybe? Havik was the one who had convinced her Emi would still be alive . . . She shook off that thought. "Okay. Park it for a second – we need to do *something* here, don't we? We have to get in. We'll keep watch until morning, see if there are any patterns we can exploit. See if their officers show their faces. And we'll know by dawn, I guess, where Kasidee stands. But even if we can't decimate the Drail, we *are* going to find Emi."

Brade nodded in grudging agreement.

She added, "And don't forget our ogres are with them. We do have a contingency. If something funny is going on, and Kasidee won't help us, Caracker will."

Brade hummed another wordless response, noncommittal, and a new fear surfaced she hadn't yet thought of. If Sister Sonseen was trying to bring them a message, something must have gone wrong. Were her ogres even safe with the Irregulars?

35

As a minority species whose mere existence tends to set humans on edge, Urlians everywhere have learnt over the course of oppressive centuries to keep quiet. Play it dumb. Do our best to appear to be helpful sluggards instead of intelligent, adaptable, thinking beings. As a result, not a lot of humans appreciate quite what we're capable of.

Don't Call Me Ogre: Rethinking Modern Urlian History, Blonc, p. 21

Caracker hadn't been fond of leaving Midpeak at night, nor the manner in which the Irregulars had distributed their heavily bound, clanking sacks of guns and ammo, expecting him and his ogres to shoulder the brunt of the burden. A long career in the military had taught him better than to protest, though; he knew a tricksy commander when he saw one. Havikare Eens was too charming by half, dangerous in the loyalty she created, and he had no intention of riling her until he knew exactly what she was up to. So he shouldered the packs without complaint, and instructed Runt and Ohno to do the same. He laid it out particularly clearly for Runt: "We're not rocking this boat until we know where it's heading."

They tramped down the mountain in the dark without so much as a farewell from Wild Wish or Brade. It was easy enough at first; the Irregulars had risen even earlier than the ogres, if they'd even slept, having collected what the monks would spare from the vaults, and they dragged their feet too wearily to make conversation. Havik, alone, walked with light energy, a cheery look on her face as she breathed in the mountain air and hopped onto rocks to take in the view, as if there was anything worth seeing under the mask of night.

Past the rocky tangle of the mountains, the Mire opened up again onto more flat bog, which they reached around sunrise. Their descent met mist rising from the marshlands, thick enough to obscure anything more than a few metres ahead. Havik happily said it meant they could move faster, unlikely to be spotted. Her men weren't as impressed, and the especially ugly one, Raltman, moaned that they were likely to get picked off by giant spiders or something. Caracker enjoyed their fear, especially as his extra height meant he could spot anything of that sort easily. They stuck to a dirt road wide enough for carriages, and despite the atmosphere, with creeping weeds and obscure distant silhouettes that might be rocks or monsters, it felt like the most hike Caracker had had since they'd left Hail Crossing.

The Irregulars broke mid-morning, tossing down their loads with great sighs of relief. Caracker suspected they were getting close to their destination, with the towers of Gauntstone poking over the horizon, but the marshland and its mist could be deceptive, and humans were weak, so he didn't complain – though Havik watched him as though expecting a disagreement. He and his ogres sat aside, heads down in quiet conference as they took water and rations. The Irregulars mostly spoke Garter, or occasionally Elmish, but at least a couple of them would likely understand Stanish. They were grumbling amongst themselves, and Caracker gathered the gist of it from Raltman: *why was there so much mist with the sun out?*

"The more I see of this place," Ohno commented softly, also watching the humans, "the more sense it makes that the world abandoned it."

"Until now," Caracker said.

"Half a mind to tell Kasidee to just pack it in when we reach them," Runt said. "Give it over to the Drail. What's the point even being here? Lugging this crap around." He toed one of the bags he'd been carrying, making the metal inside clatter. "Fighting for what?"

"For Civilisation," Ohno said, with a sarcastic smile. "It all adds up in the end, right? From the marshes to the cliffs to every other bit of unwanted land. Fight for the crap so we can keep the gold."

They laughed at her bastardised summary of half the propaganda the Comity flooded the papers and wireless with. The same messages, Caracker imagined, that the Drail fed their people.

"Seriously though, Sarge," Runt said. "This lot must have a few screws loose coming out here, don't you think? Bloody twisted humans."

"Agreed," Caracker said. "But if they're on our side, we can put that to use." He spotted Havikare moving closer as he spoke. She was smiling companionably, but her massive gun troubled him. It was the sort taverns once pointedly displayed to warn off bigger races.

"Couple more minutes and we're off, if that's good for you?" she said. That false smile probably won over most humans, her being pretty enough beneath her shabby coat and messy hair, but it didn't work on Caracker. Humans were far too soft and narrow.

"We're good to go right now if you want," Runt replied, overdoing a broad smile of his own.

"Great. Then I guess this is more to my men's benefit than yours, if you'll forgive the delay."

"No matter," Caracker said. "We're enjoying the view."

"And the smell," Ohno added. "I always wondered what it'd be like to visit a country where every inch stank like a Necostrian sewer."

"How much time have you spent time in Necostrian sewers?" Havik rejoined brightly. "I hear their lighting is bewitching. Gas-yellow glows on urine-stained bricks and rivers of shit."

Caracker snorted. Fair enough, she was quick. Ohno, likewise, looked amused, as she said, "Like I said, this place is *almost* as nice."

"We were just discussing," Runt said, "how it makes no sense you lot being here."

Caracker resisted kicking his shin. Havik cocked her head to one side, tiny in the middle of their circle even as they were sitting down. Always so hard to believe how much trouble the little people caused, tearing through the world. Giants didn't do as much damage as these soft little humans with their oversized weapons. She was still smiling.

"Yeah, it's not for everyone," Havik said. "This particular

quagmire, where no one wants to live?" She turned, waving an arm to encompass the wilderness. "They called it Bile, because the land itself could consume you. One wrong step and you'd sink with no hope of coming back up. But there's more history in these few miles than in half the continent of Boldarow. Battles have been fought here. The words of gods heard and recorded. Demons raised and slain."

"In storybooks," Caracker said, unable to resist.

She replied gamely, "Not entirely. You need to read between the lines, and you need to read a *lot,* but there are definite facts in the legends." She paused, holding his gaze, telling him she had more to say, if he asked.

Caracker sighed. "Go on then. Enlighten us ignorant brutes."

"I don't think you're ignorant. I happen to think Urlians are some of the most intelligent of the myriad creatures." Not bad; she got points for using their real name. Havik went on, *"Everyone's* been deceived about the Mire. There were big shifts in the records with each successive prophet rewriting history, hiding the truths of the earlier ones, and the Movement of Knowledge only consolidated that. But where you're sitting right now could be the same ground that Tikan travelled barefoot during his trials. This mist is of the same nature that trapped Milithrandobar for forty days, within which he spoke to Saint Druskard. Or, to take your point" – she gestured to Runt – "perhaps just where he thought up the teachings of Druskard himself. And there's modern history here, too – Gauntstone, where we're headed, was the site of a hundred executions during the Purge of the Mindless."

"A bloody graveyard?" Runt huffed, impossible to impress. "That's worth defending?"

"It's a place where people were inspired to great and terrible things. The whole Mire is, is my point. It's an awful place, granted, but people have changed the world from here on multiple occasions. It keeps happening and it could happen again."

Caracker narrowed his eyes, sensing she was serious about that. "What's the angle, then? How've you convinced this lot they're gonna win the war by preserving history?" He nodded to her uncultured gang. The one-eyed sniper watched them as the others kept their heads down, still cursing and complaining.

"Our company promises rewards, the Mire promises purpose," Havik answered.

"That's nice and obtuse," Runt said. "Seriously – what's it matter if these buildings crumble?"

Havik's smile returned, her gaze intense, and it was plain enough she was avoiding the crux of the question. Caracker was surer than ever that this little one was hiding something, and he got a sense that promise of *rewards* was part of it. He looked at the bags around their feet. Guns and ammo collected by the Irregulars and monks. Only, now he thought of it, there hadn't been any monks helping when they left the vaults. Just a couple who opened the gates and saw them out, and this lot sneaking around in the night.

"Ah fuck." Caracker grunted, leaning to take the closest bag. As he wrenched the straps loose, he noticed the Irregulars had gone quiet and were watching. He was uncomfortably sure of what he was going to find before he saw it. Not munitions, but the glint of gold. He placed it back down. "Are you kidding? That's why you're here?"

"No, that's a bonus," Havik said, hints of the smile still lingering on her face. Behind her, the men's hands were all close to their guns, and Runt and Ohno tensed either side of Caracker. "The Mire is a place of power. It's also a centre of incredible wealth. That's part of why it's mostly been untouched by war. It can afford to remain neutral. The priories exert influence in a variety of ways."

"You're thieves," Caracker said slowly. They were outnumbered, and his thump pistol was lying with the packs on the ground, with Ohno and Runt likewise unarmed. Even with their strength and size, he had to keep things calm. But of all the reasons he'd been thrown into the ugliest corners of war . . .

"It's bigger than that, trust me," Havik replied earnestly, one hand on her chest. Her other hand held the Camanese Stop Gun by the handle. "We just take care of our own, and this is a long journey we're on, requiring provisions."

Caracker held in his next response. He knew a lot about people taking care of their own. From the family friends of stuck-up officers who sent thousands into machine-gun fire through to cut-throat sergeants who dug gold from the teeth of their dead subordinates. The sort of people for whom taking care of their own meant screwing everyone else. Disappointing, really, but not surprising that these Irregulars were exactly what they appeared to be.

"You're torn," Havik noted. "Let me be clear. We're doing something bigger than the war. Beyond empires. But that only matters if you're willing to listen. The question is, Sergeant Caracker, what are *you* fighting for that's so precious?"

Again, he held in his answer, because it came to him too easily and too honestly. Honour. Personal honour. The whole damn world might be a mess and the people running this war were mad, but he had made his peace by being the best soldier he could in a fight for something halfway right. He had no illusions about the Comity being faultless, but he knew they stood for more equality than the Drail ever would, and it was on that side that he'd remain. It didn't matter how grand Havik wanted to make it sound, if they were fucking around here, they were enemies of peace. He had his honour, and these people had none.

"I wanted to talk to you before we reach Gauntstone," Havik went on, not needing his response, "because I think what we find there might surprise you too much. This way, you can decide with calmer spirits. Go in prepared. You'll like Kasidee, I'm sure; he's clever, brave, and honourable."

She said that last word like she *knew* it'd be important to him, and Caracker bit down his rising disquiet at the blatant untruth.

"Sarge," Runt murmured, growing impatient, "what are you thinking?"

Caracker frowned, the question a little too open. Not a *how should we handle this* but an *is it worth hearing them out?* He looked to Ohno and found her face impassive, only her eyes betraying concern. She'd be as unhappy as him, no doubt, but also knew that they weren't in a position to resist.

"Guess we oughta meet this Kasidee," Caracker said. "I'm dying to know what you've got going on beyond sacks of treasure."

"This ogre's too good for treasure, is he?" Raltman joined in, getting a few laughs from men who probably didn't even understand his Stanish. "What else you need?"

"Probably more than his share of food," Lost One put in.

They weren't hugely tense, fully expecting the ogres to be tempted. Because all ogres were opportunists and thugs like them, they just needed to be paid and pointed at a fight. That attitude had got Caracker shot eight times and repeatedly held him back from any position where his smarts could actually do a damn thing.

Havik was humourless now, though. Reading Caracker's face. Really quite a little thing, she was, behind her big gun. He could reach out and snap her neck. Bowl through the rest before they could aim properly. But the distance counted for something: Havik was beyond arm's length, and he wondered if she'd stood there deliberately.

No matter. Caracker could play her game, be a good boy and wait and see what was to come. Meet Kasidee, or break this party up once their backs were turned again. At the very least he'd get his own over-sized gun back in his hands and figure out the specifics later. He said, "Alright. I've been shot enough times with a lot less reason than this." He nudged the bag of gold with his boot. "But you take on ogres, better realise we demand a share fitting to the work we do. Which is a fucking lot."

The Irregulars grinned and one cursed in agreement, softening with relief. None of them wanted to tussle with ogres, and they clearly hadn't known how this would go. Runt blew out a satisfied breath and said, "Damn right. It's past time we got out of this stuffy fucking Stanish racket and got our due. This lot have the right idea." He laughed. "Had me worried for a second, Sarge. But don't you worry miss, we got no love for the bloody uniform."

That got some more enthusiastic cheers and jeers from the group of thugs, and Ohno, eyes on Caracker, echoed, "Damn right." Helping convince them, no way she actually believed it. But Caracker was acutely aware of the marksman at the back of the group, coldly glowering. If not for his more outward malice,

Caracker might've believed Havik's smile. Instead, he had an idea that the pair of them had picked up on Runt's own doubts about him.

"Sorry," Havik said. "Your mind was made up the moment you opened that bag, wasn't it?"

The men and the other ogres went quiet. All eyes on Caracker as his stayed on her. Fuck it. They were deciding this thing now, after all. Damned if he'd bow to these waifs. He twitched forward, one hand up to grab her and the other reaching for his gun. Havik was faster, and he'd barely moved when he clocked the rising barrel of her gun. Its thunderous shot was the loudest, last thing he heard.

36

Following reports of fraternising with the Enemy during the Relight Festival, Command reaffirms the following:

1. Unless sanctioned by Command, soldiers are not to communicate with enemy combatants through verbal, visual or other means under any circumstances.

2. Soldiers are not permitted to cease fire without explicit orders from their superiors.

3. Soldiers are to destroy, disable, or otherwise disband all Enemy military personnel, technology or other, at every given opportunity.

Failure to comply with these commands is punishable by execution without trial.

Imperial Edict 58, 720

They weren't coming, no matter how much Wild Wish tried to imagine Havik riding through the murky countryside with a hundred horses and lightning bolts or whatever. Her doubts had spread overnight, strangling any encouragement she tried to give herself. She might've explained Kopice and Havik's possible knowledge of Captain Tate as some weird misunderstanding, and the farm massacre and abandoned child as reasonable recklessness, but the thing she couldn't get around was Sister Sonseen's presence. She'd come to tell them something. To warn them. It had to be important, and it *had* to be about the Irregulars. In the best case, it was to say they'd been held up or even defeated at Gauntstone. For some reason, Wish didn't believe it was that. She couldn't get over how wrong it now felt to have enjoyed Havik's smile.

She makes everyone feel special.

Wish's concerns were confirmed by their scouting in the morning. Fun fact one: the entire perimeter of Carlwen had a generously distributed number of guards (barely diminished during the deadest hours of night). Fun fact two: the northern reaches, and out west towards wherever Kasidee might've been hiding, were as flat and unpleasant as the expanse of Paradise Fails. There was tall grass, low-hanging mist and large patches of glistening bog water that a sizeable force would struggle to move through. The areas that were stable were crowded by Drail soldiers. There was no realistic way that the Irregulars could get anywhere near Carlwen unseen.

It raised an additional doubt in Wish's heart: Havik would've known this. She knew poetic quotes about the Mire. She *must* have known Kasidee couldn't come around Carlwen from the north. Hell, they should've noticed it themselves from Turbulence's observatory.

"They never meant to come," Wish said at last, out loud, setting her rifle down on her lap. It was her and Brade, again, perched in a copse of trees looking towards the Carlwen gates. Graveguard was keeping watch below with the others hiding near their initial ridge.

"I suspect not," Brade agreed, irritatingly more sure than her.

"Well. Maybe we could set a fire back that way, blow something up?"

"I see two options," Brade said, ignoring her idea. "We retreat, give this whole thing up, or we face our misinformation head-on."

Wish frowned, not sure what the second one meant. "You know I'm not leaving Emi behind."

"Assuming she's even in there."

"Just tell me what you have in mind for the *real* plan."

"Right." Brade sighed. "It's about time you saw me do what I do best, I suppose."

"What's that? Talking? Knowing obscure stuff? Travelling to weird places? Not sword-fighting, I know that's third best."

Brade smiled. "Little pieces of the whole. We've been playing your game of soldiers, Wild Wish. But I'm a spy. I was infiltrating hostile territory long before there even was a war."

"Alright, great – what's the difference?"

"You aim to go unnoticed to win a fight; I aim to fit in to avoid one."

"So you're back to sneaking in pretending to be merchants? Didn't we cover that?"

"No. Much simpler. I'll go up to the gates and announce myself. Alone."

Wish gaped at him. "You're joking."

"Deadly serious. If I present myself on a diplomatic mission, with no ill intentions, and the full confidence that they will talk to me, they *will* talk to me."

"Sure, before they murder you. That's a ridiculous idea, Captain."

"Colonel Atmoor knows me. I can get in and find out what's happened to Emi. From there, it's either a case of clearing up a misunderstanding or finding a way to get her out, unseen."

"That's all?" Wish laughed, the gall too much. "And Colonel Atmoor is that much of a friend that he won't shoot you in the head for *obviously* being there to spy on them? You remember we're at war, right?"

"I've given it thought, Wish," Brade said. "If we have doubts over the Irregulars, there's a chance the Drail *didn't* start this. Meaning this *isn't* an invasion, and Atmoor may want a peaceful resolution. And I'm on this mission for a reason – it's time to put my skills to use. One way or another, I'll break this deadlock. I'll walk in there with my gun and sword, you watch."

"If it's that easy, why've we been sitting out in the cold worrying?" Wish demanded, not out of bitterness but with mounting concern. He was serious, wanting to walk right into the hands of the enemy. He smirked in his smug way and against everything she felt a quiver in her chest; this arrogant noble, too sure of himself and merciless in Low Slane, was still part of her team. He was something almost resembling a friend, and dammit the last thing she needed was him dead, too.

"No one said it was easy," he replied. "But we've no other choice."

"We can retreat, you said so," Wish blurted out, the unthinkable option suddenly preferable. She didn't care how desperate it made her sound. "Get away and send someone else to clean this up."

"You know that's not an option for either of us. And hell, if it doesn't work out at least you'll be shot of me for good."

"I don't *want –*" Wish started, her voice rising so sharply she cut herself off. She checked around her, in case the soldiers near Carlwen might have heard. No sign of disturbance, though. Through her teeth, she tried again, "I don't want you gone."

"Trust me, I'll be fine," he said, and she wished he hadn't.

Wild Wish was quite sure she was about to see Captain Rikard Brade, famed hero of the Stanish Empire, and probably lord of some stately manor, summarily gunned down for no good reason. He was on the empty road now, walking proudly towards the gates like a visiting dignity fully expecting to be welcomed inside. Having relayed the plan down to Graveguard, Wish now lay watching with the Rawboy medic, who didn't share her concern.

"I heard he once fought off four hundred ringers on the Olonian beaches," Graveguard said. He was very matter-of-fact for a Rawboy – a gaunt, very tall and somewhat skeletal man who spoke with a dry drawl that was difficult to read for humour. "Him and three men against hundreds. He had two toes cut off by an axe as they ran into the desert. There's a Coast vodka named honouring it: *Two Toes Down.*"

"Well that went from roundly unbelievable to oddly specific," Wish said, and somehow, she found it entirely plausible that the moustached gentleman with his pistol and sword had actually experienced such a thing.

"First man to set eyes on Lake Blisteria, did you know that?"

"I did not," Wish said. Nor had she ever heard of Lake Blisteria. "You sound like a fan."

"No more so than most, boss." Graveguard shrugged. "Even the Rae enjoy hearing about Captain Brade's travels, filthy Stain as he may be. Some deeds transcend borders."

Wish frowned, because the main deed she knew Brade for was trying to set off an unimaginably dangerous bomb. But that made it no easier to watch the enemy spotting him and huddling about in tense conference. She held her breath as Brade slowed down before the gates. He held a hand up in greeting to the soldiers on the battlements.

"You don't need to worry about him," Graveguard said. "That's all I'm saying."

His confidence made it worse. That Brade and this Rawboy were so damn confident meant something *had* to go wrong. She was about to watch a nobody soldier, bored on the ramparts, put a bullet through Brade without even asking who he was. Or worse – soldiers outside the walls were moving, realising something was going on. Amongst them was a pack of goblins, lively like nipping dogs as they pulled ahead with their oversized guns and jagged bladed tools. Brade didn't show a hint of fear. Someone on the wall shouted at him as the goblins hopped closer.

"Fuck this," Wish hissed, picking out the head of the closest goblin through her scope.

"It won't help anyone to start shooting," Graveguard noted, reaching towards her gun but stopping short of touching. She glared daggers at him and his hard eyes showed uncertainty, despite his age and experience and tough exterior. "Give him a chance, boss."

Wish bared her teeth, because shooting those goblins *would* give him a chance, but when she looked again they were already around Brade. One pushed at him and he bounced to the side, avoiding it without effort. He looked mildly amused. This made the goblins shudder with mocking laughs of their own, forming a mean, moving circle. Human soldiers started forming an audience behind them.

"They'll kill him," Wish said, sure of it now. Stupid, *stupid* idea.

A bolder goblin grabbed at Brade's pistol, no way for him to sidestep that one. He swatted the clawed hand away and triggered them into action. As he gripped his sword hilt, ready to draw, the goblins readied to pounce as one frenzied mass, spitting and flashing teeth, and Wish's finger found her trigger again. A long goblin limb lashed out and caught Brade, slicing his cheek and sending him stumbling as Wish targeted the biggest head in the crowd. Another goblin shoved him from behind and Brade almost tripped to his knees. The patience was gone from his unflappable face; he was about to strike back and get himself killed.

"Wait!" Graveguard said, and Wish glanced briefly over her scope – there was movement on the battlements, someone pushing through.

Brade half-drew his sword, warning off one goblin as another, unseen by him, lifted a dirty cleaver. Then there came a terrible, piercing scream, and all eyes went to the ramparts, where a soldier was falling. He hit the ground with a twisted crunch, and a gunshot followed. The goblins scattered so that they knocked over a number of green-coat soldiers. Brade remained in a half-crouch that made Wish worry he'd been hit in the gut, but he rose to stand, recovering his breath and leaving the sword in its sheath. Scratched but not shot. The soldiers, as they calmed from the goblin stampede, looked back to the walls, where a large man stood above the gates, his arm raised with a pistol pointing into the sky. He was tall, broad and bald, in a tight officer's uniform: undoubtedly Colonel Atmoor himself. Had he just thrown a man over the wall? What kind of fresh psycho was this?

No matter. Wish got his face in her sights.

New plan, she thought, as he called down to Brade. *Shoot the colonel.* An easy shot to decapitate the entire Drail army in the Mire. The men would panic, the goblins riot, probably tear each other apart and run off to make trouble elsewhere. Somewhere less damp. Or they'd react with all-out slaughter. Burn the Mire in its entirety. Starting with the scouts.

Bad plan. And besides, Atmoor had just stopped the rising trouble, though he'd maybe killed one of his own men to do so. He shouted at the goblins as they skulked about. Then he gestured Brade closer. The captain was smiling again, all forgiven despite the shocking violence. He stood below the gate with a few how-do-you-dos for their sworn enemy, after being only seconds away from having a pack of goblins tear him apart. This, Wish sensed, was what he'd been saying he was good at – but surely he wasn't going in now. They'd just seen what a lunatic Colonel Atmoor really was.

The gates squeaked open a fraction and Brade strode inside,

watched by an unhappy crowd of soldiers. Atmoor disappeared from the ramparts and the drama dispersed, a couple of men dragging the crumpled body away.

"Well," Wish said. "Guess that's done. Now they can kill him inside, instead." She sighed deeply. "I'll take first watch – go and update the others. I guess we'll know if he wants our attention. Won't we?"

She gave Graveguard a glance. His expression was blank, maybe still processing the sudden tossing of a man off a wall. He shrugged. "Sure."

"Go on, then."

The lithe Rawboy crept back down the hill, and watching his hunched back Wish wondered what the hell she was going to do if Brade didn't return. The Rebel Rawboys were all older and gruffer and more experienced than her. Could she in all seriousness keep bossing them about without Brade? But the medic was doing as she asked without question, and the little show at the gates had more Drail patrols on the move, so this was no time for second-guessing.

Once Graveguard was out of sight, Wish settled to watch the walls and windows, for any signs of movement. It was absurd. The Drail wouldn't let him out of their sight – it could be *days* before Brade got a chance to move unnoticed. If the colonel didn't just tear off his head with those bear paws. They'd probably string his eviscerated body up a flag pole. Idiot. And the Rawboys would abandon her here with one woman (a scary one) and no clear route back to restarting the Blood Scouts. When she reported this series of disasters back to Command, it'd be rewarded with a slap to the face and possibly a public hanging.

Wish tried to cheer herself up by picking out the faces of soldiers through her scope, men she could blink out of existence. Pow, dead, pow dead, and they had no idea. Some were laughing with each other, thinking they were in one of the war's few safe paces. *Wrong.*

Castor's spleen, but she was on edge. Wanting a fight to start just to know where she stood. It kept her awake. Gave her energy. Maybe. She jumped at the crunching of grass behind her and spun to find Ptrangus approaching. Scraper was slinking along behind him. He regarded her slyly, probably recognising her nerves, while Scraper offered a simple, disaffected look that reminded Wish how dark her eyes were.

"We figured you might want company, if we're in for a long wait. And seeing that none of us should be out here alone," Ptrangus explained, making Wish knot her brow. Were they being helpful or just concerned she was weak?

She brushed it off. "Either way. You might as well rest for now, it's – what, Scraper?"

The strange woman had her hand up as if to ask a question. Instead of speaking, she pointed towards Carlwen. Wish followed the gesture and frowned at the battlements, and the sight of a man preparing to use a loudspeaker. It was a big metal cone, aimed towards the road, and it amplified his voice in a tinny, unreal echo. "Lieutenant Wild Wish. Colonel Atmoor guarantees your safe passage if you agree to talk."

Wish gawked at Captain Brade, stood there so brazenly, broadcasting their business for the whole world. He was alive, then, and had the good sense not to direct the offer towards them, not giving away their position. But even so – the Drail now knew she was out here. Indeed, everyone in earshot, which was a *lot* of people, stopped to listen.

"Emi is alive and the Drail are willing to talk."

Wish's throat caught on a sudden lump of emotion. She whispered, "Emi?"

"Come to the gate, it's safe," Brade went merrily on, as if he wasn't inviting her to step into full view of an enemy army. But had he done exactly as he'd said, and defied the entire war of senseless killing to find a way for them *not* to fight? Then he added a final damning detail, "Sister Sonseen is here. She has some very troubling news you need to hear."

37

A careful survey is required to reveal the full involvement of the myriad creatures in the early stages of the war. At least before 721, we must look for "officers" recorded without rank, or by filling in gaps where the numbers of named dead do not match the recorded death toll of a battle. Only in rare exceptions were the most accomplished non-human officers celebrated.

Dueley's Comprehensive: The One War in 10 Volumes (Vol. 2), p. 130

Though disappointed with his boys' inability to hunt and butcher the enemy scouts, Bleacher was delighted to hear they'd cornered a hard-faced nun on a bloody battle beetle. After the mage, they were thankfully extra cautious about attacking random women, and had left her unharmed, waiting for him in the bleak fields of Shadow Sails. Announcing herself from the back of her beetle as Sister Sonseen, of Saintshadow, she looked tough for a tall, probably had more balls than most of the men in Atmoor's command, and her officiousness suggested some use might come from the horde's glorified guard duty after all.

Elsewhere, the company were continually disappointing Bleacher – no one seemed to know what was going on out west, between the gunfire at Gauntstone, traps in the bog and impossibly poor visibility from the mist. Then Atmoor had thrown out half-measure orders to parley with the enemy here, as if Bleacher was going to risk his boys' lives with that kind of hesitance. They were dealing with a serious hit squad, seeing how they'd evaded capture and dispatched the only competent soldier in the entire army. Carrow had been missing most of his head (well, it wasn't so much missing as not where it was supposed to be), which the goblins had a laugh about. A decent boy, kind of weak in the mind but a damn good shot, and happy to talk to goblins, because he wasn't so concerned about them judging him. But it *was* kind of funny in the irony, because he deserved a lot better, and the news had got Atmoor's back up, when the colonel was already fuming about the necessity of finding a peaceful resolution with an ever-increasing mess near Gauntstone. With the prospect of these slippery soldiers getting closer to Carlwen, coming for their mage and for *him,* Bleacher reckoned the man might soon unravel. Bleacher hoped this nun brought news that'd help complicate his life that little bit more.

"Wideskull Bleacher," he announced, a hand on his chest. She glowered with distaste, stupidly high on her beetle, a beautifully unpleasant creature. "Section 3 of the Onwail Defence Legion. I trust my boys have treated you well."

"Tolerably," she replied. "Though the same can't be said for your treatment of the Woodwings."

"Occupational hazard," Bleacher said, with a smile practised to show off maximum pointiness. The nun's icy look insisted this was *not good enough,* bless her. "We're hunting some very dangerous people out here. Keeping your pretty little homes safe. I don't suppose you've seen any Stanish cutthroats nearby? Wearing blue and likely to kill you quick as look at you."

Sonseen snorted, unimpressed by this too. "I've met the Stanclif soldiers. I have worse concerns. I wish to speak to your commander about reaching an accord."

"What worse concerns? We've got Stains out there shooting my boys without warning."

"As I said, it's a matter I'll take to your commander."

Bleacher leered. "And what makes you so sure I'm not in charge?"

Sonseen almost looked amused, but regarded the silhouette of Carlwen nestled mistily on the horizon. "If you're really a wideskull, I respect your rank, but I doubt they've even let you in that town, have they?"

That weakened Bleacher's smile. Sharp one, she was.

"Take me to your general and I'll see you have a seat at the discussions. Believe it or not, I actually think involving goblin leadership might limit your propensity for collateral damage. If your leader had any sense, you'd be after the Irregulars, not hovering around here."

"That's what I've been telling him," Bleacher said, his smile returning. He knew he'd like her. "But like I said, we have a Stain problem. If you've met them, perhaps you might tell me where they are."

"I do not intend to do that," Sonseen replied curtly. "But I have come to consider your forces aren't here on a mission of conquest, correct?"

"No, Sister," Bleacher said, curiously. "Just stamping out the filth. I'm guessing Kasidee and his crowd have made a bad impression on you?"

"You could say that. Can we get moving?"

She had no question now that he was going to oblige, and Bleacher happily did so, keen to see where this might take them. He walked alongside her beetle on the road to Carlwen, the height difference and uneven pace limiting conversation, but no matter – Bleacher's mind ticked towards fresh possibilities. With Ilscot floundering and this nun's input, he might finally convince Atmoor to set Section 3 properly loose on the Irregulars.

Colonel Atmoor was struggling to write.

He had sat for hours merely staring at the papers strewn across his desk, distantly aware of the thoughts he'd wanted to send: something for General Foul, another matter for Prognane Lightwind. Hard to focus, with Ilscot mismanaging things in Low Bile and Bleacher failing to round up these Stanish assassins. Despite his certainty that Brade could be talked to, the moderately deranged state of the mage was evidence of how dangerous the enemy might be. She could not hold a conversation without laughed threats. The death of poor Carrow cemented it. Oh Carrow. The lad had suffered so much, struggling to overcome his afflictions, and had been so talented. Of all people, Atmoor had hoped to get him through this, reinstated in the army proper, given the honours he deserved. Now, he wasn't even sure where Carrow's body was, and was too busy to organise its retrieval.

How could he write of distant troubles, advising men who never had the sense to listen, under the weight of all this shit? Colonel took in a big breath. He would prefer to write a eulogy for the best sharpshooter he had known. Couldn't even bring himself to do that.

Atmoor was stirred from his thoughts by shouting, followed by a knock at the door, a soldier calling for him. He stood, inflating with satisfaction. This was it. The enemy must be at the gate, and he would have to decide on a response. Justice for Carrow or a discourse towards peace? Would he find Brade willing to talk or riflemen who needed suppressing?

Yet when Atmoor opened the door, the messenger said, "It's Wideskull Bleacher, sir. Trying to get into town."

"For the sake of the Body!" the colonel thundered and marched out. His bubbling anger took him swiftly towards the gates and the closer he got, the louder the disagreement ahead became, with Guardian Wallace's voice shouting over a general commotion. Atmoor came up behind the armoured man and demanded, "What is going on?"

"Ah, Colonel, at last," the pompous guard said. "I should *not* be having to deal with –"

"Colonel Atmoor?" a woman shouted, arresting Atmoor's indignation. He looked over the wall to find a robed nun seated on an enormous beetle. Bleacher stood by her side with his usual sickly grin. "I have important matters to discuss, regarding the renegade soldiers in this area. But first I insist you grant access to my steed and my escort."

Atmoor was dumbstruck for a moment by this formidable nun and her beetle, but this promised unexpected progress. Progress, with these Carlwen idiots blocking the path. Wallace went to say something, and Atmoor burst out, "By Bly just open the damn gates and let them in. That man is my lieutenant and I am through conducting my command in this ludicrous manner!" Though startled, the guardian looked ready to argue, so he added, "You open those gates or I will, dammit."

And so it was done. He'd have to placate Chamberlain Furvair and Wallace later, but to hell with them. He had men with rifles everywhere now, there was no need for any pretence at deference. Bleacher's scruffily booted feet crossed the threshold into the town and a rush of shocked gasps went through the locals who'd gathered there. The nun rode ahead and Bleacher gnashed his teeth at a watching woman who gave a sharp shriek. Some green-coats laughed.

"Show some decorum!" Atmoor shouted, striding to intercept the nun and welcome her. Her beetle was stabled and they went to the keep and Atmoor's commandeered office, pausing only to invite Brother Redfire to join them. After brief introductions, moderated by Redfire with cheery questions after the well-being of her priory, Atmoor impatiently demanded her report.

The nun, Sister Sonseen, eyed him with distaste as she said that the Stanclif soldiers in the region were *not* aligned with the rabble at Gauntstone, and, despite her glare, Atmoor felt some part of his terrible load lift. He uttered, "I knew it."

"Then I'd suggest you work *together* to deal with the real problem," Sonseen admonished, like they were naughty boys.

"That was my intention," Atmoor replied. "I have already started withdrawing troops, ordering them to show restraint with the Stanish insurgents."

The nun scoffed. "It hardly looked that way with the goblin patrols in Shadow Sails."

Atmoor frowned at Bleacher. No surprise that Section 3 had not actually held back. Had they even tried to recall Carrow?

"There's only so lenient we can be, without getting ourselves killed," Bleacher said. "We've already lost some good men."

Atmoor held his gaze a moment longer. Not worth the trouble now; they needed to look forward. He said, "Sister. I do not want to engage the Stanish here, but we need *them* to back down, don't we? Do you have some way to reach them?"

"I do not," Sonseen said. "I was trying to track them when your goblins intervened."

"Dammit Bleacher," Atmoor rumbled. Bleacher merely shrugged, his amusement making Atmoor squeeze his fists closed. But he couldn't lose his cool now, in front of a nun. He went on, "What can you tell us, Sister? How many do the Stanish have? Did you meet them? Did you see Captain Brade?"

Sonseen eyed him warily, distrusting. She said, "I did. But I do not know you or your intentions so I won't divulge more that could put them in danger. Except, he is *not* their leader. That honour goes to a strange young woman with a very long gun, Lieutenant Wild Wish."

"A woman?" Was she making fun of him now? What absurdity. But then, they had a female mage here. He shared a glance with Bleacher, who appeared equally nonplussed yet irritatingly more amused. It didn't matter; they had the confirmation they needed that Rikard Brade was nearby. "Very well. We shall be on the lookout. But there must be more, Sister, for you to come here?"

"I was trying to reach *them,*" Sonseen said accusingly. "You don't need persuading that Kasidee's Irregulars are bad people, I assume. They will need to hear it from me, though."

"You've seen evidence of it, I take it?"

"I have. They were invited into Midpeak as guests and did not leave that way."

Atmoor grunted, not happy to hear the soldiers had reached that priory, but noting they had already left. This was a perfect example of a very unnecessary mess, in which some more deliberation could've avoided trouble. Could've kept Carrow alive. Quickly, Atmoor instructed Brother Redfire to accommodate the nun, so he might retire and prepare himself. He reissued Bleacher's orders, insisting there would be no violence until they saw Brade, and the goblin reluctantly slunk off to make it happen. This was all going to work out fine. Atmoor sat back at his desk, setting his shoulders, ready to write again, at last.

He started a general letter to the Arrow Council themselves. *On How We May Use International Connections to Moderate*

Misunderstandings. He would explain that Carrow had died over a misunderstanding, make his death mean something. But he was only a few sentences into it when Furvair came banging at his door, furiously shouting about goblins. Atmoor dealt with it more forcibly than he would've liked, barely even hearing his own words, and afterwards found it hard to focus again, his pen not moving. There his mind wandered again to how futile this was. He could see the solutions to so much of the war right before his eyes, had sent out so many letters explaining these ideas, but people didn't stop and think. Didn't *listen.*

Distracted by his frustration, Atmoor went out onto the battlements and asked for updates, with night falling. He learnt the line was mostly held securely, Ilscot's men finally back in order with no news of Gauntstone. Bleacher's goblins had retreated with no signs of enemy movement nearby. He wondered when it would come. If it would be with a flag of truce or a bullet through a window. He kept wondering that, tensely, through the night and into the morning. He was agitated in his own skin, grinding his teeth in the knowledge that it was still entirely possible that the Stanish would attack them for nothing. A fight neither wanted and that *he* could avoid.

Then more shouting came at the gates, and he rushed there fuming at the sounds of trouble. It was *surely* the Stanish this time, and his idiot troops were about to ruin everything.

Atmoor skidded up onto the walkway by the gates and there he was, Captain Brade, familiar even at a distance. Being accosted! About to be hurt? There were goblins and weapons about to be drawn. A soldier next to Atmoor jeered down at the mess, "Go on, get him!"

Atmoor roared and clutched the man by the lapels, to throw him screaming over the wall. He drew his pistol and fired in the air, yelling, "To hell with you all, will you never listen!"

The troops briefly scattered in fear and surprise before going still, staring up in shock, while Atmoor's chest heaved with anger. But he picked out one friendly face in the sea of miscreants. Captain Brade. Thank the Body. It would be okay.

***

Bleacher was disappointed by how quickly the civility returned to Colonel Atmoor after his unhinged outburst. The big guy had tossed one of their own off the battlements, and just as quickly was all pally and smiles for this chum from the other side. They embraced when they greeted each other inside the gates, and disappeared together with no invitation for goblins. Bleacher spat on the street. He'd done alright for himself getting in here, enjoying Carlwen's unwelcoming bars and a fluffy bed, luxuriating instead of going back out to reorganise his boys, but it wasn't much use if Atmoor was still excluding him. They emerged not long after, though, to call outside the walls and welcome the enemy's *actual* leader in.

When the whispers came that she was coming, Bleacher rushed to the front of the battlements and laughed. The nun wasn't kidding: there was a mere waif of a woman in a helmet and fatigues, about as comfortable walking up the road as a chicken in a grekkel pit. The Drail troops converged on her as they had on the captain, men and goblins hoisting guns, despite Atmoor shouting for them to keep back. Tempting as it was to let him lose his cool again, Bleacher saw a way to involve himself and said, "I'll bring her in. Keep those filthy men's paws off her."

Without waiting for permission, he ran down the stairs and out the gates. He ordered everyone back, the crowd shying away from him more fearfully than they ever would from Atmoor (even if the colonel had tossed someone off the wall). He relished the female tall's expression as she spotted him, nothing like Sonseen's calm. His head wasn't quite up to her chest, and she had a great long rifle to rival Carrow's, but she looked scared as a mouse. But what'd looks mean – Bleacher knew this woman had given his boys a run for their money, at the least. He told her, in his most refined Stanish, "Lieutenant Wild Wish. It's my pleasure to escort you inside."

"You're a goblin," the woman replied daftly, partly questioning *why him* and partly just surprised at his ability to talk. Bleacher grinned.

"And you're a bitch, eh?" he replied, and calmed her momentary alarm by indicating her curved chest. "Don't often see women talls in uniform. Are you the one did Carrow in?" She gawked, not yet over being addressed by him, so he held out his hand, spreading his three clawed fingers, longer and more jagged than frail human ones. "Wideskull Syrus Bleacher, at your service. That's the goblin equivalent of a general, to you. You'll wanna shake – no one's gonna fuck with a tall who's pally with a wideskull."

He could see the thought process on Wild Wish's scrunched face as she scanned his head. It wasn't that wide, and he wasn't big. He didn't bother to explain the title, keeping his hand out until she reluctantly shook it. He squeezed just enough to hint at his strength, soaking up their audience's laughter and the hushed comments of mock disgust or (even more mocking) awe.

"That's it," Bleacher said. "See, Colonel Atmoor's gonna promise you safety, but it's me who'll make it happen, understand?" He broke the grip and slid his long arm behind her to nudge her on, a real gentleman, guiding his date; with the height difference, he had to cup her behind instead of her shoulders.

The woman jumped out of his reach, snarling, "Don't touch me –"

"Relax," Bleacher warned her, grin thin and serious as his nearby goblins hooted with delight. There was a fire in her eyes, he saw then. Definitely not just a waif. She just needed the right provocation. "I'm only taking you inside. No normal goblin's touching a *human* the way you're thinking. Just as soon touch up a goat."

Wild Wish glowered, probably wanting to say there was no such a thing as a *normal* goblin.

"Seriously. You're too tall, too pale, too *soft*. We like our muscle hard and lean. And damn, look at how narrow your head is. Tiny mouth like that, you couldn't even fit a hand in it."

She unconsciously lifted a hand to her lips, like she'd never even considered it, and more goblins sniggered, though none would actually understand the conversation in Stanish. Bleacher grinned and she pulled her confused gaze away from him towards the town. Up to the battlements, where Brade and Atmoor had gone out of view. She muttered, "Let's just get on with this."

She walked between the columns of Drail troops, Bleacher at her side, into the town. He mugged at the goblins he passed and stuck out his tongue, getting a few more hoots and another sharp look from the tall.

"You got no idea the honour I'm doing you, lady," Bleacher said. "Your nun mate got it."

"Sister Sonseen?" she blurted. "Where is she? If you've hurt her –"

"I've been nothing but bloody civil," Bleacher interrupted. "Best friends by now, me and her. She came cap in hand saying you want my help, see. And like I said, it's *my* help you want, not bloody Atmoor."

Wild Wish didn't look convinced. She considered their surroundings, plenty of goblins in the town now, loitering by shopfronts with civilians shying away. It was a beautiful sight, bolstered by the men in Drail uniforms in between, and Bleacher noticed how the sniper girl secured her grip on her rifle. She said, quietly, "Why would I want your help?"

"With our mutual problem," he said. "There's people out here we're all gonna agree want killing and I doubt you've met anyone deadlier than me."

She laughed. Bleacher paused. It was a light, genuine laugh, and she covered her mouth with a hand to mask it, the way talls did when they hadn't meant to make fun. A minute ago she was creeping in all scared just to see him, flinching at men laughing from the sides of the roads, now she was laughing at the thought of him being dangerous? He eyed her, waiting for an explanation, and she stared back like she was holding in more.

"This way, Wish!" Brade's voice called out, and the crowd parted as he and Atmoor emerged. Wild Wish's expression lightened on seeing him, though she then frowned at the sight of the big colonel.

As they strode towards them, she leant slightly aside to Bleacher, and quickly whispered, "I took out a squad of your men lying on my back."

His mouth made a surprised *O* at her gall, but the officers were upon them, so rather than respond he said loudly, "Lieutenant Wild Wish. Meet our most *honourable* Colonel Atmoor."

The colonel looked irritated at his tone, but kept it in as he assessed Wish with beady eyes. He said, in Stanish better than Bleacher's, "Lieutenant. Thank you for agreeing to meet. I guarantee your safety in this town." He raised one of his beefy arms. "Please join me in my quarters so we can discuss our mutual problem."

She glanced down at Bleacher again and said, "What *is* this mutual problem?"

"Oh lady," Bleacher volunteered, seeing a chance to dig back. He enjoyed her expression as he said, "My boys weren't the ones you should've been killing."

38

Gauntstone, once Militace, is an oft-neglected gem in the north of the Mire with a reputation for dourness. Unfair, I say! They brew the most agreeable nettle-wine in the region!

The Mire Most Easy with Mr Zambizee,
Zambizee, p. 65

The sacking of Gauntstone had been a little messier than Kasidee intended. He had kept the fires under control, so the entire priory didn't burn down, and had managed to cajole a few dozen monks into cells rather than have them all murdered outright, but there were still incidents that got out of hand. A particularly virulent venerator had preached angrily at them about divine punishment and the men had made an example of him. His death had been put on display in the priory's main square, between rather elegant curved towers and delicate arches carved with scenes from Tikan mythology. None of the other frail, impoverished-looking monks spoke a language Kasidee's men could understand, or they were very good at pretending. Too tired to bother trying to communicate with them himself, he searched the priory instead.

Kasidee put the screams from his mind by focusing on hunting through tunnels, unlocking vaults and searching stacks of treasures. The men's violent celebrations settled before he found what he was after – chalices and saint icons of various precious metals and gems, yes, but not the discreet symbols of Bonesun. He considered it a personal mission to find them before Havik caught up (knowing the value of her smile), but first unveiled a vintage wine cellar and dusted off a few bottles. There was a Remish '96. An excellent year. Worth a fortune, he supposed, as he uncorked it to check. Perhaps he was overtired, but it tasted like liquid luxury – a depth of berries and smoke and peppery spices. As he continued his search, he swigged from the bottle, and his eyes started drooping. He climbed through the priory's keep to find a chamber to rest in. He passed broken doors, wine and food scattered about and soldiers collapsed drunk. He stepped over the occasional dead monk who'd escaped their initial incursion. Kasidee regarded it all impassively, content now just to sleep.

Daylight came, and the subdued morning mist left the priory floating in its own eerie world, cut off from reality, which Kasidee observed from the vantage point of a high window. They had successfully broken through the main gate with bodily force, leaving the walled enclose otherwise intact, but his hundreds of unruly souls were now draped between empty bottles, bloodstains, vomit and the ashes of spent fires, like festival-goers rather than soldiers. A particularly charred patch against one wall, where a structure had burnt down, warned Kasidee of how far this had gone. He went to the priory's central, narrow bell tower and took up the hammer to clang it. It sent out a mournful pang that stirred some of the men. He hit it again, and again, and shouted, "Up, the lot of you. To arms!"

That stirred them with greater urgency, the hungover mess of stumbling partisans snatching at rifles and blades or whatever else was handy, and they gradually gathered in what open space they could find beneath him. Leaning on the tower's low wall, he called down a brief speech, as stirring as he could manage so early in the morning, his own senses not quite there. The point was simple: with the damage they'd done in the night, their position was likely to be known and they could expect trouble. Ideally, they'd leave before it came, but just in case, he had dozens of men climb up to the walls on watch (never mind they couldn't see further than a few metres into the mist) and he got a team to ready the F-Apparet in the courtyard, where it could be quickly repositioned. He also organised a gang of men to return to the tunnels and continue the search he'd started. He finished by saying, "Let's find the relics before Havik gets here."

He somewhat regretted relying on her name as a motivator, but he couldn't deny that it worked. The mere mention of Havikare woke half the men up better than a splash of cold water, with many looking actually *happy* to get on with their work. Every force needed something to believe in, and the promise of Havik's favour worked almost as well as promises of glory and material wealth.

Soon, that festival atmosphere returned with the Irregulars' quick casing of the priory, as they searched for treasure, supplies and amenities. It was a chance to regroup, eat well, even wash, and the men revelled in it as well hungover as they had drunk. There was laughter in the air, and hope, with the close calls of the previous days forgotten. A fickle bunch, really. Kasidee shared their enthusiasm though. With a miracle escape from Midwood, after a miracle escape from the Black Lake, it was hard to believe they *weren't* blessed. He was sure, too, that Havik would rejoin them soon, and the final stage of their journey was all but within reach.

That faith was rewarded just after midday when a call went up announcing she was here. Men stopped what they were doing all over the priory, rushing to the southern walls, and Kasidee made his way through them, calling for quiet, especially when word came that she wasn't alone. There was a spark of uncertainty at the mention of ogres. But while some soldiers grew tense, Kasidee smiled, knowing only Havik could be gone a day and come back having recruited some of the toughest bastards out there.

She arrived to cheers, modestly nodding and smiling as she led her little victory parade into the priory, up to the courtyard where Kasidee was waiting and parts of the venerator's body were still hanging from hooks against a church wall. Havik eyed the mess quizzically and Kasidee shrugged. He was more interested in her new companions: two massive ogres resplendent in ammunition and oversized weaponry, carrying pillage sacks between them. They set down their wares and Havik explained they'd been to Midpeak. They'd gained access to a vault and taken what they wanted without anyone even realising. She had Midpeak's relics and looked forward to seeing what they'd found in Gauntstone. Kasidee assured her they'd have what she needed, if not now then soon – there were only so many chambers in the tunnels, after all. Finally, she introduced the ogres.

"Runt and Ohno. More than happy to take up our lucrative offer. Their leader wasn't so enthusiastic, but isn't that always the way?" Havik addressed the female ogre as she said this. "Officers everywhere want things to stay the same."

Kasidee found it hard to read the ogres' faces, both looking distinctly unfriendly, but he supposed that was the point of them. They watched his men milling around, wary and tense. In Stanish, he said, "Do you drink? There's a fine cellar here, to toast your arrival."

"Sounds like a good start," Runt replied, as if expensive alcohol was the least he expected. Kasidee liked his attitude: a man with simple motivations.

"But never mind them," Havik said, dismissing the marvel of *ogres* as inconsequential, "I met *her*. The leader of the Blood Scouts."

"Captain Tate?" Kasidee replied with surprise. Of all the woman's many schemes and fancies, her obsession with the fabled Stanish female scouts had always seemed one of the least likely. "She's really here?" He looked back towards the gates as if to spot her, though aware no one else was coming.

"Wild Wish," Havik corrected the name. "They went to take care of Atmoor for us. I'm sure the Drail will be suitably distracted for a little while yet. She's a firecracker. I might be in love."

It came out lightly, but the words struck Kasidee in the chest. Havik's enthusiasm was usually restricted to names from stories, long-dead or invented heroes, never for anyone real or close to them. She simply didn't see others that way. But there was a new light in her eyes. He said, straining not to sound bothered, "She made that good an impression?"

"The best. I hope they don't kill her. We have to meet again."

Kasidee nodded, not wanting to dwell on this other woman. Not when he'd come so close to realising Havik's plans himself. He said, "Come with me down to the tunnels. We'll finish up here and get marching by nightfall."

"There's no rush," Havik said. "I'm sure everyone needs a break, don't they? And I'd like to see the books here. This was once

Militace, remember? *No one* cares about Milithrandobar, which means there's probably writing here no one alive has read. I wouldn't mind a chat with the venerator, if he's still available."

Kasidee glanced guiltily in the direction of the hanging carnage.

"Ah. Well, maybe one of the lesser monks can help. There are *some* alive?"

"A few, yeah. But we're close to finishing."

"It'll be fine," Havik said, placing a confident hand on his shoulder. She passed him, towards the entrance to the church, the quickest way down to the tunnels. Like she already knew exactly where she needed to go. "And we can give Wild Wish a chance to catch up. I can't wait for you to meet her."

"Is that safe?" Kasidee said, drawing a questioning look. Her interest in the Blood Scouts had been academic before, as with most of the weird things she'd picked up in her reading. He'd never needed to question it out loud until now. "They're Stanclif elite, aren't they? Have you told them what we're here for?"

Havik's expression grew dark. "Of course not. But she'll understand. Same as her friends here." She nodded to the ogres. "Now if you'll excuse me, I have some exploring to do." She flashed another smile and strolled away towards the church whistling, her huge gun propped against her shoulder.

Kasidee lingered behind, watching her as her escort watched him. Raltman and Lost One, at their head, wore a concern that reflected his own. Discomfort at Havik being distracted or, worse, smitten, would be widely felt. He didn't want to sow doubts before their new guests, though, so Kasidee cheerily pointed, "Ohno and Runt, right? Make yourselves comfortable. If you're with us, you'll see we live well." He instructed a nearby soldier, "Take the big guys downstairs. Give them a proper Irregulars welcome."

The ogres gave him unreadable looks, not easily pleased, but they went. Damn. He loved the idea of commanding ogres, but he hadn't planned for this. He quietly asked Lost One, "What's your read?"

"This thing with the scouts? Not going to happen," the sniper said. "She's too good. Written all over her."

"Good?" Kasidee echoed with a raised eyebrow, the last descriptor he'd expected after hearing Havik's tales of the Blood Scouts. He glanced at Raltman for a second opinion.

"I dunno," Raltman admitted. "We didn't see her in action. But from what we did see, yeah. She was a fucking kid, Kasidee. A nervous, nice little girl. I don't get it."

"I guess the stories were exaggerated," Kasidee suggested. If anyone knew the power of a story, after all, it was him. Reality was always so disappointing. But the wrinkles of Raltman's forehead hinted at more. "What?"

"Well. You saw them ogres? Them and a gang of Rawboys, no less. Tough sons of bitches. They were following her, weren't they?" He huffed, adding, "Captain Brade, too, you believe that?"

"Rikard Brade?" Kasidee cooed. "He's here?"

"Here and in *her* command."

"The Rikard Brade?" Kasidee said. "You're sure? Following this nice, nervous girl?"

"With a Long 0.48," Lost One put in, in his sneering way that always preceded bad news. "She's got a gun that means business. You want my advice? If our paths cross again, we're better off shooting first and talking later."

Kasidee took that in silently. He wouldn't outright say it, not with how such thinking would upset Havik, but he suspected the sniper was right. The presence of one Boldarow's greatest heroes certainly enticed him, but they could do without distractions, either way, and what was another body on the path to glory . . .

39

With a hundred armies in a dozen theatres going after a thousand different goals, I believe it's safe to say that in this war no one, anywhere, at any given time, knows what the fuck they're really doing.

Extract from the Letters of Captain F. Miggles (Unedited), Farne, 721

Wild Wish sat in an unexpectedly comfortable leather chair, in an unreasonably well-decorated castle chamber, like somewhere lords might write lavish letters to distant friends. An old banner of house arms decorated one wall, the hunting trophies of unusual Mire beasts another, with a fire burning in a great fireplace. Colonel Atmoor stood importantly by a tall window, the goblin Bleacher leaning against a desk covered with untidy papers. They were quite a contrast, the goading goblin general with his officer's cap and medal-heavy, patchwork uniform jacket, and the veritable giant of Colonel Atmoor, bigger up close, bald and brutish with a distinctly clean uniform. They'd also picked up a monk, Brother Redfire, rotund in dark robes with a shaved head and a strangely cheerful disposition. He'd seemed genuinely delighted to shake Wish's hand and asked if he could get her favourite hot drink or alcohol, which she'd refused mostly out of suspicion. Redfire, Atmoor said, was their main liaison in the Mire – suggesting such a happy monk's endorsement was proof of Drail legitimacy. Thankfully, their own liaison was waiting in this room: the sight of Sister Sonseen, well and safe, if fixedly scowling, hit Wish with such relief that she wanted to hug the nun. She resisted, instead merely nodding at her.

Sonseen started proceedings: "Thank the Body you made it without bloodshed, but we have a serious problem. We found them only shortly after you left but I had difficulty catching up to you."

"Found who?" Wish said, skipping over the *without bloodshed* part.

"Ah. Your friend —" Sonseen cleared her throat, reconsidering her wording, as Wish felt her stomach clench. Had someone hurt Havik? But the Drail kept saying *mutual problem,* with them already doubting the Irregulars. She didn't want to hear the next sentence. Couldn't avoid it. "We found the bodies of the men entrusted with showing Havikare the vaults. Her men murdered two monks before they left Midpeak. They took their keys and more. There were relics of the Saints missing."

"Murdered?" Wish said, definitely not expecting *that.* "How? Why?"

"That's just the last thing we know they did," Brade came in, having evidently learnt more in the short time they'd been apart. "I think we best start at the beginning. Wild Wish, it was Kin Kasidee who invaded the Mire, not Colonel Atmoor."

They all let that sink in for a moment, staring meaningfully at Wish's blank face. The goblin looked far too pleased, but everyone else was Very Serious. The Irregulars were here first. *They* were the problem. Not this brute who'd just thrown one of his own men off a wall, or the goblins who'd butchered that Woodwing, or the sniper who'd killed Toothless. Kasidee had started this? That would make Havik part of the problem. But . . . Wish replied quietly, "We've discussed this. Even if they were here first —"

"They are a *blight,"* Atmoor interrupted loudly, startling her. "You'd be fools to align yourselves with these people. Wideskull Bleacher, tell them about Guiltway."

"With pleasure," Bleacher replied, meaning it. "We got to the priory about a day after the Irregulars. They'd blasted their way in with a cannon and slaughtered everyone inside. *Everyone.* The lucky ones had been shot."

"They . . . murdered an entire priory?" Wish glanced at Brade. "According to goblins?"

"Go see for yourself," Bleacher said. "Might be a few bodies the carrion haven't picked apart. You won't find goblin claw or teeth marks, and with your intimate knowledge of fighting my boys I'm sure you can spot the difference between human bullets and ours."

"There's no doubt after what happened at Midpeak," Sonseen added.

"My army is not without fault," Atmoor said, "but we are talking about a defensible position being needlessly sacked and civilians massacred. Guiltway and the Midpeak murders are only part of what the Irregulars have done. I expect Sinner's Gate was ransacked too, as their entry point to the region, and various villages and towns have been attacked on the way. *We* are here to stop them."

"And the Drail have been entirely respectful, I can vouch for that," Brother Redfire commented, brightly. "Why, until yesterday they even limited goblin access to the town."

Wish felt her face reddening from the group pile-on, suddenly feeling very young and out of place. It wasn't as easy staying brave when she wasn't hidden with a few hundred metres of space and her scope ready. She was sure that showed. She checked Brade again, the only person who hadn't joined in, and saw from his grave expression that he believed it all. But it would mean she'd really fucked up, wouldn't it? She hadn't seen any danger in Havik, despite those blatant thugs she kept company with. Some of her odd comments. But she didn't *want* to believe Havik was bad.

"I'm sorry, Colonel, everyone," Wish said. "Only, this is . . ."

"Complicated," Atmoor suggested, which was better than *upsetting.* "You intended to support Comity partisans without the full knowledge of who they are. But we have an opportunity to avoid more pointless violence here. The Drail do not *want* this territory. The Arrow Council does not want us here. I intend to withdraw when Kasidee is repelled. You can believe that or not, but I hope this is a rare occasion where our empires may be in agreement."

"So you want us to hunt down Kasidee together ?" Wish said.

Atmoor gave her another studious look. "Essentially, yes."

"After what we saw your goblins do in Midwood? And the farms in the Shadow Sails."

"We were under fire," Bleacher shot back quickly. "The tribes out here ain't exactly peaceful. But you can talk – what about

Hartland? Purnjay? Kopice? Wick? You think Stanclif's squeaky clean? *We* only fight soldiers."

Wish stared wide-eyed, recognising Wick and Kopice as locations her people had decimated (one directly involving her), and suspecting the others might be similarly bad. She felt even smaller, out of her depth, but couldn't help resisting. "We found your death wards."

"Lieutenant." Atmoor raised a hand. "I own that mobilising goblin forces always carries a degree of collateral damage. It's nothing like what we've seen from the Irregulars. And any damage you saw in the Shadow Sails was *not* my men. My patrols never returned."

Wish was silent. He sounded as calmly cold as Captain Brade, dismissing that horrific death ward, and she wanted to push him through the window. But unlike Brade, there was also weary resignation in Atmoor's eyes. Sadness. And the question of those farmers who'd been massacred. Havik had been there. The Drail had been killed, not the Irregulars . . .

"Let's get to the meat of it," Brade said. "You claim Kasidee massacred Guiltway, maybe Sinner's Gate, and the villages in between. Do you know *why?*"

Wish eyed him sideways, grateful he was cooler than her. And that he'd said *you claim.*

"Don't forget Gauntstone," Atmoor said. "My men have not reached it yet to assess the damage."

"By Bly," Sister Sonseen uttered. "We thought they were fighting you there."

Wish baulked, too. She'd sat watching those flashes of gunfire with Havik – a good-sized battle that they'd assumed to be two forces clashing. If Atmoor hadn't caught up to the Irregulars, then it was a bloodbath of innocents, not a battle at all.

"Are we on the same page now?" Atmoor said. "But to answer your question, Rikard, no I do not know their aim. We estimate at least two hundred armed men with a limited cavalry of trudge horses. They have one artillery weapon, likely an old 75, and a caravan of wagons, judging from their tracks and what was left at their Black Lake camp. There was evidence of plunder at Guiltway, but I'm not convinced they're here solely to profiteer."

"They're behaving fucking odd for thieves," Bleacher said. "They left behind – or outright destroyed – some obviously valuable shit. Paintings and even precious metals. And they're dancing around close to us – practically goblin behaviour, screwing about, picking a fight. They've also got funny little pamphlets talking about how great they think they are."

Brother Redfire raised a finger. "The good sister and I have compared notes, and suspect they're targeting specific relics."

"They took an odd mixture from Midpeak," Sister Sonseen said. "Some books of prayer rites, some Tikan bronze and old bones."

"Bones?" Wish said. She felt a couple of steps behind. "They came into the Saints Mire to raid treasuries and they're taking *bones?*"

"Artefacts of ancient saints or legendary creatures," Redfire said. "Of enormous value to certain churches. Sinner's Gate had the tooth of the Barroway Dragon, for example."

"And they took that?"

"Who knows," Sonseen said. "But they clearly have something specific in mind."

So it was back to this thieving idea, where her instincts had taken her but Brade had suggested wasn't worth considering. Wish wracked her own thoughts for some clue from all Havik had said to her, and sensed without having properly accepted it that this made sense. Havik had even called her *astute* when she assumed Atmoor was after something in the priories . . . Right idea, wrong people. Havik spoke fondly about power in the region and the value of protecting these churches. And hadn't someone said that these relics were considered too powerful to keep together? To get them all would require raiding multiple priories.

"Of course it's also possible they're directionless vandals," Atmoor droned on. "Kin Kasidee is enjoying themselves along the way. He's always promised his men adventure, in the worst ways. You met them. What's your impression – is there more going on?"

That was directed at Wild Wish, and she had to take a moment.

Mad troublemakers would be the easiest explanation, but Havik was smart. She had plans. Dammit it must've been a godsend for them, Wish rushing off to distract the Drail while they did whatever the hell elsewhere. She said, "I don't think they're religious. Or just causing trouble. At least, Havik isn't. She knows what's out here. They've been moving in a deliberate pattern."

"Poking at me, I thought," Atmoor said. "I'd been resisting the urge to follow, waiting for Kasidee's arrogance to bring him out into the open."

"Then you'll keep waiting," Wish said, before the idea had fully formed. She saw it in her head, the layout of the Mire and the path the Irregulars had taken, up the west, through the middle, around these bigger, more affluent priories. Bleacher had said they were dancing close to their hunters, but they were not engaging. She thought out loud: "They could've attacked you by now. We saw what they did to your scouts in the farms – they're not amateurs. They've been moving *around* you. Even now . . . Havik either hoped I'd push your back or didn't care, as long we were both distracted. They're not hitting the easier targets in the south, or settling in defensible positions, because they're gathering something from different sites." She looked to Brother Redfire. "Surely the crap they've taken and the priories they've raided fit together somehow?"

"Crap?" Redfire echoed, with mildly amused offence.

"Sinner's Gate and Guiltway are the most isolated priories," Sonseen answered for him. "We don't hear from them often, so they would've been obvious targets if they wished to go unnoticed."

"No," Atmoor said. "They put on a show at Guiltway. If anything they wanted us to go there, so they could double-back around the Black Lake while we were investigating."

"Wild Wish is right," Brade said. "There is a pattern. Sinner's Gate, Guiltway, Gauntstone and Midpeak are much older than the priories they've ignored. They all predate Bly Castor."

"The twins even," Redfire agreed. "Indeed, they are four of the five ancient priories."

"And this bunch of pricks would care about that?" Bleacher said.

"They have relics revering the earlier prophets," Sister Sonseen said. "Tikan manuscripts, Sandway's instruments, Venzusian jewellery – the things of myth."

"Carlwen and Prosper don't have any stuff like that?" Wish asked.

"Not as much," Redfire said. "And not as old. The twin prophets laid the groundwork for more secular interests, separating themselves from the fantastical tales of the first five prophets. The later priories reflect that."

"So what's the fifth one?" Wish said. "If they've hit four of the five, counting Midpeak, I guess we know where they're heading next?"

Redfire hesitated, and murmured that he couldn't be sure, though he obviously knew. Again, Sonseen answered for him, losing patience, "If they haven't already found what they're after, then the final target would be Drowndeep. And if it's Drowndeep, we can assume they have wicked intentions, as only the legends of Sandway would draw them there."

Atmoor grunted, breaking from a thoughtful silence. He didn't look happy, a tactician realising his flawless plans were, indeed, flawed. Wish could sympathise. But the colonel said, "The problem may solve itself yet, then. There's no sense in following them into the marshland. If they flee south, I can't follow. I'm ready to meet them here if they return, but otherwise we probably won't see them again. With luck, they'll drown in the bog."

"What?" Wish said. "You want to sit this out now? What the *fuck?*"

She didn't mean to go that far, and tensed for a rebuttal, but Atmoor merely stared grimly back, confirming it. Something about him made more sense of all this, she realised, with the way the Irregulars had gone unchecked for so long, and the mess of Midwood and the Shadow Sails. Where Kasidee had a specific path goal in mind, the Drail were directionless and passive. She addressed Sonseen rather than push it. "Is what they're doing actually dangerous? How bad could it be?"

"It depends what they're after, exactly, and what truth might be found in the myths. But the relics were separated for a reason. Sandway's instruments were particularly contentious."

Wish didn't want to ask why, not yet. Instead, she told Atmoor, "In my experience, it's best to stop people *before* they finish building their weapons. If we've guessed their destination, we've got an advantage. I parted on good terms with Havik, so maybe I can get close to the Irregulars. Figure out their plans and see if there's a way to corner them without a fight. Or slow them down at least."

"If you get them to stay in Gauntstone, I can sort this out," Bleacher suggested. "Problem is they keep running quicker than I can catch up."

This was said with some barb directed towards the colonel, recalling the goblin's earlier suggestion that he was the one Wish wanted to deal with. Atmoor shook his head and outright disregarded the suggestion. "I appreciate your willingness, Lieutenant. It sounds like you would be more mobile and able to get closer without my men. Ideally, you would find a way to redirect them towards a position we had secured, but the simplest solution, of course, may be to cut off the head."

He put it so candidly that Wish was momentarily stunned. This colonel, with his army, was actually suggesting he wait here while she handled the Irregulars? It was a ridiculous echo of Havik's same suggestion, both asking her to turn assassin while they sat out the fight. It took a moment to find the words, but when she did she split her gaze very deliberately between Atmoor and Bleacher. "He's not coming to you and I'm not here to take on an army on my own. We *can* travel separately, seeing as they'll smell Drail blood a mile off, but if we want to stop them you'll need to do *something.* At the least, I want your men close enough to help when things go wrong."

"Yet you said yourself we should stop them before they reach their destination," Atmoor pointed out. "I cannot possibly mobilise my forces quickly enough to get to Drowndeep before them."

Bleacher made a subtle sneering sound and Wish said, "I don't need all of them. Enough to surround the Irregulars, make them lay down their arms. If they're not already moving, I can get ahead of them, delay them somehow. You can come by night, get around them."

"And if they've already reached Drowndeep?" Sister Sonseen asked, unimpressed so far.

Wish considered that for a moment. "Then I'll get them to invite me in, and I'll open the doors myself." *As they were planning to do here.* She levelled her gaze at Atmoor, imploring him to accept this, to find some gumption to actually commit.

He made a low mumbling noise, and said, "This sounds like the start of something we can work with. And if they reach the coast, I have some sway with our navy in the Most Blessed Sea. I have already contacted our battleships there."

Wish glanced at Brade, who couldn't quite hide the guilt from his bland expression. She recalled Brade and Caracker unravelling the Drail code, and their assumption that the *Horrocast* had been requesting confirmation of repositioning. Orders that she had interrupted by killing all the messengers. A great stroke of luck, if they'd kept the ship at bay before, maybe not so fortunate now. But a battleship would've been overkill anyway. They had all they all needed, surely. Except for one thing.

"For this to work," Wish said, "I need my mage. You have her, don't you? You'll set Emi free, let us all walk away. Without being followed. We'll slow the Irregulars down while you gear up for a fight. Whatever their plans, Colonel, our best bet is to catch them unawares and put them in a position where they're forced to surrender. That starts with you giving me my mage."

Atmoor considered this at length and looked at Brade. "If the Arrow Council were to find out I'd released an enemy mage . . ."

"I'm not leaving without her. And you're not catching the Irregulars without us."

"Suddenly cocky, ain't ya?" Bleacher said. "This all sounds fucking woolly and hesitant to me, Colonel, respectfully. Why not make life simple – if Drowndeep's their goal, my lads can outpace them and end this on the road."

"Yeah? How'd that work out for you in Midwood?"

Atmoor tutted at the goblin for quiet, but Bleacher kept grinning broadly. Wish forced herself to keep calm, holding his nasty gaze. Out of the corner of her eye, she noticed Brade smirk, not helping.

"Very well," Atmoor sighed. "We can reach an agreement. But you might find the mage more of a burden than a help right now."

"Why? What have you done to her?" Wish snapped, but Atmoor put up a chunky hand.

"She is injured," he said. "And not very agreeable. Come, I think we're about done, I might as well show you to her now."

He walked out and Wish moved faster than was graceful to follow him. They only went a few rooms down the hall, making Wish's heart jump at the thought Emi had been so close all this time. Ignored, left out while she talked with these bastards. Atmoor opened the door and she all but shoved him aside. There was Emi, on a damn thin mattress with nothing else, shackled, *chained!* She stirred, barely awake, robed in a light tunic, her froggy face bleary and hair a scruffy mess. Wish's eyes shimmered at the sight. Emi, alive. She'd told herself over and over it was true, but hadn't really *known.* At the first hint of Emi's smile, Wish leapt forward, spreading her arms for a hug.

"Stop!" Atmoor called, and Wish turned back, teeth bared and hand flashing to her knife. Scraper's knife, made for butchering. The colonel glowered as he explained, "She's been shot in the chest, Lieutenant. Recovering as only a mage could, but still badly hurt. I wouldn't recommend touching her."

"It does sting," Emi admitted, and her voice, croaky from sleep, made Wish spin back.

"Oh Bly, Emi," Wish said, wanting to pile on her every fear and relief that had stacked up inside. *I thought you were dead. I thought I got you killed. I thought I was alone.* Emi's tired eyes showed understanding. Her faint smile was enough.

"I knew you'd bust me out," she said. "Though I didn't think you'd leave *him* alive." She almost laughed, but winced and added, "So you gonna get these off?" She shook her shackled wrists, and Wish nodded quickly. She wiped a forearm over her leaking nose.

"Yes. Yes, absolutely, yes. We're leaving. We're going to settle this. It's okay, we don't have to deal with the Drail anymore."

"Oh good. So we won?" Emi gave Atmoor a confused look; the enemy clearly weren't vanquished.

"No, not exactly. I'll explain on the way. We still have a big problem. You're gonna be fine, though. It's all gonna be fine."

"Oh Wild." Emi stifled a laugh, with that familiar, pitying smirk that always seemed to be reserved just for Wild Wish. "You know that's never true."

40

There is a centuries-long pattern of Urlians being press-ganged into military service and spat out worse off than before. Under-armed, underpaid and abusively ordered, these soldiers would also have their assets stripped with no guaranteed pensions. With the inevitable shifts of allegiance that followed, they were labelled as disloyal, miserable, unmotivated. The worker poorly managed was blamed, when we should always have been looking to the managers.

**Don't Call Me Ogre: Rethinking Modern
Urlian History, Blonc, p. 59**

"What's in bloody Drowndeep?" Runt demanded unhappily. Typical, Ohno thought, that he managed to keep up his miserable disposition regardless of who they were following. He was a born malcontent, whether faced with stuffy Stanish officers or an army of clearly deranged rogues. Though at least it helped convince the Irregulars they could be trusted; someone willing to complain this much wasn't pretending to fit in. Not like Ohno, who was, under her usual veneer of obedience, trying to think of a way to crush Havik for what she'd done to Caracker. They were now abandoning the comforts of Gauntstone, where Ohno had hoped they might end up cornered, to travel back through the cursed bog, and Runt was loudly voicing his disappointment. "We've been to bloody Drowndeep. There's nothing there worth spitting at."

"Not that you would've seen, no," Havik said, taking no insult at his tone. She was like some kind of marsh princess, in her tatty coat with that massive gun strapped on her back, riding an absurdly big horse with long, matted fur and big clomping hooves. The ogres had pride of place in the procession, two brutes tramping alongside the excessive horses with a great column of men trailing behind on foot.

"Well I'm asking now," Runt continued miserably, as if he wasn't just belly-aching. "There's no treasure there, just a load of damp. Why bother?"

"It's the lynchpin," Havik said. "The last thing we need."

"For *what?*" Runt pressed and Ohno wished he wouldn't. Any idiot could see Havik had an agenda that didn't warrant close inspection. Caracker had seen through her offers of wealth and she obviously didn't like that.

"You always gotta know everything your officers are thinking?" Raltman said. It wasn't clear how much the other Irregulars actually knew, either: Kasidee and Lost One didn't look bothered about Runt's probing, but Ohno saw how uncomfortable it made Raltman and those riding just behind. They probably preferred to trust Havik implicitly, without weighing up the details themselves.

"If you'd seen the place we're headed, you'd be asking too," Runt replied.

"What's there," Kasidee intervened, "is the means to put a real dent in this war. With a little luck, a rallying cry, a formidable weapon. At worst, something we can ransom to the churches."

Runt didn't look satisfied but Kasidee spoke with a lot more authority than Havik, making clear that it was as much as they'd get. Ohno willed her companion to be quiet. Curious as she was herself (what the hell *was* in that festering keep?), ogres weren't supposed to ask questions.

"How long have you been with the Blood Scouts?" Havik changed the subject, addressing Ohno.

"Just for this job," Ohno replied honestly. She'd seen how interested the woman was in the scouts, and her weird respect for Wild Wish, and didn't want any part of that. "About a week, maybe."

"That's a shame," Havik said. "Aren't they fascinating? How many have you met?"

"How many do you think there are?" Runt said shortly, transferring his hostility to the new topic. "There's only three of them, and none especially impressive."

"But there's a whole platoon. Dozens of women soldiers."

Runt laughed. "You wish. If there was more than those three lunatics, think they would've hired us?"

"Well, they divide their talents, there's a whole war to cater to," Havik replied, sounding slightly defensive. Kasidee's expression shifted – concern over her knowledge being challenged? She looked at Ohno again. "Tell me what you think about Wild Wish, her operation."

"She's a scared, mad –" Runt started.

"I'm asking her, not you." It wasn't angry or sharp, and all the more commanding for it. Runt eyed her, no doubt recalling Caracker and that simple, savage gunshot. Entire armies hadn't taken that man down, but this one small woman had stood unflinching before him . . . Her cold eyes found Ohno's, imploring a good answer.

"More to her than it seems, I'd say," Ohno said, truthfully. Wish had certainly put away more boulder whisky than they'd expected. And they'd all seen her shooting those degrebus out of the sky. "I don't know much about her, but anyone could tell she's seen some things. Done some things."

Havik nodded as if that was exactly what she was looking for. "And do you think –"

A gunshot tore through the conversation and men shouted and dived for cover as the bullet cracked off a rock nearby. Kasidee reined his horse back, the startled animal's immense legs lifting off the ground, and as it thundered down he shouted quick commands – *get down!* – to those too slow to react on their own. The horses broke after him, riding off the road into the shelter of a mass of rocky outcrops, as Ohno and Runt lurched in the other direction, dipping into long grass, legs sinking up to their shins. Amid the panic and shouting, Ohno listened for more gunfire as she unhitched Caracker's thump pistol, with a hope it was Wild Wish catching up to them. Reinforcements, a chance to escape. But no more shots followed, and the Irregulars settled under Kasidee's loud orders.

"Where'd it come from?" he demanded. "Who's firing?"

"Kin Kasidee!" a man called from out in the bog, and Ohno rose slightly from her crouch to see over the grass. A dark shadow by the far rocks, the clothing and voice familiar: a venerator from Midpeak. "You are surrounded. Lay down your arms!"

"Is that a fucking monk?" Runt whispered.

Ohno glanced back along the ranks of the Irregulars, the mass of bodies partly hiding by rocks and grass, some still shifting about for cover, with guns poking up all over. They stretched far into the distance, and that was just the ones still visible. All the monks in Midpeak would've had a hard time surrounding them, and she doubted very much that this man had brought even that many.

"That so?" Kasidee called from the other side of the road, down at ground level, out of sight with only the huge unmounted horses hinting at his position. Grass shifted near him where men were crawling into better positions. "And who've I got the pleasure of surrendering to?"

"Venerator Fold," the priest called back, a slight break in his older voice. Not a strong man, nor a wise one, having not merely attacked. "We've seen the evidence of your treachery. By order of the Church of the Venerate Flesh, and the authority of Midpeak Priory, I command that you relinquish your weapons and face the justice of faith."

The Irregulars did not respond immediately, letting the venerator's words echo through the marsh. He'd put it boldly, at least, with the skill of a man trained for the pulpit. Then someone laughed, and others joined in, with questions and comments as soldiers further back clarified what was being said. Ohno tensed, the amusement growing louder the further it got back, in part deliberately, she expected, to make clear quite how many soldiers were out here. Hushed orders came from Kasidee's position, calling for quiet, and when the tittering settled Kasidee called a response, stifling laughter of his own.

"The justice of faith? Venerator Fold, the world hasn't recognised that justice for generations."

"While you're in the Mire, you will respect it," Fold shouted, but less sure of himself. He'd heard the scale of the response. Only a fool could imagine he had a chance here. "You're outnumbered and we have many more weapons. Come peacefully and no one will be harmed."

This sent another cascade of laughter through the marsh, more immediate this time, and more mocking. Ohno willed the priest to give it up. Walk away, quickly, before this got worse.

"The world might have forgotten the faith," Fold shouted, "but the One God persists, and you have insulted the Saints with your presence! Your bodies are unclean, your hearts impure, and you *will* be judged!"

"Has he got a fucking death wish?" Runt hissed, as soldiers nearby echoed Fold's words in scathing tones, calling each other unclean.

"Had a bath in Gauntstone, thank you mate!" a man shouted, getting a good laugh.

"Alright enough, enough!" Kasidee shouted, though his own voice shook with amusement. "Quiet, the lot of you. You" – he stifled another laugh – "dirty bastards. Now listen here, Venerator Fold – you're a holy man and no doubt honourable, I respect that. It took a lot of guts to hide out here, thinking you could save us from our inequity. Your faith won't protect you, though. I'll give you a chance. Put *your* guns down and get out of here or we'll put your god to the test. You'll find him wanting."

Another moment's stillness, besides occasional sniggers. Ohno dreaded the answer she knew would come, wishing the priest had more sense and less pride than it seemed. She'd watched Caracker die because he hadn't been able to bend. Enough already. To whatever force might listen, she prayed, *let this priest walk away.*

"I will give you to the count of five," Fold's voice came again, met at once with derisive whoops and laughs. "Do you hear me? You have until the count of –"

A loud bang sounded not far from his position and his words cut off. Ohno looked up just in time to see the priest falling. A flurry of dark robes followed, his monks scrambling as more gunshots followed. Two or three Irregulars were shooting from the rocks off to their right, flushing out the venerator's full force of what looked like two dozen men at most. The monks weren't cut down immediately, thanks to their rocky cover, and fired back, to their credit, with shots that peppered the attackers' position. It signalled a full assault, though, with Kasidee roaring a call to arms, and the combined might of the Irregulars rose from hiding. They started sweeping past Ohno in a mad shooting wave, tripping over each other to be the first to the fight. She stumbled upright merely to avoid being smacked into, and Runt moved to one side watching nonplussed. The shots fired at the monks' position tore the rocks apart and smoke filled the marsh, within seconds removing any chance for the enemy to shoot back.

Ohno marvelled at the speed and fervour of the Irregulars' charge, before seeing an opportunity. The terrain was rife with cover, hard for them to run through quickly, leading to many tripping and disappearing into the bog. It was wide open, a good expanse stretching off into the haze, and the dark-robed men at the rear of the monks' position were running. One crumpled into the grass, hit in the head, as others pressed on.

"They're out of their minds," Runt snarled, but Ohno slapped his arm to encourage him.

"They're running, get them!" she boomed, her voice that much bigger than the others. She started a charge of her own. She built up speed quickly, ploughing through the first men ahead of her with great, splashing strides. She shouted for them to clear the path. The sight and sound of a charging ogre broke through even the manic fervour of these men, as she hoped it would, and a good portion of the Irregulars faltered, stopped firing, and paused to watch with awe. She didn't miss a step, surging past the men at the front of the charge, closing the distance on the monks' rocks. No one was firing back now, the nearby monks dead, the ones further off fleeing clumsily into the bog. As Ohno launched herself off a hard patch of ground to vault the first rocks, she glimpsed Fold himself lifeless on the ground, eyes open in dead surprise. The Irregulars picked up the charge again behind her, cheering excitedly to follow. She landed heavily on the other side of the rocks and clambered over the next ones, hunting out the quickest route through. Then she was out again, back in the slog of the marsh, bounding after the most distant monk. She sprinted with all her strength, racing up behind the panting man. He looked back with a shriek as her shadow fell over him.

Then she ran right past.

A shot came a second later and she jerked back to see the monk hit, falling. Beyond him, the Irregulars stalled again, watching her, already becoming small as she kept running. A man was up on the rocks in a crouch, with his long rifle. Lost One, the marksman she knew she'd have to beat. He'd figured it out quicker than the others and was already jamming back the bolt on his gun for another shot. Ohno gritted her teeth, twisted away from them and pressed on into the mist, ducking her head low. Their horses might have the pace but not the dexterity to catch up to an ogre sprinting through this marsh. She just had to dive deeper into the mist, to get beyond however far that one-eyed bastard could see.

Another shot came and she felt the punch of the bullet striking hard and hot into her shoulder. It made her stumble, arching her back in pain, but she stayed upright, kept running, and flung her head forward, hiding it with her body. One more chance, she imagined. If she could survive one more shot, she could make it. Hissing with pain, losing her breath, Ohno charged on, boots heavy with mud, and listened for the final gunshot.

41

Life does not end; it changes.
Faith lies in that truth.
Power lies in that faith.

The Book of Bones, Sandway,
translated by Birganio, 134:2

Wild Wish wanted to stop, to take stock, but they were in a race now, under the ominous threat of whatever was possible in Drowndeep. Brother Redfire, though he spoke cheerily, had only bad things to share when it came to the potential ancient relics and legends the Irregulars might be chasing. It didn't help that Wish had seen Drowndeep firsthand and understood the nature of those who worshipped there. Their prayers were violent, their totems connected to death.

"Of course it couldn't be necromancy," Redfire laughed, an ugly word always somehow at the edge of people's most unwelcome desires. He added, helpfully, "Perhaps something close to it. But not *actual* necromancy."

"What's close to it?" Wish demanded with alarm.

Chuckling again, he said, "Oh, there are strange legends of Bonesun raising monsters from bodies. Holding souls in limbo to fuel dark magic. Rumours of hauntings in the marsh. Stories that he did not speak to Saints, but to restless spirits. All with a common theme of communing with the dead left too close to the surface. You know the saying, *if you should die where Paradise Fails . . ."*

Wish was not familiar with the rest of that particular pleasantry.

Redfire didn't finish it, saying instead, as she'd heard suggested before, "But these were things meant to diminish the Fifth Prophet. Deliberate misinterpretations of his teachings. There's no such thing as necromancy."

That not-entirely convincing thought carried the scouts at speed along the river from Carlwen, freshly supplied with monstrously large furry horses adept in the mud. Sister Sonseen and Redfire had joined them as guides, to help when they reached Drowndeep, and only they and Brade showed any real comfort on the ride. The others jolted about as they clung on, trusting the animals to know best. Emi rode with Sonseen, the beetle a supposedly smoother ride; she made occasional pained snarls at its rough movements, but refused to slow down or acknowledge that she was seriously hurt, making Wish worry all the more. When they broke to rest the horses and take water, the mage stretched herself out, and Wish asked, for the fiftieth time, "Are you sure you're alright? You can take another route, catch us up later. Or turn back."

"Like hell," Emi growled, cracking her neck. "Do you have any idea what you let them do to me already?" Wish averted her gaze, well aware of her chest wound. A miracle she was alive. But Emi went on with disgust, "A *witlacer* touched me. Ugh."

"I think they saved your life," Wish replied carefully, and earned a hateful look.

"I need you to do something for me, Wild," Emi said, about as seriously as she'd ever spoken. Wish nodded quickly. "Promise me. Whatever happens. This is important."

"Anything, Emi."

"Don't tell Dollermore about this."

Wish frowned. The Blood Scouts' other mage, the eminently sensible witlacer, had been a long way from her mind for a long time, and this felt wholly out of place now.

But Emi evidently had her own concerns, and continued, "I would *never* live it down if she found out. Witlacers." She spat.

Wish's concerns softened. If the worst thing bothering Emi was her childish feud with her long-absent fellow mage – something that always seemed wholly one-sided – then things couldn't be all bad. With the start of a smile, she said, "Absolutely. I won't tell her."

Emi glowered, to make clear her seriousness, then she looked away to consider the river flowing past them. It was rough, murky and wide, fitting to the generally unpleasant region, and Wish doubted that the Rawboys should be filling their flasks from it. She'd strained things enough already by siding with Colonel Atmoor over the Irregulars, though, and if they wanted to drink bog poison that was their problem. As long as it didn't kill them before they stopped Kasidee – she didn't really have men to spare.

"I'm not going to be much help, you know," Emi said, guessing her thoughts. Still wearing that serious face that did not suit her. She pointed at her bandaged chest. "This sort of thing makes it hard to focus magic. Easy to reopen the wound."

Wish stared, curious at the phrasing, *this sort of thing,* as though Emi had plenty of experience being mortally wounded. She said, "That's alright. I'm not sure exactly what we can do other than slow Kasidee down, anyway. Maybe snatch what they're after and run off with it?"

"Throw it in the sea," Emi agreed. "Unless it's activated by seawater."

"What do you think it is? Actually dangerous?"

"I don't know. I told you this place isn't right. All imbalanced, weird energy. There's centuries-old secrets in these priories; the whole point is no one knows what they are."

"Until you get someone who's read all the books," Wish replied, recalling Havik's enthusiasm, the love of reading that had seemed innocent and endearing at the time. Emi eyed her oddly, the hint of her smirk returning, something Wish definitely hadn't missed. "What?"

"What indeed," Emi murmured.

Wish shook her head, not about to get into it with her. She decided to get everyone moving again.

The day was stretching out, but Wild Wish was determined to reach Drowndeep by nightfall. It was much faster going with the trails along the open river relatively even and safe, at least as far as the mountains, thanks to Atmoor's men. Their main hope was that it'd take the Irregulars longer to organise themselves than Wish's small group, and the latest reports from the Drail was that there was still movement in the priory when the Blood Scouts left. Kasidee would also need to head towards the coast, away from Atmoor's forces, before finding a suitable crossing into Paradise Fails. It wasn't just them Wish wanted to beat, though; Atmoor's greater force would be moving, too, with the goblin horde ahead of the rest, and there was no doubt in her mind that anything she could do would be better done before they caught up. She already suspected they'd become traitors to the Comity simply by talking to the Drail.

The dimming daylight saw the scouts making two river crossings, passing the base of the mountains for a clear stretch the rest of the way to Drowndeep. About halfway between the mountains and the priory, as its twisted towers came into view on the horizon, they climbed a small incline and were faced with a grim view. The shimmering water, tall grasses and rocky plains that joined Paradise Fails with the Mire's northern reaches of Low Bile stretched out before them. Far across a tributary of the distant river, there was the unmistakable dark caterpillar of a military caravan. Through her scope, Wish could make out ranks and ranks of marching men, with wagons to the rear and horses to the front. Was that a more slender shape in one saddle – a woman? And a big hulking figure accompanied them on foot.

"That's one of the ogres," Brade commented from beside Wish. "Couldn't say which."

"Only one?" Macmiddan asked, a detail that didn't bear dwelling on. Hard to say what was worse – the ogres being injured or the ogres being lost to the Irregulars.

Wish was more concerned with the woman, though. A little jab in her heart made her realise she'd really been hoping, somehow, that Havik wasn't actually connected to this. That there was some kind of mistake. But there she was, at the head of the company, unmistakably trekking south towards Drowndeep.

"About confirms it, doesn't it?" Ptrangus muttered, hunched over the front of his horse. Apparently Wish hadn't been the only one hoping some other outcome was possible. "We even got a chance of getting to the priory first?"

"They haven't crossed the river yet," Brade said, meaning they actually had a good chance, but Ptrangus's dark stare suggested that wasn't the point.

"There's a lot of open ground between here and there," Wish noted. "They'll see us. Probably speed up when they do. Maybe it's worth riding out to meet them?" The men were quiet, letting her consider it for herself. She imagined a world where she could trot up to the front of an imposing army with a wave, embodying the kind of swagger Brade had delivered to Carlwen. A little smile for Havik, maybe a comment about her hair, looking good, and some light banter to dismiss the impending trouble. *You want to go* there? *Oh no, I wouldn't bother, maybe just go home? Stop bothering people?* Wish frowned at the scale of Kasidee's force. Nowhere near as large or well-equipped as most armies she'd seen in this war, and a fraction of Atmoor's alone, but still a formidable mass of armed brutes. She could imagine every one of them as aggressive and unpleasant as Raltman and Lost One, and felt a burgeoning desire to be somewhere with very strong defences. Midpeak would've been preferable, but they weren't heading to Midpeak. Drowndeep would have to do. She answered her own question: "If there's a conversation to be had, I want some walls between us. But if we don't go out to meet them, they'll know something's up."

"In this position," Brade said, "so close to Drowndeep, we're not going to be able to slow them down for long. *If* they're willing to talk."

"There's only one ogre," Dalliance noted, and that carried about all the weight any of them needed. The Irregulars were too dangerous to meet out here in the open, and Atmoor's forces too far behind to help.

"We'll ride hard," Wish decided. "A direct line from here to the priory – anything else will give them too much time."

"About time we got to ride *something* hard in this place," Emi murmured, but the comment fell flat.

Brade steered his horse away, taking the lead. "Follow me, chaps, ladies. See you inside." With that, he gave a little *kee-ya* and propelled his horse forward, clomping down the slope into the open marshland. The others less gracefully turned after him, kicking their heels, and they began a bouncing, frantic charge. Sister Sonseen pulled ahead of Wish with Emi on her beetle as Brother Redfire followed on horseback, chuckling to himself at the clearly uncomfortable ride, his bulbous form jostling in the saddle. Wish urged her horse on, hoping it'd take care of the rest.

They trailed out through the bog at their fastest pace all day, hooves squelching and thumping, and Wish imagined them a triumphant cavalry, riding gloriously to victory. Never mind that they were riding away from trouble, towards the grimly twisted Drowndeep. As the priory's final approach came into view, the road ahead a faster path, one of the Rawboys swore from the rear. Wish glanced back, and slowed to see the tributary, where a bridge curved over it. Kasidee's troops were starting to cross. Quickly. Men were running, guns in their hands. They were too far off for her to snipe, but she made out the horse riders who'd paused at the crest of the bridge. Havik was in the middle, Wish had no doubt. She couldn't see it from this far off, but she imagined the woman was smiling. She knew the scouts were no longer on their side, *had* to know, and was ready for whatever lay ahead.

"Faster, everyone," Wish said quietly, though the others were already passing her, cantering onto the road. She shouted, "It's the final stretch, fast as you can!"

They joined Brade in his *kee-yaing,* the horses giving it all they had, and far back the sounds of the Irregulars became gradually audible. Men shouting, goading. Someone fired a gun, followed by a few more. Wish fell to the back, twisting in her saddle. She flinched at more gunshots – dammit they were already running down the road. The Irregulars' horse riders were in no hurry though, giving their foot-soldiers the first shot at this fun.

"Quick, Wish, dammit!" Brade shouted, but she looked from him back up the road. The riflemen were closing the distance absurdly quickly. In the other direction, her own squad was partway to the gates of Drowndeep, unfriendly tribesmen stirring from the village before it. Sonseen was shouting at them, waving her arms for everyone to get inside. It wasn't enough to ride in – they couldn't leave the tribespeople outside. They needed more time.

Hurriedly, Wish unstrapped her rifle from the saddle, shouting, "Go! Get everyone inside! I'm right behind you!"

More gunshots came from up the road and she snapped her attention to the Irregulars, almost within shooting distance now.

"Wild Wish!" Brade boomed.

Ignoring his protests, Wish chambered a bullet and lifted the scope to her eye. She picked out the soldier at the front of the Irregulars' charge, a madly smiling man jogging down the middle of the road as if the world ought to be afraid of him. She steadied herself in the saddle, waited for the horse to settle, and fired. The soldier fell, dead, and his mates scattered into the mud and grass. With their charge momentarily halted, Wish turned her horse to aim for the gates again. Her men were almost through, driving a confused stampede of Shore Stalkers along with them. Brade was riding back towards her. She twisted, seeing the Irregulars regrouping, picked out another soldier and fired.

"Ride, ride!" Brade shouted, steering his horse around alongside her and grabbing the reins himself. He whipped the horse into action and she almost fell off, fumbling her rifle under one arm and snatching at the saddle with her other hand. They pounded down the road together as the Irregulars' shouts and shots picked up after them. A bullet whizzed through the air, too close. Ahead, the gates to Drowndeep were open, the Rawboys forcing their way in. Another shot made Wish flinch low, and Brade yelled at the horses to move faster. They broke through the village, tripping tribespeople over, and Brade came to a sudden halt before the gates. He leapt off and hurried to help Wish down, too, then they shouldered their way into the crowded court of Drowndeep, banging into the horses that'd impossibly made it inside. Wish's troops were likewise dismounted and roaring orders, close the gate, get to arms! The monks and locals did as they were told, pushing the dismounted horses back outside to make space for the last people, rushing to secure the priory as quickly as possible. Wish watched through the closing gap in the metal doors as the Irregulars ran closer, unnaturally fast.

The gates banged shut and the monks threw their barricades into place, amid more shouting and protest. Wish kept staring at the space where the road had been, rifle raised. They'd made it, they were inside, secure. But the Irregulars were firing guns, yelling up a storm, and after a few short moments they hit the doors, banging loudly.

"What now?" Wish whispered, the clamour of an approaching army growing by the second. They'd be storming the village, quickly surrounding the walled settlement. They had artillery, she recalled. There was a body of water around part of the keep, but it wouldn't be hard to climb the walls. She threw her worried gaze about, searching for someone, anyone, to give her the answer. There were her Rawboys and Dalliance panting to catch their breath, dozens of upset tribal faces, including the mean bearded chief Shore Stalker. Emi was leaning against a wall, disturbingly worn out. There was another uniform – Latebite, the man they'd left behind, supporting himself on crutches. Sister Sonseen and Brother Redfire stood side by side near her massive cramped beetle. Every inch of space in the priory's courtyard was crowded, likewise the raised walkways and scrappy, bone-decorated walls that encircled it. Everyone, her squad of soldiers, a bunch of Shore Stalkers and a town's worth of monks, was looking at her, the one person with her gun ready to fight. Scores of frightened faces, all looking at her.

Brade pushed back through the crowd to meet her eye, drawing his pistol, and for a moment she felt lighter, with the surety he'd take charge. He said, "Lieutenant. What's the plan?"

She stared back at him, with the noises of Kasidee's mob closing in, and she held in her immediate response. *Well, shit.*

42

At the famous Last Stand of Elbuk, during the War of Unification, fifty soldiers lost their lives defending a fort against five hundred. It is still celebrated across the Rocc as a modern legend. During the One War, there were so many similar battles that few are remembered in popular culture.

Light-feet: How Hiding Changed History, Prodder, p. 135

The stillness had already dragged out for too long with the Irregulars swarming the village. Wish had to say something, no matter what, so she did: "Everyone who's armed, get to higher ground, find a vantage point. Anyone who's not, find a weapon. Anyone that can't fight, find shelter. If they get in, retreat into the tunnels, secure choke points, take no chances."

The Rawboys grunted and started moving ahead as Brade loudly translated Wish's orders. His voice was echoed by a shouting monk – Brother Estekof, up on a balcony. The monk went a step further, pointing to where people might find tools or hide. So Wish hoped. She strode off, aiming for some steps to follow her own advice.

Brade appeared next to her, a hand on her upper arm. "Where are you going?"

"Up," she said, and shrugged him off. "I've got to see them to kill them." She pushed through the crowd and another thought struck her, which she shouted over the hubbub. "Stay out of sight. Show them nothing – they've got marksmen!" Brade watched her briefly before translating this too, then he came shoving after her. Wish started up the stone stairs, exposed to the courtyard so she could watch them all racing about, and she paused again. "Sister Sonseen, can you secure the relics? Find what they're looking for? Quick as you can."

Across the courtyard, the nun nodded, alongside Brother Redfire, and together they turned to try and make their way inside the keep. Wish continued higher, onto the first level of walkways, then grabbed a rickety ladder and kept climbing. Brade followed close behind. He shouted more commands of his own, improvising details that sent the monks and Shore Stalkers hurrying to strategic positions.

"Macmiddan, Ptrangus, take the east side of the gate. Graveguard and Latebite, fall back, watch their rear. Dalliance, up the bell tower?"

"Got it," Dalliance replied, peeling off in another direction, and Wish flashed a look to the tower herself. That was the best spot. But she was on her way to the gate defences, to mirror the Rawboys Brade had sent to the other side; she needed to stay in the thick of it. As she clambered onto the tallest walkway and half-crouched past a couple of monks already hiding there, clutching bone-tipped spears, she realised that beyond the rapid activity in the priory, things had grown quiet outside. By the time she huddled down between the gaps in the wall defences, even the courtyard clamour was settling down. She glanced back to see the space was strangely empty after it had been so packed before, a sign of how expansive the tunnels inside were, to swallow up the crowd. The remaining horses stamped their feet and Sonseen's beetle tapped about in an uneasy circle, while arms and legs poked out from behind doorways, low walls and crates. The last signs of movement were those people still reaching the highest positions on the walls, and Dalliance appeared in flashes bounding past the bell tower's window slits.

Wish took a deep breath, soaking up the final calm before hell struck them, and the silence was broken by a man shouting beyond the wall. "Captain Wild Wish? That is you in there, isn't it? You're aware you killed a few of my men?"

He had an accent best described as silky, *continental,* like the smooth money-men from the southern nations. It sounded out of place here, heading a rag-tag army before the creaking darkness of bone-lined Drowndeep.

"Think they fired at me first, thanks," Wish heard herself calling back, and inwardly scolded herself for her instinctive politeness. She added, "Kin Kasidee, is that you?"

"The one and only," he replied. "What do you say to inviting us in for a friendly chat?"

"What do you say to fucking yourself up the arse?" Wish replied and again winced at herself – too far in the other direction. She heard laughter outside, Kasidee's own men amused at the insult, and she got a few impressed looks from her people cowering nearby. She spotted Emi, down at ground level near the gate, pressed deep in a shadowy nook. The mage winked up at her, but it wasn't a convincing wink, the lack of spark evident even from here. There was no sign of Scraper, Wish realised, and felt no bitterness at the thought that maybe the scout had found a place to wait out the trouble.

"Very good," Kasidee called, as the tittering died down. "This is quite a to-do, isn't it? Anyone might think you've taken a page from my book, holing yourself up in there against these odds. But at Fort Simnon we had near-impenetrable walls, a good stock of ammunition and some truly hard soldiers. What have you got in there, besides yourselves and a confused bunch of Shore Stalkers?"

"Push us and you'll find out," Wish said.

"What happened to you," Brade joined in loudly, "between Simnon and here? What made the hero Kin Kasidee turn bandit?"

"Captain Rikard Brade?" Kasidee replied. "Oh by the Body, that is you, isn't it? It's a real honour. I've read all your books. You've got a lot of fans in my company."

"Wonderful – can I persuade them to turn on you?"

Kasidee laughed again, and some of his soldiers joined in. "Come on. We don't want to hurt you. We're all on the same side, aren't we? I heard you got on famously with our Havik."

"Until she started murdering monks, sure," Brade replied.

Wish cringed at the reminder. But she needed to confirm where they stood, and added, "She was supposed to join us at Carlwen. You left us to die out there."

"Not at all," Havik finally spoke, and her voice gripped Wish by the heart. She forced herself not to lean around the rampart to look, as her emotions suddenly duelled. Wanting to see her, not wanting to see her. Hopeful, hurt. "If anyone was going to stop Colonel Atmoor, I believed you would. I'm sorry we couldn't help. But we can work together again now, can't we?"

Wish almost believed her, until the last comment. As if she might actually help them. She snapped, "Yeah. You want what we've got in here, it won't come easy."

There was quiet beyond the wall and Brade eyed Wish. She looked into the courtyard, thinking this would be an ideal time for Sister Sonseen to emerge waving some relic overhead to confirm they knew exactly what the Irregulars were here for and could thwart it. Extra collateral would be very useful right now. There was no sign of the nun in the dark doorways.

"What is it you think we came for?" Havik ventured, carefully.

"Bonesun's relics," Wish threw back. Time to improvise. "They look pretty fragile. You really think they're worth something?" More quiet, though this time Wish heard subtle movement, the leaders conferring. To stop them overthinking it, she went on, "You hearing me, Havik? You're going to have to work hard not to piss me off here."

"We've got a cannon, you realise?" Kasidee shouted, trying to sound amused but unable to hide a hint of frustration. "You must have about three guns between you."

"And a few thousand more on the way," Wish called back quickly, and realised at once it was a mistake. Never mind the traitorous implications, it sounded desperate.

"Oh? You expect me to believe that? The Comity can't help you here." Kasidee paused. "Unless you mean the Drail? My word. That's low. I'm particularly disappointed in you, Captain Brade. So what, you think Colonel Atmoor will ride to your rescue? That coward's been dragging his heels this whole time."

"He's coming," Brade shouted, thankfully committing to her folly. "Not far behind us. There's nothing for you here but death, Kasidee. Attack and we'll trash your treasure. Stay and the Drail will shoot you in the backs."

Kasidee gave it a moment before saying, "Yeah. I'd almost be worried, if Atmoor had any chance of crossing the rivers here. What do you think he'll do with no bridges? Swim?" Another brief pause. "I was waiting to catch a few of them on it, but let's demonstrate." He called something out in Garter, and a few echoing shouts followed. A signal was sent. A loud bang came from far away. Wish pressed her eyes closed for a moment, her damn words having literally explosive consequences. "That was a bridge, in case you weren't sure!" Some Irregulars clapped and cheered. Kasidee spoke over the noise, "It's important for us to be clear with one another, isn't it? So we know where we stand. You're trapped and no one is coming. But I'm magnanimous and I have a lot of respect for both of you, and your men." A quick whisper, Havik correcting him, and he added, "And your *women.*"

This was seeming more hopeless by the second.

Wish saw Dalliance's silhouette up in the bell tower, a little back from the opening but ready. If she was up there herself, she could put a bullet in Kasidee right now. She wondered if it would help or make things worse. She hoped Dalliance was smarter than her, and was watching the Irregulars' marksmen instead.

"We have one of your ogres, you know? He's brighter than the other two were. Be like him and *join* me. We'll go far together. Captain Brade, you know the adventures we've had, *could* have. Captain Tate, why keep fighting for the Empire, getting your hands bloody for someone else's gain? They're not here for you now. Isn't it time to take care of yourself?"

My home is part of that empire, Wish answered internally. *And if we don't fight then someone like you will try to take it –* She caught herself, frowning at his words, then exclaimed, "Captain *Tate?"* She'd realised Havik might have been mistaken before, but the ridiculous comment still surprised her enough to lean out from the defences. In an instant, she took in the gathered mass of the Irregulars, a truly discordant crowd of thugs with mismatched clothing, guns and spiky weapons, spread behind their leaders on huge horses. Kasidee sat at the centre, in a long, fine dark coat, wide hat, slicked hair and smooth skin fitting every bit the banker's image his voice suggested. Havik was at his side, head cocked at a curious angle as she spotted Wish and smiled. It took a moment, out in the open, before Wish regained her ability to speak. When she did, she shouted, "You don't even know who I am! Everything about you being here is wrong!"

Havik's smile faded, something finally unsettling her, and Kasidee glanced her way. She said, "What are you . . . You're the head of the Blood Scouts."

"I'm not Tate!" Wish cried again, the absurdity overcoming the threat of the situation. She rose higher, putting herself on show. "I didn't kill your people! I've never been anywhere near Kopice. I don't even know where it is! Captain Tate is *gone.* She's *dead* and all you've got is *me.*"

"I . . ." Havik trailed off as Wish looked at her imploringly. There was a chance, she considered – if at least some part of this was a mistake, might they rethink things? There would be no revenge to be had here, or whatever else she intended for Tate.

"This is embarrassing for you, love!" Ptrangus's cheerful Raw voice shouted from the other side of the gate, getting a few laughs.

"Okay, dammit Havik that's a splendid mess," Kasidee curtly cut in. "But we've got more important matters to attend to. Miss, it's splendid to meet you *whoever you are,* and my offer remains. Surrender the keep and its relics and you can walk away. We can even discuss working together. Otherwise, my patience is reaching its end."

"Oh piss off!" Wish replied, petulantly. She wanted to talk to Havik, to figure something out with her, not this damn banker-soldier and his damned army. This damn war in the way. Again. "You're out of your minds coming here, picking this fight. You don't even know who you're fucking with. You know how many men I've killed?"

"Less than Captain Tate, I imagine," Kasidee replied, bored if anything. Havik was silent, merely staring at her, studying her. "Are we going to reach an agreement here or not?"

"You can choose between leaving or dying, that's up to you," Wish replied, still eyeing Havik. Why wasn't she talking? What was she thinking? *Had* they found some connection – did it mean more, or less, now she knew Wish hadn't slaughtered her hometown?

Kasidee gave an unhappy sneer, disappointed. He looked to the gates, as if dismissing all this nonsense, and nudged his horse forward. As it clopped a little closer, he shouted in Garter, the local tongue.

Wish flinched as Brade grabbed her by the wrist and pulled her down. He hissed, "You want to get shot?" He paused to listen as Kasidee continued, then he looked into the courtyard. The bearded Shore Stalker, the tribe's chief, was coming out into the open, pushing past men who growled at him.

"What's he saying?" Wish asked.

"Kasidee's challenging the chief," Brade said. "Single-combat, blades. He promises to honour the tribe's ways and protect them if he wins. That they will be allowed safe passage out if he's defeated."

"And they're *listening* to him?"

"It's their way. It's a code of honour. He *has* to address challengers. This is bad." He met Wish's eye. "If their chief takes the challenge and loses, we'll lose the Shore Stalkers. I mean – worse, they could turn on us."

Wish quickly scanned the gathered tribe. The strong body of fighters no longer looked so reassuring, and she recalled the murdered village nearby. Those bodies impaled on sticks. It wouldn't take a great deal to imagine them joining the darker force, here.

"Do you think he'd win?" Wish asked and Brade tutted.

"I don't think it matters, seeing as Kasidee's unlikely to honour a loss. But for what it's worth, I believe he believes himself to be an expert swordsman."

The Shore Stalker shouted a response, approaching the gates. People everywhere were leaning out of hiding to watch. Brother Estekof protested, but the Stalker snarled him off, drawing his hunting blade, and the monk shied away into the shadows.

"He's setting terms," Brade said, as Kasidee responded.

"Everyone to keep well back from the gates, where they can fight without interference."

"Fuck's sake." Wish shoved Brade's shoulder. "You have to get down there. Fight him first." Brade's eyes widened in surprise. *"I'm not going to beat him, am I? Go!"*

"Kasidee already challenged him, he won't —"

"Idon'tcarefuckinggo!" Wish said, rolling the words together as she pushed him again. Brade complied, racing down the walkway. He bumped past monks and swung onto the ladder, interrupting Kasidee with a shout in Garter himself.

The Stalker shouted back at him and other Shore Stalkers began stirring into the open. Brade kept talking as he slid down the ladder and ran for the stairs. Wish heard him utter, "Worth a shot," his diplomacy apparently having failed. But he hadn't stopped, and skipped down the steps to reach the courtyard, with the gates still closed and the Stalker glaring reproachfully.

"Be ready please," Brade called up in Stanish, for the scouts, "I'm not sure if this will work." And in the next breath, he was upon the tribesman and gave him a sharp slap before stepping back. The sound rang through the keep, throwing everyone into shocked silence. Brade's stance resembled a gentleman challenging a duel in the midst of a ballroom. Except he was standing opposite a brutish savage decorated with animal parts, holding a weapon that was more cleaver than sword.

The Stalker's eyes bulged with rage, face reddening. He peeled his lips back to show off uneven teeth and rumbled a terrible, fierce roar. He surged forward and his watching tribe emerged with weapons of their own, egging him on. Wish lifted her rifle but they were encouraging the fight without joining in, as Brade skipped back, avoiding a sword-swing and drawing his own blade. The Stalker chief came at him like a pack beast, with bulky, unstoppable force, each swipe of his big weapon coming harder than the last, picking up momentum. Brade deftly dodged, ducking to one side, weaving around the other, before flicking up his own blade, a painfully frail rapier, to deflect the next few strikes. Brade's wrist twirled around the Stalker's next blow, sword moving almost too fast to follow, and the big chief's weapon was released, clattering across the ground. In the heartbeat of the Stalker's surprise, Brade's sword found his throat, and they froze, the point ready to pierce.

The chief stiffened, eyeing him with hate, and growled a fresh challenge.

Brade shook his head, and replied in sober Garter. He waited, the blade perfectly steady, until the chief very subtly inclined his head, a nod. Brade lowered the sword and nodded back, then turned to the rest of the audience and added something in their language. He'd won. He'd secured the tribe – and so quickly, Wish jumped up in celebration.

"Yes!" she said, and spun around to the Irregulars, picking out Kasidee on the road alone. He looked irritated by the noise of events he could probably predict. "They're ours, you bastard. There might be no honour in *your* ranks, but dammit you'll have a fight coming in here."

They shared a long look, Kasidee's face grave now, which filled her with satisfaction. Even better, she noticed that Havik was smiling again. She shouldn't have cared, should have wanted the woman unhappy, but she'd take the win. Kasidee huffed, "Enough. Put her down."

"What?" Havik responded, but he was looking towards the shelter of the village shacks nearby. A gun barrel poked out from the roof of one, under cover of furs, which Wish really should've noticed before. She moved as it fired, and dropped down onto the walkway feeling the rush of the passing bullet. Another gunshot came at almost the same time, a powerful blast, followed by a crash and a scream.

"God*dammit!*" Kasidee yelled, as his horse's hooves thumped back from the gates.

Wish was motionless, waiting for the pain of the bullet to hit her, eyes turned up to the dark sky. Wondering, without particular sense, if she'd already died. But she felt nothing. She heard more pitiful screaming below, the injured man wailing like a child. She flexed her fingers, blinked. She was alive. She wasn't hurt.

Havik snapped at Kasidee in Garter, sounding suddenly feral.

Kasidee responded with a frustrated, furious sound, before roaring orders at everyone else. Not knowing the language, Wish could guess the meaning: *breach the doors. Kill everyone.*

Wish lifted herself up and peered over the battlements as the sounds everywhere escalated. Brade was shouting below, reorganising the men. Kasidee was readying his troops. The shack where Kasidee's sniper had been hiding had been shredded by a large weapon; Lost One, the man who'd fired at Wish was writhing in the debris in his own blood, crying. Havik, on her horse, casually called her own orders to the scrambling men. Her Camanese Stop Gun lay across her lap, vaguely pointed towards the marksman.

Then the Irregulars parted, revealing a long-barrelled gun on waist-high wheels.

"Private Dalliance!" Wish cried, and barely finished before a gunshot came from above – Dalliance fired into the team, felling one, then another. But the Irregulars returned fire, a brief scatter of shots that quickly grew ferocious. Wish ducked to snatch up her own rifle.

"She's mine!" Havik shouted, switching languages. Surely just for her benefit. "Kill whoever you like, but Wild Wish is *mine.*"

Wild Wish took a deep breath. With the increasing gunfire and men running and shouting from all directions, that madwoman down there gunning for her in particular, Wish felt a strangely fresh calm creeping in. Her hands held her rifle. This, this felt familiar. Time to fight.

43

Advances in weaponry by no means put an end to close combat. In many regions, troops remained unequipped or without ammunition, and in the closer-fought urban territories, or when trenches were breached, the grit of hand-to-hand fighting came back to the fore. The idea that a soldier could survive on marksmanship alone is a myth.
The Great Ebb and Flow: Reflections on Modern Trench Warfare, Sommer, p. 325

The Irregulars only fired one round from their artillery cannon, which ripped through the main doors and a good portion of wall, making mist of a handful of men inside. In the next moment, soldiers started pouring in through the smoke, like insects swarming from the village shacks, screaming and shooting as they came. Wild Wish fired into the mass outside, but it was madness to stay where she was, exposed over the entrance, so she raced along the battlements towards the keep. On the opposite wall, she saw Macmiddan and Ptrangus doing the same, firing and moving. Macmiddan ripped a small black pack from his belt and tossed it over the wall, for a ground-shaking explosion. He quickly followed this with another. He swore loud insults as the blasts ripped apart dozens in the densely packed space outside. Ptrangus moved expertly by him, limbs tight and shots accurate, their skill and professionalism immediately apparent. The enemy were already in, though, and while Irregulars tussled with shrieking Shore Stalkers, clubbing at them with bone hammers and serrated blades, some crouched to fire at those on the walls. Macmiddan swore even louder as a bullet clipped him and he almost fell, but he continued, tossing one more explosive before stumbling through a doorway. Wish shot the man who'd hit him in the back, then ducked as others fired back.

It was a great bloody mess, men pressed in together snarling and grappling, guns going off and blades hacking, body parts exploding and separating. The keep was filling with the sting and stench of smoke, the yell of fighters and the patter of fleshy thunks and hacking blades. Things slowed as the tide of bodies collided; the Irregulars remained hesitant, too crowded to fire openly into the keep, with occasional shots coming from Wish's small troop – she spotted Scraper leaning out a doorway and unloading a clip of bullets into the approaching mass, ruthlessly fast. Then the violence broke, with the quaking of huge footsteps and a fierce roar, the chilling cry of an approaching monster. As Wish skidded up to a keep entrance, she saw the vast shadow of an ogre charging in. Runt burst through the smoke, tossing aside Irregulars and Shore Stalkers alike with a swipe of his big arm. He drew up fiercely tall as the last horses inside bolted for the gap he'd created, one trampling someone who couldn't move out the way fast enough. Glaring about for a target, Runt hefted his ogre-sized gun, practically a cannon.

There was a chill moment, the battle appearing to pause, as he met Wish's eye.

Her first instinct was to smile, here was hope, one of her own come to break the siege. With the size of him, he might single-handedly drive the condensed Irregulars back. But the ogre's expression was fixed, unpleasant. Of course, this ogre was a *dick.* He lifted his gun. Wish lifted hers quicker, firing from the hip, a desperate shot made easier by the size of his head. Runt jerked back, eyes rolling up towards the hole in his forehead, and he swayed like a tree, for a moment seeming like he might stay upright and shoot anyway. He dropped, first onto his knees with a crack, then sideways to smash into a wall, catching a couple more Irregulars under him.

The Stalkers cheered and surged into the open again, firing arrows and swinging at the Irregulars behind Runt, and for a moment they drove the enemy out, before another barrage of gunfire followed from outside, tearing through the gate. The courtyard was thinning now, not many defenders left, but the

Irregulars were still charging in. Wish hesitated a moment longer, sniping a few more as they came in, before she rushed inside and almost knocked Dalliance down coming the other way.

"Retreat," she ordered, as calmly as she could. "Safer inside. The tunnels."

Dalliance nodded and darted into the darkness. She followed through tight hallways, down stairs, deeper into the keep. A soldier surged through an opening, swinging his rifle in front of Wish. She jumped back in surprise and fired upwards, the bullet catching him under the arm and throwing him back outside. She edged around the opening and shot another man charging up some steps towards her, the Irregulars having mostly secured the courtyard to start pressing into the many doorways. On the far side, she saw Stalkers retreating inside, chased by shouting men. A flash of Scraper shoving Emi ahead of her. Above them, a few Irregulars had already climbed onto the battlements and one had a monk pressed against the wall as he stabbed him repeatedly in the gut. Wish was arrested for a moment by the sight of Brother Estekof's pained face, before the man tossed him aside, to fall.

Looking away, Wish snapped her attention back to the entrance as Kasidee himself hopped over Runt's body, big coat flapping about him. She chambered another bullet, but Havik jumped up behind him, her Stop Gun raised. Wish flinched aside as a bullet hit the door frame by her, another soldier having spotted her first, and she scrambled back into the corridor. Damn it, she needed to go down, follow the others into the tunnels. She ran, and turned a corner into a stairwell blocked by a soldier struggling against someone with no room for either to move. Wish shot the man upwards through the back, point blank, and grabbed his collar to pull him out of the way. She revealed Brade on the other side, his hair askew and sword raised, freshly splattered with blood. He smiled, said breathlessly, "The cellars. Harder for –"

A sound of wrenching metal and cracking stone screamed terribly over the rest of the battle, the earth shaking hard enough to knock Wish over, and she smacked into a wall. As the ground settled, an avalanche of heavy objects followed, thumping down on top of screaming men, then came the terrible, incredible cackle of a lunatic woman. Emi. Wish's heart lifted as she backtracked to look out another doorway; Emi's laughter bounced around the keep, hard to tell where it was coming from, but the effects of her attack were clear. The entire front wall and gates of Drowndeep had folded in on themselves. Bits of bodies stuck out from the great pile of debris, including Runt's legs, and men were shouting on the other side, having a hard time climbing over.

Kasidee, Havik and a few others were still in the courtyard, unhurt and suddenly looking Wish's way. A tattooed man to the left moved first, charging at her with a sword, and she instinctively fired into his gut. She darted back inside as she chambered another bullet, hearing more footsteps racing towards her. She hurtled down the stairs, banging into the walls and out into the tunnel system, which opened onto a spacious vaulted area. She jumped to one side, raising a hand, as she saw Macmiddan propped against the entrance to a far tunnel with his rifle poised, targeting the stairwell. Belatedly, she spotted Brade closer by, sword up.

Somewhere far off through the tunnels, Ptrangus' voice echoed with vicious curses, "Have it you bastards!" Gunshots followed.

"Go, get back," Brade waved a hand at Macmiddan, who nodded unsteady compliance. He retreated into the dark, swaying from a bad injury, towards the sounds of fighting. Wish spun back to cover the stairs herself and fired as her first pursuer came into view, exploding another soldier's chest. As he fell, another man leapt over him, screaming. Brade stepped in, swiping the man's rifle down with his sword so it fired into the floor, then bringing the blade up to cut through his chest and throat, in one smooth motion. The Irregular crashed against a wall gargling and spraying blood as Kasidee sprang out with his own sword raised. In the dim light of the sconces, the man looked deranged, grinning at Brade.

"Captain," he purred. "Let me cross swords with the Empire's finest swordsman."

Third finest, Wish internally corrected, quickly pulling back her rifle bolt. The Long 0.48 made her most feared sound: the hollow click of an empty clip. She looked up with alarm as Kasidee glanced her way, and she fumbled to take another magazine from her belt. He leapt towards her but Brade intercepted, turning his blade away. The two men clanged swords together, feet dancing aside. Wish was momentarily distracted by how fast they moved, in such a tight space. Then her eye went to the stairs as Havik stepped over the bodies. Her Stop Gun was raised, its wide barrel promising no chance of escape.

"Drop it," Havik commanded, but Kasidee back-stepped from Brade's blows, right into her path. She ducked around them, snarling, swinging her gun towards Brade, but Kasidee snapped at her to stop, their sword fight momentarily pausing.

"Deal with her!" Kasidee shouted. "I'll take care of him."

More gunfire sounded elsewhere, with shouts and heavy banging, and Wish flashed a look up the tunnel. There were Irregulars piling into the tunnels from other directions, no part of this keep secure. In the moment it took her to realise this, Wish found Havik upon her, and took a sharp blow to the jaw. She dropped her rifle as she fell, and tried to recover, scrambling towards a doorway, but Havik easily kept her pace. She grabbed Wish's shoulder and they briefly tussled, Wish bucking, Havik shoving. The massive Stop Gun clanged against the floor and Havik's cap flew off. A blade appeared under Wish's nose. Havik pushed her into the wall, pinning her with her body, and demanded, "Where is it?"

Wish shook her head, more in confusion than defiance, and Havik flinched as the duelling men came close again. With an irritated grunt, she shoved Wish into the next tunnel. She pushed her ahead, the knife at her throat, gun left behind, and Wish stumbled deeper into the maze. No weapon, out of bullets, not quite comprehending her situation. She needed to fight but didn't know how. Then they turned a corner and found people coming the other way.

"Wild Wish, thank Bly – " Sister Sonseen started, then froze. "Unhand her. We have the bones." The nun held something up, closed in one hand. "Drop your weapon and unhand her or we will destroy it right now."

"Ah," Havik said. "You blessed nun. *What* have you got?"

Sonseen shook her head, backing up. "I *will* break it. Right now."

Unafraid, not believing the threat, Havik pushed Wish forward as a shield. She moved much faster than Sonseen, making Wish trip up as she lunged. She caught the woman and snatched what was in her hand. The nun tried to resist, clawing back at Havik, but was shoved down, her robes audibly tearing.

"Leave her alone!" Wish shouted, trying to get up. "Dammit, we don't –"

Havik's boot caught her in the face and sent her into the wall. The woman shouted triumphantly, "Yes, you do!"

"Enough!" Brother Redfire shouted, diving in from the side. He brought his full weight into her with a hefty punch, but it was imprecise, barely clipping Havik as she dodged back. She kicked him in the knee and he gasped, collapsing, then she spun round, snatching Wish's neck and dragging her on. The knife was back between them, and Havik picked up speed, aiming for a door. She shoved Wish through it and she tripped into the dark of another tight stairwell. Wish couldn't get her hands up to stop the fall, and tumbled down, rolling and banging her joints, her head. She fell out of the darkness into dim light, aching all over, bleeding and out of breath. Up the stairs, she could just hear Havik ramming a heavy bolt into place, cutting off Sonseen and Brother Redfire's shouts. Wish tried to push herself up again, to get away from the stairwell as Havik ran down.

Havik burst into the room and paused, eyes wide with delight. It made Wild Wish pause, to take in the area herself. It was a round chamber, five metres wide, lit devil-red by a smouldering sconce. At its centre was a low circular wall – a well. There were no other decorations and no machinery for operating the well. It split the room so there was no space between them, Wish almost at the well, barely a pace from Havik.

Havik was grinning wildly, the knife in one hand and her other balled over whatever she'd wrestled from Sister Sonseen. She raised her eyebrows as Wish rested back against the well, catching her breath. If this was it, if she was trapped, overcome, then she had to fight. Just needed to catch her breath. Even unarmed, she'd do *something.*

But she wasn't unarmed, she realised, so stupid, letting it get this far. Her hand whipped down to her belt and she drew her knife. Scraper's knife, the butcher's crude weapon. She held it out in front of her and Havik regarded it oddly. She lowered her own blade, smile fading, and said, "You're bleeding."

Wish frowned at her concern, blinked a drop of blood from one eye.

"I didn't want to hurt you," Havik said.

"What?" Wish spat back, her tone, her eyes, a complete turnaround. She'd threatened her at knifepoint, pushed her down the stairs. "You kicked my *face.*"

"But we can stop now, Wild Wish," Havik replied quickly, earnestly. "I don't want to fight you. I want to share this with you." She lifted the other hand and uncurled her fingers, revealing a small, incongruous shard of bone. From a finger, perhaps? "You actually did find it. I'm impressed."

Wish pulled herself up to sit on the wall, knife raised, trying to ignore that comment – regretting now that Sister Sonseen hadn't been less efficient. She glanced behind her into the well, an opening two metres wide into a hole that fell pitch black only a short way down. Maybe five metres deep, maybe a mile.

"The Well of All Remains," Havik said, moving to the side to look herself.

Wish jerked the knife towards her, body sparking with pain. Her head was throbbing, the most notable amongst a dozen or more cruel aches. The sounds of battle were muffled above. They were secluded, even Sonseen and Redfire's shouts quiet now. Havik watched her side on, hesitating in the calm, a different woman to the fighter who'd forced her down here.

"This is fitting," Havik decided. "The perfect place for it, really."

"The perfect place for *what?*" Wish spat, tense, itching to strike but knowing her body wasn't up to it. Had to get her talking. Stall her, distract her. Regain enough energy to fight.

Havik said, gently, "To destroy the world."

44

Oh Betan, I ██████████████████. *I must write* ███
███ *to keep* ███████████. *You* ███ *understand*
███ *being here* ██████████. *The* █████████
████████████████████. *Good men* ██
███████. *Brave fighters* ██████. ██████ *knows* ██
███████████████

Extract from the Letters of
Corporal T. Sander, Balnia, 719

Wideskull Bleacher found it cute how the humans were always so ready to cut off their own feet to hinder others. The daft talls spent years making their fancy bridges to traipse across in comfort, so figured damaging them would inconvenience everyone. But it took more than a little water to hold back goblins, who always came equipped to overcome any obstacle. He grinned as he oversaw the finishing touches to their makeshift walkway, a float of twisted grass and twine shambled together and dragged into place by his best swimmers. The fireworks had already started, off in the south, but they'd join in soon enough.

He had little hope of that darling Wild Wish making a dent in Kasidee's Irregulars, but she'd slow them enough for Section 3 to catch up. Bless her, she'd give him and his lads the good ruck they'd been itching for. The rest of Colonel Atmoor's prats might even get a piece of the action, if the man put a bit of effort in. Good luck to him; there wasn't going to be much left to do once his thins got stuck in, and he doubted Atmoor's talls would dare brave this goblin bridge. They were a lot heavier than goblins, after all. A lot slower and more cautious. Humans just didn't have the same *grit* as a goblin.

Kin Kasidee was about to find that out himself.

Bleacher watched with delight as the first of his goblins reached the far bank, to filter into the bog. It was going to be a damn good night.

***

Scraper had run out of bullets, but that was okay, because this fight had got stabby fast. She knew how to stab. A man turned a corner, signalling his arrival with heavy footfalls, heavy breathing and his leading rifle, and she easily pushed the gun down the same time she brought a knife up into his neck. He collapsed gagging in disbelief, but she caught hold of him, bearing his dying weight to use for a shield as another guy leant around to shoot. In the tight hallway, there was little room to move, and Scraper shoved her victim onto his friend's gun, pinning it against the wall, so when it went off the bullet hit the floor. As he tried to wrestle the weapon free, clinging on to it, Scraper quickly struck around her shield's gushing neck to catch him in the eye. The blade went in easily, messily, but she was overstretched and had to pull back. Might not be fatal, but he fell screaming, entwined with the gusher, so the corridor was blocked by their bodies and she could retreat safely into another passage.

Drowndeep was a maze of halls, so much more expansive than it appeared on the outside, going up and down, twisting around, and she had no idea where she was going. It was best to keep moving, slipping between shadows, striking at whoever got in her way. Not all that different from the trenches of Eriqloo, except she had a greater advantage here: she had no reason to hesitate. She ran through a doorway, into a wider room where two men were moving in the other direction, between benches, guns lowered and eyes searching – already intending to loot rather than fight? They looked up at her together, uncertain in this light which side she might belong to with her blood-stained uniform and two knives. Their second's doubt was all she needed to clear the three paces to them and bring up both hands at once, knives gliding past their necks. She didn't stop, in case they had enough energy left to fight (even if their legs gave way as they reached up for help). Had to keep quiet. Keep moving.

It was easy because it didn't especially matter who she came across now. There were precisely two people in the priory who she couldn't hurt. She'd already secured Emi in a cell, the mage giggling and wincing as she reeled from her combined wounds and the impact of using her magic, and Scraper had last seen Wild Wish on the far side of the keep. The gunfire had all but stopped outside. There weren't many monks left, probably even fewer Shore Stalkers, which mostly left Irregulars. The odds were it was safe to kill without question. It was just men shouting in the halls, calming down, thinking they'd taken the priory.

Her odds might not be great – there might be another hundred or more men to come – but Scraper was a long way from done. She jogged deeper underground, following a winding staircase. She was sure Wild Wish was fighting on, and perhaps their other recruits were too. In these conditions, they could take down a lot of people before the bastards got through. Scraper wanted to, needed to. It was her element. She had killed a lot of people, but not as many as the lieutenant. At least, not since the war had started. This would make up for some of it . . .

Scraper slid out from the stairs into another corridor and saw the flash of a man passing where two tunnels connected. She silently padded after him, turned the corner and saw him turning back – a closed door blocking his path. He was encased in shadow, big and holding a gun. She whipped a knife around to its tip, ready to throw, too far away to stab. He brought his rifle up, white eyes shining in the torchlight where the rest of him was black. He gasped, "Scraper, thank the –"

Scraper caught herself, but not quickly enough to keep hold of the knife. The blade spun lethally through the air as she stared wide-eyed, a second of regret as she expected it to embed deep in his heart. But she'd faltered just enough to alter its course and he flinched aside with a curse, so it skimmed his shoulder and stuck deep into the door behind him.

Private Dalliance gawked from the vibrating blade back to her. Scraper stared guiltily at him. The hole of his open mouth showed mixed shock and admiration, then set hard as he looked past her. Scraper jumped forward, twisting aside, knowing that look, and a pair of gunshots blasted as she fell. There was a bodily impact and a man wheezed, falling down. She scrambled to her rear and watched an Irregular soldier slumping against the wall, bleeding from the chest. Dalliance hissed and cursed, sliding against a wall too. Scraper jumped up to help him.

"Flesh wound," she said without looking at it, to arrest his frightened face. She pressed her palm on his arm, at the top, where it was oozing blood. "Bandages?"

Dalliance patted limply at his pockets, hissing pain. Taking too long. Scraper ripped off his sleeve to use instead and he shrieked – probably should've used the uninjured arm. As he streamed tears, she wound the material over the wound and tied it tight. He gritted his teeth and kept the pain in. They met each other's eyes and she read his growing fear.

There were footsteps coming, echoing through the halls. Scraper watched the hallway, not liking the growing volume: there were plenty of people still to come, and this stretch of tunnel offered no real cover. Best to keep moving, but Dalliance couldn't, not quickly. They had to hole up. Scraper braced both his arms, directing him to lean against the door, and she took his rifle from the floor. She pulled the bolt back, a bullet in the chamber. It was not a standard mumbler rifle but something longer and fancier, closer to what Wild Wish used. Stronger.

"I've got more," Dalliance said, then blew out a pained breath. He was using his good hand to hold onto the injured arm, and tried to reach his pockets with the other one. Hurting himself some more. She left him to it and lay down prone. She heard him sliding down behind her, making himself smaller, with the clatter of feet coming closer. Dalliance sputtered triumphantly, "Here! More cartridges."

He slid the ammo through the dirt up alongside her.

"Got a couple of grenades, too," he said, and she nodded without looking back. She had a few grenades of her own. They'd do a lot of damage in here, so she'd been saving them. It would probably come to that later.

The first blundering soldier stepped into sight and she fired.

***

Kasidee was winning.

He might've had his doubts before, over Havik's sanity and Lost One's surliness and the whole point of this mad enterprise, but this Saints Mire expedition was all worth it just for this. Captain Rikard Brade, a living legend, here before him. An adventurer's adventurer, a champion, a true hero. A true challenge.

Kasidee could scarcely keep the smile from his face as they traded parries and thrusts, clanging around the tunnel. There was just enough space to keep his footing and keep finding ways to avoid Brade's advances, but it was tight enough to give him the advantage of crowding the man. He had no doubt that with a wider arena Brade's more creative expertise would win out. Give him a table to hop on or a light to swing from and this man would find a way through anyone's defences. But these were dull, empty chambers, nothing but stonework, and Kasidee was persistently pressing forward to limit his finesse. Strike after strike, Brade kept seeing them coming but was unable to do anything more than turn the blows away. He was tiring, sweating.

Old, Kasidee realised. Beyond his prime, out of training.

Or perhaps the legends were exaggerated.

"Has it been a while?" Kasidee asked between breaths, and dodged to the side as Brade took an opportunist swipe. He turned, quickly, to move around the man's right and brought his sword back up in a guard. Brade looked angry, too serious, his moustache ruffled. "Since you've had such a fight? A worthy opponent."

Brade's eyes narrowed, not happy about meeting his match. He jabbed fast again, two strikes, a feint, and Kasidee bounced away on the balls of his feet, hit the wall. Kasidee jerked to the side and Brade slipped in with a sting to his shoulder. He dodged out of the way, gasping at the cut in his coat. A thin line of blood seeped up.

"Well." Kasidee took a moment, with more space between them, and Brade allowed it, watching him. "Lucky blow, old man."

Brade titled his head. Was there a little amusement there?

"I must say, I'm disappointed. Where's the famous Captain Brade wit?"

"Rotting," Brade spoke at last, hoarsely. "Along with the fifty or so men you already made me kill today."

Kasidee was taken for a moment by the man's venom, but managed another smile. "Such is war, hey?"

"You're no soldier. I'll ask again, what happened to the man many called a hero? Why come to *this?*"

"You of all people should understand," Kasidee said. "After all, aren't you following a beautiful woman, too? Have you bedded her yet?"

Brade narrowed his eyes, a nerve touched. Perfect, getting him off guard.

Kasidee said her name, snidely, to twist it in – the same woman who'd thrown off Havikare: *"Wild. Wish."*

But that made the captain straighten up, and his lips curled up at last. "Oh. You daft fool."

"What did you say?"

"I called you a fool. A great delusion fool. You followed that madwoman's whim out here, did you? This was all her idea? Do you even *know* what it's for?"

Kasidee glowered. This wasn't the Brade he knew from books. No honour or decency. No *gentleman.* But he was only attempting to needle, pathetically. They had stretched this out long enough.

"She's psychotic, do you understand that? I could've told you from the moment I saw her. Whatever power you think she's after out here, it's not for you."

"Power," Kasidee scoffed and rotated his sword. He looked at the fine edge, ready at last to skewer this so-called legend. "Who cares for power? We're here for one thing, only, aren't we? What this war is all about. The glory."

Brade laughed again, lowering his sword. So condescending he'd forgotten the danger he was in. "You couldn't have come to a worse place for that. You damned fool."

Kasidee charged, sword raised, shouting. With every word a blow. "Stop! Saying! That!" Brade was pushed back, startled by his strength. Kasidee hammered at him, pounding his sword back, beating him into a corner. No grace or wit could resist this brute force. No noble blood or schooling. Kasidee felt the fury of a world of underlings, ordinary people, rising up – he was a damn bank clerk with a damn sneering father who'd found his *own* glory. He was saying *no more.* Brade stumbled, a foot slipping under the barrage, and Kasidee spat with wordless anger, knocking him down to a knee. He raised the sword high for the killing blow and

Stopped.

Stuck. His arm was up but wouldn't come down.

Something had hit him, broken his breath.

He looked down, vision blurring. Getting brighter. A long shard of metal rose straight into his chest. Captain Brade held it in place, slowly rising, fully composed. His face, inches from Kasidee's own, was emotionless. He didn't say anything, but slid the blade back out and held Kasidee by the shoulder as he lowered him to the ground.

Kasidee couldn't speak. Could barely twitch. Couldn't breathe.

It burnt. It flared with pain. Light flooded his vision.

What was – why . . .

Raltman tripped on the rubble of the priory entrance – again – and swore loudly. It wasn't even high, but the mage had made such a mess of the gate that it was hard to climb without hitting something sharp, or getting caught in a ridge. It had slowed them down no end. He grabbed a big chunk of broken wall and heaved it off with both hands, and it almost crushed a following soldier's foot. The man swore with a murderous expression before he saw who'd thrown the debris, then he quickly averted his gaze. Rightly so. Raltman kept going, sliding again but cresting the crushed mess of metal and stone, to finally survey the battlefield properly.

Ahead, Drowndeep's courtyard was a bloodbath of Mirian bodies riddled with bullets and Irregular corpses sliced apart. Their own fault: the company was full of hard-knuckled brawlers, like those Raltman had known from the Choketown Colony Prison. They should've been able to handle a bunch of damn savages with whale-hunting tools. But more than a few of his men had been opened by bullets too, courtesy of that Stanclif witch and her mates. Didn't matter now – them who'd been hiding in the keep, and them who'd pressed in to kill them, were equally dead, and the spoils were left to him and those waiting outside. Sure, it wasn't quite over, with clusters of gunfire just audible underground, but it was a clear-up operation now, nothing more. And seeing as Kasidee and Havik had run into the fray before it was all secure, too eager, and Lost One had bled out from Havik's ire, it was looking like the end game might be Raltman's to command.

He wasn't averse to it.

Looking outside, he saw roughly a hundred more hard bastards watching him, all proud at the top of his pile of rubble, with a stubby shotgun in one hand and a crude hacking blade in the other. They were awaiting assessment from an authority. Seeing him as a leader, as they should. Things had all got too complicated, with Havik promising her esoteric shit and two separate sets of troops prowling around after them. All these weird priories and their psycho tribes. With half the Irregulars dead and the mess of it all done, it was time to simplify things. He'd take the mantle of this mob as he'd been tempted to a few times before.

"Alright lads," he called out, croaking from shouting and scrapping. "Drowndeep's ours – let's make it the last leg of this journey. I see boats and no one left in our way. Take whatever shiny shit's not bolted down and load up. It's time we left this dump and set ourselves up somewhere warm and dry, what do you say?"

It met a general shout of approval, men waving their guns and blades overhead.

"First we cull whoever's left inside," Raltman continued. "Pull out Kasidee and Havik if you can, but let's not make a chore of it, shall we?"

Another roar of agreement. As he'd figured, the ones who'd held back were his sort of guys – selfish, simple. Not the more fanatical bunch who bought into all Havik's stories, who'd fought to be at the front to take the keep tooth and nail. Those who were left would follow him readily enough.

"Who's with me?" Raltman boomed, and the third cheer was the loudest. Satisfied, he turned to lead a final charge inside, but his ankle twisted in the rubble and he fell down again. He yelled, "Cocking shit of a whore!" and ripped bits of stone up around his foot, sending one chunk back into the face of a soldier behind him. He stumbled again, tearing onwards, and as he tripped this time, his men climbing around him, past him, he glanced back and saw movement in the marshland. He stopped. There were dark shapes beyond the last of the Irregulars and the shanty village.

Raltman stood again, as the others charged into the keep shouting in celebration. There were *lots* of dark shapes, and now he'd noticed them he heard far-off noises, behind the closer, louder shouts of his men. Snapping, vicious little sounds of creatures racing through the bog behind them. Dozens of shapes turned to hundreds, hurtling out of the grass, much closer than they should've been able to get unnoticed.

"To the rear!" Raltman roared, backing up over the rubble, into the keep. "Defences! We've got company!"

The Irregulars were split then, half already moving in to finish Drowndeep as the other half heard his panic and looked back.

The shadows came as they had by the Black Lake.

"Goblins!" Raltman yelled, and it sent dozens of men scattering, turning their guns the other way. How the hell had they caught up so quickly? And right as he was taking charge. But no matter. Raltman fixed his expression meanly. They could handle a bunch of goblins, as they should've done before. He gave quick orders, bracing himself for a fight. "Turn the big gun round! Get in position! Let's massacre these fucking green skins!"

Colonel Atmoor's horse splashed through a ford, the last step in getting around the broad estuaries he imagined Kasidee thought would be impassable without the northern bridges. Such a man had a predictably narrow view of a battle, Atmoor had been pleased to confirm: having come down from the plains of Low Bile himself, Kasidee assumed the Drail would follow as one mass at their heels. He hadn't appreciated that a commander with two thousand men had more options than one with a small company. And so, while the frothing clusters of Sections 3 and 5 drew attention trying to find a way over the wider tributaries, he'd steered the other three sections south through the mountain foothills. They were a little delayed, perhaps, but catching up now, with the tail end of the Stanclif scouts' defence well within sight.

Mounted alongside Major Weles and the minor cavalry of Section 1, Atmoor clomped out onto the plains of Paradise Fails with Drowndeep ahead. He took a second to assess the lay of the land. Difficult to pass through directly, but the Irregulars would have a hard time checking their approach, now that they were caught between invading the keep and defending it from Bleacher's goblins. Drowndeep itself was smoking, broken, and the gunfire coming out was sporadic and unorganised. The great wave of Bleacher's advance formed a wide arc with blunt punches of shots from their bag guns, making up in numbers what they lacked in direct power. Men were falling over themselves retreating into the very position they'd just taken – a keep ripped wide open by their own attack.

"Major Weles, take the right flank. I'll lead your cavalry down the left. Captain Hollery, set up your guns to watch for stragglers. They'll flee to the south, with an eye on the boats, if you see them?"

"I see them," Hollery replied.

"Onward then men, let's clear up this mess once and for all." Atmoor held up his pistol, a step above the pure symbolism of his sabre, to start the charge. With his army fresh for the battle, they'd make short work of what little resistance would be left after Bleacher broke his section against the tiring Irregular guns. Kasidee might put a dent in the goblins, with no huge loss there, but they'd have little left afterwards. With Ilscot's mob too preoccupied with the river crossing to get in the way, Atmoor could now put an end to this scrappy and altogether unpleasant leg of the war. "Tonight,"

Atmoor added loudly, for as many men as could hear, "we restore the Purity of the Drail to this godforsaken land! Onward, to victory!"

He kicked the horse into action and pounded towards Drowndeep, a platoon of men shouting behind him. It was a little theatrical, but they lapped it up. There were so few opportunities for a clean, just victory in this war, and this was one of them. As he rode, head down, Atmoor watched a pack of half a dozen goblins scrambling out of the village shacks and into Drowndeep, fearlessly, as flashes of Irregular gunfire resisted them. A few fell, but the others sprang over and in. More followed, with fewer enemy rifles firing back now. Weles' troop cut away to wheel around, shouting and moving fast, veterans who knew exactly what to do. There might be no fight left once he got there, but they'd make sure this was the end of it. Leave no Irregulars alive. It was unfortunate but unlikely the brave Stanclif force would survive, either.

But a sound came from beyond Drowndeep, low, deep like a ship's horn. Atmoor slowed down, glaring into the night. No sign of ships' lights on the horizon, but could a vessel have crept up on them? Surely no one would be mad enough to navigate the rocks of Paradise Fails without light. The horn was met by another, and another, spreading along the shore, and the quantity of them made nonsense of the idea it could be boats. There were too many and they were too close. Atmoor's men slowed around him, gripped as much by fear as confusion. Whatever was making the sound was formidable.

"What the fuck is that?" one soldier asked.

Something they hadn't planned for, was the best Atmoor could think of.

The horns shifted, breaking and pitching higher, lower. The ground shuddered, not just from the volume of the noise. A patch of earth near Atmoor split, a fissure as though hit by a minor earthquake, and soldiers skipped away from it in surprise. Motionless, Atmoor stared past the priory, which had calmed in response to the sounds, goblins looking around in concern, Irregulars, those with enough sense, using the lull to run for cover.

The land itself, Atmoor saw, was moving. The ground shook again and his horse stamped in fear. He tugged the reins to steady it. The walls of Drowndeep shuddered. Beyond, the dark line of the horizon shifted, as if they had angered the Saints themselves and nature was answering.

"What do we do, sir?" a sergeant shouted, the advance stilled and waiting. Atmoor stared for a moment longer. Was the world going to open up and swallow them? Just when he thought he had a handle on this place . . . But it was perhaps merely a quirk of the land. They were guaranteed a victory here, at last, easily within reach, minor quakes and strange horns or not.

"We finish this," he murmured, as much to himself as to the sergeant. He had been a step behind too often in this campaign. Always arm's length from the fighting. Not today. He raised his pistol again and shouted, fighting against the sound of the horns and cracking earth, the Rocc itself coming to life, "Advance, men! Whatever may come, we are taking that position!"

45

Over a period of roughly a century, the Movement of Knowledge saw ruthless secularisation of Boldarow, establishing everything within the laws of science. While acknowledging the mysteries of magic, it limited these to effects accepted within the four fields of witlacing (intention, will, flesh and parsing) and the field of earth-minding, expecting that even these would be scientifically explained in time.

Anything that stood outside these boundaries was considered superstition and fantasy, at best. So began the condemnation of faith-based claims and the legends of old.
A Primer of Modern Thought, H. Minant, p. 174

"This well," Havik was saying, walking slowly around the far edge of it, "is one of the oldest remaining parts of Drowndeep. Of the entire Mire. There are various legends connected to it, but the most likely truth is the simplest – it was a pit dug deep enough that they could return their dead to the land. Hard to bury people out here, with so much rocky terrain – and bodies thrown out to sea attracted predators."

"No one dug a hundred-foot well just to dump bodies in," Wish replied, finding a response despite willing herself not to engage. Havik was talking in too friendly a manner. She needed to keep in mind this woman was the enemy. Needed to watch for a chance to strike. The hole was between them now, though, and Wish sat awkwardly twisted on the wall, taking the opportunity to rest her legs.

"Not *just* to dump bodies in," Havik said. "To venerate them, in the old-fashioned way. You know, respectful, hoping your life would be absorbed back into the world. The ways that the church forgot, preferring the idea that all life should be reabsorbed into *people."* She said the last word as an insult. Shook her head. Then she met Wish's eye, smiling, and despite the death and the madness, that expression sent a tingle to the back of Wish's neck. *"Drown deep* was once a blessing. To lay shallow in Paradise Fails meant eternal damnation, to be dug up, bonding with monsters, or worse. Better to die deep in the earth and be reunited with the world. They warped that idea, using the well for executions. They made an insult – a *curse* – out of the very thing the Revery held sacred."

"Great," Wish said. "That's great, Havik, but what's it got to do with us? Any of this?"

Havik paused. "Not much, maybe. Though there is a connection back to Bonesun. Supposedly he was one of the first to be executed here, instead of buried. Depending on whose accounts you read. Some say he lived out an uneventful older life, unrecorded, others that he was martyred, and others that he mysteriously disappeared, maybe reached a higher plain."

"What's *Bonesun* got to do with anything?" Wish demanded. "Havik. You know I'm not who you thought I am. This place isn't what it used to be. Why are you here?"

Havik gave her a more wary look, enthusiasm fading. She asked, quietly, "You're really not Captain Tate? Where is she?"

"Dead," Wish replied bluntly, stinging herself with the barb. She hadn't wanted to admit it, really. Four Skills *might* have been wrong. But it was true. "She's dead and not coming back."

Havik nodded. "I thought you were far too young." Then she smiled again, a little shyly. "Prettier than I imagined. I wasn't expecting to *like* you, exactly. But . . . you fought with her? You were there at Wick? Green Rise?"

Wish paused. Havik had somehow focused on the things she *had* done. "Yeah. They were me."

Completing her circle of the well, coming close again, Havik gave Wish a long and thoughtful look, and Wish tensed, readying Scraper's knife. She said, "I'm glad you're not her. I was excited to meet Captain Tate, but I think I would've had to kill her. This is much better. You're as special as her, without the baggage."

"Dammit, Havik, you've got this all twisted, and if you're not thinking straight about *me,* can't we just . . ." Wish trailed off, imploringly. She didn't want to fight, didn't believe, now they were talking normally, that there was real animosity here. She finished, "Stop?"

"Yes," Havik replied, sitting down next to her. "We can. We are. I mean, between us." She pointed her knife from her chest to Wish's. "I get it. You took over the Blood Scouts, didn't you? You must be as formidable as Tate, but better. Your energy, it's not like her, ruthless, merciless. I'm guessing she wasn't friendly."

"You don't know anything about her, do you?" Wish said. "What are you basing all this on? There can't be books about her. Us."

"No. Not yet, anyway. I've picked up a few things from radio broadcasts, transcripts from dispatches. I make a point of reading, listening, learning. But I *did* know her, in a way. From Kopice."

"What . . ." Wish's heart sank, the question hard to bear. "What did she do?"

"Everything. She was practically in charge. There *are* records of it – Kopice was a disgrace for the Comity, with Stanclif out there screaming about Civilisation. It made tactical sense, destroying this village where insurgents might be hiding, but it was utterly immoral. I told you, I saw it. The fires. Everyone I knew dead. It was . . . incredible."

Wish stared, no words for that. Could Tate have been involved in something so brutal? Quite probably. She and Brade had got along well, kindred merciless spirits, and he had as much as admitted to Wish she was not necessarily a good person.

But Havik sounded enthusiastic about it. She went on, "Watching our homes burn was the most fun I ever had in that village. I never had friends. My parents didn't understand me. People avoided looking at me in case I said hello. No real reason why, I was just thoughtful, curious. Maybe they knew something about me I didn't, though, because when I saw them dying, I laughed. When I saw how little was made of it afterwards – no news, no one mentioning who was responsible – then I laughed even harder. Can you imagine? An entire community wiped out, all those lives, and then it's just . . . forgotten? The people most responsible were never named, let alone questioned or punished. Because it was war. A stepping stone in this great conflict to decide which empire is best."

"I'm so sorry," Wish said, horrified at the thought. Havik's unusual reaction had to be at least partly hiding how upsetting it was. Maybe her laughter was a way to cope. She had an impulse to touch her, put a comforting hand on her knee, but the woman kept up her facade.

"No. You're not getting it. It inspired me. I realised that in the midst of all this chaos there was an opportunity. We could do whatever we wanted. March under the banner of war, saying you're fighting for something *good,* and you can do anything. I asked myself, what's the most extreme thing you could do, with no one holding you back? I'd been reading a lot, for a long time, so I had plenty of ideas." She paused, holding Wish's eye. "We're a lot alike, you and me, aren't we?"

"No," Wish said, drawing slightly away. "I am *not* who you think."

"No?" Havik laughed, unfazed, and stood as Wish stood, in step with her. Wish backed up, pointing her knife, and Havik followed, ignoring it, letting the tip poke her. "You don't enjoy this? You came to the Saints Mire, Wild Wish! That takes a certain kind of person!"

"A damn unlucky one!" Wish cried. "I was an idiot. I hate all this, Havik. I hate so much of what I've done!"

"Because you don't understand yet," Havik insisted, and Wish wasn't sure if she was even listening or just following her own mad track. "You don't let yourself enjoy it. You don't understand it's in your nature. Stanclif want you to be obedient and well-behaved. The empires, they're the latest cog in a system thousands of years in the making. No better than the churches who preached duty or damnation. That's not how animals live. What we enjoy isn't necessarily moral or good. That doesn't make it *wrong* to enjoy it."

"That's exactly what it means," Wish replied quietly. "You can't tell me you signed up to make things worse."

Havik grinned again. "No. I didn't sign up at all. I think we could do without imperial authority. And how can anything that damages them be *worse?*"

"Can you hear yourself?" Wish pleaded. "How can you seem so . . ."

"Normal? Because it makes sense, Wish! But okay, I haven't explained yet. You'll love it. Here, hold this." Havik thrust her knife into Wish's free hand and absently patted the pockets of her voluminous coat. Wish stared in disbelief – she now held both knives, with Havik unarmed, within striking distance. Havik didn't care, taking out various small objects and passing them to her other hand. She explained as she tinkered with her handful, a collection of bones like the one she'd taken from Sister Sonseen. "Like with most of the prophets and what remnants of saints we have, Bonesun's relics were scattered. Some did this to profit off selling bits of holiness, or to diminish the church's power, or whatever, but Bonesun's collection was separated out of fear. His legacy was built on fear, you know that?"

"What is that?" Wish couldn't help asking, getting ahead of Havik's preamble.

"This one object was recorded in the Book of Bones, very briefly, as the Trumpet of the Dead. There's a theory that large sections of Bonesun's lost writing concerned the trumpet specifically. There are hints in the grammar of surviving passages, references to stuff that's not there. With the rise of the Church of Venerate Flesh, Bonesun was made a pariah amongst the prophets, labelled misguided and mad. Yet the very texts that deride him give clues of what they wanted to hide: who he *really* was. I don't pretend we can be certain of any of it, but I knew the answers were here, hidden and protected in a way no one could uncover through normal means."

Wish understood that part, at least: even Captain Brade had spoken of how hard it was to reach the forbidden territories of the Saints Mire. So she'd come, at least in part, for similar reasons to him.

"It's about more than sating curiosity though," Havik said,

guessing Wish's thoughts. She held up the bone structure, the relics now connected in her hands. There was a central, round shell with four hollow tubes sticking out at odd angles which resembled, in some crude and abstractly bony way, the pictures Wish had seen of human hearts. Havik continued, "They turned the world against the prophets when it suited them and elevated the ones that they liked. They spread terrible rumours, tore down churches, destroyed or corrupted their writing. They couldn't bring themselves to destroy all the relics though. The Saints Mire survived through the ages, and continues to survive, because no matter how the faith changes, or dies, there's always some part of our culture that remembers, and fears, the power it once had. You'll know some of the stories surrounding Bonesun, at least?"

"Yeah." Wish saw an end to this journey and didn't like it. "He was obsessed with death. Or the afterlife. A closet necromancer, a dark mage. Why are the worst people always drawn to the idea of controlling the dead? It's not real, Havik. Just ugly rumours. Surely you're not here for that?"

Havik nodded eagerly and stuck her tongue out between her teeth. She brought her head almost next to Wish's, breathing in her face as they both looked down at the thing in her hand, barely as big as her palm.

"Necromancy was the worst thing they could accuse him of," Havik whispered, her cheek and nose so close Wish could feel their warmth. Trembled with it. "And such a vile claim made it basically criminal to try to figure out what he was really up to. The Book of Bones is vague at best, its suppression an insult to the life of one of the most interesting prophets."

"Okay, your use of *interesting* is questionable."

Havik laughed, backing up slightly to look into Wish's eyes. Still close enough to kiss. "You want to know *my* theory?"

"I guess," Wish said. Unable to look away. Dammit this woman was dangerous and she shouldn't keep listening. But her eyes drank her in and Havik's voice drew her along.

"He was a witlacer, an expert in will magic," Havik said, purring it like a lover's secret.

Wish felt fresh tension at the thought. Out here dredging through the mud, with skirmishes and old religions, at least they'd been safe from the schools of magic complicating the front lines. The only thought she'd had of witlacers at all was Emi's resentment in Carlwen. But with Havik bringing up will magic, new possibilities shot to mind. Will mages could influence others. It was magic feared above most, almost on a par with earth-minding, given its potential for manipulation. The sort of gift that could make you like, trust, and even follow someone without reason.

Wish pulled away and raised both knives. She spat, "What are you doing to me? Making me listen. Making me care about you, making it hard to . . . You're stopping me from stopping you?" Wish clenched her jaw, tried to shake off the confusion. "You got that company of psychos to follow you out here. And now you're trying it on me. No. I won't –"

"Wild Wish stop," Havik said, a hand raised. "I'm not a mage."

"Don't. I'm not listening to another word. You're a maniac."

"I'm not a mage," Havik repeated, with sudden fierceness. "I'm ordinary. Less than ordinary! I grew up with no one even wanting to talk to me! I *wish* I could've –" She stopped herself, at the sound of her rising voice. Havik took a breath. "They called Bonesun a necromancer, Wild Wish. They spent centuries persecuting mages by spreading fear. But *they* have done far worse without magic. Look at us now. Millions of people dying because *politicians* want it. Liars and thieves have been manipulating everyone *forever* without magic. But I've never manipulated anyone. I have always been honest about what we're doing – Kasidee and his men understood. There are secrets here that could make everything different. Upset the balance of power. I'm speaking to you openly about it – I especially don't want to manipulate you."

"Then why can't I . . ." Wish started, but the look in Havik's eye was too earnest. Not persuasive, but concerned, wanting to be believed. And her own question was too uncomfortable to finish anyway. Why couldn't she simply shut this woman up? Instead, she asked, "What do you want, then? What is . . . that thing?" Wish nodded to the bone structure. Wary now of how Havik had started this conversation. Something to *end the world.*

"Ah!" Havik pointed a finger at her. "Bonesun's *real* legacy. He hated the systems in place – was staunchly critical of the Magistry, the biggest empire of the day. If you interpret his text correctly, it's not about faith and the afterlife or any of that. It's about popular revolution. His quest to connect with the Saints was, at its root, a search for the tools to topple tyrants. The Trumpet of the Dead was a deliberate misnomer. He wasn't trying to raise the literal dead – who would actually want that? You know how fragile skeletons are? No. The *dead* he wanted to raise were the idle. The dormant. The species long dominated. The people pushed down."

"Peasants?" Wish suggested.

"And everyone like them. The myriad creatures. The labourers and the poor. Everyone and everything being sacrificed on the front line right now. Do you understand what I'm saying? This" – Havik brandished the bone tool higher – "is meant to enlighten those who have been forced to listen to lies for so long that they can't hear the truth. This will change things."

"How can you possibly know that?" Wish said. It was too easy to believe, down in this morbid dungeon, after all they'd been through to get here. That such an innocuous instrument could have untold power.

Havik shifted closer again. "I don't, not for sure. Half my life has been spent in books. But now I'm living it and I *want* to know. I'm ready to make the myths a reality. Are you?"

Wish didn't move away this time, concentrating on the bone thing. She'd seen the horrors of war herself and the callousness of whoever was in charge, sending so many to die. Whatever revolution Havik was hinting at made a certain kind of sense – if only they could all just stop, say no. It made sense in *theory.* In practice, Havik had come here on a path of her own violence. They'd murdered monks, ransacked priories. Wish said, "You're not a good person."

"I don't pretend to be," Havik said, with a light laugh. "But this isn't a good world. Anything that can turn what we know upside down is likely to make it better. And if nothing else, it'll be a fun ride."

Whatever truth there was in the rest of it, Wish sensed that was the most honest thing Havik had said. Beneath her theories and justifications, the woman wanted to cause trouble. Bonesun's magical-not-magical relic of untold power *might* make things better, or it might make things a hell of a lot worse, but Havik would be happy with either outcome. New plan, Wish decided. Throw it down the well and put an end to this. It might be best to throw Havik in with it, but she wasn't sure she could do that. Might not have a choice once she upset her.

"Wild Wish," Havik said, reaching her free hand out to take one of hers. Their fingers intertwined, one knife falling to the floor. "You asked me if I had faith. I don't know about saints or gods, or even the energy that fuels witlacing and earth-minding. But I do believe whatever forces run under and through everything, they brought me here for this, and brought us together. I dreamed of having you at my side before I even knew you, can you believe that? It's a blessing that it's you here and not Captain Tate."

"You don't know me," Wish said, weakly.

"I do," Havik whispered, like a nuptial vowel.

Wish cringed at her tone, trying to focus, getting ready to take the bone instrument. But Havik's hand was wrapped around one of hers and she was *so close*. She closed her eyes. There was a slaughter still occurring above them. So many dead; maybe everyone she knew and was responsible for out here. There was a war raging and this woman only wanted to fuel the fires. But it was hard to think beyond her proximity and the sound of her voice. Her lips so close she could slip inside them. Find comfort in her touch, let herself go. Maybe she should just let this happen. The mess of bones probably wouldn't do anything anyway. Old legends and nonsense, which once tested could be forgotten, leaving them with only each other in the depths of this forgotten hell. No. She couldn't risk it. She opened her eyes, about to move, but Havik's lips suddenly pressed into hers, soft and electric. It startled her, a touch and gone again, and in that stunned second Havik pulled quickly back and raised the bone instrument to her mouth.

"Stop, no!" Wish shouted as Havik blew into one of the bones, as hard as her lungs would allow. A sound burst through the bones so strange and powerful that any hope Wish had was shattered. It was exactly the sound of dead bones screaming, thin enough to penetrate the smallest crack but loud enough to rip through walls. Something awful and awesome, and she should have stopped it.

46

If you should Die
Where Paradise Fails
Pray that you Drown Deep

Old Lomian Saying

When Havik whistled through her bone trumpet, the world answered. Fast.

The circular room shuddered, knocking dust from the ceiling and cracking the bricks of the well. As the room stilled, the earth beyond trembled, shaking in a spreading circle, and distant booms replied. Wish put out her arms to steady herself, tensed to listen as the sound circled back to them. The walls rumbled again, more bricks cracked and she tripped into Havik's side. They held onto each other for support as the volume and quaking escalated.

"What did you do?" Wish whispered, but a new barrage of shakes and booms struck, as bad as the worst artillery barrages on the front line. For a desperate moment, she considered that exact possibility – Atmoor's guns, or a ship that had arrived in support, raining shells on their position. It was worse than that, though. Atmoor had no guns that big, and she'd killed those damn degrebus before a battleship could be arranged. And whatever this was, it was rising from below. She raised her voice. "Did you set off a volcano?"

Havik gaped in wide-eyed awe. "I don't know."

"You don't know?" Wish shrieked, grabbing her by both shoulders, dropping her remaining knife. She wanted to shake her like a dog to wipe off that vacant, mildly pleased stare. "What do you mean you don't know? What did you *do?*"

"Raised the dead!" Havik cried with delight, eyes widening impossibly further. "We're going to find out what that means!"

"We're going to be buried alive!" Wish shouted.

In agreement, the room gave a particularly violent shake and they tripped to the side, towards the well, almost falling over its edge. Wish braced herself against the low, breaking wall, staring into the dark depths, and heard bubbling far below. She turned quickly away, grabbed Havik's hand and pulled her back, racing for the stairs. A fissure tore through the tiles, widening as she jumped over it, and the sconce was shaken from the wall to burst in scattering fire. Wish shouted at Havik to hurry, dragging her into the stairs, and she banged against the walls as the stairwell shook, tilting like a collapsing tower. Chunks of steps fell from above her, one glancing her head. Wish heard herself screaming as she pushed with all she had, Havik's hand tight in hers, climbing into darkness at full pace. She slammed into the door, firmly in place, and grappled at its bolt, needing two attempts to wrench it free. Then she was out, into the dusty, shaking hallway where the torchlight flickered. Havik knocked into her back and pressed close, an arm snaking around her waist. Like a drunk friend, Wish thought. A really terrible one she should've let go.

"This way!" Wish shouted, picking a direction at random. The distant booms were growing quieter, and the quakes settling, but the walls continued cracking, and the keep above groaned. Only a matter of time before it caved in. Shouts and screams echoed down the tunnels. Mostly men yelling in Garter.

Wish skidded around a corner, hit a wall, kept running. Bodies ahead – a monk with a chunk of ceiling where his head should've been. Two tatty men with rifles, necks black with gaping gashes. She hopped over them, breath quickening. She flinched as more soldiers – not really there – pressed in, shooting at her. The corridor rocked side to side, swaying like a boat, rumbling like a great engine was at work underneath them, like a –

"We need to get off this train!" she screamed, and stumbled past an opening, saw steps. She backtracked, feet tangling, and Havik caught her, the madwoman grinning, mindless as Emi. "Up, to the roof!" Wish shouted, pushing her ahead, into another stairwell, shoulder in her arse. The stairs shook fiercely and Wish scraped her hands over the steps, kept climbing. The ceiling was going to crumble, the wheels skip off the tracks! They careered out into another hall, and dodged splintering, falling rocks, aiming for the sounds of screams. It was dark, fallen torches barely revealing the contours of the collapsing tunnel, red, all bloody red, and Wish's heart was clenching, breath barely coming. Get off the train. Get out of the beast's belly. Go, go, go. There was light ahead, dust twisting in the air, and Havik turned back, reaching out her hand. Wish took it and they ran through the opening then fell, exiting onto empty space. They tumbled over broken stonework, over each other, and came to a crumpled heap on uneven ground.

Finally, Wish breathed in a huge lungful of night air, looking up past the swaying walls of Drowndeep to the sky, where dark clouds twirled and stars winked. Her vision turned dizzily, mind more unsteady than the ground. No. The ground was still moving. Men ran past as desperate shadows. Monks with flapping robes – some had survived! – and scrappy soldiers with long coats and inked skin. A goblin. Wish sat up sharply. Little green men joined the charge of people racing for the mound of scrap that had once been the priory's gate. There were more monks and soldiers up top, shoving each other over the threshold. No Drail uniforms, no Dread Corps. Not a train.

Wish blinked. Drowndeep. Not the Iron Barge. No wyrling to escape on.

No idea what was going on.

"We're not safe yet," Havik muttered, on her knees but getting up. Her coat was torn, her face and hands scratched and bloody. She grabbed Wish's arm and helped her to her feet, and they stumbled, slower now, towards the monks yelling at them to flee. The keep groaned again, a prolonged, pained screech that paused everyone. It sounded alive. An announcement that something was about to give.

"Go!" Wish yelled, and found new energy to sprint for the mound of debris, to vault up it without thinking, hands and feet working automatically. She sprang past a startled monk and over the side, followed closely by Havik, and they skidded down the far slope. Beyond them, others were charging ahead, out through the partially collapsed Mirian village, dispersing into the marshland. Wish chased them, running clear of the last shacks, as Drowndeep crumpled on itself with one last, ferocious smash. Men screamed and fell behind her, caught in the rubble or thrown down by the great gust of dust that burst over them. Wish threw herself down, sinking in mud that slapped her face, and continued crawling, blinking hard against the dust in her eyes. Everything was shrouded now, only silhouettes ahead.

The quaking finally calmed, with the general roar of the world's end reduced to aftershocks as Drowndeep's scant remains toppled. But there was something else out there, like an engine still rumbling, coming towards them. As vast and alive as the train, the ghost of the Iron Barge rising from the sea to run Wish down. Fresh shouts came, men seeing what she could not. She sat back on her haunches shakily trying to catch a breath. Havik had raised the dead. It made enough sense. Wish had killed so many people that day, outside Wick. Inside Wick, where the train exploded. If the dead were called, of course they'd come for her. Complete with their roaring, rumbling train. She twisted about, looking for Havik, and found the other woman bent over her, hands on her knees, grinning in the direction of the sound.

"Are they here for me?" Wish asked.

"I told you," Havik said, breathlessly. "It worked, Wild Wish." She opened a hand, revealing the bone instrument she'd somehow kept hold of. "Bonesun really could wake the dormant masses." She regarded the trumpet with wonder and Wish chilled at her expression.

"Don't, Havik," she said. The sounds of running men were quietening as the rumble of the approaching disaster grew louder. Other men were shouting commands, officers trying to restore order.

Havik met her eye playfully. "There's so much more it can do. There are goblins here, did you see?" She lifted the bone instrument towards her mouth and Wild Wish sprang up without thinking. As Havik's lips touched the device, Wish tackled her around the waist, bringing her to the ground. Havik heaved as the instrument flew away, and she rolled over, scrambling on her belly towards it, legs kicking. Wish grappled up, caught handfuls of her coat and pulled, crawling on top of her. Havik bucked, almost throwing her off, but she clung on tight, snarling, and tugged herself forward, to bodily slam into Havik's back. They were both stunned for a second before Wish sat back, pinning Havik's waist. She roughly rolled the woman over to face her. She got her hands on her neck, pushing Havik into the ground and squeezing. Mud clumped in her hair, head half-sinking into the bog, and Wish snarled like an animal. Havik's eyes bulged, meeting hers, afraid at last. Her mouth opened and closed, silently gagging, life gasping out of her. Her legs stopped kicking, core stopped struggling, but her hands came up to hold Wish's wrists. She didn't try to pull her off, but stretched her lips to a smile. She shuddered with something like a laugh, so unexpected Wish almost released her.

Havik's mess of fear and pain, but also happiness, made no sense.

The light in her eyes dimmed.

Wish let go, sitting back, and Havik spluttered for air, desperately. Mixed in her gasps were shudders of small laughs, but also sobs. Wish quickly stood and Havik surged up, onto her hands and knees. Like a beaten dog, partway guilty, hurt, but *smiling*. Havik tried to speak, but only managed an unintelligible rasp. Then her eyes lowered. Tracked over the ground.

There was the bone heart trumpet, sitting in the mud.

Before she could reach for it, Wish took a quick step to the side and kicked the thing over a patch of rock. She gave Havik one brief glance, no room for hesitation, then stomped on it. Havik made a sound more pained than when she'd been choking, and Wish watched her eyes tear as she ground the bones under her boot. She stomped again, twisted her toe, crushed the bone to dust.

"Enough!" Wish shouted. "You fucking lunatic, it's over!"

Men's shouts came through to her, though, calling urgently. Not sounds of retreat or panic now, but someone trying to take charge and organise a defence as the initial confusion passed. Soldiers were racing about in the parting dust, taking up positions. The thunderous sound continued to approach. Wish jumped aside as a shape rushed past her, a huffing little goblin running for its life. The power Havik had unleashed was growing impossibly loud, a patter bigger than the march of the largest armies, and it was coming fast.

"Wild Wish!" Brade's voice cut through the chaos. "Is that you?"

Alive. Thank the Saints – she wasn't completely alone.

"Wild Wish!" he shouted again, not far off.

"Over here!" Wish said. "Captain? What's happening?"

Footsteps got closer, the dust swirling and parting as more people pressed through. Brade darted into view, a hand finding her forearm. "No time. We need to retreat."

"Captain?" Wish repeated, one word for all her delirium.

"Grescinds," Brade explained equally simply, turning her to a safer direction. He started a trot, and she fell in line, looking back but making out nothing through the dust and night. Grescinds? That sound, the ground moving, the rumble, it wasn't an engine, ghosts, or the terrors of her past. It was the sound of many giant creatures combined, tearing themselves from the ground, moving together.

"How many?" Wish asked.

"A lot. Maybe all of them."

Brade moved faster and Wish matched him, but threw another look back. The dust was thin enough now that she saw them. A wave of moving bodies formed a living horizon, undulating towards them. She swore and pushed harder, off the path and into boggy ground, grass slapping her legs and boots alternately hitting hard rock and falling into cloying mud.

They blundered between men going the other way. Goblins too. Green coats and green skin almost black in the dark, the soldiers ignored them to raise rifles towards the approaching enemy. Some were stern and ready, most looked terrified.

"Here, over here!" Brade called, and she followed him through the distracted enemy up an incline, over rocks, until they breached the dust cloud and skipped to a halt. Two people were waiting and Wish almost yelped with surprise: Scraper and Dalliance. They were hunched and filthy, ready to collapse. Dalliance had an arm bound up over the opposite shoulder. Wish nodded in wordless greeting and turned to see the coming disaster. The Drail opened fire.

Wish couldn't have kept running if she wanted to then, captivated by the scene before them. The flashes of hundreds of rifles erupted from a sea of bodies, human and goblin intermingling in untidy lines through the bog and broken village, a shadow army visible in highlighted edges. A handful of men on horseback waved their arms, yelling orders. Somewhere far deeper in the marsh, cannon fired with great concussive sounds, their missiles arcing high overhead. All of it exploded into a phalanx of enormous crablike grescind, who had, at last, arrived. Mottled claws and gnashing, alien faces appeared in bright flashes under the hilly slopes of craggy shells, each creature the size of a house and moving fast. The barrage of Atmoor's army was tremendous, an entire company in the open unleashing all they had. It was absorbed with almost zero effect into the wall of grescind, as they clattered noisily through the ruins of the Shore Stalker village. Artillery shells broke into the throng with explosions that tore shells apart and scuttled small pockets of the monsters, behind their front line, but the rifle fire merely peppered them, knocking off chinks of leg or claw, occasionally bursting a face. Only a couple of creatures fell, their gaps immediately filled by others.

The rest tore into the Drail line and the massed soldiers broke in terror.

Wish's small group had maybe fifty metres of safety from the fight, just enough to allow a few moments of watching, as the grescind hit the frail men, tumbling them in groups or snapping them between claws. A couple leapt over the crowd and some shovelled squirming soldiers into their clicking mandibles, gulping down chunks of still-moving bodies. Officers were yelling for order, sweeping their hands about and shooting pistols, but the riflemen were lost, pushing over each other to get away. The goblins fled ahead of them, finding easy routes between legs and scattering into the marshland.

The artillery fired another barrage, closer to the front now, and Wish flinched as one grescind took a direct hit, its front half exploding in a great black cloud. Nearby men were thrown screaming through the air and the other monsters parted around the blast, momentarily startled, before they swept back in for the kill.

"They're done for," Brade growled.

Wish followed his gaze to a soldier on horseback. Colonel Atmoor, not far down the line, roared as he waved a sword above his head and tried to keep his horse steady. He was trying to make the fleeing men stand and fight. Wish had seen this before, an officer clinging desperately on, as if they could win through forced courage alone. The rifles were all but quiet, the officers' shouts an exception amid the screams and the terrible gnashing of the grescind's claws and jaws.

Brade pointed. "That way."

Wish had no idea what he'd seen, how he could see anything through the darkness, but she trusted his instincts more than hers. She nodded and the captain moved ahead, jumping down from the rocks. They picked up speed as he led them onto hard ground. A path. A severed arm flew past with a splat, a scream coming particularly close, and Wish shouted at her troop to run faster. They sprinted with what little energy they had, following Brade's determined example. Wish tripped and almost fell, found herself caught and held up. Scraper's skinny arm on her, stronger than she looked. A curt nod and they continued. Heavy limbs thumped over the rocks behind them, a huge shape shifting in Wish's periphery – one of the creatures was catching up.

"Through here!" Brade shouted, and disappeared into the dark. Wish ran, heart on fire, and they burst through a gap in rocks ahead, falling down together in a tumble. She blinked but couldn't see, too dark in this cavernous space. They kept moving, Brade and Scraper tugging at her, and Wish kicked feebly as she was dragged inside – just before a claw smacked the ground. The rocks over and around them shook with the patter of the creature climbing over them, and it chittered in frustration. A rush of air and a snap signalled it trying to reach in, the space too tight, and the scouts pressed themselves flat over each other, holding their breath.

The grescind kept clawing, clattering back and forth, snatching in but failing to reach them, until screams and more cannon fire interrupted it. Distracted, it pounced off the rocks and clambered away.

Wish remained frozen, lying down staring up into nothing, barely believing she was alive. It hurt all over. They were trapped in the middle of a nightmare. But one moment passed to another, with the sounds drawing further away. No more giant creatures came.

"Can she control them?" Brade asked, voice quiet.

It took Wish a second to process the question. *She* meant Havik, of course. Last seen on her knees in the mud, half choked. Just before the advance of the monsters. Wish had spared her, but surely she couldn't have escaped. Brade had the right idea, though, having guessed this disaster wasn't natural or coincidence. Wish answered, "No."

She wondered if it might've been possible if she hadn't crushed the bone instrument.

She decided not to care, and rested her head back into something soft, someone's stomach. Whoever it was didn't complain. She closed her eyes and tried to block out the screams.

Colonel Atmoor kicked his horse to full speed. He'd tired the creature coming here from Carlwen, though, and had left it too late anyway. The damned crabs were more formidable and more numerous than he'd appreciated – creatures of that size shouldn't have been able to move so fast, nor should they have been able to form such tight and efficient ranks. He only properly understood when he saw them up close, how one pounced over another, how they clambered forward shell-to-shell, with no space for men to pass. Those who weren't swept up or knocked down by claws were pierced and trampled under hinged legs thick as logs.

"Fall back!" he ordered, unnecessarily considering he was one of the only men still facing the enemy, everyone else running into the bog. He saw soldiers tripping around him, few getting more than a few metres before they sank out of sight. Occasional frantic arms grasped about for purchase as they were sucked down into mud.

The trudge horse made short work of the bog, at least, bursting through the patches it partly sank into. But it wasn't fast enough. Turning in the saddle, Atmoor saw the grescind separating at last, monsters branching off to pick out straggling soldiers. Some were still pressing forward though, advancing after the quickest, biggest targets. Major Weles, urging his horse on a short distance back, was snatched out of his saddle by a giant claw and pulled away shrieking. Atmoor looked away as the major was silenced with a terrible squelch.

He aimed for the artillery guns, the silhouettes of the massive weapons just visible on rocky terrain ahead. Abandoned; Hollery's teams had fled after only a few barrages. There was no safety or hope there, but it at least marked an escape route, positioned near the river shallows. A short charge further, that was all it would take.

The ground rumbled with the approach of a terrible beast behind him, apparently chasing him. Fast. Atmoor shouted at his horse and kicked its hinds, dipping lower in the saddle. He saw shapes of men and goblins far away, across the river or approaching it, disorderly as ever. Some of them must've started running long before the monsters reached them. If they'd put up a more unified front, held a tighter line. If he'd only had better men, a hundred or a thousand Carrows, these creatures could've been held back, however it came to this.

Even now. If he only had a faster horse, one that wasn't so damn weak.

The creature was gaining on him, making noises with its mandibles that almost sounded excited. The horse brayed fearfully, trying its hardest but slowing. Atmoor took a deep breath, eyeing the river, the artillery line. Close, but impossibly far.

With a last grunt, he urged the horse on for one more surge, then released the reins, fell from the saddle. He hit the mud hard, smacked a knee into rock and couldn't keep in a shout of pain.

Something broken, he fell onto his back, watching the horse gallop on. A final ditch hope, that the grescind would go after the bigger prey. The creature's tremendous shape scuttled over him, a multitude of legs clicking by as the horse accelerated away with new vigour, freshly liberated. The grescind continued, merciless, and Atmoor skidded back into the long grass, concealing himself as he heard the horse give a pitiful bray.

The colonel panted, trying to regain his breath as his legs sank slowly into the mud and the sounds finally began to die down. He just had to wait. Endure silently the awful sounds of the feasting creatures. But his legs were sinking, and he grunted as the mud sucked at his calves. With a moment's panic, he pulled himself upright, tugging to get free, not about to flounder as he'd seen other men doing. He stumbled to one side, out of the mud into a small clearing. He pulled up short, faced with a great boulder-like object. Momentarily frozen, heart pounding, he slumped with relief at the sight of the ugly creature. It was as tall as him and twice as wide, but nothing like as monstrous as the crabs. A mere toad of some sort, swelling with gentle breaths, completely motionless. Harmless.

Atmoor allowed himself a smile as he heard the closest grescind moving away, searching for fresh prey. He'd escaped. By the Saints, somehow he had made it. And what reports he would have to share now. The dangers of combat in proximity to monstrous fauna.

A slurping sound snapped his attention back around to the giant toad, and he frowned at its slit of a mouth peeling open. The thing had still barely moved, showed no sign of intelligence or focus in its orb-like eyes, but the great slit across its centre was widening slightly. He shook his head, best not stay here. He turned away again, to march for the river.

With a wet smack, Atmoor was punched hard in the back, and almost fell flat on his face before being pulled back, an object stuck to him hard. He managed only a brief cry as he was pulled through the air, thrust into moist darkness, and the toad's mouth closed on him.

"Release me, foul slug!" Atmoor shouted, pushing indignantly at the enclosure, but his hands sank ineffectively into its fleshy innards, as he was dragged in. He kicked, panic rising, as the creature sucked too hard for him to resist. Atmoor roared into protest – this wasn't possible – a damn toad, and he was a *colonel!* – but saliva glooped over him and he was constricted and smothered, gulped further down in pulse. He could do more than scream.

47

What happened in Drowndeep was neither mystery nor miracle. It was a structurally precarious priory in a hostile land, where both the foundations and fauna were highly agitated by an intruding force of unprecedented size. The Church resolutely condemns any suggestion of spiritual or magical abnormalities, and will not be permitting further investigation into the region.

Extract from Archvenerator Turbulence XI's Passtol Statement, 720

The scouts shifted a little, silent as the noise of the massacre became distant and quieter. Wish sat up, rested her back against a rock and avoided taking stock of her various injuries. It was enough to know she hurt everywhere but nowhere badly enough that it might kill her. She wasn't aware of anything bleeding too profusely, that was the important part, and when she asked it seemed no one else was seriously injured, either. That established, they waited.

Wish tried not to think at all, with the rapid escalation of the disaster weighing on her. The what-ifs piled up anyway, as she mentally revisited the brutal advance of the Irregulars, the fighting in the tunnels, Havik's reckless use of the bone instrument, the collapse of the keep, the rise of the monsters. A part of her insisted, with every horrible image, that there had been a way to prevent this at every stage. She could've led the Irregulars away or otherwise negotiated with them. Persuaded Havik to stop. Used the bone instrument to call off the catastrophe it had caused. Or she might have fought harder, or better, to win the day before everything was lost. Another part of her suggested none of this was possible. From the moment she'd arrived in the Mire, this had been inevitable. And she might've stopped Havik too late, but she *had* stopped her doing anything else, hadn't she?

How *did* this war keep finding ways to make things worse? And what part of any of this was going to make a difference, to anything, anywhere? She had seen Stanclif and Drail dying together for nothing. And they'd run past Drail soldiers, unhindered, alongside goblins that otherwise might've clawed her throat out, as clear as anything that their empires' differences were meaningless in the face of a horde of monsters. Why were they fighting each other when the world at large was out to punish all of them equally?

Wish's mind drifted back to Havik, wondering if she'd made it. Almost certainly not, and that made her sad. She knew it shouldn't. The woman was crazy and Wish should have killed her herself. Should have killed her before, if she'd had any sense. Should have never even led her to Midpeak. But how could she have known? And how could she quell the little piece of her that actually hoped she'd survived? There'd been a kiss, even. They'd got through it together, in part. Havik had saved her as well as put her in danger. Hadn't she?

Wish scolded herself. There were people far more deserving of her worry out there. Emi and the Rawboys, Sister Sonseen, all lost in the ruins of Drowndeep. Damn Four Skills, she found herself thinking, then. Damn Captain Brade and Command and everyone else who'd thought it made any sense to send her here. Damn Captain Tate for ever giving her this place in the war, when the woman herself might've been as bad as everyone else.

This was supposed to be a new start, and she'd lost more people than ever.

The thoughts came and went and at some point Wish must have slept, as cracks of light came in. The pale blue glow of the Mire's misty morning revealed at last the contours of this small crevice they were packed into. Little more than a break in a cluster of huge rocks, which the grescinds could have plucked them from with only a little more effort. But Wish blearily realised the sounds of the monsters had receded now. She heard the squawk of distant birds, but nothing more beyond the breathing of her companions; Dalliance was sleeping deeply.

Scraper was staring at her with a heavy brow. Sitting opposite, their legs touching. It felt like she might've been staring for a while. She was painted in blood, dried in streaks over her face and clumping her hair, clothes sodden. Her hollow eyes gave Wish a chill and she drew her knees up defensively under her chin.

"They've gone," Scraper said. Eyes not moving.

Wish listened again for sounds outside. She hoped it was true.

Brade made a noise and she noticed the captain deeper in the crevice. He'd been sleeping too, and looked especially rough in the low light. He wearily regarded the two women, and croaked, "It's over?"

"Sounds like it," Wish said. Feeling Scraper's intent gaze still on her, she raised her eyebrows to prompt the woman to speak. Scraper said nothing, so she frowned and asked, "Did you see what happened to Emi? The others?"

"They got into the tunnels, at least," Brade said. "The Rawboys were spread out down there. I didn't see them come out. I lost sight of Emi after the whole gate thing."

"She was safe," Scraper said. "But not well."

"Okay," Wish said, hardly daring to hope she'd stayed safe. "Guess we'd better take a look." She flexed her limbs, getting a little blood back into them. Pain shot through general aches, with a lancing bite from a cut on her head. She winced and crawled over Dalliance's legs to leave the crevice. He groaned and she patted his good shoulder, whispering, "Stay here."

He accepted without properly waking and she continued outside. Wish squinted against the morning light, relatively bright but with the Mire's usual muted haze. She only cautiously emerged, scanning the damp surroundings for any sign of movement. Any house-sized monsters. The grescind were apparent at once, their dormant shells the main scrappy masses that stood out in the marshland and amid the broken shacks and walls of Drowndeep. A few dozen in total, perhaps. For a moment Wish was still, dreading any movement might wake them, but when her gaze lingered on the shells for longer than a few seconds it was clear that only corpses remained. Large birds perched on some, pecking for a way in.

Scraper and Brade crept out of the rocks behind Wish and paused to take it in.

A lot of the landscape was covered by tall grass and rock formations, but not enough to conceal the scale of the carnage. Almost everywhere Wish looked there were at least hints of bodies. Or body parts. Drowndeep itself was as decimated as if a bomb had hit it, though it'd fallen in rather than out, to form a heap of bloody rubble.

Wish started walking. It wasn't easy, each step hitting her with new and imaginative sources of pain, but she found a degree of numbness for her own problems in the distraction of how much horror surrounded her. This was about as unpleasant as any battlefield she'd walked through. Severed limbs, crushed heads, guts spilling out. Wish didn't look away, sure that it was too late to ever clean her mind of such things anyway. Maybe if she saw enough, it would lose impact. She doubted it.

They trod through the marsh in silence, slowly reaching Drowndeep, and it got worse around the debris of the village, where the main strength of Atmoor's resistance had been concentrated. The bodies would've been piled higher, Wish supposed, if they hadn't also been stamped into the ground, and each other, under the merciless weight of the monsters. She walked through it trying to tell herself that her boots were sinking into slushy mud and not people.

Drowndeep's ruins presented an island in the carnage, with the bulk of the people who died there now buried under it. They climbed over the top and searched for signs of life, or a way in to anything that might've survived below. The tunnels were strong, carved directly into the rock, so there was always a chance . . .

The trio spread out, covering the short diameter of the keep between them. There was nothing to salvage, bar occasional discarded weapons. Wish considered taking a rifle but barely saw the point. It seemed unlikely anything was left to fight.

"Emi?" Scraper called out, and her voice spread with a haunting lilt into the surrounding bog. She eyed the rubble accusingly and said no more.

Wish hardened, unwilling to believe that they'd braved Drail territory and brought Emi back against impossible odds only for her to disappear again. She shouted, much louder than Scraper, "Emi? Are you here?"

No response. Brade glanced at her with sympathy. Pity maybe. It made her shout louder.

"Emi! Quit hiding!"

Birds startled from the shells of nearby grescind and took flight with indignant squawks.

"Emi, if you –"

"Lieutenant!" a voice answered. A man, muffled, but alive. "Down here!"

Wild Wish raced to the sound, tripping over the rubble. Scraper and Brade converged on her, pulling bits of stone and brick out of the way.

"We're trapped," the soldier continued, and Wish recognised the accent as she skidded down beside him, a bit of his face visible through a crack in the rubble. Macmiddan. "Can you shift it from there?"

"Hold on," Wish said, and clawed at the debris over his position. She threw away big chunks of stone which needed two hands to lift as Brade and Scraper joined her, digging their way in. They'd soon cleared off a big patch of wall, the main obstacle covering Macmiddan's hole. Wish got her hands on an edge and heaved with all her strength. It didn't move. Scraper and Brade joined her, all three of them shoving and tugging, but the blockage was bigger and deeper embedded than they had any hope of shifting. Wish pulled away, looking around for something to lever it with.

As she searched, Brade asked, "Who's in there with you?"

"Bunch of us. A good part of the tunnels held up, though I doubt they'll last long. I've got Ptrangus, Graveguard, a couple monks. Emi, too, but she's in a bad way."

"Emi?" Wish cried and threw herself at the slab again. Increased urgency didn't help.

"Wild, enough," Brade said, gently guiding her back. He scanned the area more calmly. "We can't shift this alone." He asked

Macmiddan. "Is Emi recovering?"

"Not quickly," the old veteran said. "I've got a grenade, but it's likely to bring the roof down. Is it over up there, at least?"

Wish was scarcely listening, hopping over the rubble, pulling bits aside. There was nothing. No pole to use as a lever. No chains or big animals that might help.

"Yeah," Brade answered, sombrely. She turned back, sensing his gaze, and found him staring at her. "It's over."

He wasn't telling her to give up, but to slow down. It rankled, made her want to shove him, but she did take a beat. Surveyed the damage again. How many people had been here last night, and how many had survived? Too many and not enough. But she looked past the human and goblin bodies and the mess of the ruined homes, so frail and useless now, and she took in the inhospitable wider bog land. Miles and miles of wetland that couldn't be trusted. Where people didn't belong. It had claimed them, as it had to – more brutally than anyone predicted, and in a manner that didn't entirely make sense. But what did they expect? They didn't *belong* here, with their modern war and mad empires.

Had they prodded the saints and got an answer?

She roamed the swaying grass with her eyes, and realised it was the same again and again. At Green Rise and in Wick, in all the battles before and after. None of this was natural or belonged and the result everywhere was the same. Needless, excessive bloodshed, with nothing gained. Only new ways to die. New ways to stamp death on the land, until all of it would be haunted. But as she searched the horizon, she picked out movement, a large shape hulking from the marsh. Perfect, she thought, without fear or malice. A straggling monster, one of the grescind returning to their lair. It looked like a small one, for them, but large enough, swaying as it approached. Perhaps it was injured.

Wish huffed. She scanned the rubble not for a tool but a weapon. There were a couple of crude rifles and goblin bag guns, the weaker armaments of the Irregulars and goblins. As she jumped over the keep's remains, towards the gates and where more bountiful Drail soldiers had been slain, Brade noticed where she'd been looking.

"What is it?" he said, as if there were multiple options. "Dammit. Scraper, one more try." He and her went back to Macmiddan's tunnel, for another futile attempt to shift the wall, as Wish ran onto the road. She spotted a couple of rifles not far off and jogged towards them, but paused as something else caught her eye. The remains of the shack shredded by Havik's gun, an arm poking out from under it. A longer rifle lay next to the body, one with a scope. That would do.

Wish whipped up the weapon: Lost One's unfamiliar eastern gun, bigger than a Long 0.48, weightier. It had a bolt and a trigger and a scope with dials – all she needed. She ran back up the rubble, climbing for the highest ground, as Brade and Scraper put their backs into the wall, snarling with frustration. Wish hefted the gun and picked out the creature through the scope, steadying as she searched for a weak spot.

Not a grescind.

Very big, yes, but humanoid. Wish lowered the rifle to see with her own eyes, then she raised it again, scarcely believing it. Brade and Scraper slowed at her hesitation.

"It's okay," Wish told them. "I think we're going to be okay."

48

The fact that it was impossible to say exactly how many died in the Saints Mire in the fall of 720 gave these events a particular gravitas. The numbers involved may seem insignificant in the grand scheme of the war, but the implications of where they happened, and the mystery of exactly how it came about, would have repercussions throughout the Rocc – not least because both the Drail and Stanish Empires were not immediately forthcoming about the details.

**Dueley's Comprehensive: The One War in
10 Volumes (Vol. 5), p. 25**

Wild Wish decided, as the Blood Scouts relayed what information they could about their experiences while separated, that Lost One had not been, despite his arrogance, a very good shot. Sitting on the gunwale of a medium-sized sailboat they had salvaged from the remnants of the Shore Stalker village, she cradled his ornate rifle in her lap marvelling at the weapon's quality. Expertly built, well-weighted, with a delicately rifled barrel. The scope had perhaps the strongest zoom she'd seen, with crystal clear lenses and expensive gilding around the edges. It had been crafted by someone who knew exactly what they were doing and took pride in it. It hadn't belonged in the hands of someone like Lost One, who had missed her on the ramparts and, it turned out, failed even to bring down an ogre. Realistically, if you could get an ogre in sight, there was no excuse for not being able to kill it.

It was to their great benefit though, as Ohno had come wandering in from the wilderness with the strength they needed to save their comrades. She'd been hit twice and fallen in the mud, but insisted the wounds were superficial and said the only reason she hadn't caught up sooner was the difficulty of travelling unseen. The Rawboy medic Graveguard subtly shook his head from behind the ogre's shoulder as he stitched one of the wounds, silently confiding that it was worse than Ohno made out. That was also obvious enough from Ohno's grimaces of pain and the pallor of her skin. No one called her out on it, though; if she wanted to pretend two sniper wounds were nothing, that was up to her.

In fact, regardless the nightmare they'd fought through, and the horrors it had unleashed, by some miracle all Wish's scouts had survived the Battle of Drowndeep. None of them were unscathed, but none were going to die; of them all, Emi fared the worst, barely speaking and struggling to crack her trademark smirks when they pulled her from the ground. She'd drained herself with that one act of magic, and otherwise had to avoid the fighting entirely. The lasting impact was clear as she occasionally chuckled to herself without cause, a wavering feral look in her eye, and the earth-minding withdrawal gave her little shudders of instability. She just needed to rest, Graveguard insisted, which Brother Redfire agreed with, apparently educated in aspects of magic himself. The bulky monk, in fact, did almost as much as their medic to patch things up, smiling and offering words of encouragement all the while. Though she'd only met him briefly, Wish found herself hugely relieved that he'd survived too, despite a bad leg injury courtesy of Havik. She was even more happy that Sister Sonseen was still with him — though the nun soon ventured out in search of her beetle, which she insisted would've escaped over the walls of Drowndeep, though no one had seen it go. Ptrangus (having only received what he claimed were mild grazes from near-misses) escorted her into the bog, but they returned empty-handed. Wish really hoped the beetle was okay and would show up. She'd seen enough horses killed, and she felt they deserved a break there.

The worst injury her scouts endured was a shot Macmiddan had taken to the torso, which Graveguard said had missed his guts but might've clipped a kidney. He said it blankly and Macmiddan put on a brave face so Wish wasn't sure if he was serious or not, but it didn't seem like something to joke about. Not that it mattered to her either way; the medic was doing all he could. It was up to him, now. Dalliance was almost as bad, though, unable to move his shot arm, which may or may not have been permanently damaged. Graveguard was less willing to dismiss that, but Dalliance likewise tried to smile it off, saying it was only his left arm, after all. Then there was Latebite, reunited with them, still unable to walk without aid but no worse off than he had been.

Scraper, who'd come out of the conflict bloodiest by far, somehow appeared to be the least injured. She'd still not washed the blood off, though some cracked and shed naturally, and she sat in the boat like some kind of slaughterhouse demon. No one mentioned it.

Brade had also pulled through fairly unscathed, though he'd got a few nicks and looked utterly drained. He had prepared their boat without talking, strapping the sails and setting it on the waterways to reach the sea. Everyone was reticent about floating through grescind territory, but he insisted they would be fine: the monsters had sated themselves and the boat was designed to float high in the water anyway, creating the least disturbance. From the tools he'd sifted through, he also added helpfully, it was clear the Mirians knew how to get by the creatures unnoticed. They could even have stopped them with these primitive tools, most likely – a real shame the Irregulars had killed so many of them. When the monsters' charge came, the tribe might've been more useful than Artmoor's entire army.

It was all done now, though. The military incursion in the Mire was decimated and whatever remained was not worth pursuing. At least, not without orders to do so. Wild Wish was bringing her crew home, and with a feeling of inherent rightness. She doubted, or possibly dreaded, the idea that fate had brought her and Havik together, but she liked applying it to her New Scouts instead. That they had survived in the most brutal circumstances said maybe this was meant to be. Her small platoon could be the start of something greater. A team of survivors, destined for bigger things. She wished she could've properly seen them all in action. She smiled as they bobbed along the water, leaving the Saints Mire behind, with a sense of renewed purpose.

"Would you do it again?" she asked the boat in general, without explanation. They eyed her uncertainly, all except Emi, who tried to smile too, head hanging low. "I mean work together, not come here."

"Do we have a choice?" Ptrangus replied. Graveguard nudged his knee in mock warning and he swatted it off.

"If I'm able," Dalliance said, seriously. "I'd like to stay with you. If it's not all like this?"

"Not at all," Wish replied brightly, and glanced to Emi. The mage had no energy for a snarky addition, so Wish said it herself "It's usually worse."

That got a few chuckles.

"I've got nowhere better to go," Ohno said, folded into the rear of the boat. They'd achieved an even balance with the others sitting towards the front, after some doubts the vessel could even accommodate an ogre. Brade said it was designed for hauling in large catches, so it wouldn't be a problem. She gave Wish an earnest look, the last of their group she really expected to stick with the platoon, considering the ogres had effectively been volunteers and she'd got her commander killed. That stung. Caracker was capable, stoic and excellent support, and she'd never even seen him in action. But Ohno went on, "I trust you, Lieutenant. More or less. And I reckon you could use an ogre watching your back."

"*She* needs her back watching, when you've got two bullets in yours?" Ptrangus laughed, earning a scowl from the big woman. It didn't put him off, the mission's end apparently bringing out extra cheek in him. Or perhaps it was just giddy exhaustion. "What do you think, Bite, these women likely to survive another week without us?"

"I think we put down a lot of men back there," Macmiddan answered before Latebite. "Awful lot. But it wasn't us that stopped the Irregulars or got the Drail onside. Might be worth showing her more respect."

"Aye. You know how easily she dispatched your mate?" Ptrangus glanced at Ohno. The subject of Runt had only come up briefly so far. "The Lieutenant is stone cold."

"You did that?" Ohno asked Wish, bringing a shadow back over the boat.

She nodded, dreading the response.

"Good. He was a prick."

That got Ptrangus laughing again and Latebite whispered for him to calm down. The Rawboy replied, "Ah lighten up. We're out of here. Forget this hell hole. Enjoy the sun and open air before we find a new pit of shit to fall in, huh? Probably got Drail boats waiting to sink us out there, if not a sea serpent or whatever the fuck. By Castor, what a shit-show."

"You don't have to keep going," Wish said. He frowned at her, distrusting, so she said, "You're all hurt. Enough to warrant discharges, I'm sure. What do you think, Captain?"

Brade, standing by Ohno with a hand on the boat's tiller, regarded her curiously. He'd been listening without comment, processing everything. Even addressed directly, he took a minute to think things through. His eyes were dark and he seemed worse off than he had after Low Slane and Wick, for the little she'd seen of him after that. At length, he said, "It's possible. I couldn't make any promises. Some of you, at least, could go home."

"I'd believe it when I see it," Ptrangus said.

"Not you. You're clearly too good at avoiding bullets."

"Pah. Well if I'm not leaving, none of you are. Hear me, Mac? You can be old as fuck and have one kidney, they want to make a scout out of me, you're coming too."

"No one's dragging anyone anywhere," Wish said, though she appreciated the lightness in his voice was different to before, better natured. It was a lowering of his guard, and he met her eye with a look that confirmed it. "But being a Blood Scout isn't all bad. It'll keep you out of the trenches, anyway."

"Mostly," Emi managed, a bare croak.

"Look, we're almost there," Brade interrupted, pointing ahead, and they went collectively quiet to see where the rocky marshland spread further apart, ejecting the widening river into the expanse of the Most Blessed Sea. The boat bobbed more as they approached in reverent silence, holding their breath – the last banks of the Saints Mire drifted by, a final opportunity for the innocuous rocks to come to life and sink them. Then they were out, beyond the land, leaving the shore behind, and they rocked over gentle waves into the open water.

"Thank fuck for that," Ptrangus exhaled, genuinely, and Graveguard put a sympathetic hand on his shoulder. Latebite put one on his leg. The tension they'd been holding in eased out. There was still a long line of coast to follow to get back to Hail Crossing, which wasn't entirely safe and might take days depending on the wind, but this was a big step towards their return.

They continued quietly for a while, Brade steering them along, before the captain finally took a seat and sighed deeply. Wish met his eye, down the length of the boat, wanting to convey thanks. Some part of forgiveness, too. They'd not completed the job anywhere near as cleanly as in Low Slane, but they had come out on better terms. He met her eye, seeming to understand but too weary to show much enthusiasm in response. Regardless his exhaustion, though, it was clear he was thinking. Had been wanting to say something. Wish had skimmed over the details of all that had happened, with Havik and the bone instrument and her raving about old religions. Brade had nodded as though it all made sense without offering much feedback.

Now, he said, "Our best hopes of understanding it were buried with that priory."

The others in the boat barely looked up, or raised their eyes and lowered them again. All so tired now. Wish wasn't sure she wanted to get into it herself, or if she even needed to understand it. Havik had gone after something terrible, unleashed a small part of it, and Wish had dashed her dreams of doing more. The exact details didn't matter.

"I did some reading, made some notes," Brade went on. "In Drowndeep and Midpeak. She must've been . . . incredibly astute, to have drawn the conclusions she did. What books she uncovered in her library or during her journeys, I could only guess at. She was right about some things, for sure – that the teachings of Bonesun, and the exact magics he toyed with, have long been suppressed. It's generally understood that it's for the best. Some things should be left buried."

"You want my take?" Ohno said. "She found a glorified dog whistle. The prophet made something that could call in beasts. Probably only good for grescinds, anyway. The only mystery I see is why they kept the pieces at all."

"That's precisely the question," Brade said. "If a whistle was all it was, the priories *wouldn't* have preserved it. They have records of various items of power, separated and secured in the Mire and elsewhere. The stories I found were always ambiguous. Some might've been about the Trumpet itself, if I'd had more time to explore them."

"You're welcome to go back," Ptrangus murmured.

Brade smiled wanly and Wish appreciated there was no question of it now. He absolutely could have stayed and pursued whatever curiosity had first brought him out there, but the captain was more than ready to leave it behind, just like the rest of them. He said, "Whatever that instrument's intended purpose, or potential effects, it wasn't natural, or like anything we know. *That's* the issue. It was a corruption, and an incredibly powerful one, that could bring centuries of religious and scientific dogma into question. Am I right, Emi?"

Emi narrowed her eyes. She took in a breath and let it out, then nodded. With a struggle, she said, "I've never felt magic like I did out there." She touched her chest lightly. *"This* isn't natural, either."

Wish frowned. In her usual tone, she would've read that as Emi being playfully weird, but she was too weary and worn for joking, and Wish instead saw it indicating her ailment. She wasn't just suffering from her gunshot wound, or from exerting herself, but from using her magic in Drowndeep. Just as she'd feared when they first left the priory. Wish said, "How bad is it?"

Emi met her eye. Shrugged.

"It could be a lot worse," Brade said. "This was . . . important, what we did out here. I know it might not feel like it now."

Emi snorted, half a laugh, and they all regarded her with concern, waiting for what she had to say. She took a while, hanging her head again, but shook it to be clear she was building up to a comment. At last, she murmured, "If they knew what was possible, the empires would be fighting over the Saints Mire and that alone."

"Based on a madwoman calling up crabs from the coast?" Ptragnus said. "They've got guns powerful enough to level cities by now, don't they? Who needs crabs?"

"You didn't see them, did you?" Brade replied. "Those grescind weren't just attacking at random. They came as an army. They don't *do* that in the wild."

"So what? The Comity and Drail are already pressing beasts twice as big into their forces, throwing them at machine guns the same as us."

"In small numbers. And I'll wager no one's ever seen a grescind on the front line. They're part of a good portion of the myriad beasts that are too dangerous to be tamed. The worst kind."

"Sounds like us," Latebite said, and got some laughs.

Wish smiled, because it was true enough. But Brade was talking about something bigger, and worse, and she understood where he was going. He sounded different compared to their confrontation in Reeve Abbey, where the possibility of greater weaponry was something he considered a boon. This, the promise of new powers and, at the least, an ability to control horrific beasts, was too dangerous even for him. She said, "We *have* buried that power, though, right? No one's going out there whipping up armies of recluse giants."

He didn't immediately agree, which sunk her heart for a second. He said, "I hope so," and it wasn't convincing. Seeing her expression, he went on, "No one knew to look for this before. Even if we keep what happened to ourselves, it'd only take one survivor from Atmoor's men, or one talkative monk, and the idea might spread. It's not just about the grescind; it brings into question so much more than that. The foundations of the Movement of Knowledge, the basis for suppressing the faith . . . what exactly were the prophets capable of? I pray this is the end of it, I do, but if it's not . . ." He trailed off, letting them imagine a disaster beyond all proportions. A lingering thought that the unintended slaughter of a Drail army at the hands of feral sea creatures might do what, bring back *religion* and all the conflicts and complications that offered?

"Well that's bloody cheery isn't it?" Ptrangus huffed. "Thanks, Captain."

"Yeah, a real ray of sunshine," Macmiddan agreed miserably. "Never mind we survived hell rising, we might've upset all modern thought, is that about right?"

"On the other hand," Graveguard came in, "maybe it *was* just a whistle?"

That got a few more chuckles, because plainly no one could believe that anymore, and Wish never could've, having seen, and heard, the disastrous sounds that instrument created. Their responses were almost enough for Wish to smile again, though, and Brade offered a halfhearted smirk himself. She feared he wouldn't be able to make light of it so easily. He said, "I doubt a single Irregular got out of there, anyway. If any of them even really knew what they were doing." He met Wish's eye again, with another unspoken question. Or at least, a hope. Were they *all* dead?

She held his gaze, not justifying it with an answer out loud. Havik was gone, and with her all the complications of exactly what she knew and what she was trying to do. She'd died with the rest of them and they were safe to return to the war as explosively horribly normal.

Probably.

49

*What are they HIDING from us? Something BIG happened
in the Saints Mire – THOUSANDS have died. There are no
soldiers left in Onwail and we have rumours that at least
THREE of the ancient priories have been DESTROYED! If
the Drail and Stanish forces clashed, with BIG LOSSES,
why is no one claiming VICTORY?*

*The Empires are COMPLICIT in something we are not
SUPPOSED TO KNOW. Do NOT trust your leaders. Do
NOT trust the Empire.*

Demand the TRUTH from THE MIRE!

**Questions from the Mire, Pamphlet from
the Worker's Union of Stanclif, 720**

Wild Wish was enjoying the city of Hattile, a Lome cultural hub
fifteen miles south of the current central front line, and a great
choice for Command to settle into. The narrow streets were lined
by timber-framed houses with orange-tiled roofs, with windows in
unusual shapes and sizes, the old centre a maze of grand,
repurposed churches and civic buildings. There were pastry shops
puffing out inviting scents of fresh bread and wintry spices, perfect
as the weather grew colder and the days shorter – and at night it was
lit cosily in the yellow glow of gas lanterns and fireplaces. It was a
fairy-tale city, and even the regular roadblocks, sandbags and
occasional large gun emplacements couldn't detract from that.
After a couple of weeks convalescing, enjoying the food and
company of locals who said all sorts of things she couldn't
understand, Wish was starting to think she could live in a place like
this. A reasonable second to Swelig, recreating some of the charm
she was used to but in a more expansive form. It helped that, unlike
at Rock Stable, she had friends here to share it with. She spent hours

at Emi's side as the mage recovered in a manor house commandeered for the medical care of the army's most valuable soldiers. Emi was getting back to her usual self, slower than expected but with unmistakable results. What started with Wish reading news stories and sharing pastries with a mildly inactive Emi was shifting to dodging crude cryptic comments and knowing looks that promised Emi was scheming something.

Otherwise, Wish enjoyed eating and drinking with Ohno and occasionally the Rawboys, and she even appreciated the more constant company of Scraper. Wish was still unsettled whenever she noticed her lurking, but told herself Scraper was inoffensive, content to just be nearby. She occasionally brought Wish a spiced bun or a small bottle of local wine or a warm drink; little gifts that showed loyalty. She rarely smiled, but did so when Wish thanked her for these, and that felt like progress. It was slowly wearing down the memories she had of the woman covered in other people's blood.

And all of it, the lovely food, the drink, the company . . . it was pushing away some of the other horrors. The sight of monsters tearing men apart. Gunfire in tunnels. Swarms of goblins with guns and villagers skewered on spears. Havik. Havikare, threatening everything, laughing as she choked, as Wish almost killed her. Havikare speaking of violence with a happy smile, and touching Wish. The most chilling memory of all, that touch, from that woman – an uncomfortable, wrong yearning. Havik who was mixed up, *terrible,* but had touched Wish with something real. Kissed her. Now surely dead . . .

Wish imagined snow coming soon, the season shifting with Relight approaching and the goodwill and decorations that might bring. She'd forget the rest when it came. It would be a perfect place to snuggle down for the winter, and an important enough military position that any roaming Blood Scouts might easily find her here. She could wait, let them come, relax.

Except, after only a few weeks, she received a summons in her quarters, a simple note left on her side table. *Warehouse 54 at 0930. General Macwest.*

Wish felt the blood rushing out of her, quite sure that whatever this was, with a general wanting to talk to her and upset her newly established quiet life, it was the absolute worst. But she couldn't ignore it, of course, and straightened out her uniform to go and meet the man. It was a sunny day, to be better spent in the garden at Emi's manor drinking the region's best alnon cocktails, but instead she walked, alone, out of town to a small industrial area that had been commandeered by the military. She knew some sort of mechanical work was being done out there, with its associated training and drilling, but had never needed to visit. Now, as she finally approached, wondering how long it would take to find Warehouse 54 and not sure how there could be that many buildings, she found the area a startling contrast to Hattile proper. Literally just around the bend from her storybook retreat, here were great metal-sided buildings and smoking chimneys, military vehicles strewn about in states of semi-repair, and the sounds of men shouting, tossing heavy equipment around, hammers hammering.

When she asked, she discovered there were, in fact, only three warehouses, and 54 was the largest, its designation some kind of nonsense. It was the noisiest, too. She entered through a side door to be assaulted by a very muggy heat inside and a pungent mix of gasoline and oil. She moved between vast scaffolds of shelves and tall machines to come to the centre of the building, where men in overalls or shabby uniforms were darting about, sweating, manoeuvring large bits of machinery. She spotted General Macwest, apparent from his slightly better-pressed uniform and his position standing on the side platform of a vehicle as tall as two men. He was walking across it, pointing and making comments to a group of oil-stained engineers below, and Wish crept cautiously up to a lady in a skirt who was scribbling things down in a notepad.

She cleared her throat, and the woman looked up with surprise. "Is that General Macwest?"

The woman considered Wish briefly, then turned to the general rather than answer. That was enough, apparently, for him to spot them, and suddenly everyone in the massive room seemed to be looking Wish's way. She had the feeling she'd just interrupted some Very Important work.

"Ah! Here she is!" Macwest announced, and strode quickly to the edge of the machine to climb down the ladder rungs built into its side. He wiped his hands on a dirty rag handed to him by one of the dirtier men and called out, "Everyone take five."

The general walked quickly over to Wish and held out a hand that she could see was still black from machine grime. He was younger than Wish expected, a tall and very slim man with a large Adam's apple and a floppy mop of ginger on top of his head. His uniform was slightly too big, combined with a few stains to give him the air of an unprepared schoolchild, and she couldn't help an instinctive comparison to Toothless, the sort of man who looked like an unlikely soldier. Poor Toothless – someone should have kept him in a warehouse fifteen miles from the front.

"A pleasure to meet you," General Macwest said as she shook his hand, his accent silkily upper-class Stanish. Where Captain Brade was well-spoken, this man's voice was gilded with generations of aristocracy; that alone made it clear why he was here and Toothless had died in the Mire. "The infamous Captain Wild Wish Evans. I've been looking forward to this, and wish we could've arranged it sooner. Apologies for the environment." He gestured to the warehouse around them. "I take a personal interest in the work here and it seemed a better place to meet than on the front. I hope you haven't been terribly bored in town."

"I've appreciated the break, sir," Wish replied, speaking quickly in her nerves. That voice. The importance of this man: if you believed the news, he was single-handedly masterminding the defence of Lome, without which the entire continent would fall. Her mind leapt back, though, noting his mistake, with an unwelcome memory of Havik. "But it's Lieutenant, sir, not Captain. And . . . I'm not even sure it should be that?"

"You're not sure?" Macwest raised his bushy brow. "I understand General Easter himself approved your lieutenancy after the Battle of Wick? And the correspondence I've received out of Hail Crossing has included numerous references to your rank as captain, since."

"I haven't referred to myself as that, ever," Wish hurried to say, sure it was a serious offence to claim an incorrect rank. This was making her hot around the collar, not helped by this furnace of a warehouse; being exposed as an impostor had *not* been high on her concerns here (much as the worry was never too far from her mind). "I'm not sure who's been reporting that, but I'd be happy to set them straight."

"There was a missive from Archvenerator Turbulence the Sixth, so I'm not sure you'd want to tussle with *him.*" Macwest laughed, then quickly made himself serious. "But also a rather detailed account from the nuns in Saintshadow. Tragic occurrences out there, absolutely tragic, which I believe you were instrumental in keeping a lid on."

"I did what I could, sir," Wish said, then added, "I wish I could've done more."

"Ah yes, that eponymous *wild wish,*" Macwest said. She wasn't sure how he'd understood that, or what eponymous meant, but he had a little smile and seemed too pleased with himself to question it. "Well, you'll be happy to know I consider myself well abreast of all that happened in the Saints Mire, between the written reports and Captain Brade's accounts – cracking man, that one – so let's not bore each other retreading that. I merely would like your personal assurance that it's all to stay between us."

"Sir?" Wish frowned.

"This business with the geesekind or whatever, and the fall of Drowndeep. The device that I understand was uncovered and this witch who used it? Never happened."

"Um."

"Obviously we'll have *something* made official, but for the sake of simplicity let's just say *you* don't discuss it with anyone. In fact, you were never there. Not that you shan't be rewarded: officially, there's a few medals to go around, a promotion too, I suppose, if you're saying you still need that captaincy confirmed. But we'll say you and yours were at the Palicier offensive or some such thing – enough of a goddamn mess out there no one will know the difference. Details. Important thing is, the Comity was never in the Saints Mire, understood?"

"Um. Yes. Sir," Wish answered slowly. Nothing less than she expected, but there was a bit to get her head around there. "Though, if we were never there –"

A loud bang made them both turn to see a trio of shouting mechanics trying to steady a big chunk of metal that had come loose from a chain. As they calmed, Macwest put his hands in his pockets, sighed, and regarded the vehicle he'd been standing on. "Quite something, isn't it?"

Wish gave the monstrous device a better look. The tanks she'd seen were typically about half this size, like metal carriages with large wheels and big guns mounted on top. Mostly crudely blocky. This one was made up of three large sections, the two on the side longer and flatter to support a raised central box, with tracks of metal panels under the sides instead of wheels. On top was a circular turret with four machine guns sticking out, two forward and two back.

"We call it the Crawler Mauler," Macwest said, with a little chuckle, another joke Wish didn't get. "Unlike most of our glorified cannons on wheels, *this* one can carry up to ten men, and is designed not to sink in the mud. I daresay you could've used such a thing in the marshlands yourselves."

Wish murmured agreement, not sure what the hell she'd do with a vehicle like this. It looked like a fine place to get trapped inside, if anything. She replied, not really thinking, "But I wasn't really *in* the marshlands."

Macwest laughed loudly at that, far too cheerful for a man involved in the absolute top levels of managing this war. He patted her shoulder and began marching away. "Walk with me. Where was I? Yes, we'll piece together something official. Plainly Kasidee's Irregulars turned rogue and Colonel Atmoor's forces took a rather ham-fisted approach to putting them down. Resulted in a lot of collateral damage but, rather conveniently, almost total losses on both sides. More or less as it was, really. We are in broad agreement with the Drail on this, mind; no one wants to reopen the question of the Mire for conquest."

"That's good," Wish said. She wasn't sure Atmoor deserved to take the lion's share of the blame for the fiasco, willing as he'd been to work with them, but then the man hadn't done much to help, either. And he was probably dead, so what difference did it make.

"Indeed, and we'll have none of the more esoteric questions hanging over us. I don't even want to ask."

"Yes, sir."

"And if we can ensure that sticky bit of business is out of the way," Macwest continued, going through a doorway into an office. A couple of engineers hurried out of the way with muttered words of deference for the general. Macwest went to a board pinned with charts and diagrams and scanned the numbers. "The question for us – that is, for you – becomes *what next*. I expect you've been told often enough that it'd be most convenient if you, forgive me, somewhat disappeared, but you've rather proven too useful for that. Much like those Rebel Rawboys of yours. And while there's *some* concern you may have exacerbated matters in the Mire, I don't buy it myself. Besides, I appreciate a neat path of destruction has its place, as much as a delicate touch. Leave nothing behind and all that, as you managed in Wick and Low Slane. I'm quite sure we'll have need of your talents again soon. I personally want to assure it. We're reinstating the Blood Scouts with you at the helm."

Wish stiffened to sharp attention, eyes wide. She'd imagined asking for this, rehearsed it in her head, but not yet – not for months, most likely, after more hiding away and pretending she wasn't really part of the war. And while she'd imagined they might have been her platoon in the Mire, that place was unreal, an exception – something never to talk of, now. She squeaked in disbelief, "Me?"

"Who else?" Macwest chortled. "It'll be effective immediately but I'll keep you on hiatus for as long as I can allow. Not that you'll be complacent, understand. General Easter plainly saw your potential and you're to live up to it, understand? Continue a regime of rigorous training, you and your troops. And you may be expected at a few social events. Not many – we'd rather keep this hush-hush, with you reporting directly to me when possible – but there are some people I need you to meet. Very important people. You can do as much with a reputation as with a gun, after all. Agreed?"

"Um – to be clear, sir, you realise I'm not Captain Tate?"

"Oh Saints no, absolutely." Macwest waved a hand as if that were a relief. "I dare say you're twice as dangerous and, if you'll forgive me, a damned sight softer on the eye. Crude, I know, but when people hear we have an elite female officer at hand they have certain expectations which are good to meet."

Wish just managed to keep her mouth shut, this being a twist too far. Her mind ran back to her initial misgivings, never mind all she'd been through in the Mire. She was good at shooting people. Damaging things. She wasn't a planner or a talker, much less someone who thrived when put on display. She'd barely coped talking to Colonel Atmoor and had completely failed to talk down Kin Kasidee. The one person she *had* connected with in the Mire had turned out to be psychotic. Plus she didn't like the idea of people expecting her to be pretty. She'd only ever been average in Swelig, at best, and it wasn't fair to say she was anywhere near as striking as Tate. But shoving all that aside – things she was sure would sound like childish doubts – she clung to the one practical detail that she *could* question. "With respect, sir – there were more experienced officers in the Blood Scouts than me. I've been hoping they'd resurface."

This soured Macwest's expression slightly, a complication to his otherwise smooth plans. He said, carefully, "What have you heard?"

Wish went quiet. Was there something she was supposed to have heard? She had written to Four Skills at Rock Stable but not yet received a reply. She had started to wonder if the letter had reached her, or if Command didn't want them communicating.

Macwest read her eyes, then nodded. "The *rumours* of female soldiers captured behind enemy lines are just that. Our spy network are working hard to keep it quiet. Could be embarrassing if it got out, after all. The Drail aren't publicising this yet themselves, and we're not sure why. My guess would be, if any of it's true, they're waiting for the right moment."

"Then what are *we* waiting for?" Wish exclaimed, forgetting herself and her position. Macwest's gaze reminded her, and she added, "Sir."

"No one's waiting. We have men looking into it."

"Permission to speak, sir?"

"What? You're *here* to speak with me, why are you asking permission? You're a captain now, Evans." Macwest huffed in a manner that knowingly separated them by a far berth of class. He was going to find someone to tutor her in being an officer, she was sure. "Go on, let's hear it."

"If you want me to ready a platoon, I need recruits. At the moment, I've only a couple of people to work with."

"You'll keep everyone you had in the Saints Mire, no need to worry about that. Then you'll be expected to recruit from along the line, as Captain Tate did."

"Okay. But perhaps it would be a better use of my time to track down scouts who've already been trained? If anyone can get them back from behind enemy lines, I can."

Macwest stared coldly, not surprised by her predictable demand that she'd been worrying over ever since Four Skills had appeared in Rock Stable. One of her many idle dreams, *bring back the girls, win the war, go to the farm* – but one that had suddenly become a possibility. The general said, "You're volunteering to take your men deep into Drail territory to recover our captured spies? Most likely in the most secure facilities Low Slane have."

Wish paused. When he put it like that, she realised it sounded better in her imagination. She didn't want to die doing it, really. Though it would silence her memories better than alcohol could. It would mean never having to answer the questions becoming increasingly complicated in her head. Questions about Havik. About the violence and where adventure became horror or vice versa. With those thoughts threatening to surface even here, she quickly said, "I'd go, sir, absolutely. I've wanted to go. I *need* to go. They're my girls. They need me. If I get them back I know we're infinitely more likely to avoid another mess like in Drowndeep – please." She'd gone too far, sounded desperate, and his critical gaze had grown hard.

"I've offered you the possibility of extended convalescence," he said, coldly now. "A promotion. Your own platoon and a reasonably safe position as a commander. These are excellent rewards for any soldier, wouldn't you say?"

Wish merely nodded, as she'd plainly offended him somehow.

"That is *enough*. You will not speak of the Mire again, and if I get the merest inkling that you *might,* you'll find the reverse of my generosity. Understand, Captain?" He said the title bitingly now, and she saw that for his carefree manner, he was anything but flippant about the mission that had brought her here. He had the same serious concern that she'd seen in Brade. Havikare really had been onto something in the Mire, and the mere suggestion of it threatened them. This was all about making sure she was happy enough to keep her mouth shut. Knowing that gave Wish the tiniest bit of power, perhaps, to reform the Blood Scouts. It also meant people were more likely than ever to want her dead.

New plan, she decided. Try especially hard not to think about the Mire, along with everything else. Try not to talk about it. Behave and reform her platoon with whatever they'd give her and gradually, gradually get the girls back. Little bit at a time. There was still a long war ahead, and it was only getting more complicated. She needed to be careful if she was going to make it back to the farm.

Wild Wish cleared her throat and nodded again, saying, "I understand, General, and I'm sorry if I misspoke. You can trust me."

Macwest kept eyeing her, obviously wondering whether or not he'd been mistaken about this unassuming, strange woman in uniform. As confused by her as everyone else. Except maybe Havik . . .

But as quickly as his dark side had surfaced, it disappeared into a fresh grin and he said, "Yes. I believe I can. But you're a recognised asset now, Captain. It would be foolhardy of me to release you on a suicide mission right away, wouldn't it?"

"Yes, sir," Wild Wish said. "As you wish, sir."

It didn't have to be right away.

50

The Herald has confirmation from multiple sources that Stanish troops were present in the Saints Mire; not just the separatist Irregulars under Kin Kasidee. A group including Rebel Rawboys and Ogres was seen in Hail Crossing, travelling via boat into Paradise Fails. There can be no doubt, with such troops involved, that Stanish intentions in the region were anything but peaceful. This comes as we receive growing reports of the losses of the Drail's entire defence force in Onwail, Kin Kasidee's entire company of Irregulars, and the priories at Drowndeep, Guiltway and Sinner's Gate. Serious questions are now being asked by both Khibba's Department of War and the Arbitration, expressing concern over Stanclif, the Drail and the Church of the Venerate Flesh colluding in concealing the true nature of these events.

Brickslayer Tansin of the Arbitration has voiced concerns that if Stanclif indeed had soldiers in the Saints Mire, then there may also be truth in the rumours that they, along with the Drail and the Irregulars, were not engaged in a strictly military conflict. The Arbitration are committing to a full investigation into the region, while the Khib leadership have suggested they will only be satisfied after conducting their own review. Statesman Dowel of Stanclif has said, "This really is a storm in a teacup. We have enough serious crises occurring on a daily basis that I see no need to entertain this invented concern."

Patrain Vinkent Narroway of the Drail is yet to comment.

Extract from "Rumours of Stanclif Movements in the Saints Mire Confirmed", from ***The Highscythe Herald,*** **720**

All given, Wideskull Bleacher was pretty pleased with the results of the Mire excursion. It'd turned into a great bloody nightmare in the end, but he and his boys saw a solid opportunity and took it. No sense shooting at men who weren't shooting back when you had a heap of big ugly fucking crabs charging at you. It wasn't desertion when you were faced with a stampede – it was just survival. And it was even less desertion when no one was left alive to notice it.

Topping off the opportunity to slink off, presumed dead, his fast-fingered goblins had got away with a hefty stash. Kin Kasidee proved a right greedy bugger with his wagons of treasures left up the road from the chaos of Drowndeep. Sacks and sacks of it, stacked ready for the taking. And take they did. Bleacher sat happily in a copse of trees, far from the comings and goings of the few surviving monks and tribespeople, while his goblins filtered in with the Irregulars' horde. They stacked it up and took inventory, then went out hunting for any surviving brethren, as he drew up plans to head north through the border woods. His scouts had already clocked Ilscot and his men fleeing east – bunch of cowards had properly deserted without even reaching the battle, and would likely be rounded up and punished for it. They'd report seeing the goblins running into the fray, ahead of everyone else. Surely dead. Bleacher chuckled over that.

He wasn't gonna go back and correct them.

Kasidee had the right idea, just the wrong execution. His problem, mostly, was incompetence. Poorly disciplined, poorly trained men who failed to see the enemy coming from behind. Goblins were smarter than that. They wouldn't need to raid anywhere, with the riches Bleacher had gathered already, but who knew how long the war would last? If necessary, they could hit a few more places in the confusion of the wider fighting. It was easy for goblins to hide in the shadows, sneak out after a battle or even during one. Little bit of gold here and there would go a long way. And now they'd faced the stark reality of choosing between senselessly fighting monsters or going their own way, he guessed the bigots were proved right enough at last. He and his boys couldn't be trusted. Not by humans, anyway.

He scratched a map into the forest floor, the northern border as he recalled it. The woods would give them cover past Onwail, and there wouldn't be many people left there to notice them anyway. Onwail itself would be an easy target, but better they skirt it entirely, unseen. From there, he could move east, between the front line and the Drail reserves. There was a bombed village near Grutstack where he knew the line had moved far enough away that they might settle there, unnoticed.

Bleacher was just about decided on his plans when a commotion drew his attention to the edge of the woods. Every time new boys came back, he hoped to hear Sergeant Hissle reporting in, but so far that noble sharptooth had not been found. And as he watched the goblins skipping through trees, listening to their chitters, he realised this was something more contentious. He'd instructed them to take no prisoners more to avoid having extra baggage than out of any animosity.

"It's a woman!" the first excited goblin to reach his clearing announced, spittle flying. Another came in just behind, cursing at being beaten to breaking the news. "One of them women soldiers!"

Ah, this *was* interesting. He'd liked that Wild Wish, human as she was. Like the Irregulars, she had a bit of goblin in her, spunky outcast that she was. He waved at the boys to part and let their guest through, hoping to see the lieutenant.

The woman walked calmly between the trees, through the chattering crowd, and the goblins mostly gave her space. A couple of claws reached towards her but held back, boys laughing as she smiled their way. She got it, didn't take offence, and carried on to stand over Bleacher. Almost twice his height with him slouched on his rock, head just up to her waist. Didn't matter, there were a dozen goblins hopping about and salvaged guns lying all around the clearing, making it plain enough who was in charge here. Bleacher cocked his head to one side, studying her from her big boots and ripped coat up to her bloody face and black, broken bird's nest hair. She didn't look the slightest bit afraid and he liked that.

"My boys didn't hurt you?" Bleacher nodded to her forehead, talking in Stanish for her.

"They were perfectly polite," she replied, which was utter bullshit because they were only ever polite to make fun, and they were never perfect. She had a lopsided smile that said she knew that, though, just joking. She had an Elmish accent. No uniform under that coat, just a grimy white top and peasant trousers.

Bleacher narrowed his eyes and shifted to Elmish himself. "You're Kasidee's captain, ain't ya? Got a nerve coming to me."

"I don't belong to anyone," she replied. "Our interests just aligned for a while, and I can see from your current position that ours might align now, too."

"My current position? Scratching my arse on a forest floor?" Bleacher laughed and most of the goblins in the woods laughed too. It had to be unsettling for her. What tall wouldn't be scared of a pack of greenskins? Not her, apparently. She kept smiling.

"You're planning to leave the army behind," she said. "Taking care of yourselves. I can help you with that."

"You?" Bleacher snorted. "Why the hell would I need help from a tall? Especially considering your lot just got themselves bloody murdered. Not even mentioning the whole monster scenario."

"Oh it wasn't *that* far from what I intended."

Bleacher paused. "You want me to believe you planned any part of that chaos? It was a fucking mess. A disaster."

"It was a revolution. A wave of creatures united against their oppressors. It was the potential for so much more."

Bleacher scowled. He knew the way humans worked, twisting words around, trying to get other races doing their bidding, muddled up over what anything was about. He'd had a morning of liberated thinking, though, and wasn't about to buy into someone else's schemes, not this soon. He said, "You're a long way from home, miss."

"I don't think so." She crouched before him, her smile only spreading. Big and intense as her eyes grew, there was a surety in them as unsettling as the madness. "I helped those mindless creatures use their combined strength to crush an army. Creatures with no concept of how powerful they really are. I helped Kasidee's men reach for more than petty criminals ever have before, even if . . .

they were lacking in the end. There are ways to reverse the balance of *everything*. It's something, I imagine, that even the most accomplished goblin could appreciate."

Bleacher was quiet. His boys were quiet too, hanging oddly on her words as if they made a kind of sense. These lads weren't used to thinking too much, nor planning far beyond the next prize. Why would they? He said, "You got something specific in mind, or you just singing a pretty song?"

Havikare laughed. "You're goblins, aren't you? There's something I think we've got in common: I'm just exploring what opportunities come my way. And this war is *packed* with opportunities. Don't you think?"

Get More from the Rocc

Hello again; it's me, the author, Phil Williams. I hope you've enjoyed reading *Drown Deep,* to make it this far. If you did, please let others know: leave a review, tell your friends, sound a trumpet from a rooftop, this sort of thing. The most important thing for any book's success is visibility, and it means everything for authors if enthusiastic readers help spread the word. We are a reticent bunch ourselves, after all.

As long as the Blood Scouts continue to get attention, I've got a lot more to come, as you might suspect. And if you missed it in Book 1, I have a **special offer** just for you. You can return to this world with my prequel novelette, *Oksy, Come Home,* available exclusively, and totally free, if you join my newsletter here: **https://phil-williams.co.uk/hmmd-offer**

You'll also be the first to learn about the next instalments in the series and any future offers.

Acknowledgements

While *However Many Must Die* was a book that stewed for a few years, *Drown Deep* came along a lot quicker, though at times I'll admit it felt like a mammoth task. I breezed through this a little more independently than the first instalment, in part because we'd already laid down so much groundwork in Book 1. But at the same time, all the extensive thanks that were due for *However Many Must Die* are also due for *Drown Deep*, and I offer big gratitude again to everyone who's been involved at any stage in the Blood Scouts saga (and indeed, with the rest of my publishing!).

Firstly, this time, my biggest thanks to Stefan Koidl, for the striking cover that incredibly brought Havikare herself to life. It's a remarkable thing to see such a talented artist take my words and make them a reality, and I don't doubt that a large portion of whatever attention these books receive are thanks to him.

My thanks again to my friends, readers and fellow writers who've offered feedback or otherwise supported me along the way of this journey, particularly now Richard Buxton, Adawia Asad, Travis M. Riddle, Arthur Fortune and Damien Larkin. Thanks again to Patrick Samphire and Dominic McDermott for their edits on the first book and enthusiasm for this one.

As always, thanks too to all my advance readers and reviewers, and all those who've supported me with reviews and publicity, including Lynn Williams of Lynn's Books; Timy, Jen and all the team at Queen's Book Asylum; Maddalena at Space & Sorcery; Mihir, Lukasz and all the team at Fantasy Book Critic; Julia Sarene; Jamedi of Jamreads; D.B. Rook and all the FanFiAddict team; Sam Stokes; Mark Lawrence and everyone involved in making SPFBO great; and of course YOU for giving this book a go.

A great deal is owed again to the same books and research that made Book 1 possible, though there have been a few extra books in the meantime, so thanks to any writers out there who've unwittingly helped me flesh out this world. In particular, I took some inspiration from Kate Adie's books, and it's probably worth mentioning an obvious (maybe?) element of film influence here. I'm sure war films and westerns have played a strong role in defining my style. I have an inkling Havikare Eens' first appearance has echoes of *Once Upon a Time in the West* and I doubt we'd have a Saints Mire without the likes of Conrad's *Heart of Darkness* and Coppola's *Apocalypse Now*. As to the wilder monstrous aspects and religious undertones, I guess thank a Catholic upbringing and a broad interest in the horror genre.

There are naturally historical influences again in the formation of this story, not least again Sir Richard F. Burton, whose anecdotes I will have probably roundly stolen in entirety by the time this series is done. Martin Gilbert's *The First World War* at least partly put me in the mood during this book, though I suspect more of the style and nature of the conflict harks back to my studies of the medieval crusades at university, for which I couldn't begin to recall the many books I explored then.

Finally, thanks as always to all my family and friends for their ongoing support, particularly my wonderful wife Marta. Also Herbert my dog, who reminds me to leave the computer at healthy intervals, even if I don't always listen.

Also By Phil Williams

THE BLOOD SCOUTS SERIES
HOWEVER MANY MUST DIE
OKSY, COME HOME

ORDSHAW SERIES
The Sunken City Trilogy
UNDER ORDSHAW
BLUE ANGEL
THE VIOLENT FAE

THE CITY SCREAMS

The Ikiri Duology
KEPT FROM CAGES
GIVEN TO DARKNESS

DYER STREET PUNK WITCHES

THE ORDSHAW VIGNETTES VOL. 1

ESTALIA SERIES
WIXON'S DAY
BALFAIR'S CONFINEMENT
AFTAN WHISPERS

FAERGROWE SERIES
A MOST APOCALYPTIC CHRISTMAS